ADVANCE PRAISE FOR OBSERVER:

"Robert Lanza has taken the gigantic step of incorporating his ideas into a science fiction novel with Nancy Kress. This brilliant book will take you deep into quantum physics, where these often complex concepts are illuminated through a riveting and moving story."
– Rhonda Byrne, #1 *New York Times* bestselling author of *The Secret*

"Nancy Kress is one of the greatest living science fiction writers, and her particular talent for telling stories about people on the cutting edge of science tipping into something new and marvelous is perfectly suited to the ideas that have come to Robert Lanza in the course of his groundbreaking scientific research. Together they've written a startling, fascinating novel."
– Kim Stanley Robinson, *New York Times* bestselling author

"Real science and limitless imagination combine in a thrilling story you won't soon forget."
– Robin Cook, #1 *New York Times* bestselling author

"Nancy Kress is a master storyteller, and her trademark empathy is on every page. Even as we venture into the heady territory of quantum physics and the nature of reality that Robert Lanza is known for, we never lose track of Caro, the brilliant surgeon who'll do anything to save the people she loves. *Observer* is the best of science and fiction—an intellectual adventure with real heart."
– Darryl Gregory, award-winning author of *Spoonbenders*

"*Observer* is an impressive story! . . . Lanza and Kress give us characters with science and spirit."
– David Brin, *New York Times* bestselling author

OBSERVER

ROBERT LANZA
AND NANCY KRESS

The Story Plant
Studio Digital CT, LLC
P.O. Box 4331
Stamford, CT 06907

Copyright © 2022 by Robert Lanza and Nancy Kress
Library of Congress Control Number:
Cover design by Milan Bozic

Story Plant hardcover ISBN-13 978-1-61188-343-5
Fiction Studio Books e-book ISBN-13: 978-1-945839-65-8

Visit our website at www.TheStoryPlant.com

First Story Plant Paperback Printing: January 2023
Printed in The United States of America

"The usual approach of science of constructing a mathematical model cannot answer the question of why there should be a universe for the model to describe. Why does the universe go to the bother of existing?"
—Stephen Hawking, *A Brief History of Time*

PROLOGUE

No one wanted to tell the old man.

They clustered in the courtyard outside his bedroom, under the wide overhang that sheltered the walkway. The residential wing, one of three, had been built in a square around a central courtyard at the western end of the compound to catch the slanting rays of the morning sun. This early, barely after dawn, the air was still fresh and cool, with the clean salty zing of a breeze off the Caribbean. Nonetheless, the three people could hear the AC going full blast behind the old man's closed door. James, head of household staff, wearing slippers and a flamboyant silk robe that would not have been out of place in 1940s Hollywood, had been among those alerted by the night-duty tech as soon as the police arrived.

Julian had gone with the police to identify the body.

Two of Julian's security techs, sent to inform the old man of what had happened, looked expectantly at James. He tightened the belt of his robe and said, "I don't see why we have to wake him at all. There's nothing for Dr. Watkins to do. He's old and very ill. Let him sleep."

The techs didn't answer, but their glances at each other spoke terabytes: only someone not directly involved in the project would think that Dr. Watkins wouldn't want to know instantly what had happened. But it was James who had the inspiration. "I know! Wake Dr. Weigert!"

Weigert had not been called already because Julian had left strict instructions that Weigert was never to talk to island police. The two young techs suspected the reason was Weigert's sometimes indiscreet openness. They did not say this aloud. But now the police had gone. The techs nodded, and James phoned Weigert.

He, too, arrived in slippers and robe, although his was of faded terry cloth that looked older than all three young men. James explained in great detail what the police had told him. Weigert nodded slowly and knocked on the bedroom door.

"What the— Oh, it's you, George. What is it?"

Weigert entered the bedroom, as small and white-washed as all the others set around the courtyard, although even more bare. Neither luxury nor home decoration interested Watkins; he never put personal bits and pieces on the walls or dresser. Weigert discovered that it wasn't AC he'd heard through the door but a noisy space heater. The room was a sauna. Was that necessary for Sam's condition? Weigert, a physicist rather than a physician, had no idea.

"Sam, there's been an accident."

Samuel Louis Watkins, genius Nobel laureate, switched on the bedside lamp and heaved himself upright in bed. Cheekbones sharp as chisels, bald head shining in the lamplight. "What kind of accident? *Are the data and equipment safe?*"

"Yes, they are. It's a diving accident. David Weeks. He's dead. Julian just left with the police to identify the body, but apparently there's no doubt it's Dr. Weeks." Weigert, who had known Sam since their university days and who disliked confrontation, braced himself for a tsunami of expletives. Sam had told Weeks to cease diving. No, not told: ordered.

The tsunami didn't come. Instead, Watkins adopted the intense, focused look that meant his remarkable brain was processing multiple ideas: imagining, synthesizing, evaluating. That brain had gotten them all here, in this remote island compound in the Caribbean, where Weigert, at least, had certainly never expected to be.

But all Watkins said was, "Tell me."

"Weeks must have gone out last night. Julian hasn't had time yet to check the surveillance log. The police said that Dr. Weeks's body was discovered this morning, snagged near the top of a coral reef, by some fisherman. He'd dropped his weight belt and his buoyancy device was partially inflated, which was why the body rose. His fins had the address of the compound painted on them. The police said there was no sign of any violence by sharks or humans or anything like that, and that probably Weeks had a heart attack or something and tried to get out of the water but died first."

Watkins said, "Damn idiot. I told him not to ..." He looked away, at the white-washed wall.

"Yes," Weigert said, because what else was there to say? Warmth and light abruptly poured through the open door. The sun had topped the compound walls.

Watkins was silent for a long time. Weigert couldn't tell from his old friend's face if Sam was thinking of personal memories of David Weeks, brought into the project a year ago, or of the project itself, now short a crucial member whose loss could jeopardize everything. It had not been easy to find a neurosurgeon willing to perform the unusual operations that the project called for. When the silence stretched on and on, and then on some more, Weigert couldn't stand it.

"Sam, should I ..."

"You don't have to do anything." And then, "George, I'm running out of time."

Weigert, startled by the reference to what everyone knew but no one ever mentioned in Sam's presence, didn't know what to say. He settled on honesty.

"I know."

"Of course you do. I'm sure everybody knows, right down to James's kitchen help. All right, send for Haggerty."

"The lawyer?" Bill Haggerty, another old friend of Watkins, was the only one connected with the compound who lived not only off-site but off-island. All communication with him was through heavily encrypted email.

9

"Yes. Tell him to come today."

"But today—"

"Today." And then, with a grimace on that disease-ravaged face, "Our project is too important to the future not to have thought of all eventualities. I have a Plan B."

1.

THREE MONTHS EARLIER

When Caro walked out of the hospital administrator's office, her legs felt wobbly. She stiffened them and, head held high, did not glance back at the doctors seated around the conference table. None of them followed her out—giving her time, a courtesy she recognized but did not appreciate. These people had just destroyed her future.

In the corridors of Fairleigh Memorial Hospital she willed herself to walk steadily, to return the impersonal nods of a resident, a medical student, two administrative assistants. The elevator was full; she took the fire stairwell. Its emptiness, silent except for the ring of her shoes on metal steps, was welcome.

She was catastrophizing, she told herself. There were other hospitals.

Not here, not for her talents.

She could have not reported Paul Becker.

No. She'd done the right thing.

She could have not asked Maisie to speak at the hearing.

But that one was still too painful to think about. Caro had thought that Maisie was a friend. She'd thought a lot of things that, it turned out, weren't true.

What did you do when everything you'd wanted had been in clear sight and then slipped through your highly trained fingers?

At the bottom of the stairwell, Caro pushed open the heavy door and walked past the restrooms. And there, seated

11

on a backless ottoman that was supposed to discourage lobby sitters and never did, was the last person Caro wanted to see.

Ellen jumped up. "Caro ... Oh! The hearing went against you."

Her sister could always read Caro, even when no one else could, even when Caro didn't want to be read, or even seen. "Ellen, I don't want to talk about it."

"Of course you don't. You never do. But you have to, it will just be worse if you bottle it all up."

Ellen believed in never bottling up anything. In keeping a positive attitude. In finding the bright side. Which was remarkable, considering what Ellen's life had become. Caro's respect for Ellen was enormous, but now her sense of unreality about what had just happened took on another layer: disbelief that she and not Ellen was the one in trouble. It belied their entire childhoods, girlhoods, adult lives. Their playbook had been written early: Ellen floundered and big sister Caro rescued. Today, along with everything else the day meant, was a reversal of fact that upended the universe.

"You're coming with me," Ellen said. "Now. No, don't tell me you have a patient or a meeting or a surgery, because I know you have the rest of the day free. You told me so yesterday. We're getting in my car, which is illegally parked out front, even if I have to physically drag you there." And then, in a different voice, "Caro ... You know how hard it was for me to make arrangements to get here?"

Caro knew. She knew, too, that Ellen was capable both physically and emotionally of carrying out her threat. Ellen was built like a linebacker; Caro weighed 126 pounds.

Ellen never minds whom she embarrasses. I cannot teach that child restraint.

"All right, I'm coming," Caro said.

The lobby teemed with people: a nurse pushing a smiling, home-going patient in a wheelchair, an entire happy family trailing alongside. Dr. Trilling from Radiology, in a tremendous hurry. Two med students carrying paper cups of Starbucks coffee. One said, "Hello, Dr. Soames-Watkins," and then went on talking to the other. A normal conversation: the students didn't know what had just happened to her. Theoretically, no one would know because hospital ethics hearings were not public, but after four years of medical school, years of neurosurgery residency with research, and her year of fellowship, Caro knew that hospitals did not work like that. Nothing stayed secret for very long.

Ellen's car had been ticketed. She shoved the ticket in her purse without looking at it and drove several blocks to an ersatz Irish bar.

"In the middle of the afternoon?" Caro said.

"You need a drink."

"I don't."

"You can't tell me that the … Oh, all right. You can have an iced tea or something."

The bar was dim and nearly empty. Vaguely Celtic music played, one wordless song blending into the next. They slid into a booth with hard wooden benches. Ellen, whose shaggy dark hair needed not only cutting but combing, said to the server, "Two iced teas, please."

From Ellen, this was equivalent to surrendering her sword and bending the knee. Caro forced a smile, and then all at once she was glad that Ellen had brought her here, where she could unburden herself to the person she most loved and trusted.

Ellen said, "So the disciplinary committee didn't believe you?"

Caro said, with a superhuman effort, "They didn't want to. Same outcome."

"But you had a witness! You told me that other doctor, your friend Maisie Somebody—"

"Not my friend. Not anymore." Then the hurt under the six simple words broke to the surface, and Caro put her hands over her face.

Gently, Ellen pulled them down. Caro's right hand tightened on Ellen's and did not let go. Ellen said, "Sissy?"

"The hearing came down to 'he said … she said.' Maisie wasn't a direct witness. No one else was upstairs at the party when Paul—Dr. Becker—dragged me into that bedroom. I insisted that Maisie be called to the committee because she'd seen that Becker was pretty drunk, and she knew that we were among the last to leave the party because our Uber didn't show up. Also that I went upstairs to get my coat and came down upset and with a button torn off my shirt, and I told Maisie the same night what had just happened. She *knew*. But in the disciplinary hearing, right after Becker denied everything, Maisie did too. She said that she saw nothing and I told her nothing."

"She *lied*?" said Ellen, who never lied. "Why?"

"She was protecting herself, of course. I don't think you realize how influential Paul Becker is. He's not only chief of neurosurgery, he has a brilliant international reputation, and he's the best surgeon I ever saw. A rock star. Last week I watched him tease out a glioblastoma multiforme with no clean surgical plane, one that no one else could have so much as debulked, let alone never touch the brain tissue. He—"

"I don't care. He's an asshole. He tried to rape you."

"I don't think it would have gone that far. He was just getting some cheap and drunken gropes. Although you're right, that's enough to make him an asshole." Caro tried to smile, a failure. "If I'd actually been raped, I'd at least have physical DNA evidence."

"You shouldn't need it! You should go to the cops and file charges!"

"I'm not going to do that. I'd lose, just like I lost at the hearing. He said … she said. But maybe … maybe at least the hospital might watch him more carefully now."

The server brought the iced teas. Ellen said, "And two Scotches, please. Neat."

This time Caro didn't object. After the server left, Ellen blurted, "Sissy, why aren't you angry? Why aren't you furious?"

"I *am* furious." She leaned across the table toward Ellen. "But I can't show it, not at the hospital. You don't understand.

I've trained myself not to. In the operating room, you can't show emotion." And a whole lot of good that had done her. But she wasn't going to say—not even to Ellen—that in the operating room, Caro thought of herself like a fighter pilot. Control was a necessity. Steadiness, calm, unflustered detachment. But saying that aloud sounded grandiose, possibly even ridiculous. Besides, there was never any point in trying to convince Ellen to value calm. Caro plunged into the rest of the mess.

"This means that after my Boards I can say good-bye to my chances of getting hired at Fairleigh. It just won't happen. And there are no—"

"But you're a rock star too! You told me that your evaluations or whatever they are—"

"Yes, but—"

"And your research! You did that brain mapping thing that even got published in—"

"Listen to me. I need you to listen. I'm good, yes. Very good."

Caroline is so full of herself. I cannot teach that child humility.

Caro continued, "That's part of the problem. Because I'm cross-trained in both neurosurgery and research and have done both, the only place I can work, would want to work, is a big hospital that runs clinical trials of new neurological developments. And there are no other hospitals like that in this city. Or in this state."

"I see," Ellen said. They sat in silence until the Scotches came. Ellen drank half of hers. "It's not fair, Caro."

"No. It's not." Which was why she'd thought that these doctors that she'd worked with, learned from, admired, would believe her. At the end of the hearing, Caro had looked at Dr. Borella, the only other woman in the room besides the treacherous Maisie, and Vera Borella had dropped her gaze to the polished conference table and not raised it again.

Caro had been naïve. No, it had gone deeper than that. The doctors at her hearing were faced daily with profound unfairness: The child who comes down with leukemia. The young father of three whose benign meningioma grows not in the pia mater of the right frontal lobe, where it would be easy to remove, but on the brainstem, where it destroys nerves and paralyzes him. The experimental drug that helps patients A, B, and C but unaccountably kills D. Somehow Caro had expected that physicians who experienced this profound unfairness every day would try to compensate with greater justice in their dealings with each other.

The hospital's self-interest meant it hadn't worked like that. Or, looked at another way, it hadn't worked liked that because, faced with Becker's denials, the others at the hearing had no evidence to go on, nothing tangible. He said ... she said.

A sudden, profound sense of loss swept through Caro. If only she'd left the party earlier. If coats and sweaters had not been left upstairs. If she hadn't bantered the last few weeks with Paul Becker, a banter which she'd seen as collegial friendliness, a relaxing of rank because after her Boards she would be his full colleague, and which he'd apparently interpreted as an invitation. If only just one thing of many had been different. But no, only a single "if only" mattered here, and Ellen startled Caro by voicing it.

"If only he wasn't such an asshole," Ellen said. "Because that's what you were thinking, isn't it, Sissy? That this mess is somehow your fault, because you're supposed to be able to control everything. *You can't.*"

Caro was silent. If Ellen had known anything about neurosurgery, she wouldn't say that. Caro understood completely how many things she could not control. Inoperable spinal injuries, glioblastoma multiforme impossible to remove completely, arterial aneurysms that burst in the ambulance on the way to the ER. The difference between Caro and Ellen was that Caro fought to control each of them and counted it as a personal failure when she could not. Whereas Ellen, from some mysterious mixture of courage and fatalism, accepted whatever life threw at her.

Caro said, "How's Angelica?"

"The same."

Angelica would always be the same, until one day she wasn't anything, and no longer defined Ellen's life and the life of her other daughter, Kayla. They were all the family that Caro had, and she would do anything for them—although that's what she thought she'd been doing, and now she'd screwed up.

"I'll miss you," Ellen said, "because of course you have to move where you can do your best work. My sister the hot-shot sawbones."

Despite herself, Caro laughed. "Nobody says 'sawbones' any more."

"Skull wizard. Brain editor. Gray Matter Cowboy."

"Where do you *get* these terms?"

Ellen smiled mysteriously. Then she grew serious. "I can manage, Caro. I will miss you dreadfully, but I can manage."

"I know." Her sister managed, better than nearly anyone else could have done in her situation. But with a good salary someplace else, Caro could still send Ellen money. Ellen needed it. Social services provided inadequate help for Angelica, Kayla outgrew her clothes as fast as Ellen could get them from Goodwill, and nobody, including his parole officer, had received word—or money—from Ellen's deadbeat husband in over a year. But what Ellen needed at least as much as money was adult companionship to relieve her terrible daily routine, and so few people besides Caro could stand to be in the house with Angelica.

Ellen said, "Where will you apply for a job?"

"Dunno yet. I have to start looking. Boards are next month."

"Well, right now I have to go to the ladies."

Alone, Caro pushed away her defeatist thoughts. After all, she sliced into thought every time she sent a microscope or a knife or a laser beam through the soft gray jelly of a living brain. Cutting through memories, through perceptions, through capabilities to move and speak and think. All as fragile as snowflakes, easily dissolved in a slip of the knife, a tear of a nerve. Thoughts changed nothing; only actions did. The party had happened, the hearing had happened. Both lay in the unrecoverable past, and now Caro would go forward. To a different city, a different life from the one she wanted, and she would travel back as often as she could to see Ellen and the kids. She could do this. She always had. The worst was over.

Ellen had left the second half of her Scotch undrunk. Caro hadn't touched hers. While Ellen was in the restroom, Caro got up from the booth, found the server, and paid for the liquor and iced tea so Ellen wouldn't have to. Then she pulled Ellen's purse toward her, fished around until she found the parking ticket, and stuck it in her pocket before Ellen could realize the ticket was gone.

2.

The worst was not over.

Two days later, as Caro was finishing morning rounds, DeVonne Lainhart stopped her in the corridor. Later, Caro would remember that she'd been smiling as she left the room of Hannah Glick, a young woman that Caro had operated on the day before. Dr. Fleischauer, Caro's surgical mentor, had stood back and let Caro perform the entire craniotomy on Ms. Glick, who'd been paralyzed on the right side by a frontal-lobe Grade 2 astrocytoma. Fleischauer had nodded in approval. The patient could now wiggle her right foot, and the patient's ten-year-old daughter had just declared she wanted to be a doctor when she grew up.

These were the moments Caro lived for.

"DeVonne! How are you?"

DeVonne put a hand on Caro's arm and said, "Caro, a word? Come with me. I have to show you something."

"I can't. I have to—"

"You have to come with me. Really. Seriously."

Caro looked harder at him. She and DeVonne, now a board-certified cardiologist, had been friends since med school. They'd dissected cadavers together, studied together, complained together about all the things internships and residency gave you to complain about. Caro and a now-defunct boyfriend had vacationed with DeVonne and his wife Helen in the Blue Ridge Mountains for one glorious, lecture-free, carefully budgeted weekend. DeVonne had, during one bad episode with Angelica, loaned Caro money that Ellen had needed.

He led her to an empty patient room and closed the door. The dark brown skin around his eyes crinkled with concern. "Are you on Twitter?"

"No. Who has the time?"

"Caro, there's been a backlash."

She shook her head, bewildered. "A backlash? Against what?"

"You."

"I don't—"

"Word of your sexual-harassment accusations against Becker got out. Your accusations and his denial."

She'd half expected that. There had been looks in hallways: embarrassed, mostly, but a few accusatory and a few sympathetic. Maisie? Most likely. Liars often felt a need to justify themselves to their friends, and what was it that Benjamin Franklin had said? "Three people can keep a secret, if two of them are dead." Caro had decided to just ignore all looks, of every flavor. In a few months she wouldn't be here anyway. Her fellowship would end, she'd pass her Boards, she would work in another city and leave behind Becker, Maisie, and other people's uninformed judgments.

"DeVonne—"

"Just listen, Caro. I need to … You need to know that news of your hearing got onto Twitter, the way everything does nowadays. At first the tweets were pretty sympathetic. But then other people involved themselves in your story—a lot of other people. Women's rights are undergoing a bad backlash from various men's movements, a few legit, but a lot made up of aggrieved trolls who think that women go around blithely accusing men of sexual misconduct for fun or profit. The trolls seized on a patient of Becker's, a woman whose life Becker saved with a Hail-Mary-pass operation on a clival chordoma with no good surgical plane. The patient knew enough medicine to realize how dangerous the operation was and how brilliantly Becker performed it. She Facebooked about it, and a troll calling himself 'Avvvengggger' picked it up and had his group run with it. They're a big organization, dedicated to shaming anyone they see as—I'm quoting here—'an enemy of good men.' As part of the online backlash against MeToo, they decided you're one of the enemies. These guys delight in taking somebody, anybody, down, and then other people believe what they read and just pile onto the shaming. The tweets and posts about you are terrible and getting worse, and I'm afraid there are a lot of them."

"How many?" Caro could barely get the two words past her throat.

DeVonne took a deep breath. "Over 40,000 including retweets, and counting."

"That can't be!"

"It is. Let me show you—"

"No." Caro was seized by a powerful desire to see this thing, whatever it was, without a witness.

He seemed to understand. "All right. But if you need to talk later, or any time at all, or if you want to come over tonight and discuss it with Helen and me—"

"Thanks, DeVonne. Just tell me how to find these tweets."

"Type 'pound sign, Caroline underscore doc destroyer.' No spaces." He left her after one reluctant look back over his shoulder.

Caro closed the door and stood by the sheetless bed. The room was stark and empty, the monitors silent, the over-the-bed table bare. It took a few fumbles on her phone before she had the tweets.

So *many* tweets.

> "Trying to take down a doctor who saves lives—let's crucify this bitch"

> "She should be fired"

"She should never never operate on a man."

"She should be disemboweled and burned!"

"Caro S-W: liar liar liar."

"Too many women like her trying to ruin good men"

"I like feisty bitches—I'd do her"

"Shut up, this is serious. Health care in this country sucks"

"You shut up, asshole"

"Caroline S-W needs to be thrown out of AMA"

"Isn't she related to some medical big-wig? Check your privilege, rich white bitch"

"Sterilize her so she can't pass on those lying genes"

"Protest her"

"Yeah—protest!"

"You can sign petition @firecarolinesoames-watkins"

"This kind of stuff sucks men are the real victims in this country"

"protest tomorrow Fairleigh Memorial Croyden W Virginia 8 a.m. who's in?"

"I be there"

"MeToo"

"Hah! Funny!"

"me"

"me"

"I live in Croyden and Dr. Becker operated on my sister. I'll come."

"me"

"me"

"Boil CS-W in oil"

"No, get six good men and make her—"

Caro clicked off her phone, her hand shaking.

Tomorrow. A protest against her, outside the hospital. Would anyone actually show up? Would the police be needed? Would there be violence?

Because of her.

Caro stood, felt her knees give way, and sat abruptly on the edge of the bed, holding her phone as if it were a bomb. Many of the vicious tweets had been retweeted. She didn't dare open her Facebook page, unused for months.

With Ellen's support, she had managed to regain her equilibrium after the hearing. This was different. No hospital would hire her if she were the cause of a protest that brought cops to the hospital's front steps. All her hopes and dreams, all the years of grueling work, all the loans she'd taken out after her mother disinherited both her and Ellen ... Without a good hospital appointment, how would she be able to repay her loans? How could she go on helping Ellen and the children? A neurosurgeon, unlike some other medical practitioners, could not just hang out a shingle and go it alone.

All her plans for the future ...

She wasn't sure how long she sat there. Eventually the door opened and an aide bustled in. "What are you doing in— Oh, sorry, Doctor. We have to ready this room now for an incoming patient."

"Yes, of course. Yes." Caro wasn't even sure what she was saying. But her legs, more stable than her emotions, stood and began moving her toward the door, through the door, toward she couldn't imagine what.

3.

Dr. Caroline Soames-Watkins:

We have never met. I am your great-uncle, your grandfather's brother, Samuel Louis Watkins. You have heard of me.

I am not interested in family, but since I learned of your career choice in medicine, I have followed your progress with some curiosity, including the article you co-authored with lead researcher Reuben Fleischauer on neural outcomes of direct brain stimulation. I am told that you are now a board-certified neurosurgeon. Also, that you may have trouble obtaining a hospital appointment due to recent online activity in the pernicious sewer of unthinking mob opinion.

I am in a position to offer you employment combining neurosurgery and clinical research in a private hospital in the Caribbean. The salary is above what you would be offered elsewhere. The appointment is a unique opportunity that will not suit every candidate qualified to fill it. If you are interested, my lawyer, William H. Haggerty, will arrange to fly you to the hospital in the Cayman Islands so that you and I may interview each other for mutual suitability.

Please respond within a few days to the email address below. I cannot wait too long for a neurosurgeon.

Sincerely,
Samuel Watkins

4.

"*What?*" Ellen said.

"A job offer. I think."

"Really? Where? Angelica! No, sweetie, no!"

The smell of shit billowed into the room.

Angelica, age five but the size of a two-year-old, squirmed on a plastic changing table in a corner of Ellen's shabby living room. She flailed her spindly arms and legs, her small face red with fury. Unable to speak or walk, she made her anger known the only way she could: with random movements as frenzied as her uncontrolled limbs could make them. Although her mother was practiced at restraining her, Ellen had jerked her head upward at Caro's announcement. Angelica flung herself sideways and the tube with which Ellen was suctioning feces from the child's rectum pulled out, spilling yellow-brown shit onto the table, Angelica's legs, and Ellen's shirt and hands.

Caro pressed her own strong hands onto Angelica's body. "Go clean yourself up. I'll finish here. Hush, Angie, it will be okay."

Angelica didn't hush. It wasn't okay, not any of it. Angelica had been born with both severe cystic fibrosis and a brain injury from oxygen deprivation. Multiple times each day, Ellen siphoned the abnormally thick mucus from the child's nose, throat, and lungs, and the feces from her rectum. Medicaid provided daily nursing help, but only for a few hours. Ellen, chained to Angelica's care, could not hold a job. Her public assistance was inadequate. There was never enough money.

Tenderly, Caro cleaned Angelica. The tiny body calmed. Angelica's eyes, the same clear light brown as Ellen's, gazed up at the aunt she would never speak to, never hug, never run to. Yet Caro felt that Angelica recognized her. The little girl could feel the gentleness of being stroked, the warmth of sunlight on her skin, the comfort of a full belly and a soft diaper. There was a person in that badly damaged brain, maybe even a person who, however dimly, knew that she was loved.

When Ellen returned, she dressed Angelica and then walked her up and down the shabby living room until the heavy head that Angelica could not hold upright rested on Ellen's shoulder and her eyes closed.

"Whew!" Ellen said, with her usual bright smile. "Okay, now that we can hear ourselves think, tell me about the job offer! Is it a good one?"

"I don't know," Caro said.

"You don't know? What does that mean? Where's it from?"

Caro took the letter from her pocket. Unwilling to burden Ellen more than her sister already was, and also—being honest with herself—from a sense of shame, Caro hadn't told Ellen about all the rejections she'd received in the last two months. The protest against her, although sparser than it looked in news photos, had blocked the main entrance to Fairleigh Memorial even after police had been called. The Twitter and Facebook and Instagram takedowns had continued, the viciousness apparently kept alive by some group somewhere enjoying their power over a doctor. Caro had not done the things that were the subject of the gleeful lies, and she was not the privileged, rich, man-hating harpy they said she was. She'd said as much online, but her self-defense had only fueled the pile-on. The hospitals, of course, knew the massive shaming wasn't accurate, but they also knew she'd "falsely" accused one of the most prominent physicians in the country. "We regret to inform you ..."

Ellen repeated, "Caro, where is the offer from?"

"Not where. Who. It's from our great-uncle."

Ellen stopped walking Angelica. "No! The Nobel laureate?"

"Himself."

"But where is he? Where has he been for the last fifteen years? You told me he stopped researching after he invented that drug and then just sort of disappeared!"

"He did. Only now he apparently runs, or at least is associated with, a private hospital in the Cayman Islands, and he wants to fly me out there to interview for a neurosurgeon position."

"Caro, are you going?"

"I don't know. How can I know? I Googled everything I could think of, I checked with the AMA, but Google had nothing and this facility, whatever it is, isn't in the United States, and the AMA had no information either. I talked to this Haggerty, a lawyer, and he was evasive about everything except the salary. I have no idea what's going on here, and is it a good idea to just waltz into a situation I don't understand?"

Angelica started whimpering. Ellen resumed walking her. Caro said, "You look exhausted. Give Angelica to me."

She took the little girl from Ellen. Angelica felt heavy in her arms.

Ellen said, "What is the salary?"

Caro told her.

"Holy shit! Really? And you're not even going to go see the hospital? You can't just— Is that a normal starting salary for a neurosurgeon?"

"No. It's astronomical. He could attract much more experienced people than me. Which means that there's something fishy here."

Ellen considered this. "No. Not from a Nobel laureate, because why would he endanger his great reputation with something illegal?"

"I don't know. Although, offshore, a lot of stuff is legal that isn't in the US. Particularly in the Caymans, if you have enough money. I'm not saying I haven't thought about the offer. I haven't thought about anything else since the letter came, but—"

The front door burst open and Kayla barreled through, sobbing. "I hate them! I hate them all!" She ran toward her tiny bedroom, hurling her backpack toward the sofa, which it missed.

Ellen caught her daughter as Kayla raced past. "Honey, what is it?"

"Let me go!"

Caro stopped walking Angelica and stared. Ordinarily, eight-year-old Kayla was calm and even sweet-natured in the living conditions imposed by Angelica's needs. Now tears flew off her face as she twisted to free herself from her mother's grasp. She didn't succeed.

"Kayla, I need to know what happened. Tell me what's upset you. Now. Who do you hate?"

"All of them! Jessie and Ava and Lily! They said … they said …"

"What did they say?"

"They said they won't come to my birthday party and they won't ever come to play at my house again because it always smells like shit and medicine!"

Ellen's face creased. She folded Kayla close as the little girl cried. On her sister's face, Caro saw the pain that all good parents face eventually: the inability to make things right for the child.

Kayla had been born just as Caro started med school, a few months after Ellen's jailbreak marriage to Eric. When Ellen went into labor, Eric had again been "out with the boys," and Caro had driven Ellen to the hospital and held her hand during an astonishingly quick and easy labor, especially for a first baby. When Kayla slipped into the world, Ellen cried, "Oh, let me have it! What is it?"

"A girl," Caro said, before the doctor could. "A beautiful baby girl!"

"Let me have her!"

The nurse laid the baby in Ellen's arms. "Just for a minute."

Gazing at mother and child, Caro felt herself near totally unexpected tears. Her little sister had done this miraculous, totally commonplace, utterly joyous thing, and here was a perfect new human being who'd just added a whole new layer to not only Ellen's life but also Caro's. Sister, future doctor, *aunt*. She was Aunt Caro.

Ellen said, "I'm going to call her Caroline."

"No," Caro said, before she knew she was going to say anything. "Not my name. She's ... herself. Look at her, oh just look at her, Ellen!"

"A version of your name, then. I want to. Charlotte. Caitlin. No—Kayla!"

"Kayla," Caro said, touching the baby's cheek, still covered with vernix. "Hello, Kayla."

"Why are we both crying?" Ellen said.

"I don't know," Caro said, swiping at her tears—she couldn't do that when she was a doctor!—as the nurse picked up Kayla and bore her away to be cleaned, weighed, and recorded.

Now Caro's gaze swept slowly around the tiny rented house: The stained carpet from mishaps with Angelica. The living room crowded with equipment for Angelica. The one ancient bathroom between the two doors to the bedrooms, one for Kayla and one crowded with Ellen's single bed and Angelica's crib.

Ellen crooned to her daughter, and Kayla quieted.

Was this really why Caro had come to Ellen's today? To show their great-uncle's letter to her sister, yes, but also to see again ... all this?

Never enough money.

Not enough help for Angelica.

Kayla in tears and anguish.

An astronomical salary.

Caro said, "Ellen, I've changed my mind. You're right. With that kind of salary, it's dumb not to at least check it out. I'm flying to the Caymans."

5.

"No." Dr. Lyle Luskin stood by Watkins's bed. "I'm sorry, Sam, but … no. Not yet."

Weigert braced himself. Only two people ever said no to Samuel Watkins and, although Luskin was one of them, Weigert was not. Was he going to have to agree with Luskin? Why did people have to be so confrontational? No wonder Weigert preferred numbers. One could wrestle with algorithms but not bash them over the head. Physics was so much more restful than medicine.

However, Watkins surprised him by not exploding into his usual impatient rage. All he said to his physician was, "When?"

Luskin said, "I told you I can't predict that."

Sam's voice rose. "Give me a range of time, then. Days? Weeks? Months?"

"You know I can't do that accurately. You've got the lab results right there on your mobile. Look at them again. You—"

"I did look at them! What do I have you here for if all you can do is refer me to labs I've already seen?"

"I can tell you yet again what you already know, since apparently you weren't listening. You have pancreatic cancer. The course of that disease differs radically in each patient. You also have a nasty, newly diagnosed viral infection. Until that's cleared up, you are not stable enough for elective surgery, especially untested brain surgery. You—"

"The surgery's been tested," Weigert ventured. Facts, after all, mattered. "On Julian."

"Who is thirty-five years old," Luskin said, "and strong as reinforced concrete. You, Sam, are not. Let me put this bluntly—you will not survive the operation. Not until you overcome this infection and build up your strength. And maybe not even then."

"You don't know what I can and cannot survive! You just said yourself that this cancer differs radically from patient to patient!" His voice grew louder, a threatening rumble. Weigert knew that rumble. The storm was close.

"I know *your* condition," Luskin said, a pre-emptory thunderbolt in his own voice. "You hired me as your oncologist to tell you about your condition."

"I hired you to get me well enough for the surgery! This project will lead to the greatest contribution science has ever made to humanity, and if you think it's going to be stopped by some pissant MD forbidding me to—"

"You hired me to tell you the truth. So listen to it, or find yourself a different pissant MD."

Abruptly, Watkins's voice dropped several decibels. "I know I did, Lyle. I hired you to be straight with me, and you're right to do it. I'm sorry."

Weigert blinked. As often as he'd witnessed these abrupt turnarounds in Sam's moods, at least partially the result of his medication, they still surprised him. But Luskin had said the only word that really mattered to Watkins: "truth." The only word that mattered to all of them, really. The only reason they were here, on this island, in this closely guarded compound, with this dying genius.

Watkins said, "Best estimate, Lyle?"

"If you beat this infection, you have five to six months left. Same as yesterday, Sam."

The doorknob turned and Nurse Franklin backed into the room, pushing the door open with her ample behind, carrying Watkins's breakfast tray. Weigert could never see her sparse reddish hair, blue eyes, and broad face without thinking *Irish peasant*. Even though he knew that the head nurse was actually of Polish descent and far from a peasant. Once Julian had taken Weigert to task for "thinking in stereotypes." Weigert hadn't tried to explain that sometimes stereotypes provided a useful framework for observation. Weigert, whose nanny had been Irish, associated Nurse Franklin with Nanny Kelly's basic peasant qualities: resourcefulness, stubbornness, a devoted prickliness. He was also a little afraid of her, as he had been of Nanny. Nurse Franklin was the other person who said "no" to Watkins. Julian didn't, although Weigert had noticed that Julian usually ended up getting his own way despite never directly contradicting Sam.

"Now, Dr. Watkins," Nurse Franklin said, "you're going to eat every bite of this breakfast. Not like dinner last night."

Watkins regarded both her and the tray with dislike. "We're in the middle of business, Camilla. Bring it back later."

"Now." She set the tray on his bedtable and crossed her arms.

Watkins glared. "I said to bring it back later."

Nurse Franklin, always willing to bring in reinforcements, said to Luskin, "Doctor?"

"Eat it, Sam," Luskin said. "We're done here. And you need to build up your strength."

"Oh, goddamn it, all right. Now what? Why is my bedroom suddenly Grand Central Station? Oh, it's you, Aiden. Come in. Lyle, thank you. Camilla, *go.*"

Doctor and nurse left. Weigert tried to follow them out, but Watkins said, "Stay." Weigert stayed.

Aiden Eberhart closed the door behind him. Weigert considered Aiden, like Aiden's boss Julian, too young for his position, even as he knew that to him all software people seemed too young for anything. But at least Julian was in his thirties. Aiden was twenty-four and looked fifteen. Surely Aiden was too young to be Julian's head of cybersecurity for the project? At least Julian had trained all his software people to call Watkins "sir." God knows what they might have come up with on their own. Sammy? Wizard-in-Chief? Death Lord? They all seemed to play those fantasy computer games. Weigert shuddered.

He could hear his long-dead wife, Rose, in his head: *You really are a Victorian throwback, aren't you, my darling?*

Watkins said to Aiden, "What do you want?"

"I have the surveillance report on Caroline Soames-Watkins, sir."

Watkins sat up straighter in bed. The blanket shifted, exposing the left side of his frail legs. "Good. Let's have it."

"As you guessed, when she asked for three weeks before coming here, it wasn't really 'to wrap up her affairs.'"

"Of course not," Watkins said. "She has no affairs to speak of. She wanted to check up on me, and I'd think less of her if she didn't."

"Yes, sir. She hired a hacker named Donny Cockroach, real name Donald Richard Hibler. He's not good, not bad. I don't know how she got his contact info. That wasn't in her emails. Must have been in person from somebody. But once she found him, they communicated by email. He—"

Weigert blurted, "You hacked private emails?"

Aiden and Watkins both looked at him, but here Weigert felt on sure ground. He said, "Sam, we agreed at the start that nothing on the project would be done illegally."

Watkins said, "I know, George. But this is the only illegal thing. And it's necessary. Nobody could have foreseen David Weeks's stupid and unnecessary death."

"But—"

"There are no 'buts.' Aiden, there's no chance that either my great-niece or this Cockroach person could find out that you hacked her emails?"

"None," Aiden said, looking affronted.

Well, Weigert thought, at least the boy had pride in his profession.

Aiden said, "If I can continue?"

"Go ahead," Watkins said.

"I sent the full report to you on encrypt one, but the gist of it is that she wanted info on three things: you, the compound, and its funding. All Cockroach got about you was information from public records. About the compound, he got the building history and some of the orders for our equipment—that was inevitable. Also external pictures of the compound walls, the island, everything a tourist could get from a car or drone or helicopter. Nothing that reveals anything."

"And the funding?"

"He tried, but whoever set up your multiple shell corporations and Cayman bank accounts and all the rest of it was very good. Cockroach didn't get much. I would bet anything that Caroline—"

"Dr. Soames-Watkins," Weigert corrected, despite himself.

Aiden nodded, but Weigert could feel the grin behind it. "Sorry, *Dr. Soames-Watkins*. But it's going to be confusing with a Dr. Watkins and a Dr. Soames-Watkins."

Watkins ignored this. He said, "Where did she get the money to hire Cockroach? Your initial report said both she and her sister were living pretty much on the edge, she's carrying massive med-school debt, and there are no other living relatives."

Weigert knew this part of the great-niece's history. Caroline Soames-Watkins and her sister had grown up with some money—not, of course, on Samuel Watkins's scale—but had apparently been cut completely from their late parents' will. Everything had been left to some ballet company. Weigert didn't know why (he suspected that Watkins didn't know, either), but it seemed a dreadful thing to do. Ballet! All very well in its place, of course, but ... There must have been some terrible family conflict. Sometimes Weigert was glad that he and Rose had not had children.

Aiden said, "Caroline—Dr. Soames-Watkins, I mean—borrowed the money from a friend, a cardiologist at Fairleigh Memorial. Dr. DeVonne Lainhart."

"Good, good. Now she's carrying even more debt."

"Yes, sir. All the particulars are in my report."

"Good. Nice job, Eberhart. You may go."

Weigert liked the boy better when he saw Aiden's brief blush of pleasure at Watkins's praise.

After Aiden left, Weigert said, "So she's coming."

"Day after tomorrow. Haggerty made all the arrangements, including rushing through a passport. Hers had expired."

"What do we do if she doesn't choose to stay here?"

"She'll stay," Watkins said. "What happened to her at that hospital was brutally unfair, but that's the modern world. And it's turning out beneficial for us. Her performance evaluations are excellent."

Did that mean Aiden had hacked into hospital records, too? No, Sam wouldn't condone anything that illegal. Although Weigert sometimes suspected that Watkins would do anything at all for this project.

Well, he heard Rose's voice in his head, *wouldn't you, too?*

No, Weigert answered. But—almost anything. After all, the project's underlying theory, before Sam's and Julian's separate species of genius had gotten hold of it, was Weigert's. Weigert did not forget that, not even when the other two were bending the theory to their own purposes. To their chance at immortality.

Watkins lay back on his pillows and closed his eyes. Weigert said, "Is the pain bad, Sam? Shall I call Nurse Franklin?"

"God, no. That woman is a thorn in my side, which doesn't need any more thorns. The pain meds will kick in soon. Talk to me, George. About something before ... all this. Preferably way before."

Watkins, glad to have a task he could perform for his old friend, thought briefly. "Do you remember that night at Oxford when we met? You had just arrived at college and stood in the quadrangle, looking lost, with your luggage piled around you."

Watkins, eyes still closed, smiled. Encouraged, Weigert continued.

"I happened to be passing, and you bellowed at me in all your so obvious American-ness, 'How do I find my goddamn rooms when nothing has any goddamn numbers?'"

"Not a bellow."

"A bloody bellow. I found your rooms with you, and you offered me a rather good brandy you'd bought at the Heathrow duty-free. I had been ready to dismiss you as another crass American who'd somehow bullied his way into Oxford, but I was impressed when the conversation turned to molecular physics and I learned how good you were."

"Not as good as you," Watkins said.

"No," Weigert said simply, "but still good. And then we forgot physics and got royally drunk."

"I got less drunk than you," Watkins said. "You couldn't hold your liquor, George. You still can't."

"And you couldn't find your own rooms in college. Or anything else there. Heaven only knows what would have become of you without me."

"'Dreaming spires' my ass," Watkins said, and Weigert saw that he was drifting into sleep—until the door burst open and Nurse Franklin bustled back in.

"Doctor! You haven't eaten a thing! It's getting stone cold!"

Watkins's eyes opened. He scowled at her and stuck his fork into a piece of scrambled egg. "Go away."

"I'm staying right here until I see you eat that breakfast. Every last bite."

Everyone, even Sam, had to answer to somebody.

6.

Caro's earliest memory had never actually happened. Everyone said so: Daddy, Mummy, Nanny. For a few years, Caro had stormed and insisted: "It did happen! It did!" Eventually she grew old enough to better describe the memory, but, by that time, she no longer wanted to share it, not even with Ellen. Ellen would not have understood. No one did, including Caro herself.

Yet the memory remained bright. She lay—at six years old? seven?—on a blanket in the back garden, watching clouds drift across the sky. Then, all at once, the clouds were no longer there, and neither was Caro. She was nowhere and everywhere, woven into what she much later thought of as "the fabric of the universe." She *was* the clouds, the grass, the breeze, the ant crawling across her arm. Everything was her, and she was everything.

Eventually, she would explain it all to herself as akin to well-documented mystical occurrences and wonder if she'd had an episode of temporal-lobe epilepsy. But only one episode, without recurrence? Not medically likely.

Besides, the episode—"occurrence," "neural storm," "delusion"—still, decades later, seemed as real to her as the drone of a bone saw, the scarlet of fresh blood, the cottage-cheese texture of an exposed brain. Usually Caro, scientifically wary of the inexplicable, tried to ignore the memory. However, she recalled it as the Cayman Airways flight approached the island of Cayman Brac because the memory—after all this time!—

seemed more real than the theatrically blue sea below her, the vividly showy green island, the pure white sand.

What the hell was she doing here?

But the answer to that was even less welcome than the memory. What Ellen called "your online shitstorm" still had not abated, kept alive by some vicious group of internet trolls whose motives she couldn't begin to comprehend. Ellen had said, "You're fresh meat. A change from politicians and actresses. Also, you're a doctor, and there's a whole class thing going on. Don't go online. Just don't look. I'll tell you when it dies down."

But Caro had been no more capable of not looking than of not scratching an itchy rash. Although this felt more like flesh-eating bacteria.

Did the kid next to her, his teenage scowl intent on his laptop, know about the shitstorm? Was he part of it? He'd taken one look at her, apparently decided she was too old to be of interest, and buried himself in a computer game that seemed to involve a lot of silent technicolor explosions.

The flight attendant said, "We are beginning our final descent to Captain Charles Kirkconnell Airport. Please stow all electronic equipment, lock your tray tables, and return your seat to its upright position."

The kid did none of these things. Caro touched him on the arm. He jumped as if assaulted and tore off an earbud. "*What?*"

"Announcement. We're there. Put away your laptop."

"Oh. Thanks." He gave her a sudden smile of unexpectedly childlike sweetness.

Caro turned back to the window. This was almost the worst of it: the suspicion. She couldn't encounter anyone, even a goofy kid on an airplane, without wondering if they were one of those gleefully shaming her, trying to ruin her life. It had happened to others in her position: jobs lost and friendships broken over a wrong joke, a digital misstep, an action distorted and sensationalized and amplified, made into something it had never been. Basically, an eighteenth-century public hanging as entertainment, except that now the victim didn't actually die, and the spectacle could be viewed over and over.

Professionally dead but personally alive. Unless she could somehow—how?—rebuild her reputation on Cayman Brac.

Someone named Ben Clarby was supposed to meet her at the airport. Google had offered her three dozen Ben Clarbys, and she'd no idea which this one was, or what connection he had to her great-uncle. Or very much about Samuel Louis Watkins, except for what was public knowledge.

Watkins had created and patented a genetically modified bacterium that altered the way the gut biome sent signals to immune cells in the intestinal lining. Those cells then altered signals sent to developing cells in bone marrow, creating immune-system cells that swiftly and effectively attacked adenoviruses. Watkins had sold both process and results to a pharmaceutical company, retaining a large percentage of royalties. The pharma developed Achino, now the best-selling drug in the world. Achino had saved countless people sneezes, coughs, and dripping noses, and saved industry billions of dollars in lost work time. The science won Watkins the Nobel Prize in Medicine; curing the common cold won him a fortune.

It did not, however, explain why he needed a neurosurgeon, or why his private hospital didn't search for one through normal hiring channels.

But lately a lot seemed inexplicable to Caro. She watched as the tropical island below her loomed larger and larger until the plane touched down and taxied to a stop.

≡

"Dr. Soames-Watkins? Welcome to Cayman Brac. I'm Ben Clarby. This way, please."

He was younger than she by a few years and totally unremarkable, the sort of man you'd pass three times on a street without recognizing him the fourth. A beige sort of person: tanned skin, light brown eyes, sandy hair. She followed him out of the single-runway airport filled with tourists into muggy afternoon sunlight. Ben flung her suitcase into the back of a topless jeep and opened the door for her, although from his awkwardness Caro had the impression he didn't do this often.

"Can I ask you some questions?" she said as they started off.

"Sure. You want to know about the island."

"No. About the hospital. How many beds, how much staff, the intake area, the—"

"Oh, Dr. Watkins has to tell you all that."

"Don't you work there?"

"Yes. In cybersecurity. But I can't tell you about the hospital."

Surprise warred with alarm. "Can't, or won't?"

He grinned, but there was something sour in it. "Both. But Dr. Watkins and Dr. Weigert will tell you everything."

"Who's Dr. Weigert?"

"He, Dr. Watkins, and Julian Dey founded the project. Weigert's the physicist."

Why was there a physicist? "Stop the car!"

A little surprised that he did, Caro turned to face him. They hadn't yet left the main road, lined with beach houses, ice-cream shacks, souvenir stores. "I'm getting out right here, Ben Clarby, unless you give me some answers. Now."

All at once he looked scared. "I can't, Doctor. I'm not allowed to. Please don't ... Look, there's nothing sinister about this. The hospital is doing clinical research. Actually, it's much more a research facility than a hospital. A physicist is there because it's brain research involving quantum effects. I'm not a physicist or doctor, I'm cybersecurity. But if I don't bring you back with me, I'll be in deep trouble. And this is your uncle, right? He must be somebody you trust!"

Caro studied him. Clarby was both lying and not lying. His panic at losing her was real, his total ignorance of the place's research was not. Still ... how much of her suspicion came from her online ordeal rather than anything happening in this moment? Probably most of it. It was maybe justified, but still ridiculous, to feel threatened every time somebody seemed evasive. Before the Paul Becker episode, the hearing, and the online attacks, she hadn't been so easily spooked.

She said, "I'm sorry, Mr. Clarby. I—"

"Call me Ben. Everybody does," he said, and the sour note was back again. Why?

"Please forgive my rudeness. Let's drive on, and will you please tell me about the island?"

He did, reciting facts in a voice steady but with an undertone of resentment. Her threat to leave had frightened him. *Way to get to know your new co-workers.*

Ben told her that Cayman Brac, the middle-sized of the three Cayman Islands, was twelve miles long and a little over a mile wide. Steep bluffs, ringed with reefs and sea-level mangrove swamps, raised most of the island 141 feet above sea level. There were no rivers, but many fresh springs. Christopher Columbus had sighted the island in 1503, and Sir Francis Drake in 1586. In the seventeenth and eighteenth century, it had been a base for pirates. A local stone, caymanite, was found nowhere else and was used to make jewelry and art. "Cayman" came from a Carib word for "crocodile," and "Brac" was Gaelic for "bluff." Caro already knew all this information from Google.

She learned more by simply looking around her. The western, sea-level end of Cayman Brac held the airport, beach resorts, tourist attractions, homes both shack-like and grand. As they drove into the interior, the land rose. Caro could no longer see the ocean, although she could smell the salt breeze. The road became unpaved, hard-packed dirt, mostly deserted and lined with scrubby trees that Caro couldn't identify. Bright birds flitted through the trees.

Abruptly, Ben slammed on the brakes. Caro grabbed for the dashboard to brace herself.

"Sorry," Ben said. "Iguanas have the right of way."

A huge, amazingly ugly lizard made its slow way across the road. Green with black feet, it stopped to yawn, then dragged its scaly tail over rocks leading into the forest.

Caro said, "How big is that thing?"

"Males can grow to two feet and twenty-five pounds. It's a Sister Islands Rock Iguana, found only here and on Little Cayman. Endangered and protected. Only seventy-five left on Brac."

"Are they dangerous?"

"Only if you're a plum or a leaf."

"And what was that bright-colored bird?"

"I didn't see it, but probably a parrot. There's a Parrot Preserve on the island."

He didn't elaborate, so Caro shut up and watched, although now there wasn't much to see. Palm trees, non-palm trees, stumpy pines, a coconut lying in the middle of the road. Ben ran over it. Fewer and fewer houses, until the jeep made a sudden turn, followed by another, and pulled up at a sprawling structure of high, windowless walls topped with security cameras. A wooden front gate, also windowless, resembled the thick door of a medieval castle.

What kind of hospital had no windows?

Ben said, "I did tell you it was more of a research facility than a hospital."

"You didn't tell me how this 'brain study with quantum effects' is being researched."

"No," Ben said, "I didn't." He keyed in a code on his phone and the front gate slid upwards, like a portcullis. 'Welcome to the compound."

7.

Weigert's first impression was smallness. Sam's great-niece barely reached Weigert's shoulder. Slim, dressed in something white over khakis, she looked about twenty. Then her eyes met his and he revised his opinion. They were Samuel Watkins's eyes, titanium gray.

"Ah, welcome, Doctor. I'm George Weigert."

She held out her hand. "Hello, Dr. Weigert. Caroline Soames-Watkins."

Her handclasp was firm. Ben Clarby had vanished with her luggage, and Weigert and she stood alone under the portico, a covered area just inside the gate and open on one side to the courtyard beyond. Weigert, who'd never really been at ease with any woman except Rose, wondered what he should do next.

He didn't have to decide. She said, "I'd like to see my great-uncle. Will you take me to him, please?"

Something concrete to do. But before he could speak, James bustled into the lobby. "Dr. Soames-Watkins? I'm James Warner, majordomo of the Watkins Research Compound. Welcome! I hope your flight was satisfactory. I'll have your bags carried to your room in— Oh, someone already did that? Are you hungry? Dinner is not for a few hours yet, but I can easily arrange for a tray if you're famished. Or something to drink?"

Dr. Soames-Watkins answered this effusion graciously. Weigert awarded her points for that. Manners.

"Thank you, but I'm good. Dr. Weigert is going to take me to my uncle."

She hadn't assumed the right to Weigert's given name and hadn't asked him to call her by hers. More points. Weigert was forty years her senior and there was already too much familiarity in the compound, especially among Julian's ubiquitous software team. Still, Weigert felt his anxiety mount as he led her across Wing Two's central courtyard. Planted with palm trees shading flower beds and picnic benches, Wing Two was airy, pleasant, and irrelevant. So was Wing One, a circle of tiny bedrooms with tinier baths, whitewashed inside and out, its courtyard also set with flowers and picnic tables. To Weigert, Wing One looked like a well-kept but bare-bones American motel. The only thing missing was a neon sign on the archway.

Watkins's room was the first on the left. Weigert's anxiety grew.

If Watkins disliked her ...

If she disliked him ...

If Watkins and Weigert could not convince her to join the project ...

Weigert had given his life to this. He could not see it fail now.

He knocked. The door was opened by Bill Haggerty, the lawyer. Sam was still fighting his viral infection, and today had not been one of his better days. Sitting up in bed, he looked even more frail than usual. Weigert felt the young woman's start of surprise.

Haggerty spoke first. "Dr. Soames-Watkins, I'm William Haggerty. I arranged your trip here."

"Hello," she said. "Dr. Watkins?"

Not "Uncle Sam." Although, now that Weigert considered this, he could see how unfortunate the name would be.

"Yes," Watkins rasped, and waited. Weigert knew this was a test. Did she know?

She stepped to the bed. "I'm glad to meet you. What kind of cancer is it?"

Haggerty's surprise showed on his face, but Weigert was pleased. Direct. Sam would like that.

Watkins said, "Pancreatic. Stage four."

"And your prognosis is ..."

"Terminal. And soon. Although you MDs don't really know, do you?"

"No. All we can offer are statistical probabilities. But you already know that. I'm sorry."

Weigert's tension returned. The two were regarding each other warily. What had Weigert hoped for? A softer bedside manner, a daughterly sort of concern, even a supplicant's eagerness to please? Not from this woman. At least, not yet. Of course, she had reason to be wary, having been told so little about why she was needed. Haggerty had insisted on that.

Watkins said, "You want to know why you're here."

"Yes," she said, "I do."

Haggerty cut in. "Not until you sign binding non-disclosure agreements. I have the paperwork in the security-office conference room. Sam—"

All at once Watkins's face spasmed in pain. The blood drained from his face. Caroline moved to his bedside and took his wrist, counting the pulse. "Does he get morphine? Why isn't that IV operational? Where's his doctor?"

Haggerty said, "I'll get Camilla."

The spasm subsided, leaving Watkins looking limp. He managed to get out, "Hasn't ... happened ... before. Not ... like that."

Nurse Franklin burst through the door. She slapped a patch onto Watkins's arm and passed a scanner over his forehead. "No fever."

Dr. Soames-Watkins said, "Morphine? Doctor, can I ask why you're using patches instead of that IV?"

"I'm not a doctor. I'm a nurse practitioner, and Dr. Watkins doesn't like needles."

"May I speak to his doctor?"

"Not unless you take a boat or plane to Little Cayman."

Her eyes widened. "There's no oncologist here? In a *hospital*?"

Haggerty said, "Dr. Soames-Watkins, your great-uncle seems tired now. Please come and sign the NDAs before we answer any questions."

That pretty face—Weigert only now noticed that she was pretty—stayed focused on Sam. "Dr. Watkins?"

Watkins, eyes closed, said feebly. "Better … later. George … will explain."

She turned inquiringly to Weigert.

No, no, not me! Sam and Julian were supposed to do the initial persuasive explanations. Where was Julian?

Haggerty said, "First follow me, please, Dr. Soames-Watkins."

Nurse Franklin said defiantly to the young woman's retreating back, "I can do most of what a doctor can."

≡

The security office, where a month ago the police had interviewed Weigert about David Weeks's unfortunate diving habits, was ringed with banks of computers, screens with camera surveillance of both inside and outside the compound, and locked bins. Two techs sat monitoring data. Both sneaked a surreptitious look at the new surgeon. Behind the office, a small conference room was furnished with a battered table, eight chairs, and a long shelf with coffee urns, cups, and a constantly replenished tray of pastries. Bags of crisps, used coffee cups, tubes of sunscreen, and baseball caps littered the room, since Julian's untidy techs used it as an unofficial lounge. Weigert avoided the room whenever possible.

Dr. Soames-Watkins read each of the several NDAs with care, which pleased both men. Haggerty wanted lawyerly assurance that she understood what she was signing. Weigert wanted delay in hopes that Julian would arrive and take over. Weigert expected, even desired, to explain the science to her, but not to answer the broader, undoubtedly penetrating questions she would ask about her role at the compound.

"Okay," she said, pushing the last paper across the table. "I can't say anything about anything to anybody at any time, until the heat death of the universe. Got it. Now please tell me about this facility, its purpose, and my role here."

Haggerty gathered his papers. "I'll leave you to it. Nice to meet you, Doctor. I'm sure we'll see each other again."

Dr. Soames-Watkins smiled, but her attention was on Weigert. He reached for secure ground. "Doctor, how much quantum physics do you know?"

If the question surprised her, she didn't show it. "Not very much, I'm afraid—only as it relates to the brain. Surgery works at a more macro level. I do know, of course, that calcium ions are involved in such processes as memory and excitability, to name just two, and that ions are small enough to be subject to quantum phenomena."

It was a start, but not a particularly good one. Weigert purged his explanation of double-slit experiments, entanglement, the Heisenberg principle, and a dozen other concepts critical to understanding his theory. That would all have to wait. And Dr. Soames-Watkins was a neurosurgeon. She did not need to understand the details of the physics involved. Not yet. Right now he needed only to sketch the broad outlines of the project well enough to convince her that her surgeries would serve a worthy cause. He changed levels: from ions to the entire universe.

He said, "For centuries, scientists have made an assumption about this universe: that it exists, and has always existed, independently of our perceptions of it. With a few dissenters, of course."

"The philosopher George Berkeley," she said, surprising him.

"Excellent!" Berkeley provided a place to start. "Then you know that—"

"Dr. Weigert, I don't see what Berkeley could have to do with my role here."

"No, I ... ah ... please bear with me, Doctor. It's all connected, and this is the best way to get to your role."

She nodded, and Weigert, relieved, plunged ahead. "Berkeley pointed out that all we can ever know of this universe comes to us through our senses. There is, for instance, no such objective thing as 'red.' If you see a fire engine, cells in your eyes interpret the light hitting your retina as 'red.'"

"Yes," Dr. Soames-Watkins said, in a tone that implied he was talking down to her. Hastily, Weigert moved on. It was critical that he find a level of information that neither insulted nor bewildered her. Julian, so good with people, would have known how to find that level. Weigert was trying, but his theory was so revolutionary! It had taken him years to formulate it, to bring Sam to full understanding of it, to find and convince Julian. For Julian to create the tech and software. And at least Sam and Julian had had the math necessary to fully understand. This skeptical young surgeon did not.

He made another attempt. "Doctor, do you understand the superposition of quantum foam?"

She gave him an unexpectedly mischievous smile. "Does anyone?"

Despite himself, Weigert laughed. She could be likable, after all, when she was not being wary. He said, "No, not completely. New discoveries are made every year. But here are the basics: 'Quantum foam' refers to the basic 'stuff' in the universe, the stuff that exists before you even get to basic particles such as electrons. 'Superposition' means that the quantum foam is not matter, nor energy, but just the *potential* of becoming either. It is, basically, just a cloud of probabilities. That is really important. Even when you do have that electron—as part of an atom, for instance—it too is just a quantum-foam probability of becoming a particle or becoming a wave of energy. Science has established that thoroughly and completely.

"So what determines when that electron—or any part of the quantum foam itself—becomes either matter or energy? We've known the answer to that for well over a century, as well.

Probabilities turn into matter or energy only when they are observed. That is called 'collapsing the wave.' In other words, it is the observer who actually creates what we call reality."

She sat considering for a long moment. Weigert, unable to read her expression, continued.

"Everything we just said, and more, adds up to a radical departure in the way we conceive of reality. It's just as Berkeley implied in the 1600s, although he did not say it directly: nothing exists until we observe it. Nothing."

"Nothing? This table doesn't exist? This room doesn't exist?"

"If I'm observing it, it exists for me. It's a mental construct, a creation in my mind."

She frowned. "Then this whole time you've been talking metaphorically."

"No," said another voice. "Literally."

Oh, thank heavens—Julian. Weigert hadn't heard the door open. But Julian stood there, and she reacted to him the way women always did: her eyes widened, her spine straightened, and for a moment she openly stared.

Tall, very blond, with turquoise eyes, Julian looked like an American idea of Viking heroes. What would it be like to have those flamboyant good looks, that easy effect on women? Weigert was deeply grateful that he'd never had to find out. Gossip, inevitable in such a small place, even though Weigert tried to avoid listening, said that Julian's "love life" was messy and difficult. Something about the former neuroradiologist, or was it the anesthesiologist? And hadn't some other young woman dropped out of the project because of Julian?

Dr. Soames-Watkins dropped her eyes. Her lashes trembled. It was only a tiny moment, but in that moment Weigert saw her vulnerability, such a contrast to the cool confidence she tried to project. All at once he wanted to protect her from the chaos Julian seemed to cause for women. She looked so young.

"I'm Julian Dey," he said, sitting at the table and holding out his hand. "Head of software development. You're Caroline

Soames-Watkins, and we're so happy you decided to check us out. Welcome. I'm sorry, however, that you just found out this table doesn't exist until you look at it."

"I'm not convinced of that," she said, and Weigert was pleased to see that she'd regained her self-possession. "It seems pretty solid to me."

"Precisely. To *you*. And to me, because I'm also observing it. And to George, of course."

"Are you saying that the table does not exist if no one is in the room?"

"I'm saying—actually, physics is saying—that all possible tables can exist until someone makes an observation. A fuzzy cloud of superimposed quantum information is what exists, which could become all possible tables. Then Caroline Soames-Watkins, preceded by a lot of others, enters the room and observes, and lo! There is a table."

"This is sophomore-level dorm arguing, Julian. Basic solipsism."

"No, it's not. Everything that I'm sure George just said is backed by hard science, both theoretical and, increasingly, experimental. George, your great-uncle, and I can convince you of that, if you'll only give us the chance. Would you like a cup of coffee?"

"No, thank you. And don't be so sure what you can convince me of."

Julian smiled, and his very blue eyes gleamed. Dr. Soames-Watkins turned her head and looked away. Was he flirting? Was she? If so, Weigert didn't like it. He struck into the conversation. "You're probably wondering why, if the table isn't there until we observe it, we all end up observing the same table."

"Yes," Julian said. "Why do we all see the same table, complete with that dent in the corner and that weird stain that resembles South America? Why doesn't Caroline see a Shaker straight-lined piece of furniture while I see an Italian marble console?"

Showing off, George thought. And yet, surely a woman would be the one more likely than a man to see the gilded marble table? Or was saying otherwise, avoiding what nowadays seemed to be named a "stereotype," part of Julian's so-called charm? It was very confusing.

Weigert returned to the safety of physics. "The answer to Julian's question, Doctor, lies in the creation of consensus reality, which we can discuss at a later date."

"Yes, we can," Julian said. "For now you want to know your particular role in George's theory."

"I do, yes," she said, with a return of her earlier wariness. But Weigert saw that she was also turning over what she'd just heard, probing, testing such a massive shift in the way reality existed. Of course, she would have all sorts of objections. He was confident that, given enough time, he could answer all her objections. The physics was there.

Julian busied himself with the coffee urn on the side table. "Well, *I'd* like coffee. Last chance, you two … Coffee? Yes, Caroline? Cream and sugar?"

"It's 'Caro,'" she said. "All right, black coffee, please. Dr. Weigert, you said 'this universe.' Twice.

Are you implying that other universes exist? The multiverse theory?"

"Yes," Weigert said, "although not exactly in the way that Everett branching suggests because—"

"Fine," she said. "You may have as many universes as you like. I have actually heard of the multiverse theory, although I don't know much about it. But you still haven't told me what this facility is researching, or why you need a neurosurgeon."

Weigert said helplessly, "There's so much more to understand before you can—"

"Now," she said, in a tone that startled Weigert. No one except Sam had used it with him since university. This hidden steeliness must be what had propelled her through the long, arduous years of work to become a neurosurgeon. On the whole, Weigert approved.

Julian handed her the coffee cup, sat down opposite her, and blew up all Weigert's plans for a slow, methodical introduction to his theory.

"Let me ask *you* a question," Julian said. "How would you like to live forever?"

8.

Caro gaped at Julian. Whatever she'd expected, that certainly wasn't it.

Julian said, "Okay, that was a little too abrupt. But it's at the heart of this project."

"It's not!" Weigert cried. "Julian, you're misleading her!"

"Not really. Immortality is the part of the project that the public is going to fasten on, and right now, in this room, she's the public. Let me be clear, Caro. We're not creating immortality through some sort of magic elixir or genetic tweaking. What we're doing is proving scientifically that immortality already exists because reality is not what most people think it is. George, do you like that statement better?"

"Yes. No! You've left out all the—"

"Yes, you're right, the background needs to be thoroughly explained in order to convince anyone. And to explain to you, Caro, just how you fit into our research, I'd like to take you on a quick tour of the research wing of the compound."

Caro had had time to move past shock and find words. She stood. "I think we're done here. I'd like to go back to the airport, please. If you people, including my great-uncle—if what you're doing here is using neurosurgery to alter the way the brain 'creates' reality, then I want you to know, with all due respect, that I think you're all insane."

Weigert paled. Julian said, "The definition of insanity is so mutable, just like the brain's plasticity. I'm sure you know about recent surprises in research on neuroplasticity. Your guess is essentially correct, but very incomplete. You've made a long trip to get here. Don't leave before you at least see what we're doing."

How could any tour justify everything that had already been said? But sudden curiosity, the curiosity that had led Caro to brain mapping in the first place, made her nod to Julian. A quick tour couldn't hurt, could it? Also, was she willing to lose the astronomical salary that could help Ellen, or the possible favorable professional references from a Nobel laureate that might rescue her career, or the chance to do neurosurgery?

Yes, she'd reject all that if it meant performing some version of 1950s lobotomies that turned people into zombies.

Caro said, "I don't want this coffee after all. Sorry."

"No problem," Julian said. "Let's go."

As they left the security office, Caro glanced back over her shoulder. Weigert was washing out their coffee cups in the little sink, each movement as meticulous and purposeful as if he were performing surgery.

≡

In the courtyard Julian said, "You've already seen Wing One, completely living quarters. This is Wing Two. Except for the security office, it's James's domain. He is—"

Caro smiled. "I already met James. He informed me that his title is majordomo."

"I'm sure he did. He supervises his housekeeping staff, most of whom live off-site, from his office—there, beside the gate opposite the security office. The rest of the rooms" —he pointed at each door circling the courtyard— "are the kitchen, housekeeping staff lounge, laundry, storerooms, gym, and there, just opposite with the walls folded open, the refectory. Breakfast is six to ten, lunch noon through two, dinner six till whenever, but the kitchen never really closes and food is pretty much available any time. James's staff will bring a tray to your room on request. The food is basic but edible."

Caro peered into the low-ceilinged space, now deserted: metal tables, folding chairs, bare whitewashed walls, cafeteria line with plexiglass sneeze guards. "'Refectory?'"

Julian grinned. "I know. But Weigert and Watkins attended Oxford together. George taught there afterward while doing research, and his nomenclature is still stuck somewhere between habit and hope."

Caro remembered that unlike Julian, who was dressed for the tropics in khaki shorts and a yellow polo, Weigert had worn a short-sleeved rayon button-down and a striped tie, which looked as out of place as a tuxedo on a beach. Caro could picture him in a don's robe, even though such things hadn't been worn in the United States in a hundred years, and certainly not in a physics lab.

Julian led her to a door that he keyed open with a thumbprint. "This is Wing Three."

Another large courtyard. No picnic benches or palm trees here, although it did have one flowerbed in the middle, looking less well tended than those in Wings One and Two. Clearly a more serious courtyard, circled by closed doors bearing thumbprint locks. No signs on the doors, which suggested that anyone in this area already knew where they were going.

Julian thumbed open a door. "This side of Wing Three is the hospital proper. We'll walk through, although it's not being used right now."

"Not being—"

"If you hold your questions for just a bit, I'll explain later. I promise." A warm smile, which she tried to ignore. She was not going to succumb to a sexy lunatic who clearly thought he was God's gift to women.

Labs, radiology, a single OR with scrub room, recovery, nurses' station, everything as expected except that there were only four patient rooms and two ICU beds. And no people. "Where are—"

"Most of the hospital staff isn't here right now. They'll all move back to the compound when you begin operating. Please, Caro, just bear with me. There's more to see, and it will help with explanations."

He led her out of the "hospital"—*this* was what she would be getting instead of Fairleigh Memorial?—and across the courtyard to another door, saying, "I'll take your thumbprint after you tell us for certain that you're staying. Meanwhile, this area is why everything else in the compound exists."

"I thought it existed because I'm observing it," Caro said.

He laughed. "Then observe carefully."

They walked through a conference room much larger than the one behind the security office but equipped with the same utilitarian furniture, plus a whiteboard on one windowless wall. The conference room led to a still larger space with desks and storage cabinets at one end. At the other end stood two huge computer consoles with a cot between them, plus a dazzling array of equipment.

Caro said, "You have an efMRI? Really?"

"Have you used one?"

"Yes."

Fairleigh Memorial did not have an Enhanced Functional MRI; there were only a dozen or so in the United States. Invented only a few years earlier, it took clearer, more detailed images of brain activity than anyone had thought possible. Caro and Paul Becker had traveled twice to Johns Hopkins to use their machine for brain mapping work. On those trips he'd never been "inappropriate"—what a stuffy word for something that had just altered Caro's entire life—although of course he hadn't been drunk, either.

Cables from the efMRI disappeared into the wall, except for ones that led to another large, gleaming piece of machinery. Julian said, "And that behemoth over there is the latest in Japanese tech. It does deep-image reconstruction. First you train the machine on your personal brain. After training, it uses reconstruction algorithms to optimize, display, and record the imagery of what you're thinking about. The fidelity and detail are both incredible. Magnitudes better than with previous iterations."

"Where do those other cables go?"

"To an encrypter. Data from this experimental setup needs crunching with a lot more computer power than we could have here. Sam's bought time on the MIT cluster. The data goes by satellite."

Caro stared at the cables, at the mind-reading machine, at the efMRI. The money being expended staggered her. Her salary was only a miniscule fraction. And she still didn't know what she was supposed to do to earn it.

"Julian, if this facility is conducting clinical trials on brain function, why is it being explained to me by a physicist and a software developer? What exactly is this a research trial of? Why are there no other medical personnel here, and what does all of it have to do with 'proving' immortality?"

Even saying that last made Caro feel ridiculous. Like proving ghosts, witchcraft, or the popularity of Chia pets.

"It's an unusual clinical trial," Julian said. "In fact, that's not really the right word for it. It's a research project, and we do have medical personnel. Watkins, of course. Dr. Lyle Richard Luskin, who oversees both our patients and Sam Watkins's care. You'll meet him tomorrow. Your neuroradiologist and anesthesiologist will be returning shortly to the island, as will Camilla Franklin's nursing staff. Our former neurosurgeon, David Ernest Weeks, unfortunately drowned last month in a diving accident, but your backup surgeon, Dr. Ralph Egan, is here. However, he's only temporary, since he's newly board-certified and will be leaving us for what he really wanted and has been offered, a surgical position in Los Angeles. We're already looking for a more permanent backup for you."

"How were you able to recruit someone on just a temporary basis?"

Julian smiled, his long lean body reclining negligently against the bulk of the computer console, and once again she felt the tug of attraction. He said, "Ralph is a relative of mine, but a real neurosurgeon nonetheless. We provide our patients with excellent medical care."

"They're not really patients, though, are they? They're not ill. They're research subjects."

"Yes. Volunteers eager to make a major contribution to science, starting with but not limited to ground-breaking brain mapping. And once you fully understand what we're doing here and why, I think you'll be convinced to stay."

The same thing Weigert had said. Before Caro could answer, the physicist pushed through the door. Somehow, he managed to simultaneously look both wary and eager.

"Dr. Soames-Watkins, your uncle suggested I follow you to supplement Julian's tour and explanations. With more physics, you know, to fully illuminate your function here."

Caro nodded, fleetingly amused to see that now it was Julian who looked wary. She guessed what he was thinking: Weigert would talk such high-level physics that she would be unable to follow him and would be put off the research in its entirety.

However, Weigert began simply enough. "Dr. Soames-Watkins, you already said you've heard of the multiverse?"

"In vague terms."

"Good! Mathematics tells us that the universe we perceive is only one of many. Every time an observation is made—by humans, dogs, elephants—the universe holds the possibility of other branches of itself, with all other possible outcomes of that observation."

"Every time? Resulting in—what?—an infinite number of possible universes?"

"Yes! You grasp it! You see, the wave function and decoherence—"

Julian interrupted. "I don't think Caro needs wave functions just yet. George, if I may?"

"Certainly," Weigert said, although it was clear he was bubbling over with wave functions, decoherence, and probably esoteric math. His deeply lined face glowed, and Caro felt herself warming to him. This man loved his subject with a single-minded, uncomplicated passion she hadn't seen in many neurosurgeons, who usually juggled surgery, rank, money, and hospital politics, not to mention coping with the emotional fall-out of unsuccessful surgeries. At least physics did not result in someone dying.

Usually.

Julian said, "As George indicated, there are many, many potential universes branching off from this one, created by observations—yes, even by elephants. I saw you startle a little at that. George is fond of elephants."

"Splendid beasts," Weigert said. "Very intelligent. But the moment of decoherence—"

"We are, however," Julian interrupted, "concerned here with universes branching off from *human* observations. Each one starts out the same as ours, and then evolves on its own to include things that do not happen, or happen differently, from what we perceive as 'our reality.' The research we are all doing has gone on for years—or in the case of George, who formulated the theory behind the research, for decades. We have found a way for human consciousness to enter—actually, to create—another branch of the universe. Not the body, of course—our material selves remain here. But consciousness enters another branch of the multiverse by altering all the algorithms hard-wired into your brain. Those algorithms are what interpret the information coming to your brain from your senses. Creating 'red,' for instance."

"*Enter* another branch of the multiverse?" Caro said.

"Create and inhabit. Just as your brain already creates the reality of the table we discussed in the conference room."

"How?" Caro said, although she already had a suspicion of the answer.

"Through extensively programmed chips surgically implanted in the brain, which are connected to even more extensive programming in that computer there." Julian pointed to the huge metal object whose cables dangled over the cot.

"Julian, Dr. Weigert ... How can you even believe that could ever work?"

"Three reasons." Julian watched her closely. "First, George's math shows that it can. Second, altering the way the brain perceives reality is actually something we are all familiar with: in dreams, with consciousness-altering drugs, during a high fever. Last night, for instance, I dreamed I was walking barefoot on a beach. I could see and hear the waves, even feel the beach pebbles underneath my feet. We dismiss dreams because they end when we wake up. But as George said, *everything* we experience is only a whirl of quantum information in our brains. Awake or dreaming, you're experiencing the same bio-physical process. The algorithms in my mind created that beach, those waves, the pebbles. Those algorithms are the tools your mind uses to put everything together. Life as we know it is observer-determined, which seems to trap us in the universe we're familiar with. But change the algorithms and you can create a different 'reality.'

"And third, I know what the implanted brain chip does because I have experienced it. I'm the only person David Weeks implanted before he died."

Caro said, "He did what? Implanted a computer chip in your brain?"

"Yes. I'm a cyborg."

You're a lunatic.

Before Caro could say that aloud, Weigert ventured, "If I can just explain a little more about decoherence and collapsing the wave—"

"Later, George," Julian said. "Let's allow Caro to ask all the rest of the questions I know she's bursting with."

But Caro didn't want to ask more questions until she'd had a chance to formulate them with greater precision, since *How can you be so deluded* did not count as scientific precision. She needed to sort out everything she'd already heard. How much sleep had she gotten last night? Three hours, tops. She was accustomed to going without sleep—no one got through med school without acquiring that ability—but this was exhaustion of a different sort: emotional, intellectual. More than sleep, she needed to be alone to think. Sleep, however, was a good excuse. She said, "Actually, I'm pretty tired."

"I can imagine," Julian said. "Two flights, and now all this information. Let me show you to your room."

"Thank you."

Before she could say more, the door opened and a man entered. "Julian," he said, "the police are here. I told them that Dr. Watkins is ill, and they want to speak to whoever else is in charge."

Julian rose. "Okay. Caro, this is Aiden Eberhart, my chief assistant. Dr. Weigert will show you to your room. Sixth on the left, George." He vanished through the door.

Weigert looked at her doubtfully and said, "If you'd like just a bit more clarity on decoherence—"

Caro said, "Later, Dr. Weigert. I'm feeling a little decohered myself."

And Weigert, again surprising her, went in an instant from overly erudite and possibly deluded theorist to likeable old man, and laughed.

9.

"What did the police want? More on Weeks's death?" Watkins said to Julian, who stood near Watkins's bed. "I thought that was all settled."

"It is," Julian said.

Weigert hung back by the door. Dr. Luskin had said that perhaps tomorrow Sam could sit in his wheelchair and be taken outside. Weigert hoped so. The tiny, overheated room was claustrophobic. But then Sam had never been one to take much notice of his surroundings, and none at all of their effect on other people.

Watkins said, "Then what did the cops want?"

"Two things," Julian said. "First, somebody ran over a Sister Islands Rock Iguana on the access road at the east side of the compound, which means it was probably a truck arriving at the loading dock. Supplies were delivered this morning."

"Stupid reptiles," Watkins snorted. "Let them go extinct. We're not responsible for vendors' drivers. Did you refer the cops to the truckers to pay the fine?"

"No, I paid it. Sam, we can't afford to antagonize the local authorities. You know that."

"Whatever." Watkins dismissed iguana, police, vendor, and fines with a wave of his hand. To Weigert the hand looked skeletal, translucent flesh stretched between long bones. And although Watkins's color had improved a little, pain pulled taut the skin of his thin face. Weigert could remember when Watkins could hoist a quarter cord of firewood—well, dry, green wood, anyway—looking more like a lumberjack than a genius scientist. Once, on a walking tour in Scotland, he had moved a huge boulder obstructing a Paleolithic mound he wanted to enter. Nothing stopped him in those days.

Rose said, *Nothing stops him now, either. Nothing stops either of you.*

Watkins demanded of Julian, "What's the second thing the cops wanted?"

"Another copy of our incorporation papers."

"Why? What's that, the third copy in as many months? For whom this time? We not only dotted every 'i' on the regulations, we practically engraved them!"

"This time they had a complaint about staffing," Julian said. "The hospital wing does not have enough nurses to meet medical regulations."

Watkins said with ominous evenness, "We're here in the islands precisely because the medical regs are practically nonexistent. On Grand Cayman, Vivian Grant's lab is fooling around with human cloning! And how the fuck does anyone know if we have one nurse or six or six hundred on staff? Let me read that complaint. Someone from inside the compound had to file it."

"Yes," Julian said, "and I'm afraid I know who it was. This is my fault, Sam. I had a ... a relationship with the anesthesiologist who left, Sara Doolin. The relationship ended badly, and she might have—"

Watkins's face reddened. "With Dr. Doolin? How could you be so stupid? Didn't you *think* that she might—"

"No, I didn't," Julian said, and, dear heaven, now Julian looked angry too. "I trusted her. I made a mistake and I'm sorry. But we're all cooped up here. Sara and I liked each other, and I'm not a monk, Sam!"

They glared at each other. Finally, Watkins said, "How much else is Dr. Doolin likely to tell anyone?"

"Nothing. I called Bill Haggerty right after the cops left, and he'll talk to her. She signed NDAs, of course, and she knows that if she violates them again, we'll sue her until Doomsday. She won't risk her career. This was a misjudgment on my part, as the revenge complaint was on hers, but neither will happen again."

"It better not," Watkins said. "I don't like authorities sniffing around for any reason at all. We're vulnerable, you know that. Oh, and don't start any 'relationship' with my great-niece!"

Julian flushed. "None of your business, Sam. And she's not the type to go in for revenge."

"I don't care what type she is, as long as she performs the surgeries. Has she said yet whether she'll stay here?"

"No."

"Well, do you think she will?"

Julian hesitated. "I'm not sure yet. Caro's not easy to read. Controlled on the surface, roiling with emotion underneath."

Watkins looked at Weigert. "George?"

"I can't tell yet, either."

Julian added, "She's very intelligent, but ours are such radical ideas for most people, even for someone like Caro with a prior professional interest in brain mapping."

Weigert said, "But we have *proof.*"

Watkins said, "We also have money, which Caroline needs badly both for her med-school debt and her sister's kids. Bonus money is a great motivator. So is eventual publication in collaboration with a Nobel laureate. Don't underestimate the root of all evil."

Julian said quietly, "It was the love of money, not money itself, that was named the root of evil."

Watkins said, "Same difference."

"It's not," Julian said, "but I'm not going to argue scripture with you. Any progress on finding another backup surgeon to replace Ralph when he leaves?"

Watkins said, "I'm working on it."

Weigert, surprised, said, "You're working on it, Sam? I thought that Julian ... I mean ... are you up to that?"

"I can use a laptop, George. I'm not dead yet."

Not what Weigert had meant, but this was Sam being the Sam he had become since his illness, and Weigert said nothing.

Watkins added, "I'd like to talk again to Dr. Soames-Watkins myself. Send for her, Julian."

Nurse Franklin bustled in, argued Sam into taking pills, and flounced out. Weigert, who had never been hospitalized, thought that nursing staff should be unobtrusive. Surely she could not behave like such a bully if she were not such an excellent nurse. If she were not so utterly devoted to Sam's care. If she were not Sam's cousin, known to him since childhood.

Cousins, great-niece ... Both Sam and Julian seemed able to produce relatives as needed, rabbits out of a familial hat, even after decades of neglect. Weigert, who had no family, felt wistful. But, then, he hadn't needed family before Rose died. He'd had her.

Aiden Eberhart appeared in the doorway. Julian said, "Aiden?"

"You sent for Dr. Soames-Watkins, but James couldn't find her. I checked the entry log and spoke to the on-duty tech. She didn't sign out, but she did leave the compound half an hour ago.

She's gone."

10.

Caro's bedroom, identical to Watkins's, was a whitewashed box, too small for anything but a bed, nightstand, chest of drawers, and desk. One window facing the courtyard, two doors to a bathroom and a closet that would have been inadequate if Caro had cared much about clothes. But, unlike Watkins's room, someone had hung the window with blue curtains and covered the bed with a cheerful blue-and-yellow quilt. A vase of yellow wildflowers stood on the desk. Probably James's doing. She must remember to thank him.

Caro left her suitcase unpacked. She set her laptop on the desk and Googled.

George Weigert, now seventy-six, had been born in London and educated at Eton and then Oxford, where he'd taken a double first in physics and mathematics. He'd stayed on at the great university and done research resulting in a long list of respectable articles in peer-reviewed physics journals. Married to Rose Leigh Bessborough, a distant cousin to the royal family, who'd died sixteen years ago. After his wife's death, Weigert moved to the United States and, like Watkins, dropped out of sight.

Julian Dey, Aiden Eberhart, Ben Clarby. Nothing notable on the latter two except for graduating with high honors from, respectively, Cal Tech and MIT. Much more on Julian, thirty-five, who'd apparently been some sort of boy *wunderkind* in Silicon

Valley, where he'd developed software that Caro had never heard of but which seemed to be a very big deal. Eight years ago, he'd started his own company. Five years ago he'd sold it for a sum that made her blink, and then he left the tech world.

David Weeks: board-certified neurosurgeon. A month-old article in the local paper reported his death from accidental drowning.

Ralph Egan, Camilla Franklin, both legitimate medical practitioners. Caro found nothing suspicious about the compound.

So what had the police wanted with Julian?

She called Ellen. "Hi, Sissy, I'm here in one piece and I need a reality check."

"Great. I specialize in reality. What's the place like?"

"The island is gorgeous, the compound has more security than the Pentagon, everyone is being nice to me, but—"

"Angelica! No, sweetie! Oops, gotta go! I'll call you back when I can. Kayla, come talk to your aunt!"

Caro understood. Half her calls to Ellen were interrupted or terminated by Angelica's sudden, urgent needs. There was no way around that, not if you were as devoted a mother—and as poor—as Ellen, and had a child like Angelica.

Kayla picked up the phone. "Hi, Aunt Sawbones!"

"Kayla! Did you learn that from your mom?"

"Yes, Aunt Skull Wizard!" Kayla giggled, the delicious giggle of a nine-year-old, and Caro's heart lifted.

"If I'm a skull wizard, you better watch out that I don't put a spell on *your* head."

"I can run faster than you, Aunt Gray Matter Cowboy!" More giggles.

"Maybe, maybe not. When I see you again, we'll have a race."

"Okay! Guess what happened at school today?"

"You tell me."

Kayla did, at length, a convoluted story involving people named Lucy and Morgan and Noah, a bracelet made of straw that was or was not ineptly braided, and a flurry of notes passed during math. Caro gave up trying to follow the particulars. Periodically she made encouraging noises, enjoying her niece's high spirits, which seemed to have recovered from classmates' saying they would not play at Kayla's house. Kayla finished with, "And then Noah said he liked Olivia better! He really said that!"

"Wow," Caro said. Had there been an Olivia in the story?

"I know! And tomorrow— Oh, gotta go. Mrs. Foster is here."

Who was Mrs. Foster? Caro said, "Put your mother back on."

"Can't, she's still in the bathroom with Angie. Bye, love you!"

"Love you, too," Caro said.

So … no reality check with Ellen, at least not at the moment. Caro would need to think alone.

But not here. The bedroom felt too claustrophobic. The room, the compound, the situation. She went outside, across the deserted courtyard, through the gate to the central wing. Still no one, although clatter and voices came from the refectory. Caro smelled cooking. The last food she'd had was a gluey burrito at the Miami airport, but food had never mattered much to her.

Would anyone try to stop her if she left the compound to take a walk? The thought was ridiculous; she wasn't a prisoner. The front gate was not locked, at least not from this side, and the young woman staffing the security office merely nodded as Caro left.

She started down the unpaved road. The sun drifted behind wispy clouds, muting its brassy glare. A small green lizard flitted across the hard-packed dirt. Well-worn trails branched off into the trees, which was reassuring. People hiked here. Caro took the third trail, wider than the others. Everything looked green. She remembered that October was the rainiest month in the Caymans.

She saw more yellow blossoms like the ones in her room, plus flowering bushes she couldn't identify. After fifteen minutes, sweat trickled down the back of her neck and into the cleft between her breasts, but she also felt calmer and—yes—more rational. What was she so agitated about? She didn't need to share these people's beliefs about physics to participate in any legitimate research, no more than she'd needed to share the religious or political beliefs of her colleagues at Fairleigh Memorial. She would listen to the rest of Dr. Weigert's explanations, assess the legitimacy of the research and the possibilities for conventional brain mapping, and then make a decision whether to stay or not. She was a free agent.

As free as someone could be with crushing debt and family obligations.

Around a bend in the trail, Caro rested under a slender tree only slightly taller than she was, leaning against the trunk so that the large, dark-green leaves shaded her. She could smell the ocean but neither see nor hear it. Five more minutes and she would hike back. Take a bath, have dinner, sleep. Tomorrow she would be fresher to think about all this.

Her eyes closed, opened, drifted closed again.

Another claustrophobic room, filled with flowers. Too many flowers, sickening sweet. Too many people, three of them women. Black ocean water rose in the room, swirling, grabbing at the women's black clothing. Threatening to drag them down. Only it wasn't the ocean, wasn't water at all, it was a toxic black fog that stung and pierced, a fog of Caro's own making. She'd caused it—

And Mother said—

And Ellen said—

And Caro said ... and said and said—

Caro snapped awake. Something large crashed along the trail.

She jumped up, her head brushing leaves. Were there any dangerous animals on the island? Why hadn't she checked? If—

Ben Clarby rounded the bend. "Oh, Christ, no! Doctor, get away from the maiden plum!"

The what? A sudden acrid odor drifted on the warm air.

"Did you touch it? You did. Okay, take off your clothes. Carefully. Don't touch any cloth with black sap on it. That's maiden plum, and every part of it causes itching and burns. You released sap from the leaves, too. They're really fragile. I can smell it. Take off all your clothes! Carefully! Here!" He peeled off his shirt, threw it at her, and turned his back.

Caro felt no itching. Was this some sort of crude hazing ritual? But black sap from the tree trunk had stained the back of her clothes. Caro peeled off her thin tee. Sap had soaked through to her bra. She shed bra and skirt and put on Ben's shirt, long enough to cover her nearly to the knees. It smelled of male sweat and insect repellent, mixing with the sharp odor from the tree.

She said, "Leaves touched my face."

"Not good. We need to get you back immediately. Look at the trunk. It's exuding sap from bark damage, and you just leaned your back against it!"

"How was I to know? I'm not a botanist."

"Precisely," Ben said, without sympathy. "Didn't you think to tell anyone where you were going? Come on!"

A jeep waited at the end of the trail. Ben threw a tarp over the passenger seat for Caro to sit on. She said, "Expected symptoms?"

"You're going to itch like crazy for up to two weeks, starting tomorrow. If you're really susceptible, you'll get open sores. Do you get poison ivy bad or light?"

"I've never had poison ivy."

Ben glanced at her incredulously. Apparently he assumed everyone spent a lot of time outdoors. Caro felt ridiculous. A mere four hours on Cayman Brac and she'd morphed from a doctor into a patient.

"What is the irritant in the plant called? Is it urushiol?"

"I don't know the medical name."

"Is it water soluble?"

"No. Brac has a lot of plants you want to avoid: trumpet vine, also called jasmine flower; rosary pea; machineel—*Hippomane mancinella*—which is really dangerous. Ponce de Leon died from it. The fruit—"

Caro interrupted this show of botanical erudition. "What is the protocol for contact with my particular plant?"

"The protocol is that I take you to the compound where Camilla Franklin will take care of you."

The nurse whom Caro had already offended. This just got better and better.

But Camilla was brisk, very professional. "You got here within two hours of contact. That's good. You'll get some skin penetration but not as much as you could have. Wipe your whole body with this." She handed Caro a cannister of Tecnu.

"The infection is systemic?"

"It can be. After the Tecnu, the best thing for the itching is lime juice, but it'll only help so much."

"I don't feel itchy."

"No, not for about twenty-four hours. Depends on how much contact you had, how susceptible you are. You didn't touch your eyes, did you? Even accidentally, such as swiping away sweat?"

"I don't think so."

"Good. Wipe yourself down now. Put your clothes and that shirt—"

"It's Ben's."

"Not any more. Put it all into this bag. Shoes and socks, too."

Caro's only other shoes were sandals, not good for outdoor walks. But she did as she was told. When she emerged from the bathroom, she said, "Camilla, thank you for not treating me like, well, as if I should have known better. My rotations didn't include tropical medicine. You've been great."

Camilla broke into a huge smile that changed her entire broad, stern face. "You're welcome, Doctor. I've lived in the

Caymans my whole life. Seen lots of maiden plum dermatitis. You're our neurosurgeon, not a dermatologist."

Our neurosurgeon.

The next morning, after falling into exhausted slumber and sleeping later than she'd intended, Caro lay in bed, feeling the room grow warm with the day and thinking over what Julian and Dr. Weigert had said yesterday.

A multiverse, branching each time an action was observed, including by the person doing the acting. Each branch represented all the possible results of the observation that had occurred, just as every possible outcome could occur every time an electron was observed. Until the observation, the electron was just an indeterminate bunch of possibilities. Observation "collapsed" it into a particle or a wave with a definite position, and it continued on its path. So, according to Weigert and Julian, did alternate branches of the universe, as "created" by computer chip and human decision.

How many times had Caro herself made one decision rather than another? She could visualize her life as an infinitely branching tree, with each branch a path she might have chosen. What if her mother had not said that terrible thing at Caro's brother's funeral, if Caro had not lost her temper, if family anger seething for decades had not erupted into chaos? What if she and Ellen had not been disinherited? What if she hadn't chosen to go to med school, but some other career instead? What if Ellen had married someone who wasn't a scumbag, or had not birthed Angelica, or had chosen to institutionalize Angelica and gotten a job? Those, and a million other decisions—"observations" in Weigert's language—would have resulted in very different paths through life.

Well, all that was obvious without evoking quantum physics. Trees, paths—everyone was familiar with those metaphors for life. But Julian and Weigert argued that those paths did exist, or could be created (she was still fuzzy on this point), in different branches of the multiverse. Also, that Julian had actually done so.

Electrons might not become matter until someone observed them, but Julian was not an electron. Nor was she. Only ... wasn't she made up of electrons and atoms and molecules? And the tiny, electrically charged particles in her brain that mediated neural transmission of information to each other, those particles that controlled everything she experienced and thought ... weren't they subject to quantum effects? They were. That, at least, was well-established science. Weigert's theory, what she'd read of it so far in his folders, made sense. It was based on known experiments, and she could find no flaw in the reasoning. She said aloud, "I am made of quantum foam that has been collapsed into Caroline Soames-Watkins."

No, she thought, *I am made of confusion.* Caro reached for her phone and called Ellen. No answer. Caro left a message, then followed it with an email.

Suddenly ravenous, she made her way to the refectory. Breakfast hours were nearly over, but kitchen help, who spoke minimal English, served her oatmeal and coffee. Caro would bet they were well paid to report to the compound each day, but also that none of them ever set foot in Wing Three. She wondered who cleaned there, who tended the one straggly flowerbed. Picture Julian or Dr. Weigert or Ben Clarby with a mop or trowel!

Julian dropped into the chair across from her. Caro braced for teasing or reproof about yesterday's skirmish with the maiden plum tree, but Julian said only, "Good morning! Dr. Luskin is going to check you out when he finishes with Sam. You didn't touch your eyes, did you?"

"No."

"Good. Slept well?"

"Yes, thank you. Is Dr. Weigert around? I'd like to ask him some questions about the multiverse."

"Ask me instead. That's why I'm waylaying you before George can. I'm saving you from the terror of equations. Also because, as the only person that David Weeks implanted with our computer chip, I can answer your questions about the operation."

"Which I'd like to ask Dr. Egan, an actual neurosurgeon."

He smiled. "Of course. Nobody ever said I was qualified to give any information about cutting into people's heads, not even my own. But I know, Caro, that you've done similar surgeries to implant chips for direct brain stimulation to control tremors from Parkinson's disease."

"Your research on me is very thorough."

He said, "My research on everything is very thorough," and went through a quick, exaggerated pantomime of horror at his own immodesty.

Caro couldn't help laughing. He was a gifted actor. She said with mock strict-teacher severity, "You stop that right now, young man!"

He folded his hands and looked meek. "Yes, ma'am."

God, she was *flirting* with him. But he really did have a wicked smile, and those eyes ...

She made herself turn serious. "I do have questions about your implant, both surgically and subjectively."

"Subjectively is easy. There is a recording of what I experienced in the alternate branch of the multiverse."

"A recording!"

"Yes," he said with his easy smile. "You saw our state-of-the-art deep-image reconstruction equipment on yesterday's tour of Wing Three. It records the images experienced in the brain as consciousness enters an alternate branch of the multiverse."

"Good," Caro said, although she actually had no idea how to regard this new wrinkle in an already complex situation. "I'd like to view that recording. But first, another kind of question. How long does Dr. Watkins have left?"

"Four to six months."

About what she'd expected. "You've worked with him a long time?"

"He and George founded the project fifteen years ago. They were best buds at Oxford. I came aboard a few years later."

Fifteen years. Well, that explained why both Samuel Watkins and George Weigert both dropped out of sight about then. Although "best buds" hardly seemed the appropriate terminology for either of them.

"I'd like to see your recording now, if I may."

"Of course. We can ... Hello, Ralph. I don't think you've met your new boss yet. Dr. Caro Soames-Watkins, Dr. Ralph Egan, your backup surgeon. Temporarily, anyway."

Egan nodded at Caro and plopped into a chair, obviously bursting to say something. "About that ... I'm afraid I won't be here to have a boss. The hospital asked if I can report to LA earlier than we'd agreed on. One of their surgeons died unexpectedly of a burst aneurysm and they want me to come two weeks from now. I hate to leave you in the lurch like this just as Dr. Soames-Watkins has arrived, but if you agree ..."

Julian took a moment to react, but, when he did, his congratulations sounded sincere. "We can spare you. We'll fast-track the surgical schedule, and we're already interviewing another surgeon. Congratulations, Ralph. Uncle John will be ecstatic."

Egan talked about his new position. It was the kind of offer Caro had once hoped to receive, but that, of course, was irrelevant. She congratulated Egan.

The left side of her face began to itch. She scratched it.

Julian said, "About the surgical schedule. Lorraine is still first. Maybe this afternoon you can bring Caro up to speed on ... whatever surgeons need to be up to speed on, and the two of you can operate tomorrow."

Egan said to Caro, "I have all my and David's data, including Lorraine's pre-op charting. I'll email it to you, Doctor, and we can go over it together if you like. What time is good for you?"

Events were moving too fast. Caro was not going to operate tomorrow. She hadn't even said that she was staying here, a decision she would make only when she had a lot more information. But there was no harm in looking at Egan's data, which might help her decide exactly what to tell Julian.

"One o'clock?"

"Fine. We can meet in the hospital lounge. If you'll excuse me, I need to make some phone calls. Nice to meet you, Doctor."

He hurried off. Caro said to Julian, "Uncle John?"

"Ralph is my first cousin once removed. Lorraine, your first patient, is my sister. It keeps security tight."

"Why is tight security necessary?"

Julian leaned forward, his elbows on the table. "Caro, this is a ground-breaking procedure. The surgery itself is not complicated, or so Egan assures me. In fact, it's probably far below your talents. But it's brand new, and, although eventually we'll trumpet it to the world, at the moment there are no regulations covering this. We have to be cautious."

"And you have to be out of the United States to do any of this at all."

"Yes," Julian said, and now his smile was not quite so pleasant. "Do you want to see my recording now?"

"Yes." She rose and followed him, ignoring sudden itching on her back.

≋

Nothing in Wing Three looked any different from yesterday. Julian said, "You told me you're familiar with efMRI. And maybe you already know that the deep-image reconstructor uses machine learning with deep neural networks in order to decode a hierarchy of complex brain activity from the efMRI images. Then a generator network boosts the images and refines them. A recording is made, which comes out like a video, in the same way that animation used to be created for the movies—a rapid series of images. Before even my first session, I trained the DIR on the personal visualizations in my brain. I spent a hundred and twenty-two hours lying on that bed there"—he pointed to the cot—"while viewing increasingly complicated images. A cat. A cat on a fence. A cat poised to walk along the fence. A cat on the ground. A cat—"

"I get the idea," Caro said.

"When the outputs from deep-image reconstruction almost exactly matched the pictures I was being shown, we moved onto moving images—the cat leaping off the fence. Eventually, the machine could reconstruct anything I thought about while I was hooked up to it."

"It can read your mind."

"The visual brain areas while I'm connected to the machinery, yes. Not, unfortunately, auditory areas. Lorraine has already undergone the same training. Her data is stored there too, along with that of the next few implantees after her. My team spent years programming the basic software. Later implantees won't need anywhere near as much time, because they can piggyback on elements common to previous training. With each implantee, the machine learns."

Caro looked again at the hospital bed positioned between the efMRI and the computer array. Cables lay across the pillow. All at once, it looked to her like a grisly, high-tech torture device.

Julian said quietly, "It doesn't hurt, if that's what you're thinking."

"I'm aware that imaging doesn't hurt."

"Of course you are. Sorry. The second piece of preparation, which took even longer, was programming software with information about the branch of the multiverse I would generate. For these initial efforts, the data we programmed to create the new branch of the multiverse kept it pretty much identical to this one. Keeping it as simple as possible until we saw how the algorithms worked out.

"That data, or any other we develop later, is fed into the chip through this conductor bolted to my skull."

Julian leaned forward and parted his thick blond hair with both hands. Caro saw it: the tiny titanium case which covered the ends of the connector wires leading deep into his brain.

He straightened. "What's on the chip inside my brain are new algorithms to process information. Developing those took a decade. Then, the last step, David Weeks implanted my chip."

Caro stared at him. He made it sound so clear-cut, so linear, which it couldn't possibly have been. Brain research didn't work that way. *Brains* didn't work that way. There must have been false premises, failed paths, endless trial-and-error frustration.

Julian said, "Think of it this way: a single conscious observer can completely define the quantum blur, leading to a collapse of its waves of probability into a new branch of the universe. And I was that observer, *in* that universe. Not my body, of course, which stayed right here, but my consciousness. And I controlled what I created. I could change that branch of the multiverse at will, because physical reality depends on how many observations are made and how densely they are packed together. George will have a lot more to say about that. The important point is that the universe I'm about to enter is real, and *my consciousness created it.*"

His voice held a note of exultation that made Caro uneasy. He seemed to be gazing at something only he could see.

"When I returned—which was when the computer was switched off—the universe I generated went on without me. I brought it into being by observing it, but after me there were many other observers in that universe, which I'd also brought into being. People, animals, birds."

"In other words, you think you became as a god."

"I don't think. I know."

It was too much. She said, "How do you know it wasn't just a hallucination? A really powerful hallucination that seemed real to you? You could have saved billions of dollars by just taking LSD."

He laughed, unoffended. "Caro, somehow you don't strike me as the type to ever have dropped acid."

She hadn't. Even her undergraduate years had been more about studying than partying. But that wasn't the point. "Julian—"

"You think this is just megalomania, don't you. Or wish fulfillment. Creating designer universes. It's not. It's serious research into how reality actually functions. A coherent theory that will change science forever. Some of it, of course, is uncharted territory. We're finding the proof as we go along. Right now, we have my recording, the first one ever, of consciousness creating reality. I want you to see it."

He activated the screen of the massive computer. "This first part obviously is just ordinary video."

On screen, Julian lay on the bed. Aiden Eberhart stood at one bank of screens and a tall Black woman at another. More people stood a few feet away. Cables connected Julian's skull to the machines. Caro thought of altar sacrifices, although Weigert, hovering near, hardly looked like a bloodthirsty priest, and surely Aztec sacrificial victims hadn't worn jeans and an Armani polo?

She thought she might be slightly hysterical.

Weigert nodded, Julian gave a thumbs-up, and the screen went blank for a moment. When it brightened again, the image wasn't quite as sharp although completely recognizable, as if seen through a light scrim moving in a barely perceptible breeze.

This same room. Julian stood, the cables gone from his head. Weigert and all the others had vanished. Julian walked to the door and opened it. Beyond lay not the conference room that Caro knew to be there, but the courtyard of Wing Three, ringed with its covered walkway, all the doors closed. The weedy flower bed was as Caro remembered, but next to it stood a huge, ornate fountain, water burbling over rocks crowned with carved semi-naked people and agitated horses. The whole looked vaguely familiar. Where had she seen that gaudy gusher before?

Julian strolled to the fountain and held out his hand. Water spurted over his fingers. From his pocket he drew a quarter and tossed it into the spray.

81

Trevi Fountain. In Rome. Caro had seen only photos; she'd never been to Rome. Had Julian? The fountain looked detailed and clear.

A door opened and Weigert emerged. He and Julian shook hands, Julian grinning and Weigert beaming like a lighthouse. The recording ended.

Julian turned to Caro and said, "Well?"

"Well what? I still don't see why that isn't a recording of a detailed, remarkably weird hallucination that the DIR recorded from your mind."

"No," Julian said. "it was no illusion. Look, Caro, I can't prove to you with hard evidence that it actually happened. Not yet, anyway, until we have more implantees and can analyze their results. And what I'm going to say to you next isn't something Weigert or Watkins, both scientists, would approve. I'm a scientist, too, but I can accept that there are ways of experiencing that don't meet lab criteria of experimentation but nonetheless are 'real.' Haven't you ever experienced something that had no scientific basis but you nonetheless knew had definitely happened?"

She lay—at six years old? Seven?—on a blanket in the back garden, watching clouds drift across the sky. Then, all at once, the clouds were no longer there, and neither was Caro. She was nowhere and everywhere, woven into what she later thought of as "the fabric of the universe." She was the clouds, the grass, the breeze, the ant crawling across her arm. Everything was her, and she was everything.

Carefully watching her face, Julian continued, "One of those lab criteria, incidentally, is replicability. The same experiment yielding the same results. This isn't my only DIR recording. I revisited this branch of the universe two more times, and the recordings are identical. Are drug hallucinations or dreams or any other 'altered states' known to psychology ever *exactly* duplicated, days apart?"

Caro's back and face itched again. Her own childish altered state in the back garden—dream, hallucination, delusion—had never occurred again. But it had happened.

Which proved nothing.

Her itching grew worse.

Julian said, "These first creations of a multiverse branch will all be similar to this one, because it takes less programming of the chip. But eventually, with enough information available to consciousness as it leaves this branch, an implantee could recreate the past. Enter a previous era in your life, or even the life of the planet. You could recreate a previous event and have it turn out differently than it did here, in a branch that would continue after you leave it. You could enter a universe in which you never tangled with a maiden plum tree. Think of it, Caro! You can re-live and alter the past. Not only in imagination, but in a conscious reality as solid as this one."

A claustrophobic room, filled with flowers, Too many flowers, sickening sweet. Dark ocean water rose in the room, swirling, grabbing at the three women's black clothing. Threatening to drag them down. Only it wasn't the ocean, wasn't water at all, it was a toxic black fog that stung and pierced, a fog of Caro's own making. She'd caused it—

She said, more forcefully than she intended, "Some pasts should not be relived."

He stared at her before saying gently, "That's true. But you can create a past in which your brother did not die. It's—"

"Stop," Caro said.

She was not going to discuss Ethan's death with Julian. She and Ellen didn't even talk about it, although that was Caro's choice, not Ellen's. But the terrible funeral and the even more terrible aftermath came back to her in dreams, as it had when she'd sat under the maiden plum.

"Sorry," Julian said. "But it's so important that you understand these basic ideas. Your brain isn't seeing anything 'out there' because there isn't anything 'out there' except a cloud of quantum information. Your brain uses its hard-wired algorithms to collapse the wave—many, many, many waves constantly—and so generate reality inside your head. There are many possible chains of brain activity, but the algorithms in your head limit your experience of them. Nonetheless, they still exist as *possibilities*, something even medieval philosophers sensed: 'For matter is never lacking privation, and inasmuch as it is under one form, it is deprived of another.' Thomas Aquinas. My brain chip changed the algorithms that usually deny me waking access to all but what we think of as 'this reality.'"

"So you're saying that instead of Trevi Fountain burbling away in a courtyard in the Cayman Islands, you could have erected the Eiffel Tower in Times Square. Or the Hanging Gardens of Babylon in a suburban mall."

"Put like that, sarcastically and simplistically, it sounds ridiculous. But so did quantum mechanics when it was first introduced. And Darwin's theory of evolution. And most other revolutions in scientific thinking. And let me repeat, Caro, that in terms of surgery, implanting my brain chip is no different from your work implanting electrodes for medical deep-brain stimulation."

"It's completely different," Caro said. "DBS is therapeutic."

"And this is valuable, ground-breaking scientific research. World-changing research."

"I'm a doctor, Julian. I save lives, not experiment on them."

"Compassionate use is medical experimentation. Your uncle is dying."

She gaped at him. "To call this 'compassionate use'! Those exceptions to FDA standards are only for experimental drugs for terminal patients!"

Julian said carefully, "This research *is* Sam's life, and advancing it before he dies is a form of compassionate use."

"That doesn't even ... I can't begin to say ..."

"Lorraine, plus your neuroradiologist, anesthesiologist, and nursing team, are already on their way here. Caro, please consider—"

Another voice said, "Julian. Don't." Neither of them had heard Weigert enter the room. He walked to Caro and put a protective hand on her shoulder. She looked up at the understanding in his old eyes.

"Give her time," Weigert said to Julian. "Remember how long it took you to accept all this. Caroline has had less than twenty-four hours."

"Yes, of course," Julian said. He looked as if he might say more, but Camilla Franklin rushed into the room like an exploding volcano. "There you are, Dr. Soames-Watkins! I've been looking all over for you! Dr. Luskin is here to look at your exposure to ... Oh Lord, don't scratch! Come with me. Dr. Luskin is waiting, and you need lime juice right now."

"If you have a preparation of—"

"Lime juice works better. Oh, here she is, Doctor."

A tall, gangly man followed Camilla. Caro's urge to scratch was intolerable. Dr. Luskin tilted her face to the light, careful not to touch her skin.

"Let's go somewhere I can examine you. But I can tell you right now that Camilla is right—you need lime juice."

Julian said, "And then, Lyle, Caro can perform surgery?"

Luskin looked at him. 'You should know better than that, Julian. She can't operate until I'm certain she won't develop open sores. At least a week."

Caro said to Julian, "I told you that I haven't even decided if I'm staying." Why was she having so much trouble convincing anyone of that?

Weigert said, "Julian, we need to let Dr. Luskin perform his examination. And I believe that Aiden Eberhart is looking for you."

Caro looked at Weigert as he intervened, diffidently but definitely, on her behalf. His eyes were kind in the creases and ridges of his old face. Although he wanted her skills for this project as much as did Julian and Watkins, he would not pressure or bribe her. And, for the first time, he had called her "Caroline."

"Thank you," she said to Weigert, and followed Dr. Luskin from the room.

11.

In the late afternoon, Weigert and Julian joined Watkins at a picnic bench in the courtyard of Wing One. Watkins had slept most of the day, and to Weigert he looked quite a bit better than he had that morning. Perhaps he was finally on the mend from that stubborn viral infection. Nurse Franklin had wheeled him, well wrapped in blankets, into the courtyard, where long shadows slanted across the grass and the air smelled of ocean. Weigert was glad to avoid another meeting in Sam's claustrophobic, overheated bedroom.

Julian said, "I'm glad you're feeling better, Sam. I'm only sorry to say that we have another problem. Two problems, actually."

Watkins scowled. "With my niece? If she's leaving—"

"She's one of the problems, yes, but not because she decided to leave. I think she hasn't yet made up her mind, although it's clear to me she has no other options besides us. But yesterday she went for a walk on her own, sat under a maiden plum, and—"

Watkins let out a string of curses. "How bad?"

"Luskin said she can't operate for at least a week. Camilla is dousing her with enough lime juice to float a battleship, but there's no way around it. But the problem is twofold. Ralph Egan is leaving earlier than planned to fill an unexpected vacancy at the LA hospital. He'll be here only two more weeks, which gives us only a short time between Luskin's okay for her to perform surgery and Ralph's leaving."

86

Weigert said, "Can she operate alone?"

"Without a backup? No. It's not complicated brain surgery, George, but it *is* brain surgery. She would never agree, and she shouldn't. We have to postpone the operating schedule."

Weigert calculated. Julian's sister was scheduled next, then Aiden and another of Julian's techs, and not until then Weigert himself because, as Sam had said bluntly, "We're both seventy-six. Who knows what's inside our ancient brains that won't show up on an MRI? Let Caroline get in some practice first."

Julian said, "I've already notified Lorraine to change her flight, and I can probably reach most of the nursing staff to do the same, but Barbara and Molly are already en route to Miami, so they will just have to cool their heels at the compound along with the rest of us. *Damn.* And then there's the question of another surgeon to back up Caro. I'm out of medical cousins."

Sam said, "I may have found another neurosurgeon who will agree to come."

Julian's gaze sharpened. "You have? Who? Why would they agree and why should we trust them?"

"I'm still talking to him. Let me say more when I'm sure." With the gathering twilight, floodlights came on under the eaves. Sam raised his hand to tighten the blanket around his shoulders, and Weigert saw the hand tremble. "What else?'

Julian talked of various business matters. Weigert didn't listen. He was remembering Sam as he once was, and as he might yet be again, at least for short periods in another branch of the universe.

"Time to go inside, Doctor," Nurse Franklin said. Weigert hadn't heard her approach.

Sam didn't argue. As his wheelchair was being turned toward his room, he looked back over his shoulder. "Changed my mind," he rasped. "Look up the surgeon online. Tell me what you think." A pause, while Sam summoned his strength and Nurse Franklin's strong bare arms pushed his negligible weight across the grass.

"His name is Trevor Martin Abruzzo."

On the walkway, Julian said, "At least, George, you'll have a lot of time to educate Caro about your theory. Although not this evening, I'm afraid. She's pretty miserable with itching."

"I'll prepare some reading material for her," Weigert said hopefully. "Poor girl."

"She's not exactly a girl," Julian said. "Are you going all avuncular, George?"

Weigert didn't answer. That was exactly the sort of intrusiveness that Weigert disliked. One reason he and Watkins had become friends so long ago was that Sam did not share the usual American inquisitiveness into one's personal sentiments.

Lighten up, my darling, Rose said in his head. *But, really, she is not a girl.*

In his room, Weigert Googled Dr. Abruzzo. Useful tool, Google. If he and Sam had had it as graduate students, it would have saved long hours in the Bodleian.

He was surprised to see so many citations about Abruzzo. Weigert read a few, and then did something he had not done in decades, not since he and Rose had owned King Charles Spaniels: he let out a long, low whistle.

12.

Caro tried again to phone Ellen. Still no response—unusual at this time of day. Had Ellen rushed Angelica to the emergency room? That happened regularly, and Caro could think of no other reason that Ellen would be away from home. She rarely shopped. Since babysitters were so expensive, Ellen had groceries delivered, an expense for which Caro had scraped together money each month, usually by juggling minimum payments on too many credit cards.

Camilla had given her lime juice to keep reapplying, and Lyle Luskin had supplied both steroids and sleeping pills. Caro, who knew she had a strong reaction to most drugs, nonetheless took a quarter of a pill and, despite so much sleep last night, fell into a long, fitful doze. She woke to a room in twilight gloom. Her itching had resumed. She winced at her reflection in the mirror. The flesh around one eye was swollen and red, although the eye itself seemed all right. Caro was applying more juice to everything that itched, straining to reach her own back, when someone knocked on the door. She cracked it open an inch. Julian.

"Go away," Caro said. "I look like a leper who's been in a bad fight."

"You look fine," said Julian, who couldn't see her. "I've brought you some files to read."

She opened the door two more inches. He held a thick stack of folders, blue and red and green and yellow and purple, an explosion in a child's crayon box. "If those are all physics, I don't want them."

"They're in your own field—mostly, anyway. And I also brought you another medication for your itching."

Caro let him in. Julian scrutinized her. "Not too bad. When I got entangled with a maiden plum, I had it much worse."

"You're lying," Caro said.

"Yes, I am. But not about the files. The blue one is George's theory, in more detail than anyone but a mathematician/physicist would care about, although I gather he prepared a sort of executive summary for you to read first. The red one has all the charting and operation notes from my implant surgery. Also in exhausting detail. The green file is my imaging, and you'll be interested at least in the mapping possibilities. The yellow folder has the physical and psychological pre-op work-up on Patient Two, my sister Lorraine. The purple one has signed informed-consent forms, NDAs, and all the other legal papers protecting all experimenters, including you, from any lawsuits by anybody, anywhere, at any time. In fact, you're probably protected against all future parking tickets. Both George and I are on high alert to answer any and all questions, although I doubt that will happen until you don't look like a pirate who misplaced her eye patch. Can you see all right?"

"Mostly. But where's the new medication? Neither Camilla nor Dr. Luskin said they were sending me anything more."

"It's not theirs, it's mine." Julian laid the files on her desk and drew a silver-and-calfskin flask from his pocket. "Ardbeg single malt, aged twenty-three years. As you undoubtedly know, Scotch is a nerve depressant."

"I can't take any alcohol now."

"Puritan. All right, I'll save the Ardbeg for later. Let me offer something else: an apology. I was intrusive and insensitive this morning. I should not have mentioned your brother. Please forgive me."

Caro nodded, uncertain what to say. Had she overreacted? Ethan's death was, of course, a matter of public record; the horrific family aftermath was not. But Julian had not mentioned that and he couldn't know about any of it—could he?

She said, "Maybe another time for the Scotch. Right now I think I'll look at some of those folders."

"Good idea. You don't want dinner? I can have James bring you a tray."

"Thank you."

As soon as he left, Caro picked up the phone to try Ellen yet again, but the cell rang first.

"Ellen! I've been trying all day to— What? Ellen, I can't understand you when you're crying, calm down! Is it Angelica?"

"No! Kayla!"

Kayla? Ice slid down Caro's spine. "What happened to Kayla?"

"They took her away!"

"Who?" As Ellen's voice scaled up, Caro's grew calmer, a calm created by sheer will. "Who took Kayla?"

"Child Protective Services! They took her away from me! She's gone!"

"Tell me. Start from the beginning."

Ellen made a small strangled sound, struggling for coherence. Caro clutched the cell so tight that the blood left her fingers. Ellen said, "Kayla apparently broke down at school. We had a really bad morning because Angelica ... You know how Angelica can get."

Caro knew. "Go on."

"Kayla kept saying she'd be late for school, and Angelica was having a seizure and then vomiting and finally I screamed at Kayla. Then her teacher asked her what was wrong, and apparently Kayla just sobbed and sobbed and said home was horrible, smelling of shit, and her mother hadn't given her breakfast and there was vomit on her backpack, and the next thing I know, CPS is at my door! There's a hearing in two days, and meanwhile Kayla is in some sort of foster care 'for her own protection'! As if I would ever ... I've been trying all day to get help from my caseworker or Legal Aid or *anybody* but they say they're swamped and ... Oh, Caro, I try to be a good mother! I just can't do everything all at once!"

"You're a great mother. Listen, Ellen, I'm going to take care of this. Just sit tight until I call you back."

"What can you do? I shouldn't even dump this on you. You've got enough trouble. That online shitstorm about Dr. Becker still hasn't gone away and—"

"*Just sit tight*, Ellen. Is Angelica asleep?"

"Yes."

"I'm going to call you back, but it may be tomorrow morning instead of tonight. Okay? Just don't do anything until you hear from me again. We can fix this."

"Okay," Ellen said.

"Try to get some sleep while Angelica sleeps," Caro said, knowing how futile that was. "Wait for my call." Her fingers trembled as she pressed the icon to end the conversation.

Kayla—taken to a foster home somewhere, away from her mother and her familiar bedroom and her school … Was she scared? Of course she was. Caro understood that CPS provided a valuable service for kids who were abused or neglected, but Kayla was neither. Ellen would give her life for either of her daughters. In some ways, she already had.

Caro, too, would do anything for Kayla. Caro never expected to bear a child of her own: she was too dedicated to neurosurgery, too wary of romantic relationships, too much in debt, rapidly becoming too old. But she shared Kayla with Ellen, especially since so much of Ellen's energy had of necessity to go to Angelica. Kayla, with her giggles and quicksilver feelings and spontaneous hugs …

Caro opened her door. The swift tropical sunset had ended and the courtyard, full of velvety Caribbean night lit by a half moon, was deserted. The only person she knew how to find was James, so she went back inside and pressed his call button.

"James, I'm sorry to bother you, but I need to talk to Dr. Weigert. Now. Right away."

"Of course. You should have been given a list of cell numbers already. I'll text it to you after I call Dr. Weigert."

Caro breathed deeply, thinking hard. A white moth fluttered past the dim light beside her open door. Unseen flowers filled the air with sweetness. Something small skittered over her foot and she jumped back. A lizard, darting into her room. Diagonally across the courtyard another door opened and Weigert emerged from the gloom, his tall stooped figure hurrying across the grass. "Caroline?"

"Something happened. I need your help."

"Of course. What is it?"

"It's not actually help, not a favor, it's a ... a business deal."

He peered at her face and said gently, "Shall we go inside?"

"There's a lizard in my room."

Weigert went through the door and emerged a moment later, carrying the lizard. He released it into the darkness. "These little green ones are harmless, but I quite understand, after your encounter with a maiden plum, why you might be suspicious of the local fauna as well. Now, let's go inside and you can tell me what's troubling you."

She'd had time to order her thoughts. "You—my uncle and you and Julian, the research corporation—have advanced me a small amount on my salary. I want to know if the corporation is willing to advance me more. Actually a lot more."

He said quietly, "You suddenly need much more money?"

"Yes. For my sister. She needs a lawyer. I ... She ..."

"You don't need to tell me everything, Caroline. A quick summary will do."

But she did tell him everything, about Angelica and Kayla and Ellen's bravery and warmth and Kayla's teacher and Child Protective Services, while Weigert stood gazing out the open door at the courtyard, and Caro wondered throughout her entire recitation why she had turned to him and not to Julian or Watkins. There had been no calculation, only blind, desperate instinct.

She finished with, "I want it understood that if I don't stay to do surgery at the compound, the money will be a loan that I'll repay to the corporation at five percent interest according to a schedule we'll work out."

"Not necessary," Weigert said. "I will make you the loan personally."

"You? But—"

"Taking it from the corporation implies that you are staying here because you're beholden to us. In fact, Julian would probably make that a condition of any loan. But I want you to become part of this project of your own volition—not because you are already convinced of my theory, but because you are willing to approach its possibilities with an open mind. I am quite positive that if you do that, you will come to understand and embrace what we are doing here. But, Caroline, even if you leave tomorrow, I will make you the loan. You and your sister have had an undeservedly rotten time, and I've seen enough of you to believe that you'll repay me when you can, however long that might take."

Caro had no words.

Weigert said, "I can do a bank transfer from my personal account to yours. Neither Julian nor Sam need know anything about it. Just find a solicitor and tell me how much he will cost, and you and I can draw up and sign a simple statement of our arrangements."

Caro moved toward him. Weigert shifted slightly away, and she stopped. This was not a man who would welcome gushy gratitude. She said quietly, "Thank you, Dr. Weigert. I appreciate it more than I can say."

"You're welcome, Caroline." He left, closing the door behind him against the miniature dragons lurking in the darkness.

13.

The next morning, Caro itched even worse. Despite the anti-itch med and lime juice, her face and back kept up a constant low-level prickliness that said, *Scratch me*! She didn't—the last thing she wanted was to create oozing sores—but it took an enormous effort. The itching made it difficult to concentrate. The pile of folders on her desk looked like a multi-colored bog she would never be able to cross without sinking.

Counterbalancing her discomfort was a voice mail from Ellen: "Your money arrived in PayPal and a friend found me a custody lawyer that I'm seeing at noon. The lawyer said on the phone that she thinks I can get Kayla back soon! Damn, but you're good! Thank you, thank you, thank you!" Caro tried to call Ellen but she didn't pick up. Caro wrote Ellen an email and then sat motionless at her laptop, lost in memory.

She and Ellen as children in the elaborate playroom their mother had filled with toys instead of her maternal presence. Caro and Ellen had never played with most of the toys. They'd preferred their own imaginations, two children pretending to be a cast of hundreds: Ellen as a princess and Caro as a dragon; Ellen as a shark and Caro as a swimmer. They were cowboys whose cows were attacked by wolves, explorers lost in a snake-filled jungle, knights fighting with makeshift swords until one of them decided to shriek dramatically and fall over. Attacks from dragons, sharks, wolves, snakes, jousters—children could be so enthusiastically gory. Or had the bloodthirstiness been unique to them? Caro couldn't remember Kayla playing such games. Of course, she seldom saw Kayla with other children.

It finally occurred to Caro that she was hungry. In the refectory, Julian sat at a table with two women. He motioned her over. "Caro! There you are. Two people you'll want to meet. Their plane was delayed by weather in Miami so they've just arrived. Dr. Caroline Soames-Watkins, neurosurgeon. Dr. Barbara Mumaw, neuroradiologist. Dr. Molly Lewis, anesthesiologist. If you will all excuse me, I'm needed in the security office, and I'll leave you three to get acquainted. Caro, I've already told them about your arboreal battle yesterday." He smiled and left.

"Hello," Caro said, wishing she did not look so much like the loser in her "arboreal battle." Hard to make a good professional impression with the face she'd just seen in her bathroom mirror.

"Don't try to smile," Molly Lewis said. In her late thirties or early forties, she had flamboyant orange curls, a startling Mae West figure, and a forthright grin. "We'll take it for granted that you're thrilled beyond words to meet us. Do you itch very much?"

"Yes," Caro said.

"You don't look as bad as I did when I tangled with a maiden plum."

Despite her face, Caro smiled. "When Julian said that, he was lying."

"Well, I'm not lying. It was horrible. And Julian always lies. You can't believe a word he says except about the project."

"Molly," Barbara Mumaw said with mock reproof. "Don't run down our project heads before Dr. Soames-Watkins has time to form her own opinions of them."

"'Caro,' please," Caro said.

Molly said, "I'm not running down Julian, I'm praising him. Liars are always the most charming men. They have the best imaginations."

Barbara Mumaw rolled her eyes at Molly, a mock gesture that looked practiced. A tall Black woman with close-cropped hair, Barbara projected more reserve than Molly—a puppy projected more reserve than Molly—but clearly the two were good friends. Caro recognized Barbara from the recording of Julian's session with the deep-image reconstructor. She had been standing by a bank of computer screens. As neuroradiologist, she would be interpreting all brain imaging before, during, and after the programmed chips were implanted, and would work with Caro on the brain mapping article she hoped to publish.

Caro said, "I'm told that I can't operate until my itching subsides and it's clear that I won't develop open sores, so I'm afraid you both could have stayed on vacation a while longer. I'm sorry for the inconvenience."

"No problem," Molly said. "I was glad to have my visit to my sister cut short. We don't actually like each other but, well, you know ... family. Besides, the rains have started in Seattle and won't stop until June."

"You're from Seattle?" Caro asked.

They talked lightly about their home towns, superficial information about their families, their med school days, all the while assessing each other. Caro liked them both, but how-did-you-find-Chicago-in-winter chatter couldn't answer Caro's real questions: What had made Barbara Mumaw and Molly Lewis join Watkins's edgy project? How much of Weigert's theory did they believe? Such information would have to come slowly.

She would also have liked to know if Molly, exuberant and sexy, was or ever had been involved with Julian, but since she was ashamed of the thought—none of her business!—she banished it.

Her itching increased. It was Barbara who noticed. She said tactfully, "I'm afraid we're taking up too much of your time, Caro. Julian said he dumped a pile of information on you. If you need to go read it, Molly and I can answer any questions you might have. I'm in Room 16 and Molly's in 17. We should go, too, and unpack."

"Thanks," Caro said. "I'm in 5. I should start studying all of Julian's folders. Preferably while sitting in a tub of lime juice."

Molly said, "But you probably don't want to study all day. Maybe later we three can check out a jeep and drive down to Brac Reef? I'll bet Caro hasn't seen much of the island, unless Julian took her on a tour."

Julian again. Caro said, "All I've seen is the drive with Ben Clarby from the airport, and he wasn't very informative."

"No," Barbara said. "He wouldn't be."

Molly said, "I don't trust Ben. He's the only one here that I don't trust."

That was interesting, or at least it was until Barbara said, "You usually trust everybody."

Molly gave a theatrical sigh. "True enough. That's how I end up with the men I get. Caro, would you be averse to a drink if we go to the resort hotel? Do you drink?"

"Ordinarily, yes. Right now, I'll have cranberry juice. And I'd love to go. Let me postpone my conference with Ralph until tomorrow."

"Great! I can see that it's going to be much better working with you than with David Weeks. Good surgeon, but nobody really liked him. A bark-orders-at-your-colleagues type."

Barbara said, "Caro, feel free to bark all the orders you want. Molly ... *really*."

Caro laughed. It hurt her face. "I'll bark softly and carry a big bone saw."

It was a good beginning.

＝

Two hours later, her optimism seemed unjustified.

Although, not at first. She went over Julian's imaging: pre-op, during surgery, and post-op. David Weeks's notes were meticulous, the imaging thorough. Julian's skull had been opened—something Caro had done dozens of times—and the chip inserted at a precise location. As with deep brain stimulation, thin wire leads connected the chip to a power source, although unlike DBS, the tiny battery was not under Julian's skin but external, serving as both "brain pacemaker" and connector to the external computers. For part of this first-ever chip insertion, Julian had been awake, his head held firmly in a stereotactic frame, able to give verbal feedback on what he experienced. With DBS, the lead wires would work if at least one of the electrodes was in the target motor area. But DBS was crude compared to this insane operation. Still, Dr. Weeks had done a beautiful job, and Julian hadn't experienced any of the things that could go wrong with brain surgery: intercranial hemorrhage, stroke, infection. Post-op MRIs showed only minimal scarring.

According to charting done by the head surgical nurse, Imelda Mahjoub, Julian had recovered quickly, without significant side effects. And Caro had seen for herself a Julian both healthy and coherent.

The folder with Barbara's neuroradiology notes suggested tremendous possibilities. Julian's "session" had stimulated a largely unexplored part of the brain. Mapping that area could yield critical research into brain functioning, with huge implications for understanding memory, imagination, REM sleep, any number of cerebral phenomena. Watkins had told her the truth: this data could lead to a major brain mapping article authored by Caro and Barbara, with Watkins's name to lend it prominence. It was an exciting possibility, one that could revive her entire career.

Another reason to stay, along with Ellen, Kayla, Angelica, med-school debt, credit-card debt, and the loan from Weigert. All balanced against participation in a research project unsanctioned by the FDA, AMA, NIH, or any other alphabetic codon. Although, if not sanctioned, not forbidden either.

Her back itched. She was probably single-handedly contributing to a bull market in lime juice.

After another session of standing naked in the bathtub dripping citrus juice over her shoulder, Caro dressed and turned to the folder for the first person she would implant, Julian's sister Lorraine. Carefully, she went over Lorraine's pre-surgical medical history, psychological evaluation, and imaging. It all looked good, as did a plain folder Julian hadn't mentioned, with medical bios of Molly, Barbara, Ralph Egan, and the nursing staff.

Finally she opened George Weigert's thick folder about his theory. Rifling through the pages, she saw equations, diagrams, long paragraphs dense with the language of physics. Fortunately, Weigert had written a nine-page "Brief Introduction," neatly divided into sections labeled UNIVERSE, PERCEPTION AND CONSCIOUSNESS, ENTANGLEMENT, CONSENSUS REALITY, SPACE, TIME, and, surprisingly, DEATH.

She read through the Introduction, blinked, read it again, laid it down on her desk and stared at it as if at a bomb that might explode if she touched it again.

And she had been worried about mere hallucinations of designer universes!

No professional language seemed suitable. Caro reverted to girlhood. "Oh my God," she said aloud, "you've got to be shitting me."

But she knew they were completely serious.

14.

"God damn it," Sam said, sitting up in bed. Weigert thought his old friend's color was better this morning, although with glasses perched on his emaciated face, Sam looked like a sharp-featured, intellectual ferret. He scanned the printout in his hand and said, "I thought I could trust her."

"It's not a matter of trust, sir," Ben Clarby said, smiling faintly. Weigert, standing by the door, didn't like the security tech's tone, or the smile. In fact, he'd never liked Clarby. The young man was somehow both smarmy and superior-sounding, although Weigert didn't know how that could be. Weigert said, "Let me see the printout, please."

Clarby took it from Watkins and passed it over. Watkins said, "She sent this first email the day she arrived and the second this morning?"

"Yes, sir. And her cell conversations and text messages have all been with her sister, nobody else. All innocuous from our point of view. The sister has a custody problem with her kid."

Weigert blurted, "You listened in on her cell? You can do that?"

Clarby, clearly amused, turned to Weigert. "It's not hard, with the right tech."

Weigert turned to Sam. "We agreed not to do anything illegal."

Clarby said, "Monitoring employees' electronic communications on work premises isn't illegal here. These are work premises." Pause. "Sir."

Weigert read the first email:

Ellen—

Call me tonight if you can. Did Kayla complete her salt-flour map on the thirteen original colonies? How did it come out? When I last saw it, Georgia seemed to be crumbling along the coast line.

You asked me what this project is exactly. It involves very advanced mapping of brain functions, right in my wheelhouse, using surgical skills similar to DBS (and don't tell me you don't remember what that is, because I know you do). I signed a non-disclosure agreement that says I can't tell anyone more right now. Just say that I'm enthusiastic about this study. I don't know how long I'll be here, but if you absolutely need me, DO NOT HESITATE TO SAY SO! I can arrange to fly home at a moment's notice if I have to.

Our great-uncle is crusty—think of a Dickens character with a genius scientific mind. Well, okay, that's hard to imagine. I can't name the other people to you, just say that the principals include a brilliant, rather wonky older scientist with a sweet nature, and a handsome, really annoying computer guy. The island is beautiful, and although I haven't actually seen the ocean since I flew over it to get here, I'm hoping to go—

There was more, which Weigert scanned quickly. Nothing further about the project, and the small lies (enthusiasm about the study, flying home at a moment's notice) seemed designed to reassure her sister. Weigert approved of that: family loyalty. But ... "a brilliant, rather wonky older scientist with a sweet nature"—was that him? Watkins would hate being compared to a Dickens character, even one who was a genius. And was Julian "really annoying?" Weigert hadn't noticed.

The second email was shorter:

Sissy—call me after the meeting with the lawyer. If the lawyer can't get Kayla home today, call me again—maybe I can do something more on this end. If the money I sent to your PayPal account last night isn't enough for the lawyer, let me know and maybe I can help more. My next advance of salary, I'll send you money to cover counseling for Kayla if the court mandates it. They might.

Hang on, Ellen. We can do this. You are the best mother I know—surprising, given our own mother, but absolutely true—and if I have to, I'll fly home and testify to that in court. The word of a neurosurgeon, even a disgraced neurosurgeon, should count for something.

All my love,
Caro

Weigert said, "Sam, she hasn't really violated the NDA There aren't any project details here."

Watkins said, "She wasn't supposed to say *anything* about the project. Nothing. And where did she get the extra money to wire to her sister for this attorney?"

"I don't know," Clarby said. "Trying to hack her PayPal account really would be illegal, and it would attract attention we don't want."

"No. All right, Clarby. Bring me any other relevant emails as soon as she writes them, and transcripts of any of her phone conversations you think I need to see. Tell Aiden to do the same."

"I will."

No *sir* this time, Weigert noted. And wasn't Aiden Eberhart actually Clarby's boss, instead of the other way around?

When Clarby had left, Sam said, "George, I know you don't like the security team watching my niece's emails and phone calls. It's only until she starts operating and we're completely sure of her."

"I'm sure of her now."

Sam's eyes sharpened. "You are? Why? Did she say something to you?"

"She said a great deal. She has a great deal yet to learn, but when she does, I'm convinced she'll stay. But what about you, Sam? Camilla says you're back in bed because that infection has flared up again."

"Camilla talks too damn much. I'm fine."

Sam was not fine. Weigert had a sudden quick memory: He and Sam on holiday in the Alps, just before Sam returned to America and Weigert took up his teaching post. Sam, hiking with great enthusiasm and no experience, had misjudged a snow field, fallen into a crevasse, and broken his leg. "I'm fine," he had insisted, right up until the rescue crew, muttering in German about hapless Americans, had pulled him out and conveyed him down the mountain. Weigert, who spoke German, had been glad that Sam did not.

Weigert said gently, "I'm going to find Caroline now and talk to her more about the project."

"Okay," Sam said, and closed his eyes.

He didn't hear Weigert ask, "What does 'wonky' mean?"

15.

Although at first it was difficult, Caro managed to put Weigert's physics bombshell out of her mind for the trip with Molly and Barbara to Brac Reef Beach at the western end of the island. Barbara signed out a jeep. They walked barefoot beside the gloriously blue water and then inspected the shops selling native Caymanite jewelry. Barbara bought a pair of earrings and Molly a bracelet. Caro, mindful of money, only admired. Periodically she checked her phone for any texts or emails from Ellen about her meeting with the lawyer.

After the beach, they had a drink at the resort bar. Molly, whose alcohol consumption without any signs of drunkenness was astonishing, talked about her dating life. This apparently consisted of a series of very sexy, very inappropriate men. She described her recent attempt to have sex underwater with a young diving instructor. "The problem is that the water keeps washing away all the natural lubricants."

"*That's* the problem?" Barbara said. "Not that there are, oh, sharks and stingrays and curious tourists?"

"Reef sharks," Molly said. "Not usually dangerous."

"But if you're thrashing around at all ..."

"Of course we were thrashing," Molly said. 'He was *twenty-two*. Men that age have no subtlety."

Caro said, "I'm trying to imagine *anyone* having subtlety while underwater with no lubricants."

"I don't recommend the whole experience," Molly said solemnly, then broke into guffaws loud enough that tourists at the next table turned to stare.

Caro laughed. She had not had this much fun since before the disciplinary hearing about Paul Becker. These women were already treating her like a friend. How long had it been since she'd had female friends other than Ellen?? Or any real friends, except for DeVonne? Too long.

They went on talking and laughing, telling stories of residency. "And so I'm on OB/GYN rotation," Molly said, "and this poor woman is lying in the stirrups looking worried out of her mind, and she says, "Doctor, you'll tell me, won't you, if I have fibroids of the Eucharist?"

Caro sputtered so hard that cranberry juice came out of her nose.

Eventually Barbara said, "We should go soon. I think it might rain and we have an open jeep. Also, didn't you say, Caro, that Dr. Weigert wanted to talk to you more about the project? Or was it Julian?"

"Dr. Weigert," Caro said. She hadn't realized they'd been in the bar so long. She wanted to say something, but was this the right time? Would there ever be a right time? Caro plunged in. "Barbara, Molly, I want to ask you something. Don't answer if you think I'm being too intrusive. Are you on board with Weigert's entire theory?"

The mood at the table shifted. Even Molly looked serious as she glanced around to see if they could be overheard. The tourists beside them were in the process of leaving. After they did, Barbara said, "Yes. Completely on board. You have questions, don't you. Go ahead."

"You believe that my consciousness is creating this table"—tables again!—"and that if I'm not here, it isn't, either? The same for this room, this cranberry juice, that bartender?"

"They're not here for you," Barbara said. "But they're here for Molly and me if we're at the bar without you."

"What about when no one is in the bar? Does it just not exist?"

Molly spoke, and Caro realized there was another side to flamboyant Molly, the side she must display during surgery:

sober, careful, dedicated. "It exists as possibility, like everything else, until, say, the bartender walks in to open up. When I observed the bar, the possibility collapsed for me and everyone else in it—including you and the bartender. We all share the same entangled actuality. A record of the observation remains in our memory, and when we return to the bar, our memories agree with it. To put it another way, those 'bar' degrees of freedom recorded in our memory had collapsed when we first observed the bar. In essence—although Dr. Weigert wouldn't approve of this terminology!—consensus reality 'freezes' the bar, no matter when we walk back into it."

Molly leaned across the table, as if lessening the distance between her and Caro could help Caro understand. "But the bar doesn't really 'disappear' when we leave the room. It only exists as a set of possibilities to begin with. Think of it like an old-fashioned TV set that is all static and snow until you adjust it and an image comes into view. Before your adjustments, it was only the possibility of a picture, but then you cause it to manifest. If you then turn off the TV, you don't see the image anymore, but somewhere down the street a neighbor is tuning in, so it still exists. In the same way, just because you leave the bar and aren't observing it any more, it doesn't morph out of existence, because that bar has many observers."

"Especially during happy hour," Barbara said.

"All right," Caro said, "let's posit that I accept that. I read the notes Dr. Weigert wrote for me. He says that not only is the material world the result of consciousness instead of the other way around, but that time is too. That the past only exists because our consciousness creates it now, in the ways dictated by the algorithms in our brains. Imperial Rome, dinosaurs, the formation of galaxies—"

"Also depend on the observer," Barbara said. "Time doesn't just exist 'out there,' ticking away from past to future. Einstein demonstrated that time is relative to the observer. Now peer-reviewed scientific studies take it one step further, showing that the so-called 'arrow of time' is related to the nature of the observer—us—and, in particular, to the *way* we process and remember information. Without a conscious observer, that arrow of time—in fact, time itself—simply doesn't come into existence in the first place.

"Bottom line: reality begins and ends with the observer. John Wheeler, Einstein's colleague, once said, 'We are participators in bringing about something of the universe in the distant past.' So, the observer is the first cause, the vital force that collapses not only the present but the cascade of spatio-temporal events we call the past. Time is just another tool by which consciousness makes sense of the world ... Caro, why are you smiling?"

"Something dumb. I saw a tee-shirt once that said, 'Time Is Nature's Way to Keep Everything From Happening At Once. Space Is Nature's Way To Keep It From Happening To Me.'"

Molly said, "I want that tee!"

Barbara frowned. "I was serious."

Caro hastened to repair her error. "I know you were. And I am, too. I really do want to learn. But ... it's hard to accept."

"I know. But revolutionary science always is. Astronomers would not accept that the Earth moved around the sun instead of the other way around. Eighteenth-century medicine would not accept that pathogens, too small to see, caused disease. Twentieth-century scientists, including even Einstein, had trouble accepting quantum mechanics. The multiverse theories, all of them, still have to compete with things like string theory. But science backs up Weigert's ideas of how reality works."

"And the multiverse ... You believe that Julian really entered another branch and—"

"Created it," Barbara corrected gently.

"—and that when he was disconnected from the machinery, that new universe continued on without him, on its own?"

"Yes," Molly said. "We accept that."

"And that if Julian had wanted, he could have created a branch in which, say, he didn't look like a Greek god, and that would be just as 'real' as this one?"

"Yes, as long as the laws of quantum mechanics allow for it," Barbara said, as a party of men sat down at the next table, looking with interest at the three women.

Molly seized the opportunity to change the subject. "Do you really think Julian looks like a Greek god?"

Caro was vexed to feel herself blush. "Yes, but that doesn't mean ... anything."

"No," Barbara said. And then, softly, "I don't mean to tell you what to do, Caro, but be careful there."

"Hello! Can my friends and I buy you ladies a drink?" He hovered close over their table, a big man with a paunch and a hopeful smile.

"Sorry," Caro said, "we're just leaving." She hadn't gotten to ask Barbara and Molly about the most incredible aspect of Weigert's notes, the statement she'd read last night, but all at once she didn't want to. She already had too much to take in.

Halfway back to the compound, rain began. The jeep had no top. Barbara drove faster. Caro's cell rang, and she listened to Ellen discuss her lawyer's strategy to regain custody of Kayla. The rain soaked Caro through. She shielded the phone as well as possible; her face began to itch again; Molly sang in a surprisingly sweet alto about rain and an itsy-bitsy spider.

None of which lessened Caro's resolve to find Weigert and ask him to clarify what he meant—because surely it couldn't be what his notes sounded like.

≡

She had no chance to ask Weigert anything.

When the three women arrived inside the compound, all of them dripping water onto the walkway under the covered portico just inside the gate, Julian and Luskin were waiting for Caro. She promised to meet them in the small conference room behind the security office after she dried off, changed, and applied more lime juice.

When she joined them, Julian closed the conference room door. Luskin raised Caro's face to the light, looked briefly at her back, asked questions, and then nodded. "It looks good. You're lucky, Doctor. I don't think you'll develop any sores; nothing worse than you've got now. Okay, Julian, she can do it on Tuesday. Now if you'll excuse me, I'm going back to Sam."

Caro said, "I can do what on Tuesday? And has something happened to my great-uncle?"

"Nothing that hasn't been happening." Julian's face was grim. "But he's weakening quite a bit, and although Luskin says he may rally—this is such an unpredictable cancer—he is definitely running out of time. We need to accelerate the surgical schedule. Caro—"

"I'm not operating on my uncle on Tuesday, if that's what you're thinking."

"No, we know that. He's not ready. But we do need to take advantage of the time that Ralph is still here as your backup, because the replacement Sam is talking to can't arrive here right away. Lyle just gave you the okay to implant Lorraine on Tuesday. After that, we can do Aiden, Ben, and two other people. Then we can just squeeze in Sam before Ralph leaves."

"No," Caro said. "I told you several times already that I'm not even sure yet that I'm staying here! Why don't you listen to that? And even if I do stay, each patient has to be fully evaluated for surgical complications, cerebral scarring, and post-op imaging before I'll do the next operation. I'm not just inserting under-the-skin ID chips here."

"I know that. But—"

"Each separated by at least five days, and not Dr. Watkins until I'm completely familiar with what I'm doing. That would be the schedule."

"Caro," Julian said, reaching out to take both her hands in his, "you don't understand. Sam can't die before he's implanted. He needs to experience what he's given fifteen years and most of his fortune to make possible. He *needs* to create another branch of the universe where he is young and strong and not dying."

So she'd arrived at the bombshell in Weigert's notes, after all, and it was Julian, not Weigert, that she would have it out with. She pulled her hands out of his. She'd reacted to his touch, yes—any heterosexual woman under ninety would react to Julian Dey's touch. Right now, that was irrelevant.

She said, "Last night I read Dr. Weigert's summary of his theory, including what it implied about death. If a person enters 'another branch' of the universe populated with people he remembers, Weigert says that after the implantee returns to his body here, those people continue to exist, fully alive. But even if that is all true—and it seems far-fetched to me—but even if it *is* true, as soon as my uncle's session is over, he's right back on that cot and he's still dying. His body is here. He can't *stay* there. Dr. Weigert thinks consciousness survives death, and I don't know if it does or not—that's an argument for theologians, not surgeons. But even if consciousness can't be destroyed, there's no evidence that it's going to inhabit, or create, another branch of the multiverse somewhere else. No, I know what you're going to say: There is no 'somewhere else,' no 'here' or 'there.' It's all superimposed quantum foam. But the point is, all my uncle will gain is a brief experience of again feeling healthy and strong, followed by no change in his cancer. You can't cheat death, Julian."

Something moved behind Julian's eyes, but all he said was, "That brief experience is what Sam wants. What he's worked toward for fifteen years. He's done all the pre-session training on the machines. We did it a little at a time, before you came. He's ready."

"There's a good chance that he will not survive the implant surgery."

"He's willing to take that chance. Isn't it his choice? And if he's dying anyway, what difference does it make?"

"Because I'm not going to be the one to kill him! Julian, I know you're not a doctor, but my God!"

Julian leaned forward. His face took on a hardness she hadn't realized he was capable of. "This is what Sam wants."

"He's not going to get it from me. Not in his current physical state."

Silence, during which Julian watched her closely. All at once his tone softened. "I understand your position, Caro. You're an ethical doctor, and ethical doctors don't take unnecessary chances with patients' lives. You also don't want to imperil your own career with what you see as reckless surgery. I admire that. It's one reason we chose you for this project—your high standards. And now that you're here, we all have faith in you—Sam, George, me. Maybe me most of all."

He moved toward her and Caro realized that he intended to take her in his arms.

She shoved him away. "Really? You really think that would influence me to—"

"Stop," he said harshly. "Doesn't it even cross your suspicious little mind that maybe I'm sincere in this? That my attraction to you is genuine, and so is my admiration? That maybe your snap judgment of me is unfair? That I might genuinely like you?"

She considered. He stood glowering at her, almost a caricature of masculine challenge begging to be tamed. His shoulders clenched powerfully, his thick blond hair fell forward over those astonishing eyes. But this was not some clichéd romance novel. She said, "All that did not cross my mind. Maybe you're attracted to me, maybe you admire me. I'm sure you know that I'm attracted to you, because men like you always know. But that's not what's going on here. You used that attraction to try to persuade me to do something, and that's why—"

That's why the attraction just dissipated.

"—why I won't accelerate the surgical schedule. If I even operate at all, it would be Lorraine, Aiden, Ben, and at least one more, possibly Dr. Weigert. My uncle when Dr. Luskin gives the go-ahead *and* I feel ready."

"Fair enough," Julian said. His tone was pleasant, but Caro sensed the bafflement beneath it. Julian Dey was not used to women rejecting him.

After he left, Caro sat on the edge of her bed, thinking, *I've rejected an awful lot of men.* All of them, eventually. When she'd been younger, she'd attributed her inability to have a genuine relationship to her parents' unhappy marriage: *I had no role model.* A little older, she realized that everybody used their parents as an easy justification for everything and she'd told her friends *I just have really high standards.* By the time the arrogance of that statement became clear, she'd been able to attribute her preference for light, passing affairs to the crushing press of med school, internship, residency.

Ellen had a different theory. "You're an avocado in reverse."

"A what?"

"An avocado. You know, that green veggie that—"

"I know what an avocado is, and it's a fruit, not a vegetable!"

"—has a hard pit in the middle but is soft and mushy around the pit. You're an avocado in reverse, all tough on the outside but soft and mushy inside."

"I'm not mushy!"

"Okay," Ellen said, "not mushy. But soft. Look how you are with Kayla and Angelica. And me."

"That's different."

"It's not. Some guy is going to see that someday."

Caro said aloud to her empty room in the compound, "Not today. And not that guy." And anyway, what did Ellen know about men? She'd married Eric.

Caro reached for the blue folder. This avocado had physics to read.

16.

During dinner at a crowded table in the refectory, Aiden told her that Weigert had left for Miami that afternoon. "There's a physics conference going on there that Dr. Weigert thought he'd have to miss because of activity here, but since you're not going to operate on the schedule Julian wants, Dr. Weigert decided to go after all. There's a paper he wants to hear about a big breakthrough on the topology of knots."

Since Caro hadn't known that knots even had topologies, she only nodded. The argument with Julian over the surgical schedule had only happened a few hours ago. Did everything in the compound become common knowledge so fast, and did that include her angry words with Julian when he'd tried to embrace her? Aiden didn't look embarrassed around her, so maybe not. Julian was not at dinner. Caro hoped their next meeting was not going to be too awkward.

In her room, she called Ellen again. Kayla was coming home soon. ("That lawyer is amazing!") Well, with what she had cost Caro of Weigert's loan, the lawyer should be amazing. He should be able to successfully sue God for taking Sunday off before He'd sanded the rough edges off Creation.

Caro spent the rest of the evening applying lime juice and reading through her multi-colored files. There were a lot of scientific experiments to back up each main point of Weigert's theory. She paid particular attention to entanglement, that phenomenon in which measuring ("making an observation") about one particle instantly changed a different particle with which it had been entangled—even when they were widely separated. Parts of the brain, she read, comprised an "entangled information system," operating at least partially on a quantum level, and so entanglement applied to the brain as well. Everything the brain did was only a possibility until it actually did it, and the possibilities were unlimited, although some were much more probable than others.

Even before she'd finished reading that page, her objection rose. Entangled electrons and other subatomic particles were one thing, but Caro lived in a macro-level world, not a quantum-level one. The rules were different here. Then in the next several pages Weigert addressed that objection, detailing all sorts of recent experiments that had entangled things larger than subatomic particles.

By 10:00 p.m., Caro's head spun. Nothing had clarified her questions regarding Weigert's theory and death, but the rest of his theory, when she read it slowly and carefully, surprised her with its logic and solid experimental evidence. She couldn't see any way to actually refute it.

Her room was hot. She opened the door and stepped outside, into fresh sweet night air. At a picnic table loomed a shape indistinct in the gloom beyond the floodlights illuminating the walkways. Cautiously Caro, squinting, moved forward.

Watkins sat in his wheelchair, his head thrown back at an odd position.

Dread gripped Caro. She walked closer. "Dr. Watkins?"

The head moved forward; he wasn't dead. Caro moved to face him. "Doctor, are you all right?"

"Of course I'm all right. Mars is visible tonight and I wanted to see it, but the damn floodlights are too bright. Do you ever stargaze?"

"Not really. I knew a few constellations when I was a kid, but I've forgotten all of them except the Big Dipper."

"Which you can't see over the compound walls, not at this time of year at this latitude."

Caro sat at the picnic bench, facing him. He said irritably, "No, don't play doctor with me. You're not my physician. And before you ask, no, I wasn't able to get out here on my own, and Camilla didn't bring me out, and I don't want you to call her. I got out to look at stars with the help of the only person around here willing to defy Camilla and Julian: that tech of his, Ben Clarby."

"Okay," Caro said. "What's that constellation there, with the very bright star?"

"Do you really want to know?"

She regarded him through the gloom, and decided on honesty. "Only tangentially. I'd rather ask you a question I wanted to ask George, except that I'm told he's in Miami for a physics conference."

"So it's 'George,' is it. Go ahead, ask me."

"The goal behind this compound's research is to cheat death, isn't it? You don't just want to visit another branch of the multiverse as a research experiment in physics and brain mapping. You want to 'create' another branch with you in it on the off chance that when you die, your consciousness won't die with you but will continue on in that other branch universe."

Watkins startled her by laughing, a croaky sound that ended in a cough. Caro leaned toward him.

"No, I'm ... fine ... get away. Just ... a minute."

She gave it to him, watching closely. Watkins seemed to recover. Finally he said, "I knew you were quick. The answer is yes. Do you know Donne's poetry? 'Death be not proud, though some have called thee/Mighty and Dreadful, for thou art not so.'"

"Donne wasn't talking about the primacy of the observer. And you don't know that what you hope for after death will actually happen. You can't ever have any proof because nothing in Weigert's theory makes provision for any communication between branches of the multiverse."

"That's true."

"So—"

"Did you know," he said, almost conversationally, "that Weigert wants to be implanted so that he can again see his dead wife, Rose? That he is desperate to do that?"

"I didn't know that, no." Oh God, was that the impetus for Weigert's entire theory—a wish-fulfillment fantasy borne of grief? And yet ... she had just waded through pages and pages of what looked to her like solid science.

Watkins said, "I was best man at their wedding. Theirs was one of the few genuinely happy marriages I've ever seen. I don't think my nephew, your father, was blessed with one. I met your mother only once, and that was enough. Caroline, you've made your decision, haven't you?"

"Yes." He was more perceptive than she'd thought.

"And you're staying."

"Yes." Such a simple answer, born of so much that was not simple at all.

"Good," Watkins said, without emotion. "Now, I'm getting tired. Will you wheel me back inside, please? And maybe you better ... better call Camilla."

Caro pushed the wheelchair across the grass and onto the walkway, called Camilla, maneuvered the chair inside.

"Now go," Watkins said. "She'll be here immediately, if she's not already lurking in the bushes. One more thing—"

"Yes?" Caro said.

"That bright star you pointed to is Altair. Its name in Arabic means 'the one who soars.' It's a summer star, in the northern latitudes eclipsed by the Earth during the winter, but it always returns in the spring. Always. Good night."

Arabic. Her great-uncle was full of surprises. But it wasn't Arabic that Caro thought in as she returned to her room, but rather the half-forgotten Latin she'd learned in prep school. Julius Caesar, crossing the Rubicon and knowing there was no turning his army back.

Alea jacta est.

To Caro's relief, when she saw Julian the next day he seemed not one micro-particle different from what he'd been before their embarrassing scene in the security office. Caro had spent the morning with Barbara, going over Julian's brain imagery. At lunch in the refectory with Barbara and Molly, both of whom she liked more each time she saw them, Julian slid into the chair opposite hers.

"Hello, all. Caro, Lyle Luskin says that if you check out all right today, you can indeed operate day after tomorrow. Are you still itching?"

"Only minorly."

"Good. Your implantee, Lorraine, arrived this morning and is busy unpacking. Your surgical team has been recalled and all will arrive today. Molly, if those earrings were any larger, you could throw each of them like a discus."

"I like to be armed," Molly said. She turned to Caro. "So, you didn't meet Lorraine when she arrived?"

"No, not yet."

"Oh," Molly said, a syllable so freighted that Caro's eyebrows shot up. *Now what?*

Julian said, "What Molly so charmingly intimates is that my sister is ... There you are, Lorraine. Dr. Caro Soames-Watkins, Lorraine Dey."

Caro blinked, then stood and extended her hand. "I'm glad to meet—"

Lorraine seized all ten of Caro's fingers. "Oh, steady hands. That's good, since you're going to cut open my head and turn me bionic! Don't want my chip in the wrong place. I might end up with some weird superpower. Although, on second thought, give me the superpower to drive men mad!"

"Calm down, Lorraine," Julian said. He added to Caro, "She's not really a flake. It's all a social act."

Lorraine laughed. "Don't take away my flakiness, bro! I've earned it!"

Julian said, "She has a degree in mathematics. From Yale."

Lorraine laughed again, a hearty guffaw straight from the belly that made the techs eating at the next table turn around and grin. Lorraine wore a hot pink tee cut very low, a flowered skirt with tiny bells at the hem, sandals glittering with pink stones, and chandelier earrings that made Molly's look small. The last thing she looked like was a mathematician. Although she had Julian's exuberance—raised to the tenth degree—and also looked like him, whatever the tiny extra dimension that moved "pretty" into "startling beauty" had blessed him but not her.

Lorraine declined lunch ("I only eat within a four-hour period out of each twenty-four, keeps my weight down") and left with Julian to sign papers. Caro sat back down and said quietly, "Why Lorraine for implantee number two? Why not someone involved in the project?"

Barbara said, "We specifically wanted someone not involved in the project, who has no preconceptions about what will happen but is completely trustworthy. Julian says she is. Watkins grilled her for hours—this was months ago, before he got quite as sick as he is now—and he approved her."

Caro grinned. "I would like to have been a fly on the wall during those conversations."

"One for the ages," Molly said. "Although I will admit to having my nose a bit out of joint. Until Lorraine arrived, *I* was the dramatic one around here."

Caro finished her coffee. What had her great-uncle seen in Lorraine Dey that made him trust her? Not that Caro was any great judge of whom to trust. Look at Paul Becker. Lorraine must have another, completely different side to her.

But, then, didn't everyone?

"'I am large, I contain multitudes,'" she quoted. At Molly's look of puzzlement, she added, "I wish that Ralph Egan were staying here longer. When my new backup surgeon arrives, we'll both be relative strangers to the whole project."

"When is the new guy coming?" Barbara said.

"End of next week, I think. Before then, I have Ralph long enough to implant Lorraine, do complete post-surgical observation and imaging, and then implant Aiden. Julian and I had an argument about spacing between surgeries."

Barbara said, "You won."

"Of course she won," Molly said. "She's chief of medicine." She fingered one earring. "How far do you think I could hurl this?"

≝

Overnight, Caro's surgical team arrived on Cayman Brac: surgical nurses Imelda Mahjoub and Rosita Ortega; ward nurses under Camilla Franklin; two orderlies. Julian mustered them into the Wing Three conference room. "Good morning," Caro said, as a sense of unreality overtook her that she was in charge of all these people. "I'm very glad to meet you all. Let's go over the procedures for tomorrow."

All of them had worked with David Weeks; they knew their stuff. Nonetheless, the next day there was a moment, just before Caro applied the bone saw to Lorraine Dey's partially shaved head, when she felt something close to panic. What was she doing here, in this superbly equipped operating room with this experienced team, performing medically unnecessary brain surgery? But the panic passed. She'd always believed that medical volunteers were the unsung heroes of ground-breaking research. And she, Caro, could do this pretty basic brain surgery with minimum risk to Lorraine. Not zero risk—surgery was never that—but minimum.

Then everything vanished from her mind except total, calm concentration on what she was doing. The skin was peeled back from a small section of Lorraine's skull. Caro applied the bone saw.

≝

"Beautiful technique," Watkins said. "I watched from the gallery."

Caro hadn't even noticed him; she'd barely noticed that there was a gallery. They were all there when she emerged from the scrub room: Watkins leaning on a walker, Julian, Weigert back from Miami. The Three Musketeers of Outrageous Medical Research. All for one and one for all. She couldn't stop smiling.

"Textbook," Julian said.

She grinned at him. "As if you would know. No pixels and bits and bytes."

Julian laughed. The stark white corridor felt filled with rosy light. And there was her great-uncle the Nobel laureate complimenting her, Caroline Soames-Watkins. The neurosurgeon.

Camilla Franklin raced around the corner, a ship in full sail. "Doctor Watkins! You should call me when you want to get up! And use your chair instead of that walker!"

"I should do a lot of things," Watkins said, so cheerfully that Caro's eyebrows rose. Watkins even let Camilla lead him away. Caro, suddenly ravenous, said, "I'm going to grab a celebratory doughnut, check on my patient when she comes out of postop, and then, Dr. Weigert, I'm ready for a real, in-depth lecture on the way the universe works. Bring it on!"

Weigert stared. Julian laughed again. Caro strode away from both men, feeling as if she could run for miles, could master any physics that Weigert threw at her, could indeed alter reality with sheer surgical skill.

She became even happier when her cell rang: Ellen. Caro took the call in the corridor.

"She's back! Kayla is back home! Thank you, Caro, thank you, thank you!"

"Is Kayla okay?"

Ellen's voice lost some of its exuberance. "She's upset, of course. I'm keeping her home from school the rest of the week. That new caregiver you're paying for is coming every afternoon for a few hours to tend to Angelica and I'm going to do things with Kayla. Crafts, walks, maybe a movie."

"You'll have to sit through something sloppy featuring pink unicorns or blue ponies or an animated princess."

121

"I'll face it bravely. Just let me say again—oops, gotta go! Angelica!"

The call ended. Caro had solved the current crisis and improved Ellen's life a little, but she didn't have the power to free Ellen from poverty, a deadbeat ex-husband, a special-needs child, the grinding routine of her sister's days. Just for now, however—just for now!—Caro was not going to let it depress her. One crisis at a time.

Lorraine Dey developed no post-operative complications. Despite pain meds dripping into her IV, she was coherent and cheerful, answering all the usual inane post-op questions ("Do you know where you are? How many fingers am I holding up? Who's the president?") and passed all the usual neurological tests. Caro collected more congratulations from the most egalitarian medical staff she'd ever seen; there seemed to be no professional barriers among nurses, doctors, and patient. Could that present problems in the future?

Although, according to Barbara, there existed neither future nor past. Caro found herself unexpectedly interested in learning how Weigert would justify that incredible statement. She had questions, and she wanted answers.

17.

When Ellen was three years old, she'd fallen into the fountain in the back garden. Their nanny, the latest in a string that failed to satisfy their mother, although in this case that seemed justified, had been far across the lawn on a wrought-iron bench, talking on her mobile phone. Ellen climbed onto the concrete rim of the fountain, grinned at Caro, and slipped. Caro, five, screamed, "Nanny!" but hadn't waited for any response. She threw herself into the fountain. Ellen lay face down. Caro tried to pull her sister upright, but Ellen was weighted down by her rapidly soaking jacket and pink leather boots. Then Nanny grabbed Ellen and was shaking her: "Breathe! Damn it, breathe!" Caro had hauled herself out of the water and, shivering, snatched up the cell that Nanny had flung onto the frosty grass. She'd poked 911 and said clearly, "My sister is drowning. Come right away!"

Medics had arrived within minutes, but Ellen had already begun to breathe, spewing water and puke before she began to cry. The medics did things to Ellen, and, before they were finished, Mama had come home, her high heels making little round dents in the grass. The grown-ups had all spoken angrily to each other, and afterward Nanny had been replaced by another woman also named Nanny, but not before Mama had spanked Caro hard.

"You embarrassed me in front of those men! Don't you ever do that again!"

"But Ellen—"

"Ellen was fine! Nanny had already pulled her out of the fountain and got her breathing! You called 911 just to embarrass this family, and I won't have it, Caroline! Everyone on the street saw the completely unnecessary medics arrive, and now they think I hire people unfit to supervise my children. Did you push your sister into that fountain?"

"No! She fell! And Nanny was—"

"No more lies. You've lied to me before, so how do I know you're not lying again? Are you so jealous of your little sister that you'd do that terrible thing?"

"I'm not lying!" Caro shouted. "Ellen fell! I'll call 911 again, I will!"

Her mother's face turned red. She grabbed Caro and shook her. Caro screamed, "Daddy!" but he didn't come. He never did. She screamed instead at her mother. "I hate you! I hate you!"

Afterward, when Caro could not sit down for pain, Ellen brought her toys, stroked her face, cried the tears for her that Caro could not cry for herself. *I won't cry*, she told herself fiercely, *I won't*. Ellen curled against her and Caro held onto her little sister. Caro's throat felt thick. Her face wouldn't move right, and it was hard to breathe.

I'm drowning, she thought, but she couldn't be; there was no water. She clutched Ellen more fiercely than before.

≣—

Caro thought of this memory as Weigert scribbled on the whiteboard in the Wing Three conference room. No water, but there are many ways to drown.

The session hadn't started out that way. Caro had come prepared. "George, I've read your summary of the theory behind the project, and I have three questions I hope we can discuss."

"Excellent!" He stood at the whiteboard, a marker in his hand. "Go ahead."

"First, I want to know *why* you think that quantum-level effects—collapsing the wave and so forth—apply to the macro-world of tables and planets. Second, if tables and planets exist only in my consciousness, I want evidence, not just theory, about why I see the same tables you do. And third, Barbara spoke to me about time, but what is the science behind the idea that time only exists in our head? And fourth"—she smiled at him—"I want real science but I don't want to be here for sixteen hours."

"Well. Yes. That's quite a tall order."

"I know. But can you give me just enough real science that I have a framework to read more with *some* understanding? Even though I don't have the math?"

Weigert looked thoughtful, nodded, paused, looked even more thoughtful. Caro could almost see waves of thought collapsing all over his brain as he sorted through ideas. Finally, he began.

"Your first and second questions are so closely related that I have to address them together. You want hard evidence that quantum-level phenomena apply to your macro-level perceptions. First, of course, you remember that when you 'see' a table or a planet, all you really receive is the information supplied by your senses?"

"Yes. And algorithms in my brain use that information to 'create' the table."

"Good. The universe is made up of energy in the form of particles and waves, which are actually the same thing. Energy and matter, convertible into each other. Ah, $e=mc^2$, you know. Einstein."

He swiveled to face Caro, who said "Yes," because clearly she was supposed to say something. It seemed to satisfy him.

"Let me back up to reference experiments that prove our main point, Caroline, which is that the universe is an unformed quantum blur until it is observed by consciousness. We've known for a very long time from mathematically backed, verified, replicated experiments that subatomic particles have both wave and particle natures, and that until an observer 'collapses the wave' by the simple act of observation, the so-called particle is just a superimposed blur, neither particle nor wave. Experiments also show that when scientists watch a particle pass through two slits in a barrier, the particle behaves like a bullet and goes through one hole or the other. However, if you do not watch, it acts like a wave and can go through both holes at the same time. But how can a particle 'out there' change its behavior depending on whether you watch it or not? Only if 'reality' is a process that involves our consciousness.

"Now, if we shoot that electron toward a phosphor-coated screen, its arrival will be marked by a glowing dot. However, first bounce the electron off a kind of mirror so that it can arrive at the detector by taking either of two paths, path A or path B." He sketched this rapidly on the whiteboard. "We also set up detectors on both paths. But something very unexpected happens! The electron has not taken path A *or* path B. Nor has it divided itself to take both paths. Nor has it arrived at the screen by taking neither path. Somehow it has avoided our set-up entirely."

Weigert turned to look at Caro, clearly expecting a reaction. She nodded. So far, his explanation seemed clear.

Pleased, he continued, "That happened because the electron is in a state of 'superimposition'—free to exercise *all* possibilities. It can become a wave or a particle, it can take any possible path, including going from A to B by way of the Andromeda galaxy. Granted, that's not a probable path, but it is possible. Consciousness, in the form of an observer, will determine the outcome. So it is with all other particles. And remember, a particle is just a packet of energy, a 'quantum.'

"Look at this basic concept from another angle: Heisenberg's uncertainty principle, which says that the position and the velocity of an object cannot both be measured exactly at the same time. If there really were a world out there with particles just bouncing around, then we should be able to measure all their properties. But we cannot. For instance, a particle's exact location and momentum cannot be known at the same time. But why should it matter to a particle what you decide to measure? Again, the answer is that the particles are not just 'out there.' Observation defines them."

Caro said, "I'm with you on the micro-level, but not the macro-level. Stars, rocks, this table—they're here, whether or not consciousness is."

"Are you sure of that?"

"Yes."

"How? Listen, Caroline," Weigert said, turning from the whiteboard to lean with both gnarly hands on the supposedly non-existent table, "you've agreed that we only 'know' the information that our senses perceive. You see this table only because photons reflected off it enter your eyes. You feel it only because your fingers send electrochemical signals of sensation along your nerves to your brain, signals that you interpret as 'table.' Can you grant me that much?"

"Yes," Caro said. "But you and Julian and everybody else makes the same interpretation, which argues that this particular section of collapsed quantum foam *is* a solid, macro-level table. Everyone in the compound can verify that."

Weigert's face glowed. "Precisely! Everyone in the compound will say this is a table because so many other people have already said it! This next bit is a little technical, but necessary. When observers look, their consciousness becomes entangled with the system, part of the wave function, because everything is entangled with everything else! When *you* then look at that observer, you become part of the same decohered universe. There is a growing body of research showing that multiple observers who exchange information about the decoherence of a wave *cause* the wave function to concentrate around an actual physical entity with actual physical characteristics. The research involves varying numbers of observations made by varying numbers of observers—the details are in the folder I sent you. Read the experiments I describe, including the one recently carried out at Harvard. It involves multiple observers leading to an effective increase of dimensionality of the space-time in which the physical system resides. In the presence of a large number of observers who probe spacetime just by existing in it, quantum gravity in four spacetime dimensions becomes the same as quantum gravity in 4-2 or just two space-time dimensions. No, you don't need to understand that—just this result: consciousness does not simply observe the universe. We create it, and we do so not just singly but *collectively*. And as scientists explore this new line of research, it's becoming increasingly clear how intimately we are all connected with the structure of the universe on every level. Including connections with each other."

Caro said, "I tried to read that Harvard experiment; I'll try again. But, George, it involves subatomic particles. You're still at the micro-level. Why should I believe that those same phenomena of observation create the macro-level world? Tables, rocks, stars?"

Weigert erased the whiteboard. "Let's start with entanglement. If two particles are entangled, and if you do something to one—measure it in some way—then the other is affected even if they're far apart. Math and experiments both back that up—no, I won't inflict equations on you. Unless, of course, you want them?"

He looked at her hopefully. Caro shook her head. She was growing genuinely fond of Weigert: not just his kindness but his genuine, almost childlike enthusiasm for his subject, including how much he wanted her to understand it. None of those admirable traits, however, would help her with complex equations. She hoped to just understand the basics of his theory.

"All right. The equations are in your folder. So is the fascinating experiment in which Chinese researchers found that entangled particles ten miles apart—ten miles! Think of it!—exchanged information 10,000 times faster than the speed of light, which was the limit of their testing abilities. But essentially, the communication between the entangled particles was instantaneous, confirming that quantum effects take place even on scales larger than the sub-atomic. The particles were linked—this is important, Caroline—in a manner suggesting there was no space between them, and no time influencing their behavior. And there is a growing number of experiments in which even larger objects in the macro-world have been entangled—strong proof that the principles of observation that apply to the quantum world also operate at a macro-level."

"Macro-level objects have been entangled? Like what?"

"A few examples: First, an international team successfully entangled a pair of three-millimeter-wide diamonds, big enough to be those tiny earrings that people wear on their earlobes. Anton Zeilinger and his colleagues at the University of Vienna sent huge molecules called "Buckeyballs" through a diffraction grating, and a detector beyond the grating showed the clear interference pattern of wavelike behavior. Scientists at Delft have entangled small oscillators eight inches apart—oscillators made of 10^{10} atoms.

"Another study, conducted at the University of Vienna, tested a gargantuan compound composed of about 5,000 protons, 5,000 neutrons, and 5,000 electrons. When they watched these giant molecules pass through slits in a barrier, the molecules behaved like little bullets and went through one slit or another. But if they did *not* watch, the molecules behaved in a wave-like fashion and went through more than one slit at the same time. In other words, they behaved like subatomic particles, even though they were thousands of times larger!

"Quantum effects even play a role in how living things work. In 2017, researchers at Oxford successfully entangled bacteria with photons. Do you understand the significance of that, Caroline? Science has carried the bizarre activity of the quantum world right into the macroscopic and biological world. Our world! More and more scientists are coming to agree that the quantum and macro worlds are not distinct."

Surprise kept Caro silent. If macro-level objects could be entangled ... If mere observation could affect things as big as stud earrings ...

Weigert said, "Now, your question about time—"

"Wait," Caro said. Her head felt like a disco ball, spinning with conflicting ideas she needed time to sort out. *I am drowning.*

"George, can we put off tackling the question of time? I really need to think about all this."

"Of course," Weigert said. And then, with one of the mischievous smiles that always surprised her, "Take all the time you want."

18.

Lorraine recovered rapidly from her surgery, and Caro felt confident in scheduling the next implant, Aiden. That would give her time for one more, Ben Clarby, before Ralph Egan left the island, although Julian had news about that. He intercepted her leaving the hospital after her routine examination of Lorraine.

"Caro, what are you doing today?" His manner toward her seemed as friendly as always, although without any hint of flirtation or sexual tension. It seemed that once Caro's attraction to him had dissipated, his attraction to her had vanished as well. She knew why she had changed; being manipulated had always been for her the great destroyer of sexual desire. She understood Julian less well. Had his attraction to her been faked from the start, or could he just turn it off like a faucet when it wasn't returned? Perhaps he was so sure of an endless supply of women drawn to his looks that when one moved beyond his charm, he just shrugged and moved on.

She said, "Barbara, Molly, and I are having lunch at the Brac Reef Resort and then George is going to explain the mysteries of time to me."

"Good. But you might want to Google your new backup surgeon. Sam closed the deal with him this morning, and he'll arrive three days from now. I think you'll be impressed. His name is Trevor Martin Abruzzo."

"Is he newly board-certified, or is he coming from a hospital post somewhere?"

"He— Sophy, what is it?"

One of Julian's few female software techs had rushed over to Julian. "It's Aiden! He's vomiting all over the security office!"

"Vomiting? Were you guys partying last night?"

"No! Anyway, Aiden never drinks that much! He told me to get you or Caro or Camilla."

Caro said, "What are his other symptoms?"

"He's bending over and clutching his stomach and he's sweating hard."

In the security office, Aiden lay on the floor beside a pool of vomit. Caro examined him swiftly. Fever, elevated pulse, stomach pain that he described, gaspingly, as an eight out of ten. She was most alarmed by the gasping, although his lungs sounded clear.

"It could be food poisoning," Caro said. "Aiden, have you eaten anything unusual in the last twenty-four hours?"

"N ... no."

Julian and Sophy, one on each side of Aiden, got him to his feet and then to his room. Camilla and Luskin arrived together from Watkins's room. Aiden's small bedroom was jammed with people as more of the tech team arrived to stand uselessly inside the doorway. Evidently Aiden was popular. Sophy knelt by his bedside, caressing his shoulder and murmuring.

Julian said, "Everybody out so Dr. Luskin can examine Aiden. Back to work. I'll keep you updated on his condition. Sophy, that means you, too."

Reluctantly the software team drifted off. Caro said, "Dr. Luskin doesn't need me, so I'm going to keep the lunch date with Molly and Barbara, unless you think there's a reason I shouldn't."

"No, go. You can't do anything here. But Aiden has surgery in two more days. If it's something he ate, will he be well enough for the operation?"

"Almost certainly. Twenty-four hours, usually, for food poisoning."

"You don't think it's some sort of virus that he could have passed on to Sam? We had a tech conference last night."

"I'm sure Dr. Luskin will run tests."

"Okay. Go have your girls' lunch. And be sure to try the cassava cake, an island specialty."

Caro intended to Google the new surgeon before lunch, but, as she crossed the courtyard, Molly emerged from her room dressed in a clinging pink sundress and high-heeled strappy sandals. "Caro! You're not wearing that, are you?"

"Apparently not," Caro said, glancing down at her khaki shorts and plain white tee, pretty much what she'd worn to the beach bar once before.

Molly said, "Barbara didn't tell you? Thursdays are dress-up day at the hotel. Got to give the tourists someplace to wear their fancy duds. Do you have anything? Because I'm too curvy to lend you anything, and Barbara's too tall."

"I can put something together. Come with me and give me your opinion. You look great, and anybody who can wear pink clothes with orange hair is clearly worth taking fashion advice from."

Molly pronounced Caro's yellow sundress acceptable, even with flat sandals, as long as Caro added a chunky gold necklace and drop earrings, both supplied by Molly. Barbara appeared in a simple, dramatic dark-blue maxi dress with hand-carved African jewelry.

The hotel dining room was crowded, precluding any discussion of the project. That was fine with Caro, who was still chewing over her last session with George. "So," Molly said after their wine arrived and they'd ordered food, "Tell us your story. Where are your parents, do you have siblings, do you like them, have you ever been married, do you ever want to be?"

"*Molly*," Barbara said. And to Caro, "She's really a very good doctor. She just doesn't recognize boundaries."

"I recognize them," Molly said with mock indignation. "I just jump over them. How else can I get into people's heads and see if I like them? Caro?"

Caro said, "Parents both gone. One sibling, a sister, whom I adore. Never married, wary of the whole idea."

"Why is that?" Molly said. "Bad long-term relationship?"

"Not exactly." Not true, but Caro had given all the personal information she intended to until she knew Molly and Barbara better. "What about you, Molly? Ever married?"

"Twice. Didn't we establish at our last beach trip that I have lousy taste in men?"

"Well," Barbara said, "you don't have to sound so proud of it."

Caro laughed. These were evidently their friendship roles: Molly acted outrageous and Barbara acidly objected. Clearly both women enjoyed it, and Caro, a little surprised, found that she did too.

Barbara said, "Just to complete the inquisition, I had a partner once, for five years. It didn't work out."

Molly said loyally, "Because Naomi couldn't recognize a good thing when she had it. But Caro didn't answer my question. Are you wary of men because you had a bad relationship?"

Caro, who hadn't eaten all day and could feel the wine pleasantly fizzing her head, said, "My sister says I'm a reverse avocado."

"A *what*?"

Caro explained Ellen's theory of Caro's mushy hidden depths, finishing with, "I'd rather be considered a ... oh, I don't know ... a lime. Tart but loaded with vitamin C."

Molly said solemnly, "I'm a banana because—"

"Don't go there!" Barbara ordered, and Caro laughed. Barbara added, "Tell us about your sister. Older? Younger?"

"Younger by nearly three years. Ellen has two daughters."

"You're fortunate," Barbara said. "All I got was brothers. Five of them."

Molly said, "And I'm an only child, which is why I think I'm entitled to everything. You did your residency and fellowship at Fairleigh Memorial, right? Was it a good place to ..." Molly realized what she'd just said. "I mean ... up until ... God, I'm such an idiot!" Her blush became as vivid as her hair.

"It's okay," Caro said. Of course they'd Googled her, and of course they knew about her massive online shaming. "I'm over it."

Barbara shot her a keen glance but said nothing. Molly plunged right in. "I don't know how you can be over it. You got a really shitty deal, Caro. But at least it brought you to us, and I'm glad it did."

Caro, uncomfortable with such easy warmth, was saved from answering by a server carrying lunch.

The rest of the meal passed pleasantly, without difficult questions. The island specialties, turtle stew and cassava cake, were delicious. Caro was surprised to find that the three of them had been talking for nearly two hours.

"This was as much fun as the first time," she said, a little shyly. "I hope we can do it again."

"Absolutely," Molly said, and Barbara nodded, smiling. But when they returned to the compound, Aiden was still vomiting intermittently, with fever and chills, and Luskin had had him moved to the hospital wing. "Just a precaution," he told Caro. "The diarrhea and vomiting are severe but not life-threatening." Aiden was receiving fluids and meds via IV, and Luskin was not worried about him. "I'll have some lab tests run, but I don't think it's a norovirus since no one else is sick. He'll recover fine. But James is in a rage because I suggested that something in his kitchen might have been contaminated."

Caro could imagine James in a rage. She changed back out of her dress and Googled her new backup surgeon.

Trevor Martin Abruzzo, thirty-eight, had attended a public high school in depressed Wilkes-Barre, Pennsylvania. College years at the University of Pennsylvania, graduating summa cum laude. Harvard Medical School, followed by a surgical fellowship under the nearly legendary Harold Gainer at Mass General. Then he joined Doctors Without Borders and served in the Democratic Republic of the Congo, operating under almost impossible conditions. That ended in Kinshasa, after he performed cranial surgery on the nineteen-year-old daughter of a notorious African dictator. The girl died, and Abruzzo barely escaped the continent with his life. For the last few years he'd been with the World Health Organization, sent with various short-term teams into crisis areas. He spoke French, English, German, and Lingala.

Caro found a medical analysis of the operation on the dictator's daughter, who'd had an aggressive glioblastoma multiforme in the right temporal lobe. Abruzzo's eleventh-hour operation had shown brilliant technique, but Jesus Christ Himself could not have saved this girl, a fact that made no difference whatsoever to the dictator or his henchmen.

It should, however, have made a huge difference to American hospitals hiring star-talent neurosurgeons. So why was Abruzzo coming to Cayman Brac instead of Mayo or Johns Hopkins or New York-Presbyterian?

She looked for something more personal. After some searching she found his anonymous blog, titled "Reports From A Medical Front." Whatever Caro had expected, this was not it.

He'd written one brief entry about the operation, which was how Caro's search engine had found the blog. He described the craniotomy in dry medical terms seemingly designed to either baffle or bore anyone except other physicians. The patient was not identified. The only personal note was the last sentence: "At least I could see her safely home."

What?

Subsequent blog entries were sparse and, with one exception, just as dry. No wonder he got so few hits. After she'd read half a dozen entries, Caro went back to his résumé. At Penn, Abruzzo had been pre-med but had minored in physics. He'd founded the Spooky Action At A Distance Drinking Club, a distinction that seemed at odds with the colorless scientific recitation/speculations of his blog entries. Various members of the club, including Abruzzo, had been arrested by campus police for disorderly conduct. Twice.

His picture was unremarkable. Clipped dark hair rippled with gray. Deep brown eyes behind sturdily rimmed glasses, firm chin, skin a light brown that could have been either a deep tan or some mixed ethnicity. Pleasant enough looking but no one you'd notice in a crowd. Next to Julian, he would look like an owl beside a peacock.

What brought him to this weird project in the Caribbean? Especially as a backup surgeon? He outranked her in experience, credentials, age, everything. Was she now his backup? That was not what she'd signed up for. And if she was being demoted, wouldn't Julian have told her so?

But she already knew that she didn't understand Julian. *Hidden depths, that one*, Ellen would say. Ellen, who hid nothing.

Disconcerted, Caro closed her laptop and turned to George's folders, hoping for information without too many equations.

19.

Caro was wakened at 4:30 the next morning by a thunderous noise overhead. At first a part of her dream, then it was not. She rushed to the door in time to see a medical helicopter hover into position to land just outside the compound walls.

Who? Lorraine? Complications from surgery? But it had been nearly a week … *Watkins?*

Throwing a robe over her pajamas, Caro rushed along the walkway and through the gate to Wing Two. EMTs wheeled an empty gurney through the courtyard toward Wing Three. Julian and James stood in the glare of extra-bright floodlights that Caro hadn't seen turned on before, James shivering in pajamas, Julian fully dressed. Caro grabbed Julian's arm.

"Who is it? Watkins? Lorraine?"

"No. Aiden. Lyle called for an airlift to Grand Cayman."

"What symptoms?" She felt herself shifting to professional mode.

"Blood in Aiden's feces, low blood pressure. I don't know what else. Lyle doesn't know what it could be, and there's no lab results yet."

James said, "It *wasn't* anything he ate from our kitchen. I went over everything last night, and I mean *everything*. No mold—"

Caro said, "What else did Dr. Luskin say?"

"—no spoiled food—"

"Just that the airlift to Grand Cayman is a precaution in case Aiden gets worse."

"—no cross-contaminated utensils, my staff all know not to use the same knives on fruit and meat—"

Caro hadn't felt the night breeze; now she did and pulled her robe closer.

"—and *all* fresh produce is soaked and scrubbed for pesticides or unsafe handling that—"

"It wasn't anything from the kitchens, James," Julian finally said, although probably just to shut James up, because how could Julian know what had caused Aiden's illness if Luskin didn't know? Luskin would have taken a patient history, if Aiden had been capable of supplying one. But you didn't airlift a patient ninety-some miles without a serious situation.

Julian added, "Caro, go back inside. You can't do anything here and you're shivering. The surgery sequence is changed, but not the scheduling: you operate next on Ben instead of Aiden. His imaging is on file at the hospital. You can give him any pre-op instructions in the morning."

"Okay. But, Julian, even though this isn't the best time, I have to ask: Am I still chief surgeon after Dr. Abruzzo arrives, with him as my backup, or is it the other way around?"

"You're chief surgeon. Nothing has changed, Caro. Abruzzo understands the position he was hired for."

"Then why did he accept it?"

"You'll have to ask him." Julian ran his hand through his hair. He looked distracted, and Caro had the impression—not for the first time—that there were aspects of this project she was not being told about.

The medical chopper rose into the dark sky.

≡

Lorraine's multiverse experience did not go as expected.

She bounced into the session room, looking not at all like someone who'd had brain surgery five days earlier except for the blue paper hat covering her partially shaved skull. Lorraine had affixed to the hat a violently orange artificial flower. Caro was glad that at least it wasn't a real flower. Lorraine seemed to have no idea about sterile conditions near a surgical site. She wore extravagantly studded skinny jeans with a Day-Glo orange silk shirt and three-inch-high silver sandals that showed off orange toenails.

"Hey, Jules, Caro, everybody! I'm off to another world! Let's do it!"

"Hold still," Rosita, the young nurse, said. "I'm trying to get your vitals."

Lorraine laughed. "I'm very vital, honey."

The room seemed crowded to Caro, thick with both people and tension. Julian and Barbara stood at the bank of computers. Caro and Dr. Weigert waited to one side, observers, and Caro didn't know which of them felt more anxious. The next half hour would test both his theory and her surgical skills. Had Caro been able to duplicate with enough precision the surgery that David Weeks had performed on Julian? Julian had experienced what Caro considered a lucid hallucination. Would Lorraine?

And what was everybody, frozen as flies suspended in amber, waiting for?

The door opened and Watkins was wheeled in by Camilla. The tension grew.

Only Lorraine seemed impervious to the strain that prickled like heat rash. She plucked off the foolish little hat, lay back on the cot, and winked as she opened her blouse to expose a lacy lavender bra. Camilla attached wireless sensor patches to Lorraine's head and body. The medical monitor began beeping softly with readings for her heart rate, blood pressure, oxygenation, respiration rate, body temperature, and pressure on the brain. The technology was newer and better than Caro had used at Fairleigh Memorial.

"Hey, I'm a bionic woman," Lorraine said, and wiggled her chest suggestively. "Better watch out, guys."

"Lie still, please," Rosita said.

Julian removed the tiny titanium case from over the connectors on Lorraine's skull. He hooked in the leads that tethered her to the computer and looked down at his sister as Rosita hovered nearby, alert for any change in Lorraine's vital signs.

"Ready, Lo?" Julian said.

"You know it."

Julian did something at the computer and Lorraine's face went blank. Her eyes remained open, her heart beat and lungs breathed, but Lorraine Dey was not there. To Caro it felt different from a patient in a coma, different from a brain-dead patient whose organs were being preserved by machine. Lorraine's mind had not just shut down; it had *vanished*. It was like nothing Caro had seen in any medical ward, except for death itself.

Julian's and Barbara's screens brightened with data. No one spoke. A moment later, another screen began to show the visuals flowing through Lorraine's brain, as captured by the deep-image-reconstruction software.

Her image sat up on the cot although, as with Julian's recording, no one else was present and Lorraine was not hooked up to any machinery. Her head was not shaved. She walked through the door and, as with Julian's recording, directly into the courtyard of Wing Two with its familiar flower bed and circling walkways. Bright sun winked off the studs on her jeans.

Caro recalled Julian's words: *For these initial efforts, the data we programmed to create the new branch of the multiverse kept it pretty much identical to this one. Keeping it as simple as possible until we see how the algorithm works out.*

This time, the courtyard lacked Trevi Fountain. What hallucination would Lorraine erect there? If Julian was exuberant, Lorraine was manically extravagant. Caro expected Versailles or the Alhambra or Ali Baba's cave. Caro did, however, remember what Weigert had said about the limits of alternate universes. Whatever consciousness created by collapsing the wave function, that creation must follow the rules of spatio-temporal causality. And as the wave function collapsed, so would the degrees of freedom recorded in memory as Lorraine observed her creation. If she created the Alhambra, it could not later be turned into Versailles. Nor could she erect something physically impossible to exist.

So what would Lorraine create?

She created nothing.

Instead, she knelt by the one flower bed and touched a small yellow blossom with one finger, her hair falling forward to hide her face. After a moment her shoulders began to shake, and then her entire body. Was she laughing? No. When she finally stood, holding the plucked flower, tears streamed off her cheeks and spotted her silk shirt. She raised her face to the sky and sobbed—no sound, but Caro could almost hear the sobs—and remained that way for the entire fifteen minutes until the screen blanked and the session ended.

Weigert said softly, "What the bloody ..."

Lorraine sat upright on the bed and began to cry.

Julian sat beside her and put his arm around her shoulders, despite the wires still strung between her head and the computer. "What is it, Lo? Are you all right?"

Crying.

"Lorraine, you have to talk to me! Are you in pain? What is it?"

Her sobs slowed. "Pain? No ... no ... Julian ... it was ... was ..."

"What? It was what?"

"Everything."

It took her another five minutes to recover. Except, Caro thought, she didn't recover the former Lorraine. Not really. Her gestures were not theatrical, her smile softer, her expression suffused with ... what?

Wonder. It was in her voice, her eyes, her words.

"I came into the courtyard," Lorraine said as, on the screen, the recording played, "and all at once I *knew. I felt* it.

That flower"—she pointed to her image kneeling by the flower bed—"that flower was me. I wasn't separate from it, or from the ground under my feet, or the walls of the compound, or any of you. We were all melted together, all ... one. I can't explain. But I *knew*. I still know! All of it was me and I was all of it, and I still am. Julian, I still am!"

Caro lay—at six years old? Seven?—on a blanket in the back garden, watching clouds drift across the sky. Then, all at once, the clouds were no longer there, and neither was Caro. She was nowhere and everywhere, woven into what she later thought of as "the fabric of the universe." She was the clouds, the grass, the breeze, the ant crawling across her arm. Everything was her, and she was everything.

Julian said in a hushed, odd voice, "'To see a World in a Grain of Sand / And a Heaven in a Wild Flower, / Hold Infinity in the palm of your hand / And Eternity in an hour.' William Blake."

"No," Caro said more loudly than she'd intended. "Lorraine merely had an episode of temporal-lobe epilepsy. Barbara, I need to see her mapping data."

"It wasn't epilepsy," Lorraine said. "If you'd experienced it, if you'd been there ... *Nothing* like epilepsy." She gazed directly at Caro, but it was a gaze, not a glare. Lorraine looked sure enough of her delusion to not need combat. "It was like ... like ... everything in the universe is actually one."

Weigert spoke for the first time. "Well," he said softly, "it is. Matter and energy and consciousness—all the same. Inseparable."

Watkins said nothing. He wheeled his chair out the door, trailed by Camilla. Watkins scowled as if bitterly disappointed. Why?

143

20.

Caro and Barbara worked into the evening and then the night. Lorraine's mapping data was invaluable as a comparison to Julian's. The part of the brain apparently causing both of their extremely detailed, lucid hallucinations was small and largely unmapped. Both subjects' imaging showed strong neuro-connections to the hippocampus, where memories were processed—no surprise there. More interesting were the strong connections to the nucleus accumbens, the so-called "pleasure center"; to the frontal cortex, seat of conscious cognition; and to the occipital lobe, interpreter of light and movement.

But no signs of temporal lobe epilepsy.

Caro frowned. The imaging was unequivocal: whatever Lorraine had experienced, it was not the electrical storm known to produce religious or mystical experiences. Nor was there much activity in the parietal lobe, the section of the brain that told the self where the body began and ended. Decreased blood flow there, such as practiced and skillful meditators could control, was what led to a sensation of out-of-body experiences.

This was something different. She didn't know what, except that there didn't seem to be anything like it in the scientific literature.

But the mapping data were gorgeous.

Barbara said, "If this holds up …

"… we can have our pick of top journals for publication," Caro finished.

They grinned at each other like twelve-year-olds.

⇐

Getting ready for bed, Caro checked her email. She'd almost skipped it. The hour was late, and her mind buzzed with mapping data. But she turned on the laptop. Two emails that weren't spam, the first from Ellen saying that she and Kayla and Angelica were fine.

The other was from Julian:

> Lyle just called me with Aiden's lab tests. He does not have food poisoning. The hospital still does not know what he does have, although they say it is almost certainly not contagious. He's slowly feeling better but they are keeping him for more tests. Your next implantee will therefore be Ben Clarby—pre-op work-up and imaging tomorrow, surgery the day after.
>
> Lyle says Aiden's symptoms are medically puzzling. Something here is not right.

⇐

After you've done something once, even something you never in your life expected to do at all, it was easier to do it a second time. By her next surgery, Caro thought, it might even become routine.

Ben Clarby's surgery went well. He seemed nervous, which was a little odd. Yes, he was only the third person to be implanted, but he had volunteered, and he didn't seem the type to be skittish about surgery. Still, some people reacted differently to the idea of having their head cut open right now instead of in a theoretical future. In residency, Caro had seen patients suddenly panic, change their mind, change their wills, and—once—demand a second opinion while being wheeled into the OR.

Molly put Ben under anesthesia. The chip was inserted into his brain, the lead wires connected, the small titanium case bolted to the top of his shaven skull. Unlike Julian and Lorraine, Ben didn't have naturally thick hair. The case was going to be permanently visible, but, given the addiction of Julian's software team to baseball caps, Caro doubted that many people would see Ben's case anyway.

This was the last surgery at which Ralph Egan would assist. Caro's next patient, replacing Aiden in the surgical line-up, would be another of Julian's techs: an awkward twenty-something improbably named Ivan Kyven. (What had his parents been thinking?) Ivan, skinny and long-limbed, resembled a praying mantis. Julian said he was brilliant. For Ivan's operation, Trevor Abruzzo would assist.

Ralph was leaving the compound late this afternoon, and James had organized a farewell "tea" in the refectory. Caro would have preferred not to go—she and Barbara wanted every spare minute to work on Lorraine's and Ben's mapping data—but she didn't want to offend Ralph, whom she liked. "Besides," Barbara said, "you know that Molly would never let us skip a party."

"It's just tea," Caro said. "James mentioned finger sandwiches and elegant tiny cakes. He's had his staff baking them all morning."

"For that gang of barely housebroken software kids? Well, let's check it out."

The party did indeed feature tea and coffee in tall silver urns. ("I rented them," James said.) James had recruited two of the nurses to pour. ("Traditionally considered an honor, you know.") Picnic tables in the courtyard were covered with white tablecloths, presumably also rented. Platters held petit-fours and small rolled sandwiches filled with watercress or prosciutto.

Within a half hour, everything had been devoured, Julian's team had brought out bags of chips and Oreos, and Ralph was being toasted with something mixed in a plastic storage bin from an impressive array of liquor bottles with garish labels. "No, no," James said. "This is a tea! A tea!"

Molly, standing with Weigert and Caro, laughed. "James, you can't stop them. With Julian at the hospital on Grand Cayman until midnight with Aiden, both cats are away and the mice are going at it. Actually, I think I might try some of that rotgut, simply as a medical experiment. Caro? You're not still on itch meds, are you?"

"No. But no thanks to the rotgut."

Molly looked mischievously at Weigert. "Doctor?"

"Ah, no, thank you. I must speak to Dr. Egan and then excuse myself, I'm afraid. Press of work."

"Coward," Molly said cheerfully as Weigert made his escape. "Look, Caro, Barbara's trying that concoction. If sensible Barbara is willing, won't you? Aren't you curious?"

Someone had brought out speakers, and music suddenly streamed through the compound, something with an infectious beat. The nurses had abandoned their posts at the beverage urns. One began to dance across the grass by herself, graceful and sinuous. Barbara stood with a drink in her hand, laughing with Ralph.

"Well," Caro said, "maybe just a sip."

Two hours later, Rosita was dancing with Ivan Kyven on the top of a picnic table. No one had wanted much dinner and the kitchen staff, sulkily released by James, had joined the party. They'd brought their own music, and a Caribbean beat at one end of the courtyard warred with rap at the other. Ralph had left for the airport but it made no difference whatsoever. The party rocked on.

Caro had had only one and a half glasses of the concoction in the storage bin, the second glass tasting so different from the first that she suspected it was an entirely different mixture, but it had been so long since she'd drunk hard liquor, let alone whatever potent mixture this was, that she felt floaty and pleasantly fuzzy, giggling with Barbara in two beach chairs that had mysteriously appeared on the grass. The chairs had short legs meant to rest on sand, and both women's legs stuck out straight in front of them. Molly danced nearby with a tall, good-looking busboy who spoke no English.

Caro said, "She won't—"

"No," Barbara said. "Not with anyone in the compound. Julian would have her head."

"*I* would have her head," Caro said. "I'm chief of medicine here." This suddenly struck her as so funny that she burst out laughing. Chief of medicine! Of a "hospital" with six beds, filling up with patients who believed that nothing really existed, not even time, until they themselves created it!

Barbara laughed. "I've never seen you like this, Caro. It's nice. Just as nice as your carefully making sure that Camilla is on duty for Lorraine and that I'm sober in case one of these idiots falls off a picnic table and splits his head open. I'm not a surgeon, but I can stitch up a bleeding skull."

"You are competent in every way," Caro said magnanimously. She felt magnanimous. She felt very good. "And so is Molly, and me, and George, and Julian, and my great-uncle the Nobel laureate genius, and Aiden and Ben and Rosita and Ivan and—"

Ivan made a misstep in his thrashing dance and fell off the picnic table.

"Am I prescient or what?" Barbara said, instantly on her feet. "No, wait, he's getting up. He's fine. Alcohol-induced muscle relaxation. What an idiot, even if Julian does say that Ivan is the best software engineer he's ever seen."

Caro rose too. She misjudged the low height of the sand chair and fell onto the grass. Unhurt, she felt Barbara pull her up and say something to someone else. Caro, dizzy, lurched against Barbara's shoulder as she turned to look.

A man stood beside them, quizzically surveying Caro. In the gathering dusk, she couldn't see him well. Abruptly the courtyard floodlights were turned on, and his face became clear.

"Hi," he said. "Dr. Soames-Watkins? I'm Trevor Abruzzo, your new surgeon."

"It's a party," she said—inanely, defensively, with as much dignity as she could muster.

"So I see," he said, and smiled.

≡-

The next morning, all signs of the drunken party had vanished.

Caro, only slightly hungover, met with Ivan Kyven for his pre-surgery procedures. His MRI, which she went over with Barbara, showed no potential issues with his brain. Blood tests, personnel checks, pre-op interview. Trevor watched all of it carefully, saying little. His presence made Caro a bit nervous. He had performed so much surgery, under much more difficult conditions, than she had. She didn't want to look like a newbie.

When they finished with Ivan, Caro and Trevor went to the refectory for coffee so that she could answer any questions he might have. She was *not* going to explain the entire project to him. That daunting task would fall to Julian, back at the compound with the news that Aiden was recovering slowly on Grand Cayman. Since it was after breakfast hours and before lunch, the refectory was deserted, the coffee left over from breakfast. She took a sip, made a face, and said, "You must have questions, Doctor."

"'Trevor,' please. My first question is how you can drink this stuff."

She smiled. "You were with Doctors Without Borders in Africa. Are you telling me you drank only shade-grown organic coffee prepared with a French press?"

He said, "You can't imagine what we drank over there. And now here you are laughing at me when my sole reason for coming back from Africa was better coffee."

"And look how we've disappointed you."

"Life is just a vale of tears."

Despite herself, she smiled. This was not the formal professional interview she'd expected. She looked more closely at Trevor Abruzzo. At first glance, he seemed as unprepossessing as his online photos. Maybe five-eight, a little stocky, brown-going-gray hair, brown eyes behind glasses that looked able to survive being stomped on by an elephant. A brownish kind of non-special person, until you looked more closely at his eyes behind the thick glasses. Caro didn't think she'd ever seen eyes that alive. They darted, gleamed, danced with humor, seemed to miss nothing.

She said, "Do you mind if I ask you some questions?"

"No, of course not."

Trevor answered concisely all her questions about his history of implanting deep-brain stimulation machinery, which was minimal. She went over the ways that this surgery was and was not the same as DBS, finishing with, "Do you have any questions about tomorrow's surgery? I'm not the person to discuss the overall project with you or the theory behind it. That would be Julian and George ... Dr. Weigert."

"No questions about the surgery. You've been very thorough. I think I understand Dr. Weigert's theory. He sent me the draft of the book he's writing, and we've had some interesting exchanges about it online. I'm looking forward to meeting him."

Weigert had sent him the book? They'd communicated online? Caro hadn't received any information until she'd actually arrived here. And she still hadn't seen the full draft of George's book, only the notes he'd prepared for her. Something unpleasantly like jealousy joined her increasingly jumbled reaction to Trevor Abruzzo.

She said, "I have some trouble with Dr. Weigert's theory. But you minored in physics as an undergraduate, so maybe you can follow the math."

"Most of it, anyway. Weigert's theory is the reason I'm here."

She made a sudden decision. "This is not my business, but I'm going to ask it anyway: Why *are* you here? With your record, you could get a position anywhere. Why did you come here to do this ... controversial surgery that certainly isn't going to help your career?"

He didn't seem affronted by the question, nor by the slight aggression with which she'd asked it. Nor did he answer right away. He sipped the dreadful coffee. Finally he said, "It's a fair question, and I'm glad you asked it, but not an easy question to answer. I'll try." His eyes had changed yet again, to an intensity that nonetheless seemed aimed not at her, but at something she could not see. "Have you read Kierkegaard?"

"Not recently." Or at all? Caro wasn't sure, but didn't want to admit it.

He smiled. "Understandable. What I read now is mostly detective novels. But Kierkegaard wrote something that has stayed with me for a long time. He said, 'There are two ways to be fooled. One is to believe what isn't true; the other is to refuse to believe what is true.' George Weigert's theory could change how we interpret the world. His science is convincing, but science isn't the only tool for understanding the world. Direct experience has a place, even if it doesn't meet the scientific criteria of being quantifiable and replicable."

Caro's eyes widened. "You want to be implanted."

"Yes."

"And Julian ... Did he agree to that?"

"It was the major condition of my coming here. And you, of course, will do the surgery."

"I suppose I will, if Julian says so."

Something in her words or expression caught his interest. His eyes changed expression again, but she wasn't sure to what. He didn't ask why she was here. Did that mean he already knew? About Paul Becker and Fairleigh Memorial—maybe. About Ellen and Angelica and Kayla—no. Caro hadn't even discussed Ellen with Barbara and Molly. She certainly was not going to do so with this stranger with the penetrating eyes and deceptively playful presentation.

She said, "Does your wanting to be implanted have anything to do with the blog post you wrote about why you're no longer a Christian?"

She'd succeeded in surprising him. "You read that?"

"Yes. Research on my new colleague. It was ... startling."

"Why?"

"I don't know."

He pushed his coffee cup away from him. "I actually do have a French press in my room, and some good beans. After surgery tomorrow, I'll make you a decent cup of coffee."

"Sure." He wasn't going to answer her question, and Caro felt embarrassed to have asked it. Not her business.

But then he said, "I became a Christian because that is my culture's expression of belief in something larger than this Earthly life, with ready-made rituals to embody that belief. If I'd been born in India, I'd have chosen to become Hindu; Congolese and it might have been Kimbanguism. The framework is what I wanted. I left Christianity because I found, as with most other religions, that over time the core belief in something larger had become encrusted with arbitrary rules, restrictions, exclusion of everyone who did not follow them. After I'm implanted, if I find that George Weigert's ideas about the universe are true, then they will become my framework for understanding that unseen something larger and more true than conventional science can offer."

"And how will you ever know if what you experience after you're implanted *is* true, or is just a complex, detailed, very convincing illusion?"

"I won't know until I've experienced it. But I'll tell you this, Caro. I disclosed to Watkins and Julian the usual occasional pot smoking, but not that I've done just about everything else you can think of: mushrooms, coke, LSD, more exotic substances in Africa. People I tripped with were convinced that what they saw was real, but I could always tell it was not, even as I experienced it. If Julian and Watkins had known that, they might not have hired me, afraid I'd have a flashback during an operation."

"Might you?"

"No."

"Are you always so sure of yourself?"

"Not always. But about this, yes."

She nodded, unsure what to say. Trevor wasn't like anyone she'd met before; certainly unlike any surgeon she'd met, all of whom took care to conceal from colleagues such things as chemical indiscretions, religious vacillation, or any lapse in self-confidence. The goal for a neurosurgeon was to appear in control at all times. *My goal, too,* Caro admitted, but not aloud.

Before she could respond to Trevor's last remark, Julian slid into the seat opposite her. He looked tired.

"Good morning, surgeons. I just had a call from Aiden. He feels much better this morning than he did even when I left the hospital last night, and he can return to Cayman Brac in a few days. No final lab reports yet. Apparently they're running some very esoteric tests. Caro, is everything set for Ivan's surgery tomorrow morning? And Trevor, are you ready for your grand tour of the compound?"

"Yes," Caro said, as Trevor rose, smiled down at Caro, and silently mouthed, "Coffee."

Caro sat a few minutes longer, exploring her reactions to what Trevor had said. *A framework for understanding something larger than the Earthly life.* Did that mean he would connect with Lorraine's mystical experience, whatever it had been, or with Julian's prosaic, by-the-numbers test of George's theory with the "creation" of Trevi Fountain in the Wing Three courtyard? In one sense, it struck Caro as juvenile to be searching for "a framework for something larger than this Earthly life"—the sort of thing one did in one's twenties, before the struggles of career advancement, bill paying, child rearing, or—in Trevor's case—surviving in a war zone. In another sense, however, that longing for "something more" never really died in most people, even if they did not acknowledge it openly.

Watching clouds drift across the sky. Then the clouds were no longer there, and neither was Caro. She was nowhere and everywhere, woven into the fabric of the universe. She was the clouds, the grass, the breeze, the ant crawling across her arm. Everything was her, and she was everything.

Confused, Caro took her coffee cup to the dish bin. Adding to her confusion was her awareness that, as she and Trevor talked, attraction to him, not there when they'd first sat down, had begun to tug at her. He was so unusual, so open, so alive.

Well, so she was attracted to him—so what? She'd been initially attracted to Julian, too, until she knew him better. Even Paul Becker had once looked appealing to her. She had bad taste in men, but she was hardly unique in that. (Consider Molly!) Caro had a job to do here at the compound, a job that affected not only her own future but also Ellen, Kayla, and Angelica. That was going to stay Caro's focus.

She went to join Barbara for more brain-data analysis. The job was going well.

The next day, everything fell apart.

21.

Weigert put his hands behind him and leaned against the wall, shocked to find that he needed the support. Watkins, seated in a chair with a chess problem set up on the board across his lap, had gone so pale that Julian moved his hand toward the call button for Camilla. Watkins saw him.

"No. Don't. I'm ... fine."

Clearly he was not fine. Weigert looked at Julian, who shook his head and said, "Not yet. There's more."

Dear God ... *more?* "Julian, are you sure about this?"

"Of course I'm sure!" he snapped. Then, "Sorry, George. It's just ... this is my fault."

Watkins said hoarsely, "Tell me again. In order. All of it."

Julian's mouth worked like a frog's. Curiously, this steadied Weigert. He'd never seen Julian distraught before. Angry, impatient, mocking, frustrated ... but not distraught. The sight was distressing, but someone had to remain steady and so it would need to be Weigert. He listened carefully for details he might have missed when Julian had burst in with his disaster.

Julian said, "Because Aiden wasn't here and Ben was in post-op, I did yesterday's cybersecurity check myself, after I got back from Grand Cayman. Everything looked okay. Then at 3:40 a.m. this morning, Rosita, the night nurse, woke me. She said that Ben Clarby wasn't in the hospital wing. Rosita didn't see him leave. She thought he was in the bathroom. Immediately I checked the security log. The entire system had been disabled at 3:06 a.m. this morning, including the cameras and the system-failure alarm. It had been programmed to come back on automatically twenty minutes later, which it did and—"

Watkins rasped, "You'd need a password to—"

Julian talked right over him. "—and to do that you'd need specific codes that only three people have: me, Aiden, and Ben. Not just a password, Sam, a detailed knowledge of back-door access codes and their encryption. But, more important, at 3:07 a.m. blocks of data began—"

Watkins swore and swept his hand across the chess board, sending the pieces flying. A rook struck Weigert's knee. Julian didn't even seem to notice, just kept on talking.

"—to leave the system, using all available bandwidth. It took fifteen minutes to send everything. Algorithms, chip programming, computer configurations, recordings, all of it. Ben got everything, and then he left the compound. He's still shaky from surgery and no jeeps are missing, so presumably someone picked him up in a car."

Watkins said, "I thought you have a tech on night duty at the security office!"

"Of course I do. Ben had dismissed him and said he would take the duty. He said he'd been discharged from the hospital, had just slept ten hours straight, and wanted to 'get back in harness.' Of course he was believed. With Aiden gone, Ben was in charge of cybersecurity."

"How could Clarby be sure that Aiden would be gone to the ... Oh!"

Weigert, sick at his stomach, said, "But ... the data is still all here, as well? Clarby didn't erase it, maybe just stole copies?"

"He didn't delete anything, and of course he stole copies, George! Of all our work from years of effort!"

Julian had never spoken to Weigert in that tone. Weigert felt his own temper rising but held onto it. Julian wasn't re-sponsible right now. His software had been stolen.

Weigert said, "But why? What could Clarby do with all that data?"

Watkins said, "We don't know. That's the *point*. Julian, could Clarby use the data to do what we're doing here? In a duplicate facility?"

"If he had the hardware. It would take hundreds of millions of dollars."

Surely that young man didn't have that kind of money! This facility had taken most of Sam's and Julian's fortunes. But …

Weigert's sour stomach clenched. "Clarby could sell all that data to … to whom? Where did the data get sent?"

"A secure remailer in Ukraine," Julian said, "and who knows where from there. The question is not who, but why. The best scenario is a government like China that has the talent and money to exploit it. Military uses? I don't see how, but I'm not military. Maybe just to claim credit first."

Weigert blurted, "Credit? For *my* theory?"

Julian turned from Watkins to gaze at Weigert, and his tone lost its harsh edge. "The theory is still yours, George. Anybody who can pay for this and then use it isn't interested in the physics, just in the technological applications."

Watkins said, "No. Not a government. Nothing in Clarby's background suggests those kinds of connections. And if he did poison Aiden … Julian, why the fuck didn't your background check turn up criminal contacts for Clarby?"

"Because there weren't any," Julian said. He swung around to face Watkins, and Weigert pictured a young wolf bristling with challenge to the old pack leader. "If you're implying that my background checks weren't thorough, you're wrong. Ben Clarby was clean when I hired him. But that was nearly three years ago, and people leave here for the States to see family, take holidays. Nobody is a *prisoner* here. If Ben was approached after he was hired, I wouldn't know about it."

"Maybe you should have!" Watkins shouted, and began to cough. Weigert rang for Camilla Franklin. Then, hoping to divert both their attention, he said hesitantly, "But something else I don't understand. You told me that Clarby was scheduled for surgery in a week or so anyway. Why poison Eberhart just to advance his place in the surgical schedule?"

Julian said, "We don't know. My guess is that his buyers, whoever they are, got tired of waiting, or began to doubt Ben's ability to deliver, or got nervous about the Island authorities snooping around here. They might have even threatened Ben, and he jumped."

Camilla burst in and swiped a thermometer across Watkins's forehead. He batted it away. "Get out! We're busy!"

"I'll get out when I know you're okay," she said, impervious to his shouting.

It was Weigert who got out. Suddenly he couldn't stand to be in the close, hot little room with Julian and Sam squaring off against each other. He said loudly, "I'll be back soon. You don't need me this minute." Neither of them seemed to be listening. Weigert left.

But the courtyard, fresh with morning dew, wasn't far enough. Weigert needed to think. And to think about anything other than physics, he needed to be able to talk aloud to Rose. But not in his room, another small box. He let himself out of the compound and signed out a jeep.

During his marriage, Weigert had always talked through difficult situations with Rose. She'd been a wonderful listener, attentive and non-intrusive while he worked out whatever was bothering him, and then knowing the exact right moment to offer her opinion. She still knew. Not, of course, speaking to him from beyond the grave. Weigert wasn't delusional. But they had known each other so well, for so long, that often he could guess what she would have said, and he said it for her in his head. Rose was his touchstone.

Rose was the reason Weigert wanted a chip inserted in his head.

He knew that Caroline had agreed only reluctantly to implant someone his age. But Weigert was healthy, unlike poor Sam, and seventy-six wasn't that old! Not these days! And then Weigert would see Rose again, in an alternate branch of the universe where her death had not happened. She would be there, because reality was a construct of consciousness and Rose had never, not for a moment, left Weigert's consciousness.

He was mildly astonished that neither Julian nor his distastefully theatrical sister had created a universe containing their beloved dead. They must have some; everyone did. Although, to be fair, Julian's session had been the first and had lasted only a few minutes, a test of the algorithms, the programming, the hardware, and the human brain. But ... Trevi Fountain? To use that marvelous opportunity to recreate something that, after all, still existed in the Europe of this consensual reality?

And Lorraine! "I don't really know what she did, Rose," he said aloud as the jeep bounced along the dusty road toward the sea. "She behaved not as if she'd created a new reality but rather that the new reality happened *to* her."

Maybe it did, George.

"She means something by 'Oneness' much different from what I mean by it."

But you know what she means. Brahman, Moksha, panpsychism, Tao.

"Maybe. All a bit woo-woo for me."

He could feel Rose smiling.

The jeep maneuvered around the last bend in the road and there was the Caribbean, silvery blue under the morning sun. Tiny whitecaps broke like flashing pixels. Gulls wheeled and screamed. Weigert parked, walked to the cliff edge, and watched waves break on the rocks below.

What was wrong with people like young Clarby that they could be handed the wondrous gift of truth, the truth about reality and how it actually worked, and not find it enough? That they had to try to—what was that dreadful modern word—monetize it? It made no sense.

"Rose, I don't understand."

I know. But it will be all right. You have truth on your side.

"I'm not sure any more that truth is enough."

It was one of the hardest sentences he'd ever thought.

His phone rang. A text from one of Julian's software developers, the impossibly named Ivan Kyven, which Weigert understood only because he'd received these dreadful abbreviations from young techs before: WRU? CMON NEED YR .02 1MFU

Where are you? Come on back, we need your two cents input about one more fuck-up.

Weigert drove back to the compound.

≡

Caroline and young Kyven had joined the crush in Watkins's room. The room had not been designed for six people, especially not when four of them were angry. It seemed to Weigert a constant danger that they might step on each other's feet, jostle each other with elbows, ignite each other with breathed-out fury. Sam scowled at Julian, who'd gone tight-lipped. Camilla glared at Sam, presumably because during the night Sam had gotten himself out of bed and in front of a chessboard without her assistance. Caroline was angry at Ben Clarby, her missing patient.

She said, "So he just waltzed out of here in the middle of the night?"

"It's nobody's fault," Weigert said. No one listened.

Camilla said, "Dr. Watkins, you should be in bed. I told you—"

"Enough," Julian said. "None of us could have foreseen this. Ivan, try to locate Ben electronically. Sam, I've just sent people to ask questions at the airfield and the marinas. I'm going to mobilize my entire team to check all programs to make sure they haven't been tampered with as well as copied. Line-by-line of code, if necessary. But we also need to focus on Aiden. Lyle got the hospital report and ... You weren't here, George, or you, Caro, so I'm going to recap briefly. Aiden isn't ill from food poisoning. Somehow he ingested rosary pea and—"

"What's that?" Caro said sharply.

"A native plant. The seeds are poisonous. But Aiden—"

"What's the toxin?"

Julian looked at a text on his phone. "Abrin."

Caroline's eyes widened. "How much?"

"Lyle doesn't say. Maybe he doesn't know. He says there's no reliable test to detect abrin, which is why the lab screen wasn't helpful, but Aiden's symptoms indicate it. What does abrin do?"

"It penetrates the body's cells and prevents them from making certain proteins they need, eventually harming organs. It all depends on how much he ingested, since abrin doesn't have an antidote. Is Aiden having hallucinations or seizures?"

Julian said, "Lyle doesn't mention those."

"That's a good sign. Does he—"

"Caro, I don't *know*. It's a text, not a complete medical chart. What I do know is that Aiden knew better than to eat anything wild on the island."

Caroline said slowly, "Ben knows all about the native plants. On the way back from my contamination from that maiden plum, he was showing off by naming all those that are dangerous."

Weigert's spine curdled.

Watkins demanded, "Did he mention rosary pea?"

"I can't remember."

Silence. Weigert surprised himself by being the one to break it. "Call the police. They can find Clarby more quickly than we can and arrest him for attempted murder."

Watkin's voice rose. "No! No cops! They're already uneasy about what they imagine we're doing here, thanks to that woman *you* dumped, Julian!"

Weigert watched Caroline's gaze swivel to Julian.

Watkins said, more calmly, "And we don't actually know that Clarby poisoned Eberhart in order to jump the schedule for surgery. There have been so many delays already, starting with that fool David Weeks's senseless death. Police will just slow everything down more, maybe stop it entirely. No cops."

Caroline said, "But if it was attempted murder ... And why would Ben even want a—"

"No cops! And doctor, you need to move up *my* implant!"

Caroline persisted. "Covering up a possible crime is also a crime, isn't it?"

Ivan said, "But I'm still scheduled for surgery next, right?"

Camilla said, "Dr. Watkins, I told you, and Dr. Luskin told you, about the dangers of getting up by yourself and falling, and you just go and—"

Julian said, "Sam, Caro already told you that she won't operate on you yet because—"

Help me, Rose. It's all coming apart. Help me.

But there was no answer inside Weigert's head.

22.

Caro had never seen Julian so agitated. This was a different Julian from the urbane mastermind who juggled people like wooden pins. As they left Watkins's room, she caught at his arm and said, "What do you want me to tell Trevor? And the medical staff?"

He stopped walking. "Christ, I haven't thought ... Call them together and tell them about the theft. Just the minimum details. No, wait, you need to tell Trevor all of it. He's senior staff too. Caution them—this is important, Caro—that they can't talk or email or text any of this outside the compound, or discuss it with any of James's people. And don't tell them that we think Ben might have poisoned Aiden with rosary pea. In fact, don't tell them Aiden was poisoned, just that he's going to be all right and will be coming back to the compound in a few days. I guess you better talk to Trevor first, then the others. I have to get my team together to start checking code. We'll use the big conference room in Wing Three, and we may need the security-office rooms, too."

"Then I'll use the hospital," Caro said.

In the hospital break-room she comforted a tearful Rosita ("I thought Ben was just in the bathroom! The light was on in there and he'd said he was having constipation!") and then sent her to summon the entire rest of the medical staff for a 7:30 meeting.

Trevor entered the lounge, tucking his shirt into his pants, as she was making coffee. "Caro, what's wrong? What's happened?"

"Close the door, Trevor. The entire medical staff is going to be arriving soon, but Julian wanted me to tell you more than I'll tell them."

They sat at the round table in the middle of the room and, to the incongruously cheerful sound and smell of brewing coffee, Caro related the night's disaster. Trevor didn't interrupt, his brown eyes fastened intently on her face. Caro finished with, "Nobody seems to know exactly what Ben will do with the data, since doing anything with it will take millions of dollars."

Trevor said, "I can think of a few things." Abruptly he rose, walked to the coffee machine, didn't touch it, walked back to the table and sat down again. He ran his hand through his thinning hair: Julian's gesture, handicapped by having only ten percent of Julian's mane. His face was rigid except for his eyes, which shone with a controlled fury that startled Caro.

He said, "To take this incredible breakthrough ... this thing of wonder and awe and ... *transcendence*, proof of the kind of transcendence that humanity has hungered for since pre-history ... to use that for—" He broke off.

"For what, Trevor? What do you think Ben can do with it?"

Trevor rose again and went back to the coffee, this time pouring two cups. He handed her one. "I don't know for sure. How could I? But George's theory and Julian's software and hardware allow a person to create and enter a new branch of the universe just as 'real' as this one, do anything they wish there, and then leave it to continue on without its creator. In Africa I saw what that kind of unfettered power can do to a helpless village. An alternate universe in the wrong hands ..."

Caro said carefully, "I can't judge George's theory because I don't have the math. But I've seen no evidence that what happens during post-surgery sessions hooked to the computer is anything more than an engineered hallucination. And"—she felt compelled to add this, although she didn't know why—"both Julian and Watkins know that's where I stand."

"Well," he said, surprising her yet again, "I'm not sure I believe George's entire theory either. I won't be sure until you implant me. I'm keeping an open mind. No, I'm not implying that you aren't ... Caro, I really hope you're not a poker player. Your face might as well have your thoughts scrolling across your forehead like a Times Square billboard."

Stung, she retorted, "Nobody else seems able to read me so easily."

"No?" he said, sipping his coffee and making a face. "Then only me."

Before she could think of anything at all to say to that, Rosita opened the door. "Doctor, everybody's here."

Caro nodded and rose. Her medical staff, including Barbara and Molly in various states of hasty dress, crowded around the nursing station. Caro told them about Ben Clarby's theft, and Julian's insistence on a quarantine of all information to outsiders. She finished with all the good news she could summon up: Julian's staff was working to check and secure all data. Ben was being searched for. Aiden was recovering well and would return to the compound, maybe tomorrow. The surgical schedule would continue as planned, with Ivan Kyven next.

"The project is going forward," she said reassuringly, "no matter what. Does anyone have questions?"

No one did, because either they were too stunned or she'd been so thorough. After they left, however, Barbara asked Caro, "Did Clarby steal the mapping data, too? And the work we've done on it?"

She hadn't thought of that. All her and Barbara's work, their future spectacular publication ... She felt suddenly sick. "I don't know. I'll ask Julian."

She did. Ben had not stolen any patient imaging, brain mapping data, neural research files, personnel information—nothing but the knowledge to program chips and computers, in order to create ... what?

≡

When Caro and Trevor left the scrub room after Ivan Kyven's surgery, Barbara waited for Caro in the corridor. "How did the operation go?"

"Smooth as cream." Ivan, master of the inappropriate comment, had the most beautiful brain Caro had ever seen. Opening up some brains—usually but not always on older patients—revealed problems not picked up by dye in MRI images. Slow-growing low-grade astrocytomas. Incipient aneurysms. Small knotted snarls of blood vessels. Not Ivan. His brain had been as innocent of anomalies as his personality was of social skills. The chip insertion had gone flawlessly.

"Beautiful work, Doctor," Trevor said. He'd watched her every step, and Caro had surprised herself by not being nervous while being studied by this much more experienced surgeon. In the OR, at least, she was still sure of herself.

Barbara said, "Caro, Watkins wants to see us later this afternoon. He wants a report on the mapping data."

"Did you send him our files?"

"Yes. I think he's going over them now so he can ask us questions later. Although who knows? Maybe he'll say we knocked down Dr. Weigert's entire theory."

"Did we?"

Barbara smiled. "No. We put floor beams under it. But Watkins's summons isn't the only reason I've been stalking you. Lorraine arrived on the island this morning for her second multiverse session, and Julian sent me to bring both of you to Wing Three right now."

Trevor said, "I thought her session was tomorrow."

"Was supposed to be. But she's here now."

Caro said, "Can I at least get a cup of coffee first?"

"You drink too much of that stuff," Barbara said.

"I'm a surgeon. Of course I drink too much coffee. Without caffeine, nobody would ever receive any surgery at all. Didn't you go to med school?"

"It seems a million years ago," Barbara said. "I was a different person. Speaking of which, wait until you see Lorraine. Trevor, you haven't met her before, so you won't have any comparison, but Caro will."

When they reached the session room, Caro clutching a double espresso, she looked at Lorraine and blinked.

She almost didn't recognize Julian's sister. Gone were the dangly earrings, heavy eyeshadow, low-cut tops. Lorraine wore jeans and a loose crew-neck sweater that, after a moment, Caro recognized as one of Julian's. Her walk had lost its sexy bounce. Lorraine *glided* forward, her face serene. "Hello, Caro," she said.

"Hi. Good to see you again." *If it's really you I'm seeing.*

Weigert nodded at Caro and Barbara. Julian said, "We're about ready to start."

In contrast to his sister, Julian looked terrible. Since Ben Clarby's theft and disappearance, he seemed to have aged a decade. The skin beneath his eyes sagged; his face looked pasty and hollow-cheeked, as if he hadn't slept. Meticulous checking showed that the compound's data had not been compromised by Ben Clarby's theft, but neither electronic nor physical searching had found any trace of Ben. Most likely there had been a boat waiting for Ben on one of the reef beaches. Julian blamed himself for the entire debacle.

Weigert said to Lorraine, "Just lie down on the cot, Ms. Dey, and let your brother connect you."

"Okay." Lorraine smiled, so compliant and non-snarky—so un-Lorraine-like—that sudden unease washed through Caro.

As Lorraine glided toward the machinery, Caro put one hand on Julian's arm and whispered, "Lorraine isn't … Do you see a personality change in her?"

"Yes, but not from your surgery, Caro. From her multiverse experience."

"How does—"

"I only know what she told me."

Barbara and Julian took their places by the computers. Caro, having no choice, waited with Trevor and Weigert. Annoyed to find her heart thumping—why?—she drank off the rest of her coffee, which did not help.

The program switched on and Lorraine switched off, her face going blank in the way that was, and was not, like patients in a vegetative state. *Not there.* Elsewhere. But with a subtle difference from any vegetative or coma patients that Caro had ever seen, a difference she could not name.

The screen brightened. Lorraine's image, alone in the room, rose from the bed and walked out the door, but not into the courtyard programmed into the chip. Darkness lay beyond the door, a peculiar darkness suffused with flashes of golden light. Lorraine walked into it and vanished.

Weigert gasped. "The program—"

"It's not the program!" Julian said. And then, "I think that's what she's creating!"

Nothing? Lorraine was creating nothing? Caro's hand wobbled and droplets of coffee splashed onto the floor. What if Caro's surgery had affected Lorraine's brain in some way not obvious until electrodes connected her to the computer's power sources? What if Caro had unwittingly destroyed some critical neural connections that—

"Stop the program, Julian!" Weigert said. "Now!"

He did. The screens went dark. Lorraine stirred, sat up on the bed, and blinked once.

Julian spoke gently to his sister. Caro saw that the gentleness was costing him every last fiber of will power. "Where were you, Lorraine?"

She said, "Everywhere. Every time."

Normal speech. Caro's relief was so great that she sank, boneless, against the wall.

Barbara said, "Everywhere? You were gone less than a minute."

"No," Lorraine said. "I was gone for all time. And no time. And now I don't ever need to do that again. It's with me for good now. Caro, you can remove my chip if you like. Use it for somebody else."

Julian said, "*What's* with you for good?"

"The Oneness," Lorraine said. "It's all One. I'm you and you're me and we're everything, and once you know that, you can't not know it. I'm sorry I can't explain it any better than that. There aren't words." She swung her long legs off the bed and stood up. "You have to experience it. Everyone should. Then you *know*."

Weigert said, "You agreed to more sessions, Ms. Dey. For after the input is reprogrammed."

"Okay, if you want me to. I just meant that I don't need to do it again for myself. Fuck, I wish I could give you all what I now have!"

Those words sounded more like Lorraine. The tears in her eyes did not. Nor her obvious pity for everyone else in the room, which Caro resented. She didn't need pity.

"I have to go now," Lorraine said. "There are people at home that I need to apologize to. I haven't always been a kind person."

Barbara blurted, "Are you kind now?"

"Probably not," Lorraine said. "But they're me, you see, and I'm them. I didn't know that before. I didn't know how I'd hurt them. I have to make some phone calls."

She walked—no, glided—out of the room, leaving them all standing there.

"Julian," Barbara finally said, "I think I'd like some of that Scotch you're always waving at everyone."

23.

They didn't have the Scotch, or at least Caro didn't. She needed, all at once, to be alone. In her room she locked the door, lowered the blinds, and tried to order her thoughts.

So much was coming at her at once: Ben Clarby's theft, her unexpected conversations with Trevor, her and Barbara's soaring hopes for their journal article, and now Lorraine. Although ... Why was she so agitated about Lorraine? Nothing, really, had happened except that a very extroverted woman had been in a quieter mood—everybody had those—and experienced a moment of spiritual reflection. So what?

She was lying to herself, and she knew it. What she didn't know, didn't understand, was what had happened to Lorraine, and she didn't like not knowing. What exactly had occurred? How? Why?

Those were the questions Caro's medical training had taught her to ask about the brain. She didn't like not having answers. She especially didn't like that the answers she didn't have seemed somehow tied to the question Julian had asked the first time she'd met him: How would you like to live forever?

As what? As a disembodied spirit floating in Lorraine's nothingness that was "everything"? No thank you.

But Lorraine, like Caro, was a scientist, a mathematician. In contrast to her over-the-top-sexy clothing and flamboyant manner, her psych profile was stable, productive, logical. But she wouldn't be the first woman to have covered up feelings of social awkwardness with its opposite, an ill-calculated theatricality. Especially if, like her brother, she had a high sex drive.

None of that fit with a religious conversion. If what Caro had just witnessed actually *was* a religious conversion. Caro and Barbara would go painstakingly over the brain mapping from Lorraine's one-minute hallucination, but Caro suspected the mapping wouldn't differ from her first session. No pronounced activity in the brain centers associated with religious ideation.

It seemed to Caro that Trevor had been right when she'd asked him about his blog post on Christianity: religion reflected humanity's need to codify natural impulses of curiosity about nature and a desire for order, plus perhaps gratitude for life itself. Start with feelings and then build up around it beliefs and strictures that got thicker and thicker, like layers of nacre around a grain of sand. You ended up with rigid laws—cover your hair, no meat on Fridays, sit this way during meditation even if it hurts your spine, build points on roofs to keep out evil spirits. *Or else.* The original impulse to worship life was smothered in rules and fear.

Had Lorraine stripped all that away with her vaguely mythic "Oneness"?

Or was her hallucination dictated by her familiarity with Weigert's physics, which insisted time and space are tools of the mind instead of hard physical realities? A suggestible mind might have been strongly swayed by Weigert's brilliance and conviction.

Or—a third possibility—had Lorraine created a unified and kindly universe from some need of her own, something that hadn't been in her psych profile? Had Lorraine's lucid-dreaming illusion come from Freudian need?

Of all her medical training, Caro had most disliked her psych rotation. She'd chosen neurosurgery partly because it dealt with something tangible: the three-pound mass of electrochemical machinery that was a brain. Solid. Real.

All at once, she wanted even more solid reality. She phoned Ellen.

"Ellen? How are you all?"

"We're good. Is everything all right there? You sound a little weird."

"I'm fine. Tell me what you're doing right now, this very minute."

"Well, I'm hanging Angelica's things on the drying rack set up in the living room because the dryer's broken and it's raining outside. Angie is asleep. Kayla is doing homework at the table, it's— Kayla! What's your homework? Aunt Caro wants to know."

The house was so small that Caro could hear Kayla's answer without Ellen repeating it. "Math. Fractions. I hate fractions!"

Caro shouted, "You're right! Fractions are terrible! Let everything stay whole!"

Ellen said, "Jesus, Caro, you just broke my eardrum! And everybody needs fractions. What if"—this was clearly for Kayla's benefit—"we had to divide a loaf of bread?"

"Let them eat cake," Caro said.

"What?"

"Never mind. It's just good to hear your voice. What are you making for dinner?"

"Meatloaf."

"I love meatloaf."

"Since when? You're acting very strange, Sissy."

"This is a strange place. I miss you all so much."

They chatted a few minutes more until Angelica woke. Caro could hear the wailing. She ended the call, refreshed by the dose of mundane, tangible, everyday normalcy.

It didn't last. Caro's thoughts would accept no discipline. They shot back to Lorraine like a dog after a squirrel.

Would Lorraine's hallucination—conversion, insight, whatever—stay with her? It could be merely a temporary high, even though nothing in her or Julian's brain imaging indicated any involvement of the addiction center. Lorraine herself had said that she'd been "gone for all time," even though her session had lasted for less than a minute.

Caro's own childhood "session" in the garden had also felt both instantaneous and eternal.

She had postponed George's lecture about time once, twice, thrice. But it seemed that the concept of time was more intimately bound up with consciousness than Caro had realized.

She went in search of George.

≡

"The thing you have to understand about time, Caroline, is that it doesn't really exist."

Caro said, "Always good to lead with a right hook."

"I beg your pardon?"

"Never mind." They walked along the beach at Spot Bay. Caro had found George signing out a jeep and invited herself along. It somehow seemed typical of George to prefer this rocky beach to the far more picturesque ones near the resort. George wore thick-soled boots, and Caro was glad she had at least changed her sandals for her new sneakers. She said, "Time doesn't exist?"

"No, at least not as a real objective or external 'thing.' We only believe it does because our brain's algorithms are wired to interpret information as occurring sequentially. Otherwise, we couldn't make sense of the world at all."

"I should think not," Caro said. A pebble wedged itself into her shoe. She bent to remove it. Round, worn perfectly smooth by the sea, the pebble was reality proven mutable. But time?

"Let's start with the basics," Weigert said. "You know that the equations for Newton's laws of motion, Einstein's special and general relativity, quantum theory—they all function independently of the notion of the passage of time. They operate backward as easily as forward! And you also know that Einstein proved that time is relative to the observer—that there is no one definite 'present moment' for everyone in the universe."

Caro did know these things, at least in a vague way, but that was all she knew about physics and time.

He continued, "So since the so-called 'flow' or 'arrow' of time has no direction in physics, what makes us believe that it moves forward like an arrow? Three things: motion, the second law of thermodynamics, and dinosaurs. Motion first. Do you know who Zeno of Elea was?"

"Ancient Greek philosopher," Caro said.

"Yes, fifth century BC. He said that nothing can be in two places at once, obviously, so an arrow flying through the air occupies only one place at any given moment. At that moment, it is therefore at rest. Thus, motion is really just a series of separate events, not a continuous one. Time isn't a feature of the external world; it's a projection of something within our minds as we tie together things we're observing."

Caro frowned. "But we all age. That's time."

"That is a series of events, too, that we interpret as time. It's just an idea in a person's mind, no more than a collection of thoughts, each of which occurs in the present moment. So it shouldn't come as a surprise that time has no existence as a separate entity. Time as we conceive of it is change, and only observers can experience change. Without observers, there is not even any reality to begin with.

"The reason we *experience* growing older is that we observers have memory and can only remember events observed in the past. Quantum mechanical trajectories 'future to past' are associated with erasing memory, since any process that decreases entropy—any decline in order—leads to the decrease of entanglement between our memories and observed events. In other words, if we were to experience the future, we wouldn't be able to store the memories—you can't go back in time without that information being erased from your brain. By contrast, if you experience the past, the usual route of 'past leads to present leads to future,' then you accumulate memories and nothing violates the law. So, a 'brainless' observer doesn't experience time, or a world in which we age. And it's not just because you don't experience things if you lack a brain. It actually goes deeper than that. The arrow of time—indeed, time itself—simply doesn't come into existence at any level in the first place! Aging is truly all in your head.

"You, Caroline, are young in one 'now', and you will experience wrinkles and graying hair in another 'now'. But, in reality, they all exist in superposition. Think of it like one of those old phonographs. Listening to the music doesn't alter the record itself. Depending on where the needle is, you hear a certain song. This is the present—the music before and after the song is the past and the future. In like manner, every moment endures in nature always. The record doesn't go away. All 'nows', like all songs on the record, exist simultaneously, although we can only experience it piece by piece. That superposition is why Einstein said 'the distinction between past, present and future is only a stubbornly persistent illusion.'"

"But ..." Caro said, and wasn't sure what to say next. Barbara and Molly had made the same arguments, although less technically, and she hadn't known what to say then, either. Weigert had stopped walking and, framed by the ocean, stood gazing at her with so much excitement about his own explanations that affection for him rushed over her. Affection, however, was not understanding.

He said, "Consider dreams, or drug experiences. During those, you are the only observer. Your consciousness can construct reality any way at all. Don't your dreams construct space and time in weird ways?"

"Yes, but dreams aren't real."

"They aren't our consensus reality. But they show that your mind constructs its own time when freed of the algorithms hard-wired into your conscious brain. More evidence that time is an emergent property of consciousness. Now, consider the second law of thermodynamics."

Caro hoped he wasn't going to ask her to define it. She was pretty sure it had to do with decay but was fuzzy on the details.

"The second law of thermodynamics," Weigert said, walking again and waving his arms, "says that when energy changes from one form to another form, or matter moves freely, entropy in a closed system increases. Differences in temperature, pressure, and density even out horizontally, evolving toward thermodynamic equilibrium. Total entropy can never decrease over time for an isolated system."

He turned to face Caro. "In other words, ice cubes don't unmelt, you don't get younger, and the universe eventually runs down."

"Yes," Caro said, relieved that he'd said something she could agree with.

"But interestingly, Ludwig Boltzmann, who created the laws of thermodynamics, didn't believe that entropy proved the existence of time. Using statistical mechanics, he pointed out that there are a huge number of states in which those ice cubes can exist, and nearly all of them are disordered. Full of entropy. A state in which ice cubes *don't* melt at all is only one state, and statistically the chances of observing it are infinitesimally small. Entropy is merely a fact of statistical behavior. So we see a lot of disordered states, and the algorithms in our consciousness interpret that as 'time.'" He smiled whimsically. "Unless, of course, you just took those mushroom thingies and see the ice cubes unmelt."

Caro would bet her life that George Weigert had never taken magic mushrooms, or possibly anything stronger than aspirin.

Weigert talked next about why the laws of quantum gravity and the decoherence of the wave function describing the universe were inadequate to explain the emergence of time. Caro, who'd never supposed that quantum gravity did explain time, got lost in terminology. She found herself again when Weigert reached his conclusion, for which he again stopped and faced her.

"So you see, my dear, the emergence of the arrow of time is related to the ability of observers to remember information about what they observed. If you lack a brain—as, for instance, a rock—then time does not exist for you in the first place. Time is a relational concept—one event relative to another. 'Before' and 'after' have no meaning without association to another point. Thus, time requires an observer with memory, since without that you can't have the relational concept that underlies the whole idea of 'the arrow of time.' A simple example: your cell phone rings. But the ring doesn't happen until you compare its sound to the silence of the second before. Do you understand, Caroline?"

"Not completely," she admitted, and seized on something he'd said minutes ago, something she could at least visualize. "Dinosaurs had brains, right? Small brains, but weren't they observers?"

"Yes! They did and they were! I just use dinosaurs as a shorthand for geologic time. People like dinosaurs. I don't know why, but they do. Nasty beasts. Go back further, to the formation of the solar system. If there were no conscious observers—and there were not—then the sun and planets did not exist. Physical reality begins and ends with the observer. All other times and places are things we've invented, serving only to unite knowledge into a logical whole in our minds. Think of a globe in a classroom—it's merely a representation of places that are theoretically possible to visit. Until, say, Paris was actually observed, it dwelt in the sort of blurry probability state that we've discussed before. The uncollapsed wave function. Paris, the sun, the moon, dinosaur fossils—they now exist in consensus reality because consciousness created them. The collapse of the wave function is a material object's birth moment."

"No, wait," Caro said. "There was no sun, moon, primitive Earth?"

"There is now. Geological reality is now part of our consensus reality. But it extends no further back than an entity capable of observation."

She struggled to formulate her objection. "But that's circular reasoning. There was no earlier existence because consciousness wasn't there to observe it, and so there existed no reality to *create* observers in the first place."

"You're going to ask the big question, aren't you?"

Was she? Yes. She saw it.

"So where did consciousness come from?"

"The question is actually a bit daft. Since 'before' and 'after' have no absolute meaning independent of the observer, the question of what came 'before' an independent observer is completely meaningless. It's like asking what's north of the north pole, or whether death is a state of 'being nothing.' Most people do imagine death as nothing, but the verb 'to be' so completely contradicts 'nothing' that you might as well announce you're going to 'run not run.'

"The question only arises from a lack of understanding of physics. I deal in equations and observations and experiments, and this is what those three things reveal. Consciousness creates the past, not the other way around. Which, incidentally, was what Stephen Hawkings said, too: 'The past, like the future, is indefinite and exists only as a spectrum of possibilities.'"

Caro said slowly—she didn't want to offend him— "I'm sorry, George, but I can't buy this explanation of time. It just doesn't make sense to me. The rest of what you've said about the primacy of the observer ... Well, maybe. I'm still thinking about it. But time? It passes. I've seen it pass for my entire life."

Weigert smiled, such a gentle and accepting smile that Caro had a completely irrelevant thought: *His late wife was a lucky woman.* But all Weigert said was, "You don't have to accept it yet. I know it's hard when your whole idea of reality gets upended. I do know. How is your sister doing, Caroline?"

She had given him updates on the legal proceedings he had paid for. He already knew that Kayla was back home. This question felt different, more personal. She said, "Ellen always sees the best side of everything. She's managing, just as she always does. Nothing breaks her."

Weigert regarded Caro for a long moment before saying, "I'm glad."

She was left, however, with the impression that he'd wanted to say something else but had drawn back. Upper-crust British manners? His natural reticence? Whatever it was, she didn't ask. Weigert was different from Watkins or Julian. He put less value on directness and more on trust. And Caro trusted him.

If she and Ellen had had a father—or grandfather—like Weigert, would both their lives have turned out differently? Would Ellen have not been desperate enough to make a jail-break marriage? Would Caro be less wary of romantic involvement?

No way to tell. Not unless you were George Weigert, and Caro was not that.

24.

Ivan Kyven recovered from his surgery with almost inhuman haste. When the nurses insisted he stay in bed, he squinted for hours at his laptop. "Working," he said, although each time Caro checked on him, he seemed to be playing video games. The titanium box gleamed on the top of his shaved head, making him look even goofier than usual.

Barbara and Caro worked on the mapping data from Lorraine, Ben, and Ivan every spare moment. When Watkins summoned the two women for a progress report, Caro, groggy from too little sleep, groaned.

"Come on," Barbara said, "we can do this. Just put on your medical-school persona, when nobody slept."

"I was younger then. But okay, we're ready, even if Watkins rips our work into tatters."

He did not. "Good," Watkins said in his overheated room as Camilla hovered in the background. "Very good work. I commend both of you. Keep it up and you'll have an eminently publishable article." He turned to Caro. "Abruzzo is working out all right?"

"Yes. We implant George—Dr. Weigert—next, as you already know. Trevor will open and close and I'll do the surgery. But that raises another issue. Trevor says you promised him that eventually he can be implanted. Who will be surgical backup for that operation?"

Watkins said, "Not settled yet. In good time. Before then, you'll implant me."

Caro had half expected this. She said, "I haven't heard from Dr. Luskin that he's cleared you for surgery."

Watkins scowled, a horrible inverted rictus on that ravaged face. "All you doctors are too afraid to take chances."

"If that were true," Caro said evenly, "I wouldn't be here at all, would I?"

Watkins tried to answer but coughed instead. The cough intensified and Camilla sprang forward. Caro waited until her great-uncle's spasm subsided. When it did, Camilla threw her a eloquent glance. Caro and Barbara left.

Barbara said quietly to Caro, "Do you intend to implant him ever?"

"When I think it's safe to do so," Caro answered, aware that both she and Barbara recognized that it was no answer at all.

※

As Caro stumbled toward her room for a nap, Molly accosted her. "Where are you going?"

"Sleep," Caro said. "I was up most of last night working and—"

"I know you were. Barbara, too. Good, take a nap, because we're going out tonight to dinner. Everybody except me and Trevor looks like shit. So I made a reservation at the beach hotel for everyone under seventy and over thirty except Camilla, who won't leave Watkins. No, don't protest, Caro. We need this."

"I—"

"No need to dress up."

"I—"

"Be at the gate at 7:00."

Caro gave up. She was too tired to argue. Molly looked more determined about this outing than Caro was about anything except sleep, and maybe a dinner out would be fun.

And dinner *was* fun, at least after everyone had a drink and began to relax. Because the dining room at the hotel was packed, they couldn't talk about the project, which in itself was refreshing. Conversation settled on travel stories: Europe, Hawaii, New York City, Mexico, Rio de Janeiro. Julian had been to Katmandu, but that was his only contribution. He drank steadily, growing more and more quiet.

Caro limited herself to one glass of wine, which she nursed. As the meal progressed, she became increasingly aware of Trevor seated beside her: of the turn of his head, the length of his long fingers on the stem of his wine glass, the glow of his bright brown eyes whenever he turned in her direction. Why had she not noticed before how broad his shoulders were on his stocky body?

He never mentioned Africa, nor Doctors Without Borders.

After dinner, Molly said, "Anybody up for a quick walk on the beach? It's a lovely night."

Trevor said, "Sure."

Julian finally spoke. "Not me. I'll wait for you here."

Barbara said, "I think I will, too. I hurt my foot earlier and I'd better not walk on sand."

Caro, who hadn't noticed or heard anything about a foot injury, looked at Barbara, who almost imperceptibly glanced sideways at Julian, now on drink number what? Completely unlike him. Barbara, Caro realized, didn't want to leave him alone. Kind Barbara.

The brief walk was hauntingly lovely. The sand under Caro's bare feet was cool and firm. A first-quarter moon made a silver path on the water. A slight breeze, ruffling the water, smelled of salt tang. Molly took off her shoes and dashed into the waves, squealing.

Trevor said, "Caro?"

"I'll stay on dry land. I think— Trevor, what is it?" He'd stopped walking and put one hand over his eyes. A moment later, the gesture was over.

"Sorry," he said. "It's just that this looks ... not even like a postcard, but a parody of a postcard. And three weeks ago WHO sent me to a village in Somalia that had just ... No, never mind. Sorry."

"Don't apologize. I can imagine how terrible the contrast must be."

"No, you can't. And I don't want to tell you, at least not now. Please don't get the idea that I'm not glad to be here. I am. Caro—"

Before he could say more, Molly dashed up to them, laughing and shaking water off her legs. "You should both wade! It's so warm! Of course, I'm comparing it with my last post, in Maine, famous for freezing over in October."

"I'll match you," Trevor said lightly. "I grew up in Fairbanks."

"You win!" Molly said. "Let's go collect Julian and Babs."

Babs? How much had Molly drunk?

Caro didn't find out. She drove everyone home and they separated. In her room, Caro prepared for bed, even though it was only ten o'clock. Her sleep deficit, aided by the wine, demanded to be paid.

Only ... What had Trevor been about to say when Molly pelted toward them?

What had Caro hoped he would say?

She barely knew him. Pulling on her sleepshirt, she eyed the pile of folders on her desk. That's where her focus should be, not on random attractions to men who bantered well. Paul Becker, Julian Dey, Trevor Abruzzo ... Why wasn't she ever attracted to silent types? Solid types who did not found bizarre research projects or grope female colleagues or work in traumatic war zones?

Someone knocked on the door, lightly, and then harder. A key turned in the lock.

Caro dashed to the door. "Who's there! I'm calling security!"

Julian's voice said, "I *am* security. Please open, Caro."

"Julian, go away!"

"I can't. I'm too drunk. And I have to tell you something."

"In the morning!"

She heard him sob, just once, stumble away from the door, and fall down.

Caro unlatched the chain. Julian lay sprawled half on the walkway, half on the grass of the courtyard. He sat up slowly. Caro demanded, "Did you hit your head? Is anything broken?"

He looked at the Scotch bottle in his hand. "No. It's fine." After a moment he added, "I have to tell you something. I screwed up."

In the glare of a walkway light, she studied him. He looked terrible. She said roughly, "Come in, then. For two minutes."

He did, stumbling a little, and fell heavily onto her desk chair. Caro yanked a robe over her sleepshirt and said, "What did you screw up?"

He looked astonished. "You know. Ben. Stealing all the data."

"I thought cyber protection was Aiden's job."

"Aiden was in the hospital," Julian said. "I thought you knew that."

Of course she knew that. Maybe he was drunker than she'd thought.

He said, "Do you want a drink?"

"No. And neither do you." Gently, she took the Scotch bottle away from him. He didn't protest. "What did you want to tell me?"

"Ask you two things. 'Simportant. Will you stay here if the FBI shows up?"

"The FBI? Why would they come here?"

"Not completely sure. But they might. Did you know that you saved us from them once?"

"I did? How on Earth—"

"Sam. He was going to make Ralph Egan implant him if you hadn't come here."

She said instantly, "Ralph wouldn't have done it. He wasn't board-certified and had no backup surgeon."

"What Sam wants, Sam gets. Although maybe not that time cuz ... George. Anyway, you came."

"What about George?" Julian was evidently a loquacious drunk. Not like Caro's father, who kept everything locked in his alcohol-sodden mind until it was too late. She pushed that thought away.

Julian closed his eyes, his body so loose in her desk chair that he seemed in danger of slipping out of it. But he wasn't slurring his words, and one thought followed another in logical order. He said, "George. Said if Ralph implanted Sam, George would tell authorities we have an unlicensed neurosurgeon operating here. Entire project would end."

Caro gaped at him. "*George?* He loves this project!"

"George is very ethical. So am I, believe it or not. Which you don't."

Did she believe Julian was ethical? It depended on how you defined that word. But, then, ethics always did depend on individual perception.

He surprised her by saying, "Lorraine is the key, you know."

"Lorraine?"

"Even when you construct a new universe, even when you can put into it anything you want, there is—are—is—differences. In people. What the rest of the algorithms in your brain let you construct. Your personality. Who you are with all your experiences. That."

Caro untangled this. Now Julian did sound drunk. She said, "I think you should go to bed."

"Can't sleep." And then, "I gave up everything for this project."

"I know." Caro felt sudden sympathy. She knew what it felt like to have your dream shattered. "But the project itself is intact. It can still go forward."

"You don't understand what ..." He lost his thread, found it again. "What Ben could do. But you're sweet to say that. Din't know you could be so sweet."

He lurched toward her and tried to plant a sloppy kiss on her mouth. Caro shoved him away. She wasn't afraid of him. Julian was no Paul Becker. Nonetheless, she moved toward the door as she said sharply, "Don't."

Caro's cell rang. It lay face-up on her desk and she glanced at it: Ellen. At this hour? She snatched up the phone and answered. "Ellen?"

Her sister screamed, loud enough that Julian stumbled sideways. The scream was followed by wailing so primal it sounded animal rather than human.

"Ellen! Ellen! *What*?"

"Angelica! Angelica died! My baby died!"

The room tipped as a swirling black wave swooped over Caro. Julian gripped her elbow to steady her. "What is it? Anything you need, we'll get it. Caro? I can't ... Fuck it! Why the fuck did I drink so much? I can't ..."

She said to him, "George. Please. Go get him.

I want George."

25.

Early the next morning, Caro flew to the States. Weigert had arranged everything, or maybe Julian and Weigert together, or with Barbara or Molly? Her room had been full of people. Barbara had offered to go with her, that much penetrated the fog of grief and worry, but Caro refused. Her flight from Miami was delayed and then canceled: mechanical difficulties. Caro rebooked. It was evening before she reached Ellen's shabby little house.

A strange woman opened the door. Two more women sat on the sagging couch, eating from Ellen's plastic bowls. "Yes?" the stranger said briskly. Sixty-ish and heavyset, her face militarily stern, she looked capable of leading armies. Patton in a flowered apron.

"I'm Ellen's sister," Caro said.

The woman's face softened. She said in an up-country Southern accent, "Oh, thank the Lord. None of us know nothing about how to help her. Come in."

Caro did. The other women put down their bowls and rose, nodding politely, introducing themselves. They were neighbors, called to duty by the woman who'd answered the door. None of them offered a first name. Mrs. Foster—Caro vaguely remembered hearing that name before, from Kayla—Mrs. Carruthers, Mrs. Green. They addressed Caro as "Doctor."

"We cleaned up a bit," Mrs. Foster said. "The place needed it."

The living room and kitchen were immaculate, the table crowded with casseroles and cakes. Someone had removed

Angelica's changing table and crib, although Caro had no idea where they could have been put in the tiny house. Everything smelled strongly of pine disinfectant, like an entire hospitalized forest.

"Thank you," Caro said. "Where are Ellen and Kayla?"

"Kayla is finally asleep in her room," said Mrs. Foster. "And Mrs. Kemp ... Well, you better see her for yourself." She moved purposefully to Ellen's bedroom.

This room had not been cleaned. Clothes lay strewn on the floor and on the unmade bed. The room smelled bad. Ellen sat in the corner in an upholstered chair that had once been yellow. She stared unmovingly ahead, not raising her eyes when Caro walked over to her.

"Ellen?"

No answer.

Caro knelt on the floor. "Ellen, it's Caro."

"Yes," Ellen said. And then, "Angelica's dead."

"I know. I'm so very sorry. I'm here now, Ellen."

"Yes." And then, "Angelica's dead."

Caro took her hand. It lay cold and limp, unresponsive. "Ellen, have you talked to Kayla?"

"Yes." Pause. "Angelica's dead."

Caro, blinded by sudden tears, blinked them away, angry at herself. *Not now.* But Ellen's condition shocked her to the core. Ellen, who'd always seemed so strong!

Caro stood and turned to Mrs. Foster. "How long has she been like this?"

"Ever since the ambulance come and take that poor dead child away." Mrs. Foster jerked her head toward the bedroom door and Caro followed her back to the living room. "Betty Green has a car and she was gonna drive Mrs. Kemp wherever, the hospital or the funeral home, but Mrs. Kemp, she just sank into the chair like that. She never moved since yesterday, and what you heard is all she says. Even Kayla crying and carrying on didn't rouse her none. I slept here last night but nothing changed. The hospital keep calling about what to do with the remains but we didn't know what to tell them. Fairleigh Memorial. I wrote down the number."

"I'm grateful for all your help," Caro said.

"You should eat something, Doctor. The stew is still hot."

"Thank you. A little later. It smells delicious."

"You want us to stay or go?"

The question, so straightforward, penetrated the fog of unreality enveloping Caro ever since Mrs. Foster had opened the door. Ellen, resourceful and courageous Ellen, loving and blithe Ellen, had collapsed in on herself. Caro had seen this reaction to grief before. Not talking, not eating, not washing. Grief that gnawed away from the inside, body and soul, the inconsolable mourning for a lost child.

She had seen it before, and the memory sickened her, but … no. Not Ellen. Ellen was nothing like their father.

Mrs. Foster waited for an answer. Caro reached for one. "I think I'd like to be alone with my sister just now, thank you. But if I need someone to stay with Kayla while I take Ellen …" Where?

"My number is right there under the hospital's," Mrs. Foster said. "Along with Jackson Funeral Home. They won't gouge you on the cost. I'm leaving you the stew. You both got to eat. And our prayer circle will pray for you."

"Thank you."

At some invisible signal, the other women scraped their stew bowls into the garbage, washed them, stacked them in the drain, and patted Caro's arm on their way out, murmuring condolences. This all took only a few moments. Caro had seen surgical teams less efficient.

Caro opened the door to Kayla's room. The little girl lay in stained pajamas on top of her faded quilt, nose red, eyes open.

"I'm here, sweetheart," Caro said. "I'm here. Don't cry."

"I wasn't crying," Kayla lied.

"Okay." Caro sat on the edge of the bed, drawing Kayla beside her. "Can you tell me what happened?"

"God took Angelica to Heaven," Kayla said. "That's what Mrs. Foster said. Only there isn't any heaven and I told her that and she went like this: 'Tsk tsk tsk.' I didn't like it."

"No," Caro said. "What did happen to Angelica?"

"Mom was changing her and she had a big seizure and then made some terrible noises and then she died. Mom called you and after that she grabbed Angelica and took her to her bedroom chair and sat there. Angelica was all floppy and Mom wouldn't answer me and I got scared and ran next door to get Mrs. Foster."

Kayla gave her terrible little history in a tough, matter-of-fact voice that Caro suddenly recognized: it echoed her own tone in a crisis: *"I'm sorry, our best efforts couldn't save the patient." "I'm furious about Becker but I don't show it." "It will be all right, Ellen. Don't listen to that bitch."*

Caro said, "You did the right thing, Kayla. Mrs. Foster said an ambulance came and took Angelica away?"

"Mom wouldn't let go. They had to fight her. And then Mom got ... like she is now. She won't talk to me. But I don't care."

Too much bravado. No nine-year-old should have to deal with this. Kayla needed help as much as Ellen did, and right now the best thing was to get the little girl moving. Caro drew her close and said gently, "Of course you care. But I'm here now. I want you to do something for me, Kayla. Take a shower and get dressed while I make some phone calls. Then we'll heat up some of that stew. We should eat."

"I'm not hungry."

"We'll see. But first shower and dress."

Kayla stumbled into the bathroom. Caro steeled herself and made the phone calls: the hospital morgue, the funeral home, the hospital again, Mrs. Foster. Kayla emerged, dressed, and Caro heated the stew. She didn't want food but both of them needed to eat, and when she spooned some into her mouth—it was delicious, church ladies always cooked superbly—Kayla did too.

Ellen would not eat, move, talk except to say, "Angelica is dead." Kayla would no longer even glance toward her mother's bedroom door. In the shower she seemed to have fallen into a remote stoniness more disturbing than tears.

Mrs. Foster returned to stay with Kayla while Caro took Ellen to Fairleigh Memorial for psych evaluation. They admitted her immediately. When Caro explained to Kayla that her mother was going to be in the hospital for a little while so the doctors could help her, Kayla didn't ask what kind of help, how long her mother would be away, or anything else. She just nodded with a willed toughness that Caro knew all too well. She saw it in her mirror, had seen it there for nearly a decade, all through med school and fellowship training. Ever since that other funeral that had changed everything.

The only thing Kayla asked was, "Will Mom be back for the funeral?"

"Sweetie, I don't think we're going to have a funeral. Your mom said she wanted cremation and no ceremony that—"

Kayla's stoicism shattered. "There still has to be a funeral! There's always a funeral!"

Where had Kayla gotten that idea? Before Caro could ask, Kayla erupted.

"If you don't have a funeral, it means you didn't love the person!" she shouted. "We loved Angie! There has to be a funeral! There has to be!"

"All right, yes, we'll have a funeral."

"Promise? Promise me!"

"I promise."

"Okay."

Caro tried to hug Kayla, but Kayla pulled away, marched into her room, and closed the door.

When she didn't come out, Caro searched the house. She found the kitchen drawer with Ellen's financial records. She also accessed her own bank statements on her laptop and sat crunching numbers for an hour.

Not good.

Caro's large advance from Watkins was nearly gone: spent on home help for Angelica and overdue payments on Caro's med-school debt. Weigert had paid for the expensive lawyer for Kayla's custody hearing, but that money was also spent. Her salary at the project had seemed astronomical—by her standards anyway—but she had ongoing med-school loans, and Ellen had unpaid bills for rent, electricity, heat, a credit card. Medicaid would cover a portion of Ellen's hospital bills, but would there be uncovered portions? And now: a funeral.

She paid the utility bills with her credit card and sent the minimum amount to Ellen's credit-card company. The Jackson Funeral Home's website listed estimated costs. After reading them, Caro hunted through all Ellen's cupboards for wine or, better yet, liquor. She found a single bottle of cheap wine and drank half of it.

She also found a book for children called *A Funeral Is A Sad Thing*, which told a story designed to help kids through "this sad but important occasion that shows how much you loved the person who is gone." Had Ellen bought it to prepare Kayla for the inevitable about Angelica? Probably. And yet Ellen's collapse showed how little she herself had been emotionally prepared for Angelica's death.

This important occasion that shows how much you loved. Caro cursed the author and hurled the book into the trash.

26.

The memorial service was held two days later, at Jackson's. Caro had been afraid that nobody would attend, but she'd underestimated Mrs. Foster, who possessed the organizational skills of a presidential campaign chairman. Mrs. Foster borrowed Ellen's address book (who kept a paper address book anymore?) and made calls. The small room, with an urn holding Angelica's ashes and a picture of Ellen holding Angelica, was crowded. Old friends that Caro hadn't realized Ellen had kept in touch with. Neighbors. Church ladies. The home-care help for Angelica. The mechanic who kept Ellen's shaky car on the road.

Ellen was not able to leave the hospital.

"I'm sorry to tell you," Mrs. Foster said, "that I couldn't get no relatives to come. I tried, Doctor. I called Angelica's father's parole officer and—"

"That number was in the address book?" Caro said, startled.

"—and he said that man just got sent to jail somewhere in Nebraska. I called the number for Ellen's mother, and somebody there said both your parents are dead."

"Yes," Caro said. "They are. Thank you for all you've done, Mrs. Foster."

"She's a good woman, your sister."

Kayla, who'd insisted on wearing her darkest clothing, a black tee-shirt with a polka-dot navy mini-skirt, sat dry-eyed and tight-lipped through the brief service. She refused to hold

Caro's hand. People stood and spoke, more about Ellen than Angelica, and Mrs. Foster must have organized that, too. Caro braced herself for the inevitable questions afterward, but Mrs. Foster took the microphone last and said, "Now, Doctor Soames-Watkins got to get Kayla home, so thank you for coming. Anybody who wants to make a donation in Angelica's name can send a check to the Fairleigh Memorial Children's Services. Now please let Kayla and her aunt pass on by."

Caro rose, grateful, and led Kayla along the aisle between the rows of folding chairs toward the exit. In the last row sat Julian.

She almost stumbled, so surprised to see him. Only after she had Kayla seat-belted into Ellen's ancient Chevy did Caro wonder if she was supposed to have Angelica's ashes with her.

Mrs. Foster would bring them.

At Ellen's, Kayla went straight to her room and closed the door. Since yesterday, her grief had turned from intermittent sobbing in Caro's arms to a stony silence that refused all contact. Caro, both hurt and confused, found all her efforts to talk to Kayla were rebuffed. Why? What was going on in the little girl's mind?

Weary, Caro made herself a cup of coffee, which tasted sour in her empty stomach. She was waiting for the inevitable. Nobody flew from the Cayman Islands to attend a forty-five-minute makeshift funeral and then go away again.

A knock on the door. "Julian. Why are you here? Did my great-uncle send you?"

"No. Yes. It's more complicated than that. May I come in?"

She didn't answer, which he took for assent. To Julian's credit, he not only didn't comment on the shabby living room, he appeared to not even notice it. She did not ask him to sit down, the memory of their last encounter raw in her mind. The drunken attempt at a "farewell" kiss, the upsetting reference to her staying "even if the FBI arrives." Had Caro misjudged? Maybe Julian had crashed Angelica's funeral simply to apologize?

No. As he began to talk—the old poised Julian, sure of himself and his plans—she realized that he was never going to apologize. His drunken behavior and Caro's second rebuff of his kisses had, in his mind, simply been erased, an artifact of the Julian who'd been so thrown by Ben Clarby's death. Now he had recovered his "real" self, so therefore anything he'd said or done then did not exist.

He said, "Caro, I'm going to come right to the point. Sam didn't send me here, but when I told him I was going anyway to attend your niece's funeral, he and I had a long talk. Well, it was actually more of a shouting match. You know Sam. But underneath the bluster and tyranny, he's scared. I think you already know that. Maybe everybody is scared of death when it's staring you right in the face. Before he dies, he wants to create another branch of the multiverse with himself in it, young and strong again, both for the experience and to leave that healthy version of his body ongoing in a branch universe. You already know this, because both he and I have told you."

"Yes," Caro said. "Although, as I've told you, I'm not convinced that anything he would experience wouldn't be just a hallucination. And I don't believe he's 'scared' of death. Furious at it, more likely."

"You're entitled to your own opinion, although I don't think your opinion is as unwavering as you're pretending now. But are you going to deny Sam what he passionately wants?"

"Until Lyle Luskin says that Watkins can survive the surgery."

"You told me once that a patient has the right to make informed choices about his own treatment."

"Implanting a chip is not treatment. For my uncle, it's dangerous elective surgery. Julian, we've gone over this before. Nothing has changed."

"Yes. It has. Your situation has changed. Your sister is hospitalized with a mental collapse which—"

"How do you know that? *How*?"

"—is serious enough to need rehab, possibly for a long time. You and I both know that state-run mental hospitals here are understaffed and inadequate, and that private care costs money that you don't have, and that your salary from us wouldn't begin to cover. Kayla needs a home and someone to take care of her. You still have massive med-school debt, and don't insult both of us with indignation because I already know exactly how much you owe. See, I'm laying all my cards out on the table. We need you. Sam could die at any time. And you need us, or at least you need a lot of money for Ellen and Kayla ... No, don't interrupt, please let me finish.

"There's a superb mental hospital on Grand Cayman, built for all the billionaires and their friends that keep homes on the island. We'll fly Ellen there and pay for everything as long as she needs it, including outpatient care. We'll hire a nanny for Kayla and you can either keep her with you in the compound, or else we'll rent a cottage as close to the compound as possible for her, the nanny, and eventually Ellen. We'll hire whatever help they all need. Caro—no, look at me—this is what it comes down to." Julian held his two hands in front of him and moved them alternately up and down, like scales. "I'm sorry it's come down to this, but it has. Choose: your comfort level with Sam's surgery, or Ellen's and Kayla's welfare."

Caro whispered, "You son-of-a-bitch bastards. You, my uncle, Weigert."

"George? Come on. George doesn't know about any of this. Just me and Sam. Promise to do Sam's surgery now, Caro, or at least soon, in exchange for Kayla's and Ellen's welfare."

Ellen. Kayla.

Julian's implacable face.

She said, "I want all the money for their care for a year put in escrow up front, unable to be withdrawn if anything happens to me or the project ends."

"Done. Bill Haggerty will arrange papers for that."

"And I implant Watkins after George. My uncle is not going to die in the next week."

"Okay. George first."

Caro was exhausted, physically and emotionally. Julian, so sensitive to others' moods even though he acted on them from self-interest rather than kindness, lifted one hand to take hers, sensed her recoil, and instead merely softened his voice.

"I'll do everything we can to make this easier for you, Caro. I'll book a flight for you and Kayla tomorrow, and I'll stay here to close up this place, put Ellen's stuff into storage, and arrange for her transfer to Grand Cayman. There'll be papers for you to sign, but a courier will bring you those if electronic signatures aren't acceptable."

"And you already know who Ellen's landlord is, what rent is owed, how to break the lease."

"Yes," he said simply. "You're too valuable for sloppy surveillance."

"Unlike guarding that data from Ben Clarby," she said, and immediately regretted her cruelty.

He said only, "You should prepare Kayla."

"Did Ivan develop any complications from surgery?"

Julian smiled. "Ever the surgeon. No, no complications."

"Have you found Clarby?"

"No. I doubt we will. And Caro, one more thing. Barbara, Molly, Trevor, and George all wanted to make this trip with me. I wouldn't permit them, but—"

"Of course you wouldn't," she said. "Mephistopheles doesn't let anyone else witness his bargain with Faust."

"—but I want you to know that they all offered. You have friends on Cayman Brac, good friends who care about you. That's all." He turned and opened the door.

Friends who care about you. A genuine attempt from Julian to console her, or another manipulative reason for her to do what the project wanted? With Julian, nobody would ever know. Maybe he himself didn't know.

She went into Kayla's bedroom to prepare an nine-year-old, who'd just lost her sister and her mother, to lose everything else in her young life.

How, exactly, did you do that? No children's author was going to write that book.

≡

After Kayla was asleep, the doorbell rang. Mrs. Foster, bringing the urn with Angelica's ashes. Caro had no idea what to do with it. She asked Mrs. Foster to keep the urn for now and told her that Caro and Kayla would be leaving the next day and the house vacated. Mrs. Foster said in her soft accent, "Honey, you just take care of yourself and that child."

"Yes. Thank you for everything. I couldn't have managed all the ... Thank you."

Caro sat alone at the rickety table and finished the bottle of cheap wine. Maybe it would help her sleep. Maybe it would block out the funeral that kept replaying in her mind. Not Angelica's funeral—Caro's brother's.

There had been no kind Mrs. Foster at Ethan's funeral six years ago. No kind, compassionate, knowledgeable older person to lean on. Just her parents, her mother screaming at Caro and Ellen after they and their father had been left alone with the ostentatious casket, the nineteen huge flower arrangements turning the air sickly sweet, the printed programs left on the seats of gilt chairs, the musicians packing up their violins and flutes and pretending not to listen to a family's final unraveling into cruelty and hatred.

Caro didn't want to remember Ethan's funeral.

She couldn't stop remembering.

Their mother had adored Ethan. Everything he did was wonderful, and everything Ellen and Caro did was not only lesser, but wrong. It was as if Lauren Soames-Watkins had only so much attention to take away from herself, and believed that giving any to her daughters would somehow deprive her son. When Caro was a senior in college, Ethan died in a car crash on an icy New England road. After the funeral, Caro had bent over the coffin to kiss Ethan good-bye, a trigger that exploded her mother's fragile control. She screamed, "Don't touch him! It should have been you or Ellen who died, not him! Why wasn't it you or Ellen instead! "

Ellen crumpled to the floor, and it was that, not her mother's words, that had ignited Caro's years of anger and pain. She couldn't stand to remember all that she'd said, and she couldn't stop remembering it.

You fucking bitch! If anybody has to die, it should be you! I hate you!

And:

You, our supposed father, letting her bully and demean and neglect Ellen and me all our lives without saying a word because you're too weak to ever oppose her!

And:

It will be all right, Ellen. Don't listen to that fucking bitch!

And ... and ...

And.

The day after Ethan's funeral, Caro had left home for good. Her mother changed her will—the money was all hers—to cut off both Caro and Ellen. Two weeks later, their father collapsed into a profound, unspeaking depression.

Like Ellen, Caro thought now, drinking off the last of Ellen's terrible wine. Ellen, who had always been so cheerful, so resourceful, so brave. And all the while, Ellen too had her breaking point, and now she'd reached it.

But Ellen was not going to end up like her father. Three months after Ethan died, he'd killed himself with a nine-millimeter Beretta no one even knew he had. Ellen was stronger than that, and Ellen had Caro to help her. No matter what it took.

Even implanting a computer chip into the brain of a dying Nobel laureate who would probably not survive the operation.

Her laptop was flooded with messages. Caro ignored them all and set about packing Kayla's things for their flight to Cayman Brac.

27.

The atmosphere at the compound had changed. Caro could feel the edginess as soon as James greeted them. "Welcome back, Doctor. And this is Kayla?"

Kayla said nothing. She ignored the hand James held out to her, as she had ignored everything else on the trip to Cayman Brac. Caro barely recognized her lovable niece in this silent, sullen child. Kayla had questioned nothing, not why her mother was left behind at a hospital, nor Caro's assurances that her mother would be joining them soon. Caro felt helpless. Kayla's withdrawal was not like Ellen's, not a complete shutdown of the will to function. It felt as if Kayla blamed Caro for something, and thought that Caro should already know what. But Caro didn't know, Kayla wouldn't tell her, and the little girl's misery tore at Caro's heart.

Maybe the nanny or the therapist, both hired remotely by Julian from his inexhaustible supply of island contacts, could reach Kayla.

The nanny, a middle-aged, motherly looking Islander, apparently knew not to touch the child. "I'm Jasmine," she said. "I'm going to be taking you to school and helping with whatever you need. There's a lot of fun things on this island, Kayla, for when you feel like doing them. Can you swim?"

"No."

"You want to learn?"

"No."

Caro said, "'No, thank you,' Kayla," and wondered if it was right to correct her.

"No, thank you," Kayla said in the same sullen voice, and Caro looked helplessly at Jasmine.

"We'll be fine," Jasmine said to Caro, and Caro nodded, hoping it was true.

Caro's new bedroom, located next to Kayla's and Jasmine's rooms, looked exactly like her old one except for doors connecting all three. The doors were so new that they smelled of sawdust. In Caro's room, Molly waited. She hugged Caro and then held her at arm's length to examine her. "You look terrible. And you have every right to look terrible."

All at once, and for the first time in five days, Caro wanted to cry. She didn't. "You don't look too great yourself."

"Nobody does. We're all on our last nerve here. Well, maybe the second- or third-last. But I'm so glad you're back. And you don't have to explain about your sister or niece. Everybody always knows everything in this place."

"I don't want to talk about it, Molly. Not yet."

"I'll spread the word. Just hole up here and spend time with Kayla."

"I need to check on Ivan in the hospital."

"Oh, Trevor released him already. Nobody heals from surgery as fast as a twenty-two-year-old who's already convinced he's immortal. Are you coming to his multiverse session today?"

"Yes." The faster she got back into the routine here, the better she would feel, and so the better her chances of helping Kayla. As long as no one expected her to spend time alone with Julian or Watkins.

"Great," Molly said. "Four o'clock."

⇜

Ivan Kyven was perhaps the only cheerful person in the compound. His head had healed beautifully, although the tiny titanium case holding the connectors on top of his shaven head made him look like an alien in some B movie. But, Caro realized, Ivan was already alien to her. He reminded Caro of the boys in high school who hunched over their tablets playing video games, everywhere they could: at lunch, on the school bus, in any class with unvigilant teachers. Nerds. Caro had been a nerd, too, but not that kind. Science wonks and digital geeks had an overlap, but she hadn't been in it. She'd stayed after school to do extra frog dissections. Ivan's tribe sat on the picnic benches outside, arguing about battle passes and abandonware.

"You comfortable, Ivan?" Aiden asked as he hooked Ivan to the session machinery in Wing Three. Caro hadn't even realized that Aiden was back from Grand Cayman. He looked thinner but otherwise recovered from his bout with rosemary pea. Watkins sat in a chair at the side of the room. Caro refused to look at him.

"I'm good," Ivan said. He squiggled his scrawny frame on the bed until he found an optimal position and then asked a long string of software questions, of which Caro understood none. Aiden answered each, also incomprehensibly. Ivan finally said, "Cool." A moment later, his face went into the eerie session blankness and the computer screens brightened.

Barbara, stationed at the other imaging screen, suddenly snorted. Aiden shook his head. Caro thought: *What the hell?*

The image of Ivan stood up from the bed, walked out the door, and entered a landscape that was ... what? Some sort of structure superimposed on the Wing Two courtyard, a series of undulating wooden scaffolds ringing the compound walls and rising higher and higher even as Caro watched. Small brightly colored blobs with spindly legs appeared, peering down from higher levels, scampering from tree to tree on those levels that, all at once, sprouted trees in huge pots. The blobs were some sort of robots. The image of Ivan climbed nimbly up a ladder to the first level of scaffolding and aimed a gadget at a pink amoeba. The gadget gave off a burst of light and the pink blob turned green. Ivan went on jumping and shooting and laughing for another half minute before the screen went blank. The Ivan on the cot blinked, and Aiden erupted.

"What the fuck was that? What did you do, you moron?"

Ivan blinked again. "It's a game I'm inventing, for kids. Why did you cut me off? If I get seven greenies, I get a reward!"

"You had the chance to create an alternate reality and you turned the compound into a *video game*?"

"Why not? This game will earn me a fortune someday. And anyway, it's my reality to create!"

"And it will continue on now without you! Those blobby robots are real! It's a real universe!"

"I know," Ivan said, somewhere between defiant and abashed. "The goobods will be okay. They're happy little robots."

The blobby creatures *had* looked happy. All at once, Caro wanted to laugh. It came out a strangled *unnnhhhh*. A video game hallucination, tailor-made to whatever went on in the head of this intelligent, emotionally stunted, man-child. Ivan could have lucid-hallucinated anything, and he'd chosen a video game full of "goobods."

Aiden was not laughing. "You're lucky Julian isn't here! When he finds out how you wasted an opportunity for real information about the multiverse—"

"I got real information," Barbara said, and Caro would have sworn that she, too, was suppressing laughter. "Interesting cerebral mapping data. It's all right, Aiden."

Caro stole a look at Watkins. He'd fallen asleep in his chair, morphing from a manipulator of Caro's life to a frail, sick old man.

"Well," Ivan said, sulky now, "you should have let me finish my game, Aiden.

I was *winning*."

≡

Kayla remained silent and withdrawn. Nothing interested her. Caro suggested a card or board or video game, exercising together in the gym, a jeep ride to the ocean, a movie on her laptop. Kayla shook her head, mute.

"Kayla, do you want to talk about your mother or Angie? Sometimes when we're sad, it helps to talk about it."

Another shake of the head before Kayla turned away.

Jasmine said privately to Caro, "That child needs to see her mama."

"I know," Caro said. "I'm working on it."

"Good. Because until her mama comes here, or Kayla goes to her, Kayla is just going to keep on acting out."

"Has she mentioned Angelica to you?"

"No," Jasmine said. "Not once."

Caro phoned Julian yet again. He said he was still working on the documentation to transfer Ellen to the hospital on Grand Cayman, and that there was no change in Ellen's condition. "Is she eating?" Caro asked.

"No. But she didn't fight having an IV with nutrients. I got this, Caro."

She washed her face and brushed her teeth, caught sight of herself in the mirror, and scowled. When she'd been eleven or twelve, someone had remarked how much Caro resembled "your beautiful mother." Caro's immediate response—"No, I don't!"—had not been true, so Caro tried to make it true. She bought a box of Clairol with her allowance and dyed her light brown hair a ghastly flat black. She'd cut ragged bangs. She smeared on cherry-red lipstick, the shade farthest from her mother's tasteful rose. She'd vowed to gain weight to cover up the delicate bones that Lauren Soames-Watkins maintained by fanatic dieting and three-times-a-week Soul cycling. And none of it, in addition to causing a huge fight, had helped. Caro had still looked like a clownish version of her mother.

Ellen looked like their father, big and athletic. Over the years, Ellen had somehow managed to forge a relationship with him, which Caro hadn't realized was so important to her, and which Caro had destroyed at Ethan's funeral. Because of course Ellen had sided with Caro. Ellen, never academic, had been a community-college freshman when their father committed suicide. Almost immediately she'd gotten pregnant by Eric the Drug Dealer and dropped out of school to marry him. And then, four years later during one of Eric's brief paroles, became pregnant with Angelica. Would any of that have happened if Caro hadn't lost control at Ethan's funeral? Might the fragile, miserable household have held together?

Another timeline, another branch of another universe. For just a second, Caro fervently wished she could believe wholeheartedly in Weigert's theory, in Julian's software, in the possibility of what life does not furnish: a do-over of moments one profoundly regrets.

≡

"Are you busy the entire rest of the day?" Trevor asked her. They had just finished the pre-op imaging, interview, and blood-work for Weigert's surgery, scheduled for the next morning.

"Most of it," Caro said. Mapping data with Barbara, check-ins with Julian about Ellen, attempts to reach Kayla, or at least to show she cared by sitting nearby as Jasmine supervised the child's schoolwork. "Why?"

"If you have, say, forty-five minutes, we could take a short drive to the cliffs on the east side of the island. They're spectacular."

"How is it that you've been on Cayman Brac for, oh, five minutes and you've seen these cliffs while I've been here so much longer and have not?"

He smiled. "I'm a tourist at heart. I walk around European capitals in a Hawaiian shirt with a fanny pack around my waist and a camera around my neck."

"And sandals with black socks."

"You know it."

She looked deliberately at his Converse high tops. Trevor laughed. "Come for a drive later today, Caro. I promise to keep away from any maiden plum trees."

She agreed, her mood already lifted by his playfulness, by the promise of a brief absence from the compound, by his wanting to be with her. Maybe she could return from the cliffs with a fresh plan to reach Kayla, or at least a different perspective on why Kayla was shutting her out so painfully.

After he signed out a jeep, he said, "I lured you out on false pretenses. My license expired while I was overseas. You'll have to drive."

"I can do that. You navigate."

"If you knew how terrible my sense of direction is, you wouldn't ask that. Fortunately, it's a small island. Head north."

Eventually he directed her off the main road and down an unpaved side road bordered mostly by thick scrub. When they could go no further, Caro parked and they walked toward the sound of the sea, with gulls wheeling overhead and the occasional bright flash of a parrot.

The cliffs were indeed spectacular, falling in irregular shelves and boulders of limestone 120 feet to ocean rocks below. The tide was in and waves surged restlessly against the cliff. Under gray clouds, the water was a dark turquoise flecked with white.

"People climb these cliffs," Trevor said, "and rappel down."

"Do you rappel?"

"No. Far too much of a coward."

"Right," she said. "A coward who joins Doctors Without Borders. This is lovely, Trevor. Thanks for bringing me here. Even though I'm afraid of touching any plants or—"

He interrupted her. "What the hell was that?"

A huge lizard disappeared into the brush. Caro smiled. "A Sister Islands Rock Iguana. They're protected." She remembered that Ben Clarby had told her that during her first hour on Cayman Brac. It seemed a lifetime ago. "Aren't they ugly?"

"Yes. That thing— Oh oh, it's starting to rain."

Only a few drops, but Caro had already learned how quickly storms blew up in the Caribbean. They ran for the jeep and Trevor said, "Don't go back to the main road, take the first right. It leads to Spot Bay."

They beat the rain, but just barely. Following Trevor's directions, she parked by a bar in the village wedged between the parrot preserve and the sea. Together they wrestled and fastened the rain tarp over the jeep, darting inside the bar just as the sky opened and rain fell in heavy sheets.

The bar décor featured parrots: stuffed, sculpted, and photographed, plus a live bird in a huge cage. The tropical feel was slightly diluted by a large TV over the bar displaying a soccer match between Montreal and Orlando. Caro ordered chardonnay; Trevor asked for Lagavulin. "Ah," he said after the first sip, "you can't get this smokey Scotch anywhere in the Congo."

"Will you tell me more about Africa?"

"Yes, but not now. Caro, I have to ask you something. Several somethings, but the first is this: Can I do anything to help your niece?"

Trevor was the only one to defy Molly's stricture that Caro did not want to talk about her family. Caro said stiffly, "No, thank you."

He gave her a long look but said only, "Okay. But if you change your mind, just say so. I'm good with kids."

She nodded, believing it. His combination of playfulness and empathy would appeal to children. Away from the compound and its multiple complications, Caro was very aware of how much it also appealed to her.

"Second question," he said. "This one is also none of my business, but I'm going to ask it anyway. Are you in love with Julian?"

She nearly spilled her wine. "*With Julian?*"

"Yes. I've picked up a lot of emotion between you two, and if you're involved with him, I'd like to know that."

"I'm not in love with Julian. I've never been in love with Julian."

"Then what—"

"We have a … a complicated if brief history, half him giving me genuine help with Ellen, and half him manipulating me, again through Ellen, to stay and do exactly what he and Watkins want. Julian is more complicated than he seems. But there was never anything romantic between us." Not quite true, but close enough.

"Good. I just thought I better find out."

She took the risk. 'Why?"

"Because I'm attracted to you. You must know that, a perceptive woman like you."

She hesitated, then said, "I haven't always been perceptive about … about men."

His gaze softened. "See, that's what I like about you. One thing I like."

Caro was confused. "What is?"

"Your honesty. You tell the truth, even to your own detriment. For one thing—and I've listened to you carefully on this—you refuse to say that you believe George's theory, although pretending to would have made things smoother for you here."

"I believe part of it. Just not the hallucination delusion." The words had just slipped out.

He smiled. "Interesting term. But see? You just proved my point. I like your honesty. I like your uncompromising intelligence. I like your fierce loyalty to Ellen— Yes, I know the whole story. Do you think anything is private in that compound? And I've always liked spiky women."

"Am I spiky?"

"Like a yucca. Do you know what I'd like to do, Caro? Have a normal conversation so we can get to know each other better."

She said, "And what do you imagine would constitute 'normal' in this situation?"

His brown eyes—such alive eyes!—sparkled. "All right, not 'normal.' How about this, put in George's terms: We need to generate a universe in which we converse in ways that other people in this universe would consider normal."

"Okay," she said, playing along. "What is your favorite pie?"

"My favorite *pie*?"

"Yes."

"Cherry."

"Mine's lemon."

'Of course it is. Sweet and tart."

"What music do you—"

"No," he said, reaching across the table for her hand. "I want to know you in ways that actually count. Tell me where you grew up, what kind of childhood you had. Why you became a doctor. Why neurosurgery. Tell me everything."

She was not going to do that; her natural wariness kicked in as soon as he said it. But she could tell him a little: about her childhood closeness with Ellen, the games they'd played, her decision to go to med school, which intern rotations she'd liked and which not. Nothing about Ethan, her father's suicide, her previous superficial relationships, Paul Becker. Although she was fully aware that much of that information could be found online, if he'd wanted to look. The facts, anyway—but not how those facts had affected her.

Trevor was far more forthcoming. He told entertaining stories about growing up working class in Boston, but also about his college years, his sister and brother, the woman he'd once been engaged to before she broke it off. Caro shook her head at that: she couldn't imagine any woman who'd accepted Trevor later changing her mind.

He was attracted to her. Like all pretty women, Caro always knew when a man desired her. But not once during the hour they talked did Caro feel he was trying to maneuver her toward sex, or toward anything else. So why not show her attraction to him, too? Why not go to bed together?

An uncomfortable question, although Caro already knew the answer. Her casual affairs had been just that: casual. Trevor Abruzzo did not do casual. He would want more, would want her to let him into her life in a way that might be temporary but not shallow. She couldn't risk that. She had too much going on in her life, and too much heartbreak already. If that made her a coward then, well, okay, she was a self-preserving coward.

They were just finishing their second drinks when Caro's cell rang. The sound startled the live parrot, who in turn startled Caro by squawking, "Oh my fucking goodness!"

"It's all set," Julian said. "I'm flying to Grand Cayman tomorrow with Ellen and a nurse. But first you have to sign, scan, and email back the additional papers I just sent you. God, it's like buying a new house. Sign, initial, and don't miss even one place. Get whoever's on duty in the tech office to do the printing and scanning, or James in his office. Can you get them back to me in half an hour?"

"I'm not at the compound."

"Where are you?"

"Spot Bay."

"Why are you … Never mind. Just get back and do this as fast as you can, okay?"

"Of course. But I want to see Ellen as soon as she arrives. Tomorrow."

"I don't think the facility will allow a visitor on the very first day, but I'll ask. And you're still implanting George in the morning, right?"

"Yes. Let me know when I can see Ellen. And … thank you." The two words came out more intently than she intended; everything now was so fraught with emotion.

Caro said to Trevor, "We have to get back. I need to deal with papers for Ellen."

"We should leave anyway," Trevor said, signaling for the check. "Will you have dinner with me Saturday night, assuming there are no more crises at the compound?"

"Yes." The word came out without her willing it. Trevor paid the bill. "Okay, one more time, based on your intensity during that phone call and my insecurities: Are you sure about Julian? He's charming, smart, and about a dozen times sexier than I am."

It took a real effort for Caro to remember that she had once thought Julian charming and sexy. What she did realize, for the first time, was that Trevor, like her, had insecurities. Unlike hers, his centered on his appearance. She looked straight at him, at his stocky body and nondescript features and receding hairline. At his warm, intelligent, kind brown eyes. She said in the most meaningful tone she could manage, "No. He's not."

To her surprise, Trevor actually blushed.

She drove back one-handed, the other held in his. But for Caro the spell had been broken and only half her mind was on Trevor. Julian's phone call had yanked her back to reality, *this* reality. Ellen was being transferred to Grand Cayman. Caro had checked out the hospital online: it was as upscale as Julian had said, with a strong reputation. Surely they would be able to help Ellen. And Caro could visit her sister there and, when Ellen was well enough, bring Kayla to see her mother. It would be all right. Caro—with George's and Julian's help—would make it all right.

Ellen would not end up like their father.

≡-

Weigert's surgery went smoothly, despite his age. Caro thought she'd never seen anyone happier to have his skull cut open. When Molly, poised to administer anesthesia, told him to count backwards from one hundred, he smiled at her and said, "By ones, primes, squares, Fibonacci sequence or—" Caro never did find out which he chose; he was out.

His brain presented no hidden anomalies. His vitals during the operation never wavered from the expected. Caro, relieved, did the closing instead of leaving it to Trevor, who didn't question her decision.

During surgery Trevor was all detached professionalism, but of course their drive yesterday had not gone unnoticed. Molly had begun her inquiry with "Oho!" and, despite Barbara's tactful attempts at restraint, asked so many questions that Barbara finally lost all tact.

"Oh, for heaven's sake, Molly, can't you see that Caro doesn't want to talk about Trevor? Leave her alone!"

"There's nothing to talk about," Caro said. "We went for a drive to see the cliffs." She was determined to say no more. After all, she barely knew Trevor Abruzzo.

Only ... it didn't feel that way.

28.

Weigert recovered much more rapidly from surgery than most people of seventy-six, which Caro ascribed to not only a strong constitution but also to an even stronger desire for his session in another branch of the universe. Although glad of George's progress, Caro's promise to implant Watkins next weighed on her. As did Kayla.

Jasmine again talked privately to Caro. "Doctor, something you should know. Kayla destroyed all my cosmetics this morning. Smashed the lipstick, squeezed out the foundation, sprayed all my hair spray on a flowerbed until the can was empty."

"I'm sorry," Caro said, her belly turning sour. "I'll pay for them."

"Thank you, but that's not the point. Has she been destructive like that before?"

"No. Never. It was … everything …"

"The therapist is coming this afternoon to start work with her. Right now, she isn't fit to go to school."

"No. Please tell the therapist not to leave until I talk to her."

She met with the therapist, who had nothing useful to say ("I just met her, Doctor. Give us a little time.") Caro signed out a jeep and took Kayla for a drive to see the ocean from Cayman Brac's famous bluffs. Startlingly blue, the water broke into whitecaps on the rocks below and flew upward, crystalline in the sunlight. Caro had waited for the expansion of heart that open water, with its suggestion of limitless possibilities, always gave her. It did not come.

Kayla was unimpressed. "Pretty," she said listlessly, followed by, "When is Mom coming?"

"Soon," Caro promised. "Really soon."

Kayla folded her arms and said nothing during the drive back to the compound.

Caro was touched by how hard everyone tried to draw Kayla from her sullen grief. Molly and Barbara offered to take her to the beach or shopping or to the resort hotel for lunch. Trevor brought out a deck of cards, did a few simple tricks—he told Caro he'd used them to amuse and distract his little patients in Africa—and offered to teach them to Kayla. Even Julian, not quite able to hide his lack of interest in children, offered Kayla a new video game. She responded to nothing, not even an extravagant gesture made by James.

Caro entered Kayla's room to find the little girl, still in pajamas, sitting on the bed facing a beleaguered Jasmine and a bewildered James. All three of them stared at the floor, where a mewling kitten sat in a towel-lined cardboard box. The kitten, black with a white-tipped tail, had the wide eyes of all kittens and a paw raised to one edge of the box.

Kayla looked up, her bottom lip stuck out. "I don't want it. I told them I don't want it. Take it away."

Jasmine said, "You once told your aunt that you did want a kitten. She told me."

"That was before," Kayla said. "Take it away."

James turned to Caro. "I have a friend at Spot Bay whose cat had kittens. He's desperate to give them to good homes. We're not supposed to have pets in the compound, but in this case, I thought ..."

"It's not your fault," Jasmine said. "You were only trying to help."

Kayla moved her foot as if to kick the box. Maybe she was just going to nudge it, but Caro was strung taut. From frustration, from yearning, she said in a quiet, deadly tone she'd never used with Kayla, "Don't you dare."

Kayla, startled but not cowed, demanded, "When is my mother coming here?"

"When she's ready and I say so."

Kayla's face reddened, reminding Caro uncomfortably of Watkins. Kayla burst out with, "I hate you!"

"I'm sorry to hear that," Caro said in the same tone, "because I love you. Now get dressed and start your schoolwork. I'm coming back to check on you in one hour. James, will you please return the kitten to your friend?"

"Yes," James said quickly. "Yes. I will!"

"Good. I'll see you later, Kayla."

No answer. But as Caro followed James and the still mewling kitten, she caught Jasmine's glance of respect. And Kayla obeyed, going to her dresser and pulling jeans out of a drawer.

So why did Caro feel even worse than before?

≡

Trevor chose a smaller, more intimate restaurant for their dinner together. This time, she asked him to talk about Africa.

He said, "It's not exactly light conversation for a second date."

"Will you tell me anyway?" She gave him his own words from their cliff drive back to him: "I want to know you in ways that actually count."

His brown eyes held hers. "Well, Africa certainly counts," he said. "If you're sure you want to know."

He told her about the children blinded by schistosomiasis, whom he could not help to see again. The soldiers, some as young as ten, with limbs mangled and torn by bullets in the latest of Congo's never-ending wars. Renal failures for which he had no dialysis machines. Wounds for which he could not devise sterile dressings, drugs he had to apportion, deciding who lived and who would have to die. Caro, a doctor, knew that all this happened. She even knew it must have happened to Trevor. But his vivid, personal images brought it, and him, into almost unbearable focus.

215

He was so open with her, so trusting. How did people do that?

"Trevor, did you always want to be a doctor?"

"No. In my college years, I wanted to be a monk."

"A monk!"

"Yes. What I told you once before. I wanted a framework to understand the world, both the seen and unseen parts. Religion seemed to satisfy that, for a while anyway."

"And you couldn't just become an ordinary Catholic? You had to try for monkhood?"

"I'm afraid I find it hard to do anything by halves."

He looked at her as he said this, and the entire conversation abruptly shifted into something else.

She said slowly, "I can't ... it's hard for me to ... I haven't dated anybody for a long time. Years."

"Years! And you so beautiful, sitting there with soup on your chin."

"Oh, God, why didn't you tell me earlier?" She swiped with her napkin at her chin.

He smiled. "Didn't want to. And Caro ... I know you're dealing with a lot just now. Is there anything else I can do to help?"

"No. I visit Ellen tomorrow. Then I'll know more. I want to ... Another question, Trevor, this time about the compound. Do you ever get the feeling that there are things about the project that we haven't been told? I mean ... I don't know what I mean."

"I do," Trevor said. "I've noticed it, too—certain glances among Julian, Aiden, and Watkins. Although not George. I don't know what they mean."

"Would you tell me if you did? If they'd told you something they hadn't told me?"

"Yes. I would."

They left the restaurant only when it closed. In the jeep, Trevor kissed her deeply. Without discussing it, they left the jeep parked and walked to the beach. Many people strolled the dunes and water's edge, and Caro didn't know if she was glad or sorry that she and Trevor weren't alone. She took off her sandals and let wet sand squish up between her toes and warm water swirl around her ankles. She and Trevor stopped talking. They held hands as they walked, and Caro felt his strong, long fingers warm around hers, felt the salty ocean breeze on her face, felt a return of something so long gone from her life that it took her a moment to give it a name.

Happiness. Maybe temporary, but nonetheless real.

≡-

Weigert's multiverse session stunned her.

He lay on the cot in Wing Three, wired from the new titanium case on top of his head to the computers. Julian and Barbara stood at their screens. Watkins sat in his wheelchair with Camilla beside him.

Weigert said, "I'm glad you're here, Caroline. Julian, I'm ready." The old man folded his hands across his chest, suddenly reminding Caro of Ethan in his coffin. *Stop it*, she told herself. Although Weigert looked nothing like a corpse. He smiled wide enough to show an ancient gold-capped tooth in the back of his mouth, his expression as expectant as a child on Christmas morning, right up until the moment his face went slack and the computer screens brightened.

The same room. Weigert rose eagerly and rushed to the door. When he opened it and walked through, it was not to the courtyard that Julian, Lorraine, and Ivan had altered in their hallucinations, but to a room that Caro had never seen. Old-fashioned furniture, some of which looked like genuine antiques. Books lining one wall. A leather chair was drawn up to the fire burning in the grate. Pictures and ornaments on the mantelpiece, daisies in a cut-glass vase on a side table, heavy curtains drawn over the windows. A full-length portrait of a man in a powdered wig dominated one wall. In a basket by the fire, a brown-and-white dog lay asleep.

A woman rose from a wing chair by the fire, white-haired and straight as a birch, her face welcoming. She spoke, but of course the deep-image reconstruction didn't include sound. Weigert rushed over and took her in his arms. She kissed him, then drew back slightly to look at his face, her expression almost maternal. Caro didn't need sound to imagine her words: "What is it, George?"

They stood there, talking, Weigert holding her tight until the session ended.

He sat up, real tears on his wrinkled cheeks. "Now she's still alive somewhere. Still alive. In that reality. The reality I created for her." Forgetting the wires, he tried to stand. Julian raced over and freed him. Weigert walked out the door, leaving the other four people staring at each other. Julian started after him, but Caro said, "No, give him a minute," and Julian stopped.

Barbara said, "Did you notice the sharp detail? I hadn't realized that the other recordings were slightly blurry until I saw this one!"

Julian said, "He knows that room completely. When we were programming his chip, George described in incredible detail the reality he wanted to create. Also, there were two people in that multiverse. The greater the number of observers, the more probability waves are localized and the less a given reality can deviate from consensus. So, to us it looks sharper."

Caro followed Weigert to check him for post-session physical complications. She could tell that Weigert wanted to be alone but was too polite to say so, so she ran her neuro-tests quickly and went to her own room.

Weigert's hallucination had made him happy. A physicist devoted to data, he nonetheless completely believed that his wife was, in some branch of the multiverse, now alive, along with an entire world around her. She would leave that cozy living room to go to the supermarket, or visit friends, or walk that dog. And when she did, she would encounter more people that were part of her expected reality, and their additional observations, plus even the dog's, would extend' and harden that consensual reality more. Or so Weigert believed.

Did he believe a hallucination or an actuality of physics that her mind rejected because it was so revolutionary? Caro was no longer sure. Her only certainty was that Weigert's session had brought him inestimable comfort. He was revitalized through seeing—or thinking he saw— what Julian had once called his "beloved dead."

Revitalization was what Ellen needed.

Caro sat on the edge of her bed, thinking hard, for a long time.

29.

It had worked.

And what a strange thing, Weigert thought, to experience your life's work for yourself. What a strange thing to know that Rose lived on elsewhere, and that he had just held her in his arms and could do so again. What a strange thing reality was: strange and, now that they had the key, miraculous.

Weigert spent the rest of the day in his room, with bouts of unpredictable weeping from joy.

People interrupted him, of course. Lyle Luskin, Caroline Soames-Watkins, Camilla Franklin, all checking on his physical condition. Lyle nodded in satisfaction, Camilla fussed, Caroline said softly, "I'm so glad for you." Sam, Julian, and Aiden "debriefed" Weigert. The debriefings were recorded: what Weigert said to Rose, what she said back, the auditory and tactile and olfactory sensations in the multiverse room that had not been captured by deep-image reconstruction. The clock ticking on the mantel—that clock had been a wedding gift from Rose's parents!—the feel of the carpet under Weigert's feet and of Rose in his arms, the scent of his wife's hair. Vanilla and roses. She'd always smelled of vanilla and roses, and she still did.

Somewhere in the multiverse, alive. His theory had worked.

≡-

The next morning, Weigert woke stricken with guilt. He'd been selfish; joy had made him selfish. He hadn't asked Caroline about her poor sister. He hadn't even said anything to reassure Sam about Sam's own surgery, scheduled for this morning.

He dressed hurriedly and made his way to the hospital in Wing Three, not even stopping for breakfast. No one was there except a nurse doing inventory of a supply closet. Weigert said, "Where is everybody? Dr. Watkins's surgery—"

"The surgery was postponed," she said, staring at his skull. Damn, he'd forgotten to put on his hat. The tiny titanium box sat exposed on his shaven skull. "Dr. Soames-Watkins left for Grand Cayman this morning."

Weigert said, "Oh, yes, thank you," and went back to the residential wing. Sam was not in his room. Weigert found him in the Wing Three session room with Aiden and Julian. Sam looked better than he had for a while.

"Sam, your surgery's been postponed?"

"Yes. My great-niece convinced herself that she had to fly off to Grand Cayman today. She also convinced herself that she can't leave again for the entire week following my surgery, even though Abruzzo will be here. I don't know why I hired him if she's not going to let him do anything."

Weigert ignored this. Sam knew perfectly well why he'd needed to hire a second surgeon and why he and Julian were still hunting for a third.

Julian explained. "While you were in hospital, Caro received permission to visit her sister. She'll be back this afternoon and Sam's surgery will happen at 7:30 tomorrow morning."

"I see," said Weigert. While he was in hospital, he seemed to have missed several key events.

Weigert went to his room to put on his hat before breakfast. On the way to the refectory, he stopped dead. Caroline's niece was stomping on a flower bed, methodically flattening and ripping the flowers.

"Kayla! You stop that right now!" A middle-aged woman, from her accent island-born, rushed through the gate from Wing One. The little girl looked up defiantly, but at least she stopped stamping and kicking her feet.

Weigert strode forward. He kept his voice gentle. "You can't do that, you know, child. The flowers belong to everyone."

"I don't care!" she shouted, and kicked him. Weigert rubbed his shin at the same time that his heart suddenly ached because it was so clear that she did care, that she was hurting badly.

"I'm so sorry," the nanny said. "I was only in the loo for a minute and she ... Kayla, apologize."

"She doesn't need—" Weigert said at the same time that Kayla mumbled, "Sorry."

So, not a bad child, just distraught with grief. Weigert had never known how to handle grief, not even his own when Rose died. All he'd been able to do was immerse himself in physics. He could hardly recommend that to this little girl.

The nanny led Kayla away. Weigert ate breakfast and went back to his room to work on the galleys of his book. He had trouble concentrating, distracted by the image of Kayla's furious, scared little face that didn't even know how scared it was. Weigert turned on his laptop and sent an email.

Dear Caroline,

I know you are having difficulties right now with both your sister and your niece. If there is anything I can do, anything at all, please let me know.

Most sincerely yours,
George Weigert

It wasn't much. In fact, it wasn't anything, just the meaningless words everybody said when an acquaintance was in trouble. But it was all Weigert could think of to do. So he was surprised later in the day when Caroline answered.

Thank you, George. There is something you can do, the most important thing anyone can do for me. It's not more

money. I arrive back at the compound tonight. Please wait
for me in your room.

Caro Soames-Watkins

Weigert's face crinkled. He couldn't imagine what she ...
Until he could.
Oh, dear God.

30.

Caro took the morning's first express flight to Grand Cayman. Trevor, Molly, Barbara, and Julian had each offered to accompany her. All of them understood when she refused.

The Grand Cayman psychiatric facility—"Linden Cliffs" although there were neither lindens nor cliffs anywhere in evidence—was a revelation. The psychiatric wing of Fairleigh Memorial had been built mid-way through the last century, when nurses wore starched white uniforms and a brutal version of electroshock was overused for everything. Since then the wing had been maintained, barely, on a scrawny budget. Patients' rooms were small and shared. The dayroom badly needed painting. The nurses' station had looked like a shabby fortress.

Not so at Linden Cliffs, which was not a facility for patients dependent solely on health insurance. Caro, torn between gratitude that Julian had brought Ellen here and resentment that on her own she could never have afforded this for her sister, marveled at the luxury.

Single rooms with tasteful furnishings. Original art on the corridor walls. A dayroom like a country club. Periodic entertainment brought in from Miami (Fairleigh Memorial had the high school glee club twice a year). A staff-to-patient ratio comparable to a fine spa. Three psychiatrists with impressive reputations. Caro had researched them.

She met with Ellen's doctor, Edward Silverstein. Dr. Silverstein was not happy with Ellen's proposed transfer to Cayman

Brac, but Bill Haggerty had produced enough legal papers to release Ellen to anywhere, even against all medical advice. "You understand, Dr. Soames-Watkins, that your sister eats only minimally, participates in no activities, including therapy, does not move unless led, and says nothing except 'Angelica is dead.'"

"I do understand that," Caro said. Silverstein had compassionate eyes and a genuine concern for his patient, but right now he was an obstacle in Caro's way. "Ellen will have medical supervision on Cayman Brac. And we won't remove her from here until you can certify that she has improved substantially."

"And why do you seem so confident that will happen soon?"

"I can't say for sure, of course, but despite this temporary collapse, Ellen has tremendous resilience and courage. Grief and her meds make that hard to see right now, I know."

Finally Caro was led to Ellen's room on a non-violent floor. Ellen sat in a leather wing chair that could have graced an Oxford University commons. "Mrs. Kemp, your sister is here to see you," the orderly said. "Dr. Soames-Watkins, if you need anything, just call out."

"Thank you." Caro pulled up a second chair to face her sister. "I'm here, Sissy. How are you doing?"

Ellen said, "Angelica is dead."

"I know. It's Caro, Ellen."

"Caro." A glance of acknowledgment, gone in an instant. "Angelica is dead."

"Yes. But, Ellen—no, look at me—I'm here to tell you something important." Caro took a deep breath and glanced over her shoulder. She didn't want to sound unbalanced, not in this place. "I know how much you miss Angelica. I miss her, too." *Angelica looking up from her crib to give Caro one of her rare smiles, Angelica's sweet baby warmth as Caro walked her up and down the living room.* She fought to keep her voice steady. "But listen to me, Sissy: I know how you can see Angelica again."

"Angelica is dead."

"Yes. But listen—no, keep looking at me—I want you to trust me."

Caro took her sister's hand. This was it, then. She'd needed to see Ellen for herself before she made her decision, before she set the machinery in motion to carry out that decision. Now she had seen her sister. Ellen was in great need—just as their father had been. But Caro was here for Ellen. No one, after the sisters' disinheritance, had been there for their father.

She said, "We've always trusted each other, haven't we? And you know that I've been working with our great-uncle on a secret project about the brain. You remember that, don't you? Of course you do. You're smart and you can follow what I say. The secret project involves your mind going into other universes, and in some of those universes Angelica is still alive. Alive and healthy. You can go there with your mind. Not in imagination, for real, with your mind. You can't stay long, but you can go there and see Angelica. Alive, in a real place. *Real*, Ellen."

"Angelica is dead," Ellen said, but was it with a shade less torpor? Ellen added, "I want to die. Kayla is better off without me. And Angelica is dead."

Caro struggled to hide her shock and keep her voice steady.

"In *this* universe Angelica is dead, but not in the other universes. You can see her, hold her, talk to her."

Ellen's face came to life. Her eyes blazed. Her head jerked up. She socked Caro in the face so hard that Caro's teeth rang and her mouth filled with blood.

The blow shook something loose in Ellen, some old sisterly feeling, some sliver of who she really was. She said, "Oh! You're hurt!" snatched off her own sweater and pushed it against the blood streaming down Caro's face and onto her shirt.

Caro gasped, spat blood onto the sweater, and felt her face. Pain like a fireball shot across her jaw and up through her skull. But her nose wasn't broken and her teeth seemed intact. And now Ellen was staring at her instead of at nothing, and Caro grabbed the moment.

Ellen said, *"Angelica is dead."*

"Trust me one more time, damn it to hell! I'm Caro!"

Ellen nodded slowly, as if her neck were a rusty winch coming to life. "Caro." And then, "See ... Angelica ... again."

"Yes. In another ... place. You can visit there." *An echo of George's voice saying: But there is no "there" or "here"—you understand that, don't you?*

"I'm sorry," Ellen said next. "I'm sorry. But I ... can I ... can you ..." She burst into tears.

Footsteps in the corridor. Quickly Caro stood, blocking any view of Ellen from the doorway and keeping her own back turned. The orderly's voice said, "Everything okay here, Doctor?"

"Yes, thank you!" Caro sang, and wondered for days after how she found the lilting voice, the cheery tone. Lilting and cheery were not her style even when she hadn't just been punched in the face. The footsteps moved on.

Caro wiped the rest of the blood from her throbbing nose. She had only a short time before her face swelled and her bruises turned purple. "Ellen, listen. To see Angelica again you have to be released from here and come to my project on Cayman Brac. That means you have to eat, have to talk in group, have to do whatever they say. And this is very, very important. You can't tell anyone about this, no one. It's a *secret*. If you tell anyone, you can't see Angelica."

Cruel to be kind. Where was the quote from? Trevor might have known.

"Yes. A secret."

Did she understand? Caro peered from her rapidly closing eye at her sister, and decided that she did. Ellen was Ellen again, in the same way that Lorraine and Weigert and Ivan hooked to machines were not themselves until they were unhooked. There was nothing medical about this perception. It was of the spirit, not the brain, and Caro didn't want to go there.

She shoved the bloody sweater into her purse, grabbed another from Ellen's closet and put it on over her stained shirt.

The sweater was far too big for her. Caro leaned over and kissed her sister, who said only, "How long?"

"Depends on your behavior here. Do everything they say. I have to go now."

"Yes," Ellen said. And then, "You saved me from drowning in the fountain."

Where was Ellen's mind now? Somewhere in the past? Did she really understand?

Caro's face felt on fire. She walked rapidly down the corridor, her face turned sideways toward the wall. If she'd had a hat, she could have pulled it low over her forehead. Why hadn't she brought a hat? Why didn't she own a hat?

She signed herself out of the floor, watched by a desk clerk who looked at her curiously but said nothing. Outside the building, she called for an Uber to take her to the cheapest hotel near the airport. She was supposed to catch the next plane, but right now she needed a hotel room, if only for a few hours. In the car, she used her phone to send an email to Weigert. She needed him again. He was the only person who could, or would, help her with this.

The hotel clerk barely glanced at her. Maybe this particular Econo Lodge saw a tsunami of women who'd been slugged in the face. On that depressing thought, Caro found the ice machine on her floor, sat in a chair in her room, and applied an ice pack made of a thin scratchy washcloth. She had ibuprofen in her purse. Her cell phone rang: Julian. She ignored it.

Ellen was back. Sort of. Temporarily. And perhaps only if Caro could deliver what she'd promised: the illusion of Angelica alive in an alternate universe. Ellen, always more romantic and suggestible than Caro, might believe the illusion was real and be comforted. Be saved. Already Ellen's personality had begun to emerge from her depression, like a sunken boat being raised from the sea bottom.

And what did that say about personality? That it was completely the result of circumstances, and when those changed, so did a person's fundamentals? Caro's father, going from an abject, dominated mouse to a man with enough resolution to kill himself. Kayla, going from talkative and sunny, to a sullen child acting out rage. Ellen, resilient enough to joke her way through anything, until she couldn't.

Caro iced and paced. The hotel room was ten steps in one direction, eight in the other. The blood did not wash out of her shirt, but cold water did lighten and smear the stain. She dried the shirt with the hotel hair dryer and put it back on under Ellen's sweater. Ice and pace, pace and ice.

Julian called again, and again. The fourth time, she answered and told him through swollen lips that she would arrive on Cayman Brac on the last express flight, landing at 8:00 p.m. Trevor called, but although she didn't pick up, she was nonetheless warmed by the mere fact of the call. Then she made the call that counted: George. Her email had said she'd talk to him when she got back to Brac, but she couldn't wait. Ellen couldn't wait.

They talked for a long time.

When she eventually left for the airport by a side door—her credit card would be charged automatically for the room—her face was turning the colors of several varieties of squash.

Spirit and brain. One, at least, was solid matter. But if George could believe that the brain itself was a mental construction, part of consciousness-generated reality, Caro would help Ellen believe that, too. Sometimes, you had to take what you could get.

Assuming that George could convince Julian and Watkins to give it to her.

31.

After considerable thought, Weigert decided to tackle Julian first, without Sam, and before Caroline arrived from the airport. Weigert did not want this meeting interrupted, which meant it needed to be held in either his room or Julian's. He decided on his own, asked Julian to come "on a matter of great importance," and set about tidying the piles of page proofs, physics journals, and diagrams on the desk and the extra table he'd jammed into the small chamber.

"Working hard on your book, I see," Julian said. "Why do you need to see me right away?"

"It's Caroline. She—"

Julian's face tautened. "Is she all right? Oh god, was there an accident?"

"No, no, nothing like that. Caroline is fine." Was she? Weigert determined to stay on track. "But she emailed me and then she called. She needs ..."

"She needs what? She's gotten everything she asked for from us."

"Yes. But now she needs something more, for her sister. She ..."

Go ahead, my darling. Just say it.

"... wants Mrs. Kemp to be implanted, in order to see her dead child again. To pull Mrs. Kemp out of her crippling mental state."

Julian's eyes widened. He said nothing for a long moment, but George could almost see his brain crunching away, arranging arguments *yea* and *nay*, searching for the best advantage to the project and himself. There were times, Weigert realized, when he wasn't sure he liked Julian.

"Well," Julian finally said, "that's an interesting idea."

Which meant what? Cold fusion could be called an interesting idea, but it hadn't worked and wouldn't ever work.

"I think," Weigert said, "that if Dr. Luskin agrees, we should do it."

"Why?"

From compassion. To honor Caroline's long struggles to help her sister. To let this poor woman see her dead child and be comforted. "To obtain a unique set of mapping data from a brain with severe depression. That will add another dimension to Sam, Caroline, and Dr. Mumaw's journal article, which in turn will add luster to the project."

"True enough," Julian said, and stood longer in thought. Weigert could not read his expression. Finally he said, "Yes, I think you're right. We should do it. Ellen is young enough that if her MRI checks out, there probably isn't much risk. But you know the rule, George. The decision must be unanimous, and I'm not sure Sam will agree."

Nor was Weigert. He'd said that to Caroline on the phone, adding, "I'm afraid you endow me with more power than I have."

She had said simply, "It's your theory."

"Caroline, my dear, I—"

"My sister says she wants to die. Her doctor told her that right now her thinking is so disordered that Ellen believes Kayla will be better off without her. George, *that is not my sister.* If you knew what she's been through, what her life has been … And through all of it she's been strong. But everybody has a breaking point, and a lot of people need help getting past it, so they can go on at all. Can you understand that?"

Everybody has a breaking point. Weigert's had come when Rose died. Afterward, he'd clung like a barnacle to his theory, with its promise that not only could Rose still exist somewhere, but that he could see her again. Without that hope, that comfort, would Weigert have been able to go on?

And so Weigert had said, "I'll try." Apparently he had succeeded with Julian ... but with Sam?

Julian said, "We have to get Sam to agree now, tonight, before his surgery tomorrow. That's imperative."

"Why?" Weigert said. He'd envisioned softening Sam slowly.

Julian said, "There's a chance that Sam might die during tomorrow's surgery—you know that, George. Not a small chance, either. The project will continue anyway, but there must be no ambiguity surrounding the outcome of Sam's operation. I want it crystal clear to any potentially hostile observer that Caro's surgery did *not* kill Sam just so she could get Ellen implanted. We all need to agree on Ellen's chip *before* Sam's surgery, then fully and legally document the agreement, to protect Caro from rumors of malpractice and the project from eventual negative publicity. I can get Bill Haggerty here tonight if I—"

"Wait, wait. Are you saying someone might suspect *Caroline* of murdering Sam so that he couldn't oppose Mrs. Kemp's implant? Who would ever say such a thing?"

"I don't know who. That's the whole point, George. But we need Sam to agree before his surgery, and we need fire-proof legal documents saying so."

Weigert would not have thought of any of this. He looked at Julian with a mixture of respect and horror. "All right, yes."

"We'll go to Sam together, right after I make a few phone calls. You're the best person to persuade him, George. His oldest friend, and you lost your wife. If you can work on Sam to see that if only Ellen could see Angelica, as you saw Rose ..."

Weigert closed his eyes. What he saw was not Rose but a fight with Sam, on the eve of his dying friend's surgery. But, if it would help Caroline ... "All right. I'll try to persuade him."

"No," Sam said. "Absolutely not. Are you both crazy?"

He sat up in bed, wearing not pajamas but an incongruous plaid shirt which made him look to Weigert like an emaciated and elderly lumberjack. His eyes were brighter than Weigert had seen in a long time, his color better. He didn't look like a man who would die during surgery. Nor did he look like a man who was going to agree to anything he didn't want to. Combat crackled off him like static. Did Julian feel it too?

Weigert said, "Sam, *you're* making a radical choice to risk surgery in your condition. Surely Caroline and her sister have the same right." He paused, steeling himself to refer to what only Sam and he knew. "As did my Rose, to make her choice at the end."

"Your wife's action and mine are not similar. When Rose took that overdose"—Weigert ignored Julian's start of surprise and concentrated on Sam—"the cancer had left her no options. I have options, and I've made a decision. Ellen Kemp isn't stable enough to make any decisions. Jesus Christ, George, I know you're not a lawyer, but think what potential lawsuits we'd be opening ourselves to if a psychiatric patient underwent elective brain surgery as part of our clinical trial! Especially if she dies!"

Julian said, "The surgery isn't entirely elective. It's necessary to save her life because otherwise she might end it. Luskin will swear to that, and Haggerty will cover us legally."

"You've already talked to Luskin and Haggerty on this? Without telling me?"

Weigert said, "Please stay calm, Sam. We're telling you now. Caroline's sister won't receive surgery until she's discharged from the hospital on Grand Cayman, however long that takes. And her mapping data will aid the project, not hurt it. You must know I wouldn't risk our work here unless I was sure it will be all right in the end."

"You are risking it, George! You know you are!" Watkins turned his face, now purpling, to Julian. "He's risking everything for that woman. What hold does she have over him?"

Julian said sharply, "Come off it, Sam. Caro has no hold over George."

"Then what hold does she have over you, Julian? Are you sleeping with her, against my express orders?"

Weigert felt anxiety fall away from him. Sam was clearly not himself, probably as a result of his medications. Weigert stepped closer to the bed. "No one has any hold over anyone, Sam. Stop being so melodramatic. This is *my* theory, and even though you're funding it, even though you believe in it, even though decisions on surgical candidates must be unanimous, on this one you should listen to me. I've created a new branch of the multiverse and, as yet, you have not. Caroline has implanted chips flawlessly into four people, and she will do many more. All of them are risks—we take risks with this work every single day. If Caroline and Julian and Lyle Luskin, who have all seen Mrs. Kemp—as you have not—believe she will eventually be a candidate for this surgery, then I think you must listen to them. For once in your life, Sam, *listen to other people.*"

Watkins glared at him. Weigert stared back. Astonishing himself, he added, "And nobody cares if Caroline sleeps with Julian."

Silence.

Julian said, and Weigert would have sworn there was amusement in his voice, "But just for the record, she's not. I'm not."

Watkins said, "All right! But if I'd known that she would be this much ... all right. Set it up with Haggerty and I'll sign his damn papers. As long as I get my implant in the morning!"

"You will," Julian said. "Thank you, Sam."

"Get out," Watkins rasped.

They did. Best to escape with victory. On the walkway, Julian said, "Do you want to tell Caro or shall I?"

"You," Weigert said. All at once, he wanted to go back to his room, papered with the comforting facts of physics, and work on his page proofs. Enough with all this drama! But when the Rose in his head said, *You did right, my darling,* Weigert felt himself smile.

32.

When Ivan picked up Caro at the airport, he stared openly at her face. "What happened to you?"

Caro asked him to tell everyone that she had walked into the edge of a door and didn't want to talk about it. That wouldn't stop some people, of course—Molly, Trevor, maybe Julian. She would tell Trevor what had happened. Everybody else could spread whatever delicious gossip they chose. A mugging. A fight with a secret lover on Grand Cayman. Resistance to an alien abduction. Whatever.

It turned out that her request for privacy didn't stop Weigert, either. She went to thank him for his help in getting agreement for the project to implant Ellen. He said, "Caroline! What happened? Are you all right, my dear? Julian said to not interrogate you, but ..." He trailed off helplessly.

She should have known Weigert would ask questions. Asking questions of the universe and everything in it—that was what he did.

"I'm fine, George," she said gently. Affection for the old man welled up in her. *So sweet-natured, so brilliant.* "I walked into the edge of a door."

"You should be more careful!"

So innocent. "I will," she said.

≡

The next day, it seemed to Caro that no one exhaled between 7:00 and noon. The entire compound held its collective breath while she and her surgical team worked on Samuel Louis Watkins, Nobel laureate, ruthless genius, her great-uncle. What had become routine was no longer.

This surgery was low-risk compared to, say, a glioblastoma deep in the brain. But Watkins was old even for his actual age. He was dying from pancreatic cancer. And, Caro discovered, there was an oligodendroglioma, a cancer of the glial tissue, near the site where the leads would go. The slow-growing tumor, which had probably been there for years, hadn't shown up on the pre-op MRI. Although 70% of low-grade tumors eventually morphed into more aggressive tumors, Caro left the oligodendroglioma alone. Trevor concurred. Watkins would die long before the oligodendroglioma became a problem to him.

It was a problem for her now, however. She had to maneuver around it to insert the leads, guided by the images on the screen at the end of the operating table. A sub-optimally placed lead meant she would have to go in a second time to reposition it. That had not happened with any of her surgeries so far, and, in this case, it must not happen. Watkins would not survive a second procedure.

Caro wasn't sure he would survive this one.

But he did.

By the time Caro asked Trevor to close, she had sweated a waterfall in the cold room. As she left the OR, she glimpsed Julian standing behind the glass of the tiny gallery. He met her in the scrub room.

"Is he okay? Did it go all right?"

"Yes," Caro said. "He's not going roller-blading or bungee jumping, but he came through okay. However, the risk isn't over, and the next two weeks are critical. He stays in the critical-care unit and nobody goes in except me, Trevor, Molly, and his nurses. Not even Camilla, who's not trained for this. I mean it, Julian. And don't try to discuss business with him by phone. Sometimes with these small holes for wire leads, air can enter the space between the brain and the skull and cause confusion for up to two weeks. You and George will have to make any necessary decisions without Watkins."

Julian nodded.

The rest of the day she and Trevor took turns sitting with Watkins. Molly oversaw his morphine drip. "Well," she said to Caro at mid-evening, "a brain chip has not improved his personality. He's just a more bad-tempered version of himself, which I didn't think possible."

Caro laughed, a weak gurgle. She was nerve-weary. It was amazing that Watkins had survived the surgery; it would be even more amazing if he recovered well enough to lie on the cot in Wing Three and have a multiverse session.

"Caro, go rest," Molly said. "You look as bad as Watkins does. Well, no, not quite—but rest now." She hugged Caro, who was surprised at how much comfort was brought her by the simple human touch of a friend.

Watkins did not develop post-surgical complications, but neither did he recover as fast as Caro would have liked. Dr. Luskin moved temporarily into the compound. (And how he could do that and still maintain a medical practice on Grand Cayman, Caro didn't ask.) Watkins was a bad patient, brusque and fretful. The eighth or ninth time that he demanded an exact date when he could "create a branch of the multiverse," she had difficulty restraining herself.

"When I say so. You do understand that you're lucky to be alive at all, don't you? The Hallucination Delusion will just have to wait."

To her surprise, he actually smiled. "Call it that, do you? Your loss." And then, surprisingly, "Thank you, Caroline."

The next day, Trevor implanted Aiden, with Caro as backup. For the first time, the hospital had two patients at once, a harbinger of things to come.

During Watkins's post-surgical recovery, neither Caro nor Trevor left the compound. They found ways to be together, although not yet in either of their bedrooms. Their growing attraction to each other would inevitably lead to sex, but Caro shied away from that. She wasn't …

Wasn't what? She'd had casual affairs before. But that was the point—intimacy with Trevor would not be casual. With the others, it had been sex. With Trevor, it would be making love.

He didn't press her, even though she'd never put into words why she was behaving as if she were thirteen instead of thirty. Finally, she put it into words for herself: she was afraid. Of loving him and being loved in return, of being that vulnerable to heartbreak.

Only … didn't the endless talking that they'd so far substituted for sex render her even more vulnerable?

Not at first. At first it was all light-hearted excitement. More of a night owl than she, Trevor wrote her late each night, and each morning she woke in a glow of anticipation. The emails contained random anecdotes from his childhood, funny stories about his surgical residency, descriptions of his favorite cities (Venice and New York). Questions about her. What did she think of the president, country & western music, Northern Italian cuisine? Did she like to cook? Watch football? Garden? Play chess? Go to the movies? What did she think of Louis Quatorze furniture?

"I've never thought at all about Louis Quatorze furniture," she told him over lunch in the refectory.

"Good," he said. "I hate it. Prissy fragile stuff."

"You like a good leather wing chair."

"Damn straight."

"What if I like Louis Quatorze?" she said, and held her breath. This was the closest they'd ever come to suggesting a future where furniture tastes might matter.

"Then you should have it," he said, and she was both relieved and unhappy at the ambiguous answer.

She said, "I might like Louis Quatorze beds. Although I understand that Louis himself was always too busy while in it to actually look at his bed. That might be nice ... Trevor, don't choke on that sandwich because I don't remember how to do the Heimlich maneuver."

"And you call yourself a doctor."

"Who hates most but not all Louis Quatorze furniture."

"That's not good, because I lied when I said I hated it. Have all Louis Quatorze in my room. I had Sam put it in my contract."

"Damn. And all I got was heavy Tudor oak."

Playfulness was safe, and it left her feeling buoyed up and cheerful for the entire day, even as it brought them closer. Until the night the conversation changed.

≡

At nearly midnight they sat at a picnic table in the Wing One courtyard. Only a few lights still shone from the windows ringing the velvety darkness. Stars glittered around a crescent moon small and curved as the paring from a child's fingernail. Caro sat across the table from Trevor, peering through the darkness to make out his features. She cupped her hands around her water glass full of wine. Trevor, on call, had only actual water.

They were talking of something inconsequential, although Caro's body reacted to his every remark as if it carried the fate of nations. Her pores tingled with him. Later, she could not even remember what their subject had been. There was no clear transition, unless it came from the night-blooming flowers beside the picnic table. Caro breathed in their scent, thought, *Too sickly sweet,* and said abruptly, "Trevor, I had a brother who died."

"I know," he said gently.

"But you don't know what happened afterward. What I did. What I caused."

Even in the darkness she felt his attention sharpen. He said, "I'll know only if you want to tell me."

"I do. Ethan died in a car crash and at his funeral I tried to … I wanted to …" She lifted her glass to gulp her wine and found that Trevor was holding her hand. But she didn't need the wine. She needed to tell him, to make him understand who she really was and what was wrong with her.

"There was a formal wake. After everyone had left, I bent to kiss Ethan good-bye in his coffin. My mother … my mother lost it. She screamed at me not to touch him, he was hers, it should have been me or Ellen that died instead, she wished it had been us. Ellen started crying and my father just stood there, like he always did, head down and silent. I screamed back at her that she was a bitch, she should die. I couldn't stop screaming. It all came out, all the years I knew she didn't love me or Ellen, only Ethan. All those years.

"She disinherited us—the money was hers, not my father's—and threw me out. Ellen was still in high school so she stayed, but she was barely seventeen and couldn't help our father with the clinical depression that deepened after Ethan died. Eventually he killed himself. And then Ellen married a no-good—"

"Stop," Trevor said, in a tone she'd never heard from him before. Anger. For a world-paralyzing moment she thought the anger was directed at her.

"Caro, it was not your fault. None of it. I know, love, that you know what you're telling me is your emotional reality, not your rational beliefs. Emotions matter—Christ, do they matter—and I'm telling you from my emotions that you are lovable no matter what your mother said or did. Or didn't do. You are not responsible for your father's suicide or your sister's jailbreak marriage. Those kinds of actions are the result of years of behavior, not of something said at one funeral, even if the something was a massive loss of temper after years of neglect and emotional abuse. You exploded spectacularly, but everybody does at some time."

"Not you."

"Oh, God, why would you think that? You're wrong. I once …"

He halted, and Caro saw that he labored under a memory at least as painful as hers. She said, because suddenly it was the most important thing she would ever hear, "Tell me."

"I lost it at a rock concert."

"At a rock concert!"

"Yes."

He took a while to go on. "I think my rage, like yours, was a long time building. In Africa, I put back together child soldiers with missing arms, holes in their chests, feet that had been deliberately cut off. And worse, torture that I'm not going to tell you about. For months I asked myself: Why? Why so much hatred, so much cruelty? And eventually everybody who stays there—a lot don't—learns the answer, which is that there is no answer. Not really. There are long-standing historical and political reasons, there are horrendous individual experiences warping people, but there isn't any really good answer why the torturer does it. Why he enjoys it. All I could do was accept it and do what I could. And then I came back to the States on leave, stayed with my sister, and took my nephew to a rock concert. Some terrible punk band in a not-very-big venue. But Gabe idolized the lead singer, the way kids do, and he brought along his cherished guitar that he'd just gotten for Christmas. My sister scrimped and saved to buy it. She's a widow and neither of us ever had much money.

"The lead singer leaned down from the stage and asked if he could see the guitar. Gabe was thrilled, an eleven-year-old handing over his guitar to this guy he admired. The singer took the guitar, played a few chords, and then smashed it onto the stage, grinning. And the crowd howled and cheered.

"I looked at Gabe's face and I lost it. I climbed onto the stage and grabbed the guy and got in two good punches to the face before security dragged me away. They got in their punches, too, and if a kind woman hadn't taken Gabe out of the place and found me, I don't know what would have happened. But I wasn't just punching that asshole who'd smashed a kid's prized guitar, I was punching every monster in Africa who'd recruited kids as soldiers or shot them or cut off their arms or all the rest of the senseless cruelty over there. But of course my stupid action didn't help them, or even Gabe, who saw his uncle give in to violence that helped not at all."

Caro moved around the picnic bench, put her arms around him and hung on. This was a side of Trevor she hadn't seen before. The reverse side of idealism: pain when you failed your own ideals.

They stayed that way for several minutes before she said, "Make love to me, Trevor. Please."

He pulled away to peer at her face. Moonlight glinted off his glasses. "Are you finally sure?"

"Yes."

Because of what you just told me about yourself. Because you know enough about me to even ask that question. Because I love you.

Because I can love you.

Quick the first time, slow the second, sweeter than even her imaginings. She didn't even need to say, or hear, *I love you.* They both knew.

33.

"Spill," Molly said eagerly.

"Oh, for God's sake, stop," Barbara said to her. "Caro will tell us whatever she wants or doesn't want."

"I don't want," Caro said.

Molly clapped both her hands dramatically over her mouth. Between her fingers she said, "Women say that only when it's serious, or could be serious."

"Molly," Barbara said, "shut up. Caro, ignore her."

"I am," Caro said, smiling at both her good friends. The reports from Dr. Silverstein were encouraging. Ellen was improving much faster than expected. George was busy with the publication of his book and his deeply satisfying sessions with Rose. And Trevor ...

Trevor was a miracle.

"Well," Molly said, "you look happy."

"I am," Caro repeated, and hugged them both.

"Doctor," Rosita said, appearing from nowhere, "Dr. Watkins has developed a fever."

≡

Fever meant infection. Postoperative intercranial infection was serious. A subdural empyema, cerebral abscess, or infected bone flap would mean another surgery. Another operation, or meningitis, or a dozen other infections, could kill Watkins. Post-op patients were always vulnerable.

Relief swept through Caro when further work-up established that at least the infection didn't involve the brain. The old man had a urinary tract infection, possibly from his catheter. That was still serious. Anything was serious in an elderly patient with stage-four cancer, even before you added in the immune-weakening steroids necessary to control post-op brain swelling. Caro prescribed broad-spectrum antibiotics and hoped the infection wouldn't go septic.

Her great-uncle looked small and pitiful in his ICU bed.

Julian said to her privately, "Is he dying?"

She said gently, "He was already dying."

"I mean—"

"I know what you mean, Julian. But I can't give you the answer you want. Medicine isn't yes-no. It's up to his body now, and he's a fighter."

Watkins held on, not dying but not improving much, fretting constantly that his multiverse session was being postponed. Caro let Trevor deal with that; he was better at it. Twice a day Caro phoned Dr. Silverstein at Linden Cliffs, to increasingly favorable reports about Ellen. Aiden, Sophy, and nurse Destiny Tattersall all recovered quickly from surgery and had their sessions. Caro did not attend. She spent her time in brain mapping analysis with Barbara, in trying to reach Kayla, and in sex with Trevor. Activities one and three went well.

All that Kayla would say to her was, "When is Mom coming here?" Over and over. Caro had no answer. All she could do was try to keep Kayla's resentment from growing. Caro's door connected to Kayla's, and, although Caro and Trevor made love each night, it was always in his room, and afterwards Caro returned to her own room in case Kayla needed her in the early morning. So far, this had not happened.

Then, on a morning so fresh and vivid that it seemed the world had been created just moments ago, Caro took her coffee to her favorite picnic bench in the Wing One courtyard, shaded and partly secluded by palm trees. The soft air smelled of loamy earth, newly cut grass, and a gentle salt breeze. Caro breathed deeply and opened an email on her phone.

> Sissy—Dr. Silver Beer Mug says I can leave here next week. Can you come get me? I'm sorry I was—like that. Like Dad. I want what you promised. Ellen

Before Caro could process this, James hurried toward her across the grass. "Doctor, I've been looking all over for you! Julian wants you right away in the security office.

"The FBI is here."

≋-

Weigert hurried from the hospital, where he'd been sitting with Sam, to the security office. Julian and Aiden stood there with two strangers. Julian said formally, "Dr. Weigert, this is FBI Special Agents Hannah Kaplow and Greg Logan. They have some questions for all of us."

"And for Dr. Watkins," Agent Kaplow said. She was almost as tall as Julian, with the strong features that Weigert thought of as "handsome." Agent Logan looked insubstantial beside her, but he had watchful eyes that made Weigert nervous. Although what was there to watch? Or to be nervous about? Nothing.

Julian said, "Dr. Watkins is very ill. He had brain surgery recently and has developed an infection. You can observe him from outside the ICU but I doubt his doctors will let you question him."

"That would be Doctors Lyle Luskin and Caroline Soames-Watkins?" Agent Kaplow said.

How did she know that? Was the compound under FBI surveillance? How? Why?

Julian said, "Yes, Doctors Luskin and Soames-Watkins. She's in the compound now. He will be here shortly to attend Dr. Watkins. What is this about? I didn't think the FBI had jurisdiction in the Caymans."

Agent Kaplow said, "Only if American citizens are directly involved."

"Involved in what?" Julian's tone was just as pleasant as Agent Kaplow's, but Weigert could feel the air in the room tighten. Behind Julian, surveillance screens showed various views of the compound gates, inside and out. A seagull flew close to one screen, a flurry of white wings, strayed too far from the sea.

Agent Kaplow said, "We'd just like to ask you and your staff some questions, Mr. Dey."

"Certainly. This way, please."

The five of them filed into the conference room behind the surveillance office and sat down. Julian did not offer coffee, even though a full pot sat on the cluttered sideboard along with baseball caps, empty soda cans, and the latest offering from James's kitchen: ginger cookies. Their spicy fragrance wafted through the room. Agent Kaplow said, "We've been told that you're doing scientific research here, under Dr. Samuel Watkins's direction. Is that correct?"

"It is," Julian said. "We're properly registered with the Caymans government."

"Yes, we know. You're doing brain mapping, which involves inserting lead wires into human brains, wires that can pinpoint what occurs at different brain locations."

"Yes. As I'm sure you already know, various scientists have done extensive research into this area, using both animal and human subjects. We're extending that research. Our subjects are all volunteers, and I can furnish you with complete sets of legal contracts for each volunteer, including me."

"That won't be necessary," Agent Kaplow said. Agent Logan looked curiously at Julian's head, but the tiny connector boxes on both him and Aiden were hidden by thick hair. Weigert, whose hair was thinning, had taken to wearing a jaunty Irish fishing cap over his connector box. Should he remove the cap? Only, he decided, if he was told to. He was not a freak to be stared at.

Julian said, "I'd still like to know what you—"

Agent Kaplow interrupted him. "Can you tell us more about the nature of your research?"

Julian's eyes got a sudden gleam. "Certainly. Dr. Weigert is the guiding force behind our entire experimental design. George, would you like to explain what we're doing here in more detail? From the beginning?"

Solid ground! Weigert began, "Everything we do here starts with the concept of reality. You see, quantum physics has proven for well over a hundred years the basic principles of quantum interaction, starting with the series of experiments that demonstrated beyond a doubt the probabilistic nature of subatomic particles. John Wheeler—"

Six minutes later, he had arrived only as far as quantum entanglement. Agent Logan squinted and frowned, looking lost. Agent Kaplow's tone lost some of its pleasantness. "Thank you, Dr. Weigert, but I don't think we need the theoretical underpinnings. Is it true that these wires you insert into people's heads—"

"Oh, I don't insert the wires! I'm a theoretical physicist, not an MD."

"Yes, I understand that," Agent Kaplow said. "And we want to talk to your chief surgeon. Mr. Dey, please have her brought here. Dr. Weigert, the end result of your theory is that people with these wires are hooked to a computer and their brain functions recorded while information is fed into their brains. Is that roughly correct?"

"Very roughly. You see—"

"And this information causes them to have particularly vivid and detailed hallucinations, which they remember afterward, and which deep-image reconstruction software records. Is that correct?"

"Not hallucinations," Weigert said indignantly at the same moment that Julian said quickly, "That is essentially correct. The hallucinations are experienced as real, and the resulting brain mapping data are invaluable in decoding how the brain processes memory and imagination."

Weigert frowned. Rose was not a hallucination! But if Julian wanted the FBI to think so, then Weigert had best let Julian talk to them. All would be clarified when Weigert published.

"I see," Agent Kaplow said, although Weigert doubted that she did.

The door opened and Caroline entered, carrying a coffee cup. "Julian, you sent for me?"

"Yes. Sit down, Caro." Julian made the introductions. Caroline sat, looking wary.

Agent Kaplow asked her a lot of medical questions about the surgeries she performed, her training specifically with surgical implants, and her reasons for coming to, and remaining on, Grand Cayman. Weigert felt, rather than saw, Julian stiffen slightly. But Caroline answered everything in a cool, professional voice.

"The surgery is similar to Direct Brain Stimulation, an established technique of inserting permanent wire leads into the brains of tremor patients, usually, although not exclusively, those with Parkinson's disease. I have an interest and background in brain mapping, which I'm sure the FBI already knows. You probably know, too, that I filed an unsuccessful sexual harassment complaint against Dr. Paul Becker, head of neurosurgery at Fairleigh Memorial Hospital, and that led to a concerted cyberattack on me via Facebook, Twitter, and other social media. I came to work with Dr. Watkins because Fairleigh Memorial no longer provided a viable workplace for me. Also because of my interest in brain mapping, and because Samuel Watkins is my great-uncle and a Nobel laureate that any young surgeon would be honored to work with."

Agent Kaplow looked unsurprised to hear any of this. Julian smiled faintly.

Agent Logan spoke for the first time. "Did you implant experimental wires into a former employee here, Benjamin Hunter Clarby?"

Julian's smile vanished.

"Yes," Caroline said, "I did."

"When was that surgery performed?"

Caroline looked at Julian, who supplied the date.

"Was the surgery successful? No complications?"

"Not during the first sixteen hours post-op. Sometime after that, Ben Clarby left the compound."

"Against medical advice?"

"It would have been against medical advice if I'd had the chance to give any. My understanding is that he left suddenly in the middle of the night."

"Do you know why Clarby did that, Dr. Soames-Watkins? Please let me remind you that although you're not under oath, under Title 18, Section 1001 of the United States Code, it is a federal crime to knowingly make false or fraudulent statements to the FBI."

Caroline's chin lifted. "I have no idea why Ben Clarby left."

"Have you heard from him since? With, for instance, medical questions?"

"No."

"Have either you, Dr. Weigert, or you, Mr. Dey, had any communication with Clarby in any form since he left?"

"No," Weigert said. "But he stole some data." Should he have said that? But it was the truth.

Julian said, "That's correct. Clarby copied proprietary scientific data. None of us knows why, or what he did with it. Do you? If not, I'd like to know why you're questioning legitimate scientific research."

"It's not the research we're questioning, Mr. Dey. And if you access the internet news feeds, as I'm sure you do regularly, you'll learn as soon as it goes public why we're talking to you, and why we want to talk to Dr. Watkins.

"Last night Ben Clarby was found murdered in his mother's New York apartment."

≡

Weigert felt sick in his stomach. He hadn't liked Clarby, but ... murder? Who? Why?

"I don't understand," he said to Aiden, the only one left in the security office. Julian and Caroline had gone to conduct the agents to Watkins, futile though that would be. Aiden, bent over his phone, apparently didn't even hear Weigert.

"I found it," Aiden said. "Very brief article, just that his mother came home from shopping and found he'd been shot in her guest room in Brooklyn. She called the cops ... no real information ... graduate of Stanford ... but why the FBI? Murder is usually a state crime, not federal."

Weigert hadn't thought of that. He'd never had reason to learn about the American jurisprudence system. He recoiled from the images that flooded his mind: the mother, the guest room, young Clarby. Shot where? In the head? In the heart? Had there been much blood? Before Aiden could tell him, Weigert left the security office.

Rose—

Steady, my darling.

The project is about science, not criminal activity! We're not some ... some cheap TV show!

It will remain science, no matter what else happens.

Yes. It would. But if the FBI somehow shut down the research ... Could they do that? Would they?

Evidently Caroline had the same thought. Fifteen minutes later, she knocked on the door of Weigert's room. "George, can I talk to you?"

"Come in, Caroline. How is Sam?"

"Serious but improving. Did the FBI tell you or Julian anything else before I arrived?"

"Nothing important. Did Sam say anything to the agents?"

"He was asleep. They didn't seem to really need him anyway except, I guess, to see that he exists. The agents are still talking to Julian and Aiden. George, what is this about? Please tell me whatever you know that I don't about Ben Clarby."

Weigert sat on his desk chair. It was rude to not offer the chair to Caroline, but he felt shaky, and she was thirty-one years old and Weigert was not. How could someone so young and slight look so formidable?

He said, "I don't know anything that you don't know already."

"Does Julian know more than that?"

Weigert hesitated. An image came to him: Julian, Aiden, and Ivan conferring by the computers in the session room, cutting off their conversation the moment Weigert appeared. Caroline's eyes sharpened.

Weigert answered her as honestly as he could. "I don't know. Once I would have said that Julian, Sam, and I share all knowledge about this project. Now I'm not so sure, although I have no substantiated reason to believe that. But I don't ... it isn't ..."

She found the words for him. "You don't like the ambiguity."

"Yes. I mean, no. Caroline, I've heard that sometimes young people, hackers, they steal data just to show that they can. To show off to their friends. Do you think that's what Clarby did?"

She gave him her affectionate smile. "I don't know for sure, but I'm afraid not. Hackers don't get murdered for showing off." She was silent a long time before adding, "My sister will be here before too long. I want her implanted as soon as possible, in case the FBI does somehow shut us down."

"I understand," Weigert said, because it was all he could offer her. "I'll make sure she receives her implant as soon as the physicians at her facility release her to you. Doctors control everything."

"Not this doctor," Caroline said.

34.

The speed with which Julian arranged for Ellen's eventual arrival dazzled Caro. Of course, she thought, enough money could do anything. Then, however, she was ashamed of her cynicism. Money needed someone to spread it around, and Julian was doing that on Ellen's behalf.

A cottage was rented or bought (Caro didn't ask) a quarter mile from the compound. Household furnishings arrived in a steady stream. Aiden's techs installed a security system that connected to the one at the compound. Julian found a nurse for Ellen and a local woman to come in daily to cook and clean. He and Caro zoomed every day with Dr. Silverstein and with Ellen herself.

Caro held off telling Kayla any of this until Ellen's actual return. Any broken promise would only deepen Kayla's mistrust.

The FBI did not return. If they were in contact with Julian, he didn't tell Caro or Trevor.

Watkins's condition remained the same: critical but stable. Caro spent more time than necessary sitting by Watkins's bedside in the ICU. Often he slept through her visits, but one afternoon he opened his eyes and croaked, "Caroline."

"I'm here," she said, putting aside her book. Was he rallying? His vitals on the monitors said no. "Do you need anything, Uncle?"

She had never called him that before; it just slipped out. He noticed, giving her a fleeting skeletal motion of his mouth that was meant to be a grin. He said, "Talk … to me. My … nephew."

Caro's father, who, as far as she knew, Watkins had never met. What should she tell him of Devon Watkins's pathetic history and how much of it did he already know?

With Watkins, honesty was paramount.

"My father is dead," she said steadily.

"Killed ... himself."

"Yes. He'd been clinically depressed for a while. A few years later, my mother died. I do remember my grandfather, your brother John, but only dimly. I was just a small child when he died."

Watkins said something that might have been, "Idiot," but Caro couldn't be sure. The old man had closed his eyes.

What else could she say? "My father was a quiet person, intelligent but self-effacing." *Who was completely controlled by my horrible mother.* "He and my sister were somewhat close." *Which I ended the day of Ethan's funeral.* "I don't think he looked much like you, at least not from the pictures I've seen of you when you were young. Younger." *God, what a mess she was making of this!*

"Brother. Dead."

She'd already said that her grandfather, Watkins's brother, was dead. Then she realized whom he really meant: not his brother but hers.

She said steadily, "Yes. Ethan died, too." So much death. Why was Watkins doing this?

"Die. Me."

"Yes. But not, I hope, of this infection. You may rally."

"No," he rasped. And then, more clearly than anything else he'd said, "Good for the project."

It was good for the project for Watkins to die? Puzzled and disturbed, Caro leaned closer to her great-uncle. But he had fallen back asleep.

Ellen's flight from Grand Cayman was scheduled for tomorrow. Caro would tell Kayla in the morning. She had no idea how Kayla would react.

After making sure the child was asleep, Caro was preparing to go to Trevor's room when something heavy hit her door.

Now what? She flung open the door to find James picking himself up from the walkway as a small furry bottom with a white-tipped tail disappeared into a bushy flower bed.

"I slipped. And no, I never took the poor little thing back," James said crossly. "She's been living behind the kitchen. And now I can't catch her!"

"You never took the kitten back? Why not?"

"Just because!" He picked himself up. "Look at that, grass stains all over my new chinos. I have to catch her. What if she eats a lizard?"

"What?"

"A lizard! What if lizards poison cats? Do they, Doctor?"

Caro had no idea. "Have you been feeding her cat food?"

"Of course I have!"

"Then she probably won't eat a lizard. She'll be fine overnight in the courtyard. Leave her until morning."

"But—"

"The kitten will be fine."

In the morning Kayla burst through the door adjoining their bedrooms. "Aunt Caro! Why was my cat out all night? I found her in the *bushes!*"

Kayla stood with the kitten in her arms. Fur matted with dirt, a flower petal stuck in one ear, the little thing meowed like fingernails on a whiteboard. Kayla cuddled it protectively. While Caro blinked herself awake enough to keep up with events, Kayla advanced a step closer to the bed.

"I don't care what you say, I'm keeping her."

"I never said—"

"Fluffy is *mine*. You can't separate us!"

"I don't—"

"Julian said at breakfast that Mom will be here today. Do you think she'll like my cat?"

Brain surgery was easier than children.

≡

Easier, in fact, than all family ties. When Ellen arrived at the cottage so carefully prepared for her, Caro ended up having only a few minutes with her sister, and those minutes were full of shocks.

She planned to bring Kayla later in the afternoon. First, Caro wanted to judge both Ellen's condition and her mood. Caro stuffed a rudimentary version of a "doctor's bag," instruments and basic meds, into a large purse. She didn't want Ellen to view her as medical personnel but rather as her sister; nonetheless, Caro wanted to be prepared to examine Ellen if warranted. Since she also used the old purse as a traveling bag on airplanes, it was stretched out in odd places from defunct laptops larger and clumsier than Caro's current model. The purse, once dark red, resembled mottled cow skin dotted with some terrible disease. Two of its myriad zippers were broken. Ellen had always made fun of the object, and Caro hoped she would do so now. That would be a good sign.

Ellen's emails and phone conversations over the last few days had been brief and coherent, but almost exclusively focused on Angelica. When could she get the "transporter" put into her head that would let her visit Angelica in the other universe? When would she be recovered enough from the operation to visit Angelica? Could Kayla somehow go with her to visit Angelica? Had Kayla been told that Angelica was living and healthy in another dimension?

Caro had answered each question as fully as she could, which was not what Ellen wanted. Never academically inclined, she didn't want to hear about Weigert's physics, or how the implant worked. She just wanted to see her dead child alive again.

Caro couldn't leave Watkins, recovering too slowly, to accompany Ellen on the flight from Grand Cayman. Nor was Julian willing to leave Brac again. Barbara had been chosen. But when Caro arrived at the cottage to await the jeep from the airport, the car was driven by one of James's household staff, a huge islander named Mick who spoke some difficult-to-understand dialect, and it was Lorraine who sat in the back seat with Ellen.

That was the first shock.

The second was Ellen herself. Although still thin and frail, with lusterless dry hair badly combed, her eyes no longer looked dead. But they held a laser focus that disturbed Caro. Lorraine helped Ellen down from the jeep, and Caro hugged her.

Ellen pulled away. "Angelica? Kayla?"

"I'll bring Kayla later. How was the trip? The flight?"

"Okay."

"Yes? Any ... any turbulence?" Oh, God, she was talking in banalities. To *Ellen.*

Ellen said, "It was okay."

A whole sentence, at least.

Then Ellen said abruptly, "I'm still not well, Caro."

"I know. But here, you will—"

"Yes." Long pause. Caro felt sick inside. This wasn't how she and her sister were with each other. But then Ellen smiled. A forced smile, but the next words were sincere.

"I still ... I will be all right, as soon as I see Angelica. As soon as I *know.* Caro, thank you. To you and to Julian. He's wonderful, isn't he? I never knew a man like him."

Oh ... no. *No.*

Caro said carefully, "He's been very helpful."

Then Ellen gave her a genuine Ellen smile, that grin that said she understood more of what Caro meant than Caro had said, and for a brief flash she was the old Ellen again. "Are you two—"

"No. There is— Ellen, you don't want to ... I mean, with Julian ..."

Ellen put her hand on Caro's arm. "It's okay. I'm not."

Lorraine listened to this exchange, making what of it? Who knew? This tranquil, centered Lorraine was almost as disturbing as Ellen. Was Ellen, after her implant and eventual multiverse session, going to be as smoothed out, as un-spiky, as focused on the internal and eternal as Lorraine? Oh gods, no. Don't let that happen. She would no longer be Ellen.

Lorraine said, "This sun is really hot. Would you like a drink of water, Ellen? Tea, coffee, maybe a smoothie? Let's go inside." She took Ellen's arm.

Caro, instantly and irrationally resentful, trailed behind.

The cottage's three bedrooms opened directly off a comfortable, open-plan space decorated in classic sea resort. Wicker chairs with blue cushions, white wooden tables, curtains printed with starfish. A woman rose from a chair by the fireplace. Another turned from the stove, which wafted spicy odors from three pots. Lorraine said, "Ellen, this is Nadjla, your nurse, and this is Mrs. Cary, who comes in daily to take care of us all."

Ellen nodded but didn't answer. Mick came in with Ellen's suitcase, and Lorraine pointed at the largest of the bedrooms, which had two single beds. A pink stuffed turtle, which Kayla was way too old for, rested on one bed. Mick put Ellen's suitcase on the other bed.

An unwelcome suspicion invaded Caro. On the dresser of one of the two smaller bedrooms sat a picture of Nadjla with a young woman who so closely resembled Nadjla that she had to be her daughter. The third bedroom had a large, colorful dream catcher on the wall. And *Mrs. Cary comes in daily to take care of us*. Us.

Caro said, "Lorraine, are you staying here?"

"Yes, for a while. Julian thought it would be a good idea for me to be able to answer Ellen's questions about the multiverse."

Caro said stiffly, "I can do that."

"Yes, of course. But you have duties at the compound."

"Don't you have teaching duties somewhere? College classes that—"

"I'm on sabbatical." Lorraine smiled at Caro.

Ellen said gratefully, "Thank you, Lorrie. I have lots of questions."

Caro wanted to tear out Lorraine's hair. She recognized her jealousy as petty, as childish, as ridiculous. *Lorrie.* But she controlled herself to say, "Julian's idea?"

"Yes," Lorraine said.

"So kind," Ellen murmured.

Before Caro could answer—and what would she have said about Julian anyway?—Mick exploded back inside. "Doctor, we go right now. Julian call, say come now."

"What is it?" Caro said. 'What's happened?"

"Dr. Watkins. We go *now.*"

35.

Pancreatic cancer was a capricious killer. Weigert knew that. People could live for years after the diagnosis, or die within weeks. As Weigert sat with Sam, abruptly Sam became agitated and his breathing shallower, less regular, and noisier. The nurse said, "Fluid in the chest. It doesn't seem to be causing him any pain. But I'll notify Julian to call Dr. Luskin."

It hurt Weigert to see his old friend like that.

Rose, I don't think it will be long now.

I know, my darling. I'm so sorry.

Astonishing how much more comforting it was to "talk" to Rose in his head than it had been before. Yes, at the moment it was just Weigert creating both sides of the conversation, but it wasn't that when he was in a session with her. How did someone like Caroline, dear girl that she was, manage without that comfort? Of course, Caroline had never been married and her closest relative, her sister, was still alive in this universe. In fact, wasn't Ellen Kemp arriving on the island today?

Weigert sat with Sam, who did not wake, for another hour. He ate lunch and then returned to his room to answer queries from the publisher of his forthcoming book. In the early afternoon he walked to the hospital wing to see Sam again, perhaps awake this time. The ICU nurse stood talking to other nurses, a few of whom were crying.

Then Weigert knew.

As soon as the nurse saw him, she walked over. "Dr. Weigert, I'm so sorry. Dr. Watkins died fifteen minutes ago."

Weigert nodded. He knew that for a short time, before the real grief started, he would be numb. He'd been here before, with Rose. Numbness was a blessing that did not last.

"I'd like to sit with him for a few minutes, please." Weigert started toward critical care.

The nurse's voice changed. "He's not in the hospital wing."

"Where is he? I thought he was—"

"Dr. Watkins died in the session room."

"Why would he ..." Weigert didn't finish his sentence. The answer to that question was clear, if not to the next ones. "Is Julian there? Why wasn't I called?"

"I don't know, Doctor."

He felt her bewilderment; she really did not know. "Thank you," he said brusquely. He hurried to the computer complex, fumbling his first attempt at the thumb lock. Sam must have felt the end coming and had wanted a session in the multiverse before he died. Weigert would have done the same thing, and he hoped that Sam had had at least a few minutes connected to the computers, a few minutes in whatever other universe he'd entered. But ... why hadn't Weigert been called along with Julian? Someone was going to have to explain that!

A shock ran through him when he saw Sam lying on the cot between the computer consoles. The wire leads were still connected to the tiny titanium box on the top of his bald skull. Camilla was just now closing Sam's eyes, her own shiny with tears. Julian and Aiden stood by the computer screen, talking in low voices. They turned abruptly when Weigert entered, and a strange expression flitted across Julian's face.

Weigert knew what he was seeing, but it was a long moment before he could find words. When he did, they were addressed to Rose.

He died during his session.

But his brain could not devise an answer from her.

"George," Julian said. "It was just a little while ago. He went peacefully. He—"

"But it wasn't only a little while ago that you brought him here," Weigert said. "Was it? You had to load him on that gurney"—he pointed to it, shoved into a corner—"and hook him up, which means there was plenty of time to call me before his session started."

"I'm sorry," Julian said. "It was so sudden and unexpected—"

"No, it wasn't," Weigert said. Only a few times in his life had he felt towering anger, but he could recognize it. "Why didn't you send for me, Julian?"

Camilla said, "Doctor—" and stopped, glancing sideways at Julian.

"And," Weigert said loudly, "where is Dr. Luskin? Are you telling me he wasn't here either? That he left after Sam took a turn for the worse this morning?"

"Of course Lyle was here," Julian said. "He's in the security office filing the death certificate. Please calm down, George. I'm so sorry we didn't call you, but the main thing is that Sam had a peaceful death, just sliding away after his session and—"

"After? Not during?"

"No, after. It's a short session because his breathing became so raspy that we turned off the computer. But he was happy with just the few minutes he had in a branch universe. We have the recording of the session, and you can see it and—"

"Caroline told me yesterday that Sam wasn't strong enough yet for a session. That he needed to stay in hospital. So why did you do it?"

"Because he was dying anyway and that's what he wanted." Julian's voice was harder now, his gaze challenging. But Weigert didn't back down.

"You don't know that he would have died anyway. He's had bad spells before and he rallied from them. But the stress of the session ... He died *during* it, didn't he?"

"No. After."

"The session might be what killed him!"

"No. You know the cancer had almost run its course. And Sam made his own decision. Even though Lyle wasn't happy about it, it *was* Sam's decision to make. He—"

"I want to talk to Lyle. And to Caroline. Aiden, send for her."

Aiden spoke for the first time. "She isn't here. Her sister arrived on the island today and she's at the cottage."

Weigert repeated, "I want to talk to Caroline. And Lyle. Now."

Again Julian and Aiden glanced at each other, and again Weigert could not read Julian's expression. But, consummate fixer that he'd always been, Julian dropped his voice and said soothingly, "Of course, George. Aiden, phone Mick to bring Caro back here. Camilla, please get Dr. Luskin. George, if you want to sit with Sam for a bit ..."

"I do. Alone."

"Certainly."

They all left. Weigert pulled a chair next to Sam's cot. Sam's mouth was slightly open. Someone, probably Camilla, had propped a folded towel under his chin to partially close his lips. Weigert's rage left as abruptly as it had arrived. Supposing he had been called? Would it have made any difference? If Sam, even in this weakened body, had decided that he wanted his session now, it would have happened no matter what Weigert said. Sam always got his way. And Weigert wasn't a physician. Lyle Luskin had allowed this, so anything Weigert could have said would have been overruled anyway. Sam had wanted his session in the multiverse before he died, and he could not have known that the session would last only a few minutes before his body reached its end. Despite the accusation that Weigert had hurled at Julian, a multiverse session did not kill. It could not change cancer.

"Sam," Weigert said softly, "what did you create in your new universe?" A stupid question. Weigert would know soon enough, when he viewed the truncated recording. He just hoped it had been satisfying to Sam. Even so, it was a tragedy that his old friend had not lived to see the publication of their joint project, with its revelations that would change physics forever.

He remembered when the project had started. And then farther back, when he and Sam had both been young fellows at Oxford, roistering in the pubs on King Street. Later, when Sam's fanatical research developed the Achino, the cure for the common cold with all its other applications to anti-virals, Sam had practically lived in his lab and Weigert had seen less of him. He'd emerged, though, to stand as best man at Weigert and Rose's wedding. Then Sam's Nobel Prize: Weigert and Rose had journeyed to Stockholm for the ceremony. And so back to the project: its start fifteen years ago, recruiting Julian, finding the site on Cayman Brac, building the compound ...

Weigert sat there what seemed a long time, his hands on his bony knees, remembering.

Lyle Luskin entered quietly and drew up a chair beside Weigert's. Weigert said, "He's not there any more."

"No," Luskin said. "The body is an empty shell."

Something in Luskin's voice made Weigert turn away from Sam to look at the physician's face.

Ask him, my darling.

"Lyle," Weigert said to the only person whose friendship with Sam went back almost as far as Weigert's, "is there something about this death that I should know?"

A pause before Luskin said, "No. Sam was very ill near the end. Julian turned off the computers as soon as Sam was in real trouble. And death comes differently to everybody."

The door opened again, this time not quietly, and Caroline rushed in, trailed by Julian. She stared at Sam, and then put a hand on Weigert's shoulder. He covered it with his own.

"George, I'm so sorry for your loss."

Her loss, too. Sam had been her great-uncle, after all. Family, even if not close.

Caroline leaned over the cot and felt for Sam's wrist.

"That's not necessary," Julian said. "Dr. Luskin certified the death and filed the certificate. Come away, Caro, the first-call car from the funeral home will be here soon."

"Tell them to wait," Caroline said. "George, were you here for my uncle's death?"

"No," Weigert said, offering no explanation because he had none. The gurney in the corner, the wire leads hooking Sam's head to the computer, the truncated multiverse session—there would have been time for both him and Caroline to be called. From her face, she thought the same thing.

She said, "Dr. Luskin, do you have the record of his last vitals?"

"Yes, of course."

"Taken how long before he died?"

"A few minutes." Luskin rose. He and Caroline looked at each other, and Weigert could feel something pass between them.

"What were his temperature, blood pressure, all the rest?"

Before Luskin could answer, Julian said, "Caro, stop. The man is clearly dead."

"Yes," Caroline said. "Dr. Luskin?"

Luskin handed her a small electronic device, presumably displaying the figures she'd asked for. Caroline frowned at it and said, "His temperature hadn't dropped. His skin isn't pale, let alone gray- or blue-toned. From what you've said, he wasn't confused about his surroundings or unduly agitated. His lips aren't dry."

Julian said, "Those things aren't conclusive."

"I know that. But how do you know it, Julian? You're not a doctor. Are you requesting an autopsy?"

"*No*," Julian said, his face suddenly so unpleasant that Weigert was startled.

"Then I am," Caroline said, "as his other physician."

"No," Luskin said. "I'm his oncologist and I certified his cause of death. An autopsy isn't necessary."

Inside Weigert's head, Rose said, *There is something Dr. Luskin doesn't know and doesn't want to know.*

Caroline's voice broke. "Julian, what aren't you telling me?"

"Nothing." Julian was once again the man Weigert knew: diplomatic, concerned. "I'm sorry I yelled at you, Caro. I think we're all a little overwrought. Sam will be missed so much, by all of us. But at least he got to experience a session, however brief."

Caroline stared at him, her face uncertain.

But not as uncertain as Weigert, who understood none of it, except that he needed to see the recording of Sam's session in the reality that his old friend had created.

≡

Later that day, after Sam's body had been taken to the crematorium, after the staff had been gathered together and been assured that the project would continue, after Bill Haggerty had arrived to go over all the necessary legal procedures with Julian and Weigert as the two remaining owners of the research facility, Weigert went to the computer room to view the recording of Sam's session.

Aiden and Julian were there, studying screens filled with data. Aiden was saying, "It may be that first he has to—" He stopped speaking as soon as Weigert entered, and both young men turned to face him. Again he had the brief impression that they didn't want him there, and again Julian smoothed it over—whatever "it" was—with his easy charm.

"George. Come in. You want to see Sam's recording, and we both want to see it again with you. It's comforting."

Weigert nodded, saying nothing.

The recording started as they all did, with the subject rising from the cot in this same room, his leads to the computer having vanished. That much was programmed onto the implant. How the subject looked was not, and this Sam was young, strong, dressed in the chinos and lab coat that had been his inevitable uniform for decades.

Involuntarily, Weigert leaned closer to the screen. What reality would Sam create once he left this room? Sam had no wife, no children, no closer kin than Caroline, whom he'd never even met until he hired her.

But unlike every other implanted person, Sam did not walk through the door into a new reality. Instead, the door opened and Julian entered the room. They spoke briefly—saying what? Weigert would never know; no living Sam remained in this branch of the universe to recap the conversation the way Weigert had reported what he and Rose had told each other. In silence, Julian held out his hand. Sam reached to take it, and, just before their fingers met, the recording went dark.

This was the moment, here in this universe, that Sam had gone into his death rattle and Julian had turned off the computers. Or—

Weigert felt every muscle in his body tighten. He opened his mouth to speak, but no words came out. Sudden panic took him, breaking in waves over his mind so that he nearly staggered slightly sideways. He had not considered this.

Somehow, *he had not considered this.*

Not even its possibility.

If Julian and Luskin were lying to him because it would be very bad publicity to say a subject died during the active phase of an experiment, that was one thing. That made sense.

But if Sam had actually died *during* his session, if his body had died here while his consciousness was in a new reality ... Did that mean that Sam got to stay there? Alive? And ... and young?

"Julian—"

"He died after I ended his session, George. After."

"Then for the sake of argument—" Where did Weigert get the strength to even phrase this question? But questioning steadied him, as it always had. "Sam asked you to take him here when the end was coming. If he *had* died during his session, if that's what he'd hoped would happen, was he trying to cheat death? To continue on in a branch universe because there was no living brain here for his consciousness to return to? Was that what he'd been hoping for?"

"I don't know what he hoped. But of course it didn't happen that way. Sam died after I ended the session."

Now Weigert's mind was clear again, racing over the solid scientific underpinnings of his theory, the equations and experiments and data so far ...

He said to Julian, "We'll never know. We can't know. It's possible that when his body died here, the body with his brain in it ... the brain that consciousness creates ... it's possible he disappeared from the alternate universe too. Or that he didn't. Julian ... *I don't know which.*"

Julian said, a little louder, "Sam died after his session ended. No one has ever died because of this project. Sessions do not kill people."

Which was, of course, what Julian was concerned with— the eventual reputation of the project as a whole.

Weigert looked at the empty cot as if Sam's lifeless body had not already been taken to the crematorium. Consciousness could not be ended by bodily death because consciousness created reality, and since time itself didn't exist outside of consciousness, there was no "after death" except of the death of someone else's physical body in another person's now. But nothing in Weigert's theory indicated exactly how consciousness persisted, only that it did. And neither Weigert nor anybody else could now ask Watkins the crucial questions: What does your reality feel like now? Are you complete in your newly created branch reality, down to every detail of your childhood: what TV shows you watched, your favorite breakfast cereal, the name of your fifth-grade teacher, the feel of your dog's fur?

Julian repeated, "There's no way to know, George."

No. There was not. Weigert looked at the screen where the recording of Weigert's session had played, but the recording had ended and the screen gave him back only the reflected image of Weigert's own face.

36.

Caro found Luskin in the small lobby leading to the main gate, his roller bag beside him. She said, "Lyle, a word, please."

"Mick is driving me home."

"He can wait. Did my uncle die during or after his session?"

"You heard Julian," Luskin said evenly. He looked exhausted but more composed than before, a man who had committed to his version of events. Or to somebody's version.

"I did hear Julian, yes. My uncle was in distress, Julian ended the session, and a few minutes later Watkins died."

"Yes."

"His vitals—"

"Caro," Luskin said, "you're a talented neurosurgeon and I admire your skill and your caring. But you're not an oncologist. I've seen scores of patients die of cancer, and only a few followed the exact set of steps that you've apparently got stuck in your head. Sam's end was consistent with his disease, and he died of pancreatic cancer, not his multiverse session."

"Or during it."

"No."

Luskin's gaze did not meet hers. She'd found out what she wanted to know, and it sickened her. "I believe you. You didn't do it, you didn't even know about it beforehand, but you suspect it now. Julian injected my uncle with something lethal, didn't he, just as Watkins told him to. So that Watkins could

... what? Stay in his hallucination after he died? You know that isn't possible, Lyle!"

He didn't answer her. He thumbed opened the gate, walked to the waiting jeep, and climbed in.

It wasn't as if she didn't know that doctors sometimes performed illegal euthanasia. No one talked about it, ever. But it did happen, and from motives of compassion. Caro had seen terminal patients in terrible pain and suffering, and hoped that the end was near for them. Only—

Watkins had not been in extraordinary pain. He had even, when she'd checked on him early this morning, rallied a little.

First of all, do no harm.

Had Luskin done harm? Had Julian? She had no doubt at all that Watkins, who commanded everything in the compound, had ordered the lethal injection, if that was indeed what had happened. Had it? If so, it was something far stranger than mercy killing. Mercy resurrection?

Caro wanted to talk to Trevor, needed to talk to Trevor, a need as palpable as thirst. She found him in his room, working on his laptop, and told him everything that had just happened, including her suspicions. Trevor listened carefully, his gaze never leaving her face.

"I can't say I'm sorry he's gone," Trevor said, "because it sounds like an easy death, as deaths go. But, Caro, you can't know what happened to Sam after death. Nobody can know. But, love, that's always been true, for all people at all times."

"I'm not talking about after his death. I'm talking about the cause of his death."

"You can't know that, either. And despite our Hippocratic oath, I believe that patients have the right to decide the circumstances of their death. Sam is dead, and he wanted to die. You have to let this go."

Trevor was right. Caro's uncle was dead. He'd wanted to die.

She said, "I was sitting with him in the ICU a few nights ago and he wanted to talk. He said he was going to die. I said he might yet rally. And he said, 'No. Good for the project.' He meant that his death was good for the project."

"I don't know what he meant," Trevor said. "I've read about near-death experiences—tunnels, lights, the whole show—and probably you have, too. Maybe Watkins was experiencing something like that."

"He didn't say death was good for him. He said it was good for the project. Trevor, how much exactly do you believe of George's theory?"

Trevor reached into a drawer of his desk and took out a bottle of cabernet sauvignon and two glasses. "I believe we should both have some wine if we're going to have this discussion. Also, we can toast Sam. Caro?"

"Yes." She watched him open the wine, pour it, hand her a glass with his strong, long surgeon's fingers. In the light from his window, filtered by bamboo blinds, the liquid glowed redly. She took a sip, then a longer drink. Almost immediately, warmth spread through her.

Trevor said, "I believe all of the hard science underlying George's theory, of course: quantum effects, entanglement, the way observation changes the behavior of what we call 'energy' and 'matter,' the subjective nature of time ... Well, Einstein pretty much nailed that one over a hundred years ago. And the subjective nature of space does follow, mathematically, from the rest. Mathematics also establishes at least the possibility of the multiverse. The two key areas—and I think these are the ones you question too—are whether microlevel effects really can apply wholesale to the macro universe, and whether consciousness really does create everything. And, by implication, can alter everything in a branch of the multiverse. That's why I want to experience a session for myself. To see if they feel like reality, or like an elaborate hallucination created by Julian's software."

"You're saying that subjective experience should have as much weight as scientific evidence."

"I'm saying that subjective experience has some weight, and I don't yet know how much. And I don't think you do, either. You told me, remember, about your experience in the garden, when you were a child—the feeling of being 'woven into' everything. Can you say that wasn't real? Was just a hallucination? You told me you were never a fanciful child."

She said slowly, "I don't know." *The clouds were no longer there, and neither was Caro. She was the clouds, the grass, the breeze, the ant crawling across her arm. Everything was her, and she was everything.*

Trevor said, "I don't know yet either. That's why you're going to implant me as soon as a backup surgeon arrives, which will be in two more weeks. Not a new surgeon, although Julian is working on that. Your backup for my implant is Ralph Egan. He's only flying in for one day for my surgery, a favor to Julian. Caro, your turn. How much of George's theory do you believe?"

She studied his face, unusually tense. Both of them knew how important this could be to any future they might have together. Weigert's "primacy of the observer" was the elephant in the room, and, in the first flush of love, they'd been stepping around it.

She said slowly, "Like you, I believe the underlying science, to the extent that I can follow it without the math. And I can see how George's conclusions follow from both the science and from his premises. But I can't shake the idea that there are other possible explanations, the chief of which is that Julian's software, both on the chips and in the computers, causes unusually consistent, detailed, directable hallucinations. And I can't see any way of proving otherwise."

"Not even that, when implantees go back for a second session in the branch of the universe each created, things have evolved there on their own? George told me that during his third session with Rose, he discovered that their house smelled of smoke and workmen were swarming over the kitchen. Evidently there'd been a small fire. Nothing on Julian's programming had included a kitchen fire, and George had certainly not thought about hallucinating one. It happened because that branch of the universe had, independently, evolved. Did he tell you about the kitchen fire?"

"Yes. But, of course, no one plans or even 'thinks about' what a hallucination will contain. The content of a hallucination is unpredictable."

"In that case, everything else about George's three visits to Rose should have been equally unpredictable: her, the house, all of it. And it didn't partake at all of the chaotic randomness of hallucinations. You can't have it both ways, Caro."

He was right. And yet ... "I'm not convinced."

"But you're not unconvinced, either."

"No," she said reluctantly. "Just confused. George is a great mind, but great minds have been wrong before. The history of science is full of wrong turns."

"Yes. But now let *me* go from the macro to the micro, from the universe to you and me, and ask the big question. How much does your confusion—no, that's not the right wording. How much does it matter if I end up believing totally in the primacy of the observer and you don't? How will it affect our life together?"

"Do we ... Will we have a life together?"

"I hope so. I want a real future with you."

She felt her heartbeat go irregular, her throat tighten. "If you believe George totally and stay with the project after it goes public ... I wasn't planning on staying here indefinitely, Trevor. This isn't the only kind of neurosurgery I want to practice. And I have to ... There's Ellen and Kayla. But I ... I couldn't bear to lose you, either."

He nodded. They didn't touch; the moment felt too solemn and too fraught to add any other element to it.

Trevor said, "Do you think you will ever choose to be implanted yourself?"

"No. Is that a condition of ... of us?"

"No. Neither is your continuing on with the project indefinitely. People do manage long-distance relationships, Caro. If necessary, we can do that. Or I may become disillusioned about the project after I'm implanted. Or you may become convinced. We have to wait and see. Not completely satisfactory, but there it is."

"Yes," Caro said. *There it is.* A life together. He wanted her even if she disagreed with him on the fundamentals of the universe. She wanted him. So much happiness flooded her that she was ashamed. All over the compound, little knots of people were grieving. Watkins had just died—this was a time for grief, not for this warm, all-encompassing happiness.

Unless Samuel Louis Watkins was also happy. Somewhere.

37.

The day after Watkins's cremation, James organized a memorial service in the Wing Two courtyard. Caro sat between Trevor and George, holding George's hand. Julian was the only speaker. He talked about founding the project and its long development. Because the service included James's staff, who never entered Wing Three and knew only that the scientific study concerned brain mapping, Julian's remarks were general and vague. He spoke movingly, but, to Caro, the ceremony had a weirdly deceptive feel. James's workers might be uneducated but they were not stupid. Surely they'd heard rumors, made speculations. However, none of that was evident from their closed, respectful faces.

It was a relief to escape the compound to take Kayla to Ellen.

Trevor offered to go with her, but Caro didn't want anyone else—nothing extra to confuse Ellen. Trevor kissed her and said, "Good luck, love."

Kayla refused to hold Caro's hand as they walked, trailed by Jasmine, from the jeep to the pretty little cottage where Ellen waited. *Let this go well. Please let this go well.*

The sliding glass door to the tiny back deck stood open. Ellen sat in a lawn chair, facing the garden. Nadjla, her nurse, noticed Caro and rose. Ellen did not turn.

Nadjla came swiftly into the cottage and addressed Kayla. "Your mama is waiting for you. She gets tired real easy, though. You won't say or do anything to tire her out, will you, honey?"

Kayla didn't answer. She pushed back her thin shoulders and marched out to the deck. Hastily, Caro followed.

Please don't let Ellen start with "Angelica is dead." Why hadn't she thought of this before? It would only upset Kayla more. Why hadn't—

"Hi, Mom," Kayla said. "I'm here."

Ellen's head swung slowly around. Before Caro could ask the nurse if Ellen was having a bad day, Ellen reached out one tentative finger and just touched Kayla's chin.

"Angelica died," Kayla said, "and I miss her too."

"I know," Ellen said, and then added, her voice as tentative as her touch had been, "But I have you?"

"And I'm not going away from you again. Aunt Caro can't make me." She looked defiantly over her shoulder at Caro, who felt the ground fall away under her.

So that was why Kayla had been so furious with her! Too young to fully understand Ellen's clinical depression nor the danger of suicidal ideation, Kayla had blamed Caro for what the little girl saw as Caro's unnecessary separation of mother and daughter. Then Kayla's rage had spilled over onto everyone else in the compound. Caro should have known, should have foreseen …

Ellen's voice in her head from months ago: *You can't control everything, Caro.*

"Miss Jasmine," Kayla said, " will you go back to that place and pack my suitcase so somebody can bring it here. I'm staying here to take care of Mom."

Ellen said, "Kayla—"

"Okay, will you pack my suitcase *please.*" And then, to Ellen in a softer voice, "She'll bring my kitten, too. You'll like my kitten, Mom. She's white and black and her name is Fluffy."

⪮

Ellen improved daily, but Luskin had not yet given the go-ahead for her implant. Caro and Trevor did more surgeries: a nurse, two techs, Camilla. The new sessions yielded new brain mapping data, which she and Barbara analyzed minutely. The days were full of work, the nights of Trevor. In spare half hours, Caro studied the folders with George's science with greater attention than ever before. She wanted to see what Trevor saw—as long as it did not require abandoning her rational judgment.

Weigert's theory had a lot of respectable antecedents, going back over a hundred years. A great many physicists had seriously posited an ultimate substrate of reality made up of consciousness, or something like consciousness, or something not quite like consciousness but able to be controlled by consciousness.

Nobel laureate Max Planck, regarding consciousness as fundamental to the universe: "I regard matter as derivative from consciousness."

Astronomer Royal Martin Rees, who insisted that the universe could only come into existence if someone observed it, even if that observer turned up "several billion years later. The universe exists because we are aware of it."

And more Nobelists: Wigner, Schrödinger, Matloff.

Finally, she tried to read Stephen Hawking, who believed that "there is no way to remove the observer—us—from our perceptions of the world ... the past, like the future, is indefinite and exists only as a spectrum of possibilities."

The past as a spectrum of possibilities. If Caro could create a new past for herself, what would that look like? How far back would she go—childhood, med school, Fairleigh Memorial before Paul Becker's party?

No. Because then she would not have met Trevor.

Then all such theoretical speculation shattered when the FBI returned, this time bringing with them Island police and New York City homicide detectives.

38.

The little conference room behind the security office had not been intended to hold so many people: Julian, Aiden, Weigert, Caro, Trevor, and the FBI agents Caro had met before, Hannah Kaplow and Greg Logan. The three strangers were introduced as Captain Sebastian Ebanks, Area Commander Royal Cayman Islands Police Service; Detective Nicole Bodden, NYPD; and FBI cyberforensics expert Henry Smith. Smith was dressed in khakis and an ill-fitting sports coat and looked about fourteen years old. He looked, in fact, uncannily like Julian's young techs, with an expression that somehow combined abstraction with hectic frowns.

Julian said to Caro and Trevor, "I've already told the agents that we're not answering any questions until our attorney arrives. Fortunately, Mr. Haggerty happened to already be on his way to Brac on an unrelated matter."

Agent Kaplow said, "Then we'll just use this time for a general update. As Mr. Dey already knows, the FBI formed a joint task force with the NYPD to investigate Benjamin Clarby's murder in New York."

That was more than Caro knew, although it explained Detective Bodden's presence. Julian had not kept Caro up to date. In his eyes, this was not her or Trevor's concern; only surgery was. Unless ... Was it possible the cops were here to investigate Watkins's death? Did they somehow suspect that Julian ...

They didn't. Agent Kaplow said, "You already know that we are looking at a person of interest for Clarby's murder"—

Caro did not know that, either—"and we're pursuing that. But now we're concerned with your research here, and the theft of brain mapping data which you claimed occurred. Henry?"

The cyberforensic expert might look fourteen, but his voice was deep and assured. "What I'm going to show you is a website with restricted, password-abled access, taken off the Dark Web. If you're not familiar with that term, it's the often-criminal underbelly of the worldwide web, on which you can buy or sell pretty much anything, from arms to child pornography. Users and locations can't be traced due to a heavily layered encryption system. This laptop has no Internet connection; you're viewing a stored copy of the website."

Caro had heard of the Dark Web, but only vaguely. She watched Henry Smith open a laptop, turn it on, and bring up a program. Caro peered at it through an opening between Weigert's and Trevor's shoulders.

Flashy graphics of assault weapons, missile launchers, grenades in action, all set to raucous music. A title appeared: ALTERNATE MAYHEM. The music stopped and a voice disguised by some sort of synthesis said, "Want to assault anything and anyone you choose in a universe you design? This is not a video game—this is a genuine alternate universe with real people in it who will continue on after you've had a satisfying day of revenge and go back to your usual life. How is that possible? Science, my itchy-triggered friends, creating another branch of the multiverse just as real as this one. Science pioneered by a Nobel Prize winner, and soon to be explained in a book by a major physicist. Science and justice—for *you*. Create whoever you want in your personal universe—and do whatever you want there. Like this, with one of our users and a bitch who tried to use him."

The graphics disappeared, replaced by an image of a man in a black ski mask, lying on a cot. Familiar lead wires connected his head to a computer. The image jolted slightly, the wires dissolved, and he rose and walked past a bank of computers toward a door. Something turned over in Caro's stomach. Was it possible she was looking at a duplicate of the machinery in the sessions room? Dimly she recalled someone—Julian?—saying that Clarby could have been feeding information to his "buyer" for years.

The man stepped through the door into a small chamber, where he strapped on a belt of grenades and picked up an AR-15 assault rifle. He opened a second door.

A shopping mall. Target, Chipotle, Nordstrom, a food court, more. People with colorful shopping bags, strollers, soft pretzels. Self-conscious teenage girls, mothers pulling along reluctant children, men and women in business suits. Someone saw the armed and masked man and opened her mouth in a silent scream.

He smiled slowly, a grin made more horrible by the ski mask surrounding his mouth, and aimed his weapon at a woman who turned just in time to see him, but not in time to run before he fired. And then went on firing.

Caro couldn't look away. There was no sound, but her horrified mind supplied it as bodies jerked and splattered, some propelled several feet. Blood, limbs, brains ... Oh God, brains ... *minds* ...

After what seemed like hours but must have been only a few minutes, the man stopped, smiled again, threw a grenade, and vanished.

Back to graphics of weapons. The disguised voice-over said, "That guy got to give that bitch and her friends exactly what she had coming to her. And so can you. Remember, this is not a video game. This is a real, alternate universe, and we can put you there. Not cheap, no, but what price the chance to return again and again to your own private playground, where you are untouchable and they have to cope with whatever you choose to do? Payment can be in Bitcoin, WebMoney, Perfect Money. Or, if you prefer a sexier version of an alternate universe, here's what you can have with any partner, or partners, you want, willing or not, legal or not—"

Agent Kaplow said, "Stop there," and Smith turned off the program.

"We found this," Kaplow said, "because we were following leads to Clarby's murder. His body had a strange patch on the skull where it looked like skin had been torn off, and the autopsy revealed what the pathologist said were lead wires for Deep Brain Stimulation therapy. There's no record of Clarby having any medical condition that would require that. Then, last night in Manhattan, a man went to an ER with a bad infection. A doctor saw that the skin on his skull had been ripped the same way as Clarby's, and that spot was the infection site. He notified the police. We talked to both doctor and patient.

"This website is connected with Clarby, isn't it? To the data that you claim Clarby stole. The mall is a real place; we've identified it. Nothing happened there. But what we don't know is what this so-called recording is. Smith says the programming code is not remotely like any video game—"

"*Not,*" Smith said, with surprising force. "*Definitely* not."

"—that he's ever seen. So tell me, Mr. Dey and the rest of you who have something to contribute—what exactly are we looking at here?"

39.

Weigert felt paralyzed.

Bill Haggerty arrived, and Weigert listened to him and Julian discuss the situation, away from the authorities. Julian stressed cooperation; Haggerty stressed legalities. Then, with the lawyer paying close attention, Weigert answered the FBI's questions. He explained the physics of "exactly what we are looking at here." Julian translated that physics into non-scientific metaphors. Caroline and Trevor answered medical questions. And all the while Weigert stood paralyzed while a tsunami of horror swelled just beyond his small safe island of physics. A monstrous, sickly wave rolling toward his island to drown him. To drown everything.

The officers were there such a long time. An eternity.

The officers were there no time at all.

Subjective time, objective time … but there was no objective time, there never had been, only the dark wave sweeping endlessly toward him …

"So you're telling me," Agent Kaplow said, "that this 'implant' enables a person to enter an alternate universe and commit the consequence-free murder of actual human beings?" Clearly she didn't believe a word of anything Julian or Weigert had said, but the terrible phrase echoed and re-echoed in Weigert's mind.

Consequence-free murder of actual human beings … *consequence-free murder …*

He was going to vomit. Was going to faint. The wave the wave the wave—

Then Rose's hand was under his elbow, steadying him. Only of course it wasn't Rose, it was Caroline. "George, you should lie down. Agents, can't you see"—anger in her voice—"that Dr. Weigert isn't well? Do you need any more answers from him?"

They did not. They didn't want physics, they wanted only to measure the horror, which wasn't measurable because it was infinite. Caroline said, "Dr. Abruzzo can answer the rest of your medical questions," and led Weigert from the conference room, through the security office, to the lobby. Then she was saying something he didn't understand and leading him toward the hospital wing.

"No, no ... I don't ... no ..." Weigert broke away and all at once he was back in his own room with no memory of walking there. He sat on his desk chair, Caroline's arm around his shoulders, and the tsunami rushed ashore and broke, drowning him.

He had done this. His knowledge of how the universe really works. Now living men and women and children—God in Heaven, *children*—shot and bleeding and screaming in pain even after the shooter had left the branch of the universe that his twisted mind had created. A shooter that could return there again, and again, as often as he was connected to the programs Ben Clarby had stolen.

Consequence-free murder—

Rose, help me—

No answer. His mind could not conjure a Rose who co-existed with this loathsome horror.

Which he had made possible.

He wrapped his arms around Caroline's waist and hung on, his life raft.

She said, "George, it isn't your fault."

"It is! It is!" He let Caroline go and, suddenly full of anger, stood to face her. "It is our fault! How could it not be? *We* did this, Sam and Julian and I. And we didn't foresee where it could lead, how it could be used!" And then, more quietly, "Oppenheimer."

"No," Trevor Abruzzo said quickly, and when had he arrived? Weigert raised his voice and recited Oppenheimer quoting the *Bhagavad Gita*: "'Now I am become Death, the destroyer of worlds.'"

Caroline said, "Sit down again, George ... All right, you don't have to if you don't want to. But let's consider this logically. You were doing science, looking for truth. I know you still believe in the science behind your theory."

"Of course I believe in the science! It exists! But look what we've done with it!"

"And look what else we've done with it," Caroline said. "You've seen Rose again. My sister will see her dead baby. You've brought hope and comfort to people, and will bring those precious things to more people."

Weigert stared at her. Anger had banished paralysis. All at once his heart hammered in his chest and he couldn't breathe. Sweat poured down his face. His arms flailed, as if he could grasp air with his hands and force it into his lungs.

He couldn't breathe, couldn't breathe ...

"He's having a massive panic attack," Caroline said from a great distance, but it didn't matter because there was no longer any air in the room. After some time or no time, a faint prick as a needle slid into his arm.

≡—

He woke to find himself in the hospital wing. Caroline sat beside his bed, frowning at a tablet. "Caroline?"

She put down the tablet and took his wrist. "How are you, George?" And then, as if she knew it was a stupid question, "Your pulse is normal. I'm going to take the rest of your vitals. Are you still groggy from the meds?"

He was. "You ... drugged me?"

She forced a smile. "That sounds like we addicted you to heroin. It was just Valium, to which you reacted unusually strongly. There, let me just ... Okay, your vitals look good."

His head felt clearer by the second. "Where's Julian?"

"Gathering documents and hard drives for the FBI. They obtained subpoenas. Maybe he's done by now. Do you want me to send for him?"

"No. I want ... The FBI took the hard drives? Everything?"

"Julian said not to worry, he had duplicates of everything in a warehouse somewhere, and his entire army of techs is re-installing hardware and software and running diagnostics. It's a digital factory in Wing Three."

"I want a session. Now."

"The equipment isn't working yet."

"I have to see Rose. I have to."

Caroline said gently, "And you will. Maybe tomorrow. I promise, George."

He nodded, defeated. But tomorrow would come. Then he could replace the image of the shooter from the Dark Web, black ski mask over his face and bloodshed staining his brain, with the image of Rose. His Rose, savior and sanctuary, who would help him find understanding, just as she had always done before.

40.

It was shocking to Caro that after the FBI's shattering revelations, life at the compound went on as before.

In theory, only six people knew about Alternate Mayhem: Julian, Aiden, Weigert, Watkins, Caro, and Trevor. But Julian's techs were all wizards at digital investigation, there were several romantic relationships among techs and nurses, and Caro overheard Ivan Kyven make a joking comment in the refectory: "Well, even if the Fibbies do decide to believe us, they don't have jurisdiction over alleged crimes committed in an alleged universe!" Not funny, and no one laughed. Julian hauled Ivan away and gave him hell.

Weigert spent his time either in his room or in multiverse sessions in Wing Three. Caro and Trevor performed more surgeries. She studied an electronic copy of George's book, spent every night with Trevor, and worked with Barbara on fresh mapping data. Every few days she visited Ellen, usually to find her, Lorraine, and Kayla together. Ellen's nurse had been dismissed. Lorraine made Ellen take walks, play board games with Kayla, pet Fluffy. Lorraine's efforts were only semi-successful; Ellen improved but remained fragile, focused almost solely on seeing Angelica "the way you promised me."

To Caro, accustomed to snow in March, summer came shockingly early to Cayman Brac. Even at night the air stayed hot and humid, disrupted only by the occasional, spectacular afternoon thunderstorm crackling and booming. People checked hurricane warnings every day. When the trade winds blew, a welcome brisk breeze smelled of the sea. Everything not already in flower produced blooms with hectic speed, in preternaturally bright colors. Insects hummed and droned.

"All right," Lyle Luskin finally said after examining Ellen. "I don't think there's anything to be gained by waiting longer. Mrs. Kemp can be implanted."

≡

The OR, like all ORs, was cold. The nurse wheeled in Ellen, Molly administered anesthetic, and Ellen's eyes closed. Trevor cut through her skin, peeled it back, and was handed the bone saw.

Another surgery, like so many before. But this was *Ellen*. Every move that Trevor made tautened Caro's nerves another notch, until they felt ready to snap. If he found something unexpected in the brain, if he made a mistake cutting … But of course he did not.

Ellen woke on schedule in recovery. "Ellen, do you know where you are?"

"Caro … hospital … hurts."

"I'm starting the morphine drip. Just answer a few questions for me. How many fingers am I holding up?"

"Two … Angelica?"

"In a few days. Remember, I told you that first you have to heal from surgery."

"Yes." Ellen's eyelids fluttered, closed, opened again. A faint, woozy, in-pain smile.

Caro had seen that smile on other patients: relief that the surgery was over, that they'd survived it, that a physical problem had been solved. But Ellen did not have a physical problem. She had a vision, a hope, and Caro had given it to her.

"It will be fine," Molly said as she hooked up Ellen's morphine drip. "The multiverse session won't fail her."

"How can you know that?" Caro said. Molly wasn't even implanted.

"I just know it," Molly said, uncharacteristically gentle.

Caro didn't push it. Molly was trying to reassure a friend. But Caro didn't know what she would do if the reality did not live up to whatever images Ellen had already created from longing and loss.

≡

Five days later, Ellen had her session in Wing Three.

She had been quiet and docile during her stay in the hospital, touching the titanium box on her head through her paper hat, eating and walking and doing physical therapy as she was instructed, a model patient but still not Ellen. She had lost a lot of weight. Her tall body, always so solid, had thinned so much that her shirt flapped loosely around her breasts. Her jeans were held up with a belt loaned by one of the nurses. She lay on the cot while Julian explained what was going to happen.

"I know," Ellen said. "Caro told me. I'm ready."

Julian removed the cover of the connector box and hooked the leads to her skull. Caro pulled her chair closer to her sister. Behind her stood Trevor, George, and Molly, but Caro was scarcely aware of them, not even of Trevor.

Ellen's face went blank.

Caro made an inarticulate sound and leaned forward in her chair. She had seen this so many times—but this was *Ellen*. To see her sister in the not-alive-not-dead state, a Schrödinger experiment, disturbed Caro more than she'd expected.

The screen beside the cot brightened.

The image of Ellen rose eagerly from the cot, lead wires gone. She rushed to the door and opened it. The Wing Three courtyard lay beyond, just as Caro had seen it twenty minutes ago, drenched with rain, except that now a toddler squatted on dry grass, trying to shove thick plastic shapes, squares and circles and triangles, through their corresponding holes in the wide lid of a red plastic box.

A sentence from her intense study of George's book came to Caro: *Brain dynamics at the quantum level allow all parts of consciousness to be simultaneously connected: sensory input, memory, imagination, processing algorithms.*

Angelica looked up, saw her mother. Her little face broke into a rosy smile. She stood up on chubby legs in miniature denim shorts and rushed toward Ellen.

Ellen snatched up her daughter—her living, healthy daughter—and hugged her so tightly that Angelica squirmed. Tears coursed down Ellen's thin cheeks.

What would happen if we could change the algorithms that collapse the quantum waves in the brain?

Angelica squirmed harder. Ellen set her down on the grass. Angelica grabbed her mother's hand, tugged her to the plastic pail, and plopped herself down on her diaper-padded bottom. Ellen knelt beside her, and Angelica handed her mother a green plastic circle.

You are the observer. You create the universe every day, every hour, every nano-second. Everything that can exist, will exist, somewhere, including your beloved dead. They can once again be alive, walking around, solid as the chair you sit in now, solid as this book you hold in your hand.

Ellen pretended to put the green circle into a square hole. Angelica scowled, grabbed the plastic shape from Ellen's hand, and showed her how do it right. Mother and daughter put in all the rest of the shapes, took the lid off the box, and dumped out the shapes. Angelica picked up one and ran away with it, squealing happily. And Ellen did what she had never been able to do in this universe: chased her baby in a game of tag.

Kayla appeared from nowhere and joined the joyous running.

Playing with her children, Ellen looked weightless, as if she skimmed over the grass without her feet ever, not even once, touching the ground.

Caro left her chair and slipped from the room. George, finally smiling, didn't even notice her walk past him. Trevor made a move to follow, but Caro waved him off. She needed a minute without even him.

Delusion or reality—and Caro was no longer sure what that word even meant—the session had brought Ellen comfort, had brought Ellen back to herself.

And had made all Caro's choices and compromises and uncertainties worth it.

41.

Caro and Barbara's article was peer reviewed and accepted: "Frontal Lobe Stimulation and Memory-Imagination Imagery Formation," *New England Journal of Medicine*, Caroline J. Soames-Watkins, M.D., Barbara Mumaw, M.D., Samuel L. Watkins, Ph.D. It looked wonderful. Caro had already seen the article online, but that was no substitute for holding the actual journal in her hand. The reproduced mapping images looked amazing, and *NEJM* had used more of them than she and Barbara had initially dared hope.

She had promised Julian a year at the compound. This article was her ticket to eventual interviews for a surgical position in the States, where she could take Ellen and Kayla and support a new life for the three of them. And she and Trevor would manage a long-distance relationship. It wasn't what she really wanted, but they'd discussed it again and again, growing more sure of their need for each other but never coming to a completely satisfactory conclusion. She couldn't imagine what a completely satisfactory conclusion would be.

In the weeks since her implant, Ellen had recovered rapidly from surgery, from hopelessness, from grief. She no longer required therapy. She was Ellen again.

And Kayla, slowly, became Kayla. Once the little girl felt assured that her mother would not leave her again, she began to enjoy the island, the beach, the colorful parrots in the trees. She lost her sullen withdrawal, but she was still wary around Caro.

Caro said, "Come for a drive with me, Kayla. There are new puppies at James's friend's house in Spot Bay."

Kayla looked up from her book. "Mom too?"

Ellen said, by pre-arrangement with Caro, "I'm really tired, honey. You go with Aunt Caro and see the puppies."

"Can Lorrie come?"

"Lorraine went grocery shopping."

"I'll wait for Lorrie."

"Well, all right," Ellen said, "but then you won't see the puppies. They're going tonight to their forever homes on the big island."

Kayla chewed her lip. Puppies were a powerful lure. "Okay, I'll go."

The dogs, brown and white Labs, tumbled over each other to get to Kayla. After a half hour of play in the sunshine, Caro drove her to an ice cream stand. As they licked dripping cones at a picnic bench, Caro said, "You've been mad at me a long time, Kayla."

Kayla said nothing. Her gaze dropped to her sticky hands.

"Are you still mad at me?"

"No. Yes. I don't know!"

"I think you are still mad. You thought I sent your mother away."

Kayla's head jerked up. "You did!"

"I sent her to a hospital because Angelica's death made her very sick. You saw how she was, Kayla. Then I brought her here so she could be with you and so she could see Angelica again in another world. Your mom told you that."

"But you could've sent me with her! To the hospital and to the other world!"

"No, I couldn't. They don't allow children into either place. Would it be fair of me to blame you for things you can't do, like surgery? Would that be fair?"

"Noooo ..." Kayla's ice cream had melted down the sides of the cone and onto her hands. She didn't seem to notice.

"Then please don't be mad at me anymore for things I couldn't do."

"I'm not," Kayla said. And then, stunning Caro, "I'm mad at me."

"Why are you—"

"Because you helped Mom and I didn't. I can't do anything right!"

"Oh, sweetie, you did help! You help every day, just by being Kayla! That helped your mom, and me too. You're a big part of why Mom got better. We both get happier when we see you happy."

"Is that true?"

"It is."

Kayla jumped up and hugged Caro, squishing both their cones into Caro's breasts. Caro didn't care. Kayla had Ellen's bravery—how many nine-year-olds could recognize their own errors of judgment, let alone admit them out loud?

But mixed with Caro's pride and relief was the small, inevitable sorrow known to anyone who loves a child's unfiltered emotions: Kayla was growing up.

≡

Trevor left for a long weekend in Boston, to see his sister and nephew before his own implant surgery. After Caro drove him to the airport, she headed to the beach to meet Ellen, Kayla, Molly, Barbara, and—it turned out—Lorraine.

After everyone had a swim, Caro, Ellen, and Molly lounged on blankets. Barbara went to find a bathroom. Kayla and Lorraine built an elaborate sandcastle, Kayla running excitedly back and forth with pails of water to moisten the white sand. "Lorrie, let's make a tower!" Kayla said happily. "A really tall tower with a feather on top! Mom, you and Aunt Caro help, too!"

Ellen said, "Sure! I'll go find the feather."

Caro said, "I'll stay here with Molly. You have plenty of builders already."

When they were alone, Molly said, "Caro, what's your problem with Lorraine?"

Caro almost said she had no problem with Lorraine, but this was Molly, who had only the haziest notion of personal boundaries and who, in Barbara's temporary absence, would dig and dig until she got an answer that satisfied her.

Caro said carefully, "Lorraine is so changed since her implant. It makes me uneasy."

"Why?"

"Well, she's the only one whose personality seems different than before. Nothing about insertion of wire leads should have that effect."

"I don't think it did," Molly said. "I've known her a lot longer than you have, and I always thought those hyper-theatrics—unlike *my* theatrics, of course—were a cover for ... I don't know, some kind of despair that the world didn't make sense to her. Now it does."

"I guess. Everybody's different."

Molly propped herself up on one elbow and looked sharply at Caro. "Don't give me half-hearted platitudes, Caro. Or evasions. You have some deeper problem with Lorraine. Everybody's noticed it. It's Ellen, isn't it?"

"What gives 'everybody' the right to gossip about—"

"Oh, don't resort to indignation. We care about you. You're jealous of Ellen's friendship with Lorraine, and you're upset because Ellen wants to stay here permanently even if you leave. But that doesn't mean ... Oh Christ, Ellen didn't tell you that yet. Did she?"

"Stay here?" Caro repeated. "Why would Ellen—"

"She likes it. She and Lorraine are going to rent a cottage together in Stake Bay. I'm sorry, I thought she already told you and that's why you and she seem so—"

"She can't! What would she live on? Julian isn't going to just support her forever!"

Molly brushed sand off the edge of the blanket and spoke very carefully. "Ellen has taken a job as secretary at West End Primary School, where Kayla will start school in September. I'm sorry. I really thought you already knew all this."

"I didn't!"

"I see that now. But, Caro, as your friend, I have to add one thing more, and you're not going to like it. I know, from what you've said, and what Ellen has said, that you've rescued Ellen all your lives. You've been wonderful, and she knows it. But she doesn't need rescuing any more. She wants to stand on her own two feet."

"Or on Lorraine's!" Caro said furiously, stupidly, painfully, just as Barbara dropped onto the blanket with a string bag full of sodas and said, "Let's toast the publication of our article with a nutritionally terrible sugar high!"

At the compound, just after Caro had shed her sandy bikini and showered, Ellen knocked on her door.

"Caro, it's me. We have to talk."

"It's not really a good time," Caro said.

Ellen opened the door and walked in.

"Damn it, I just said—"

"I know what you said, Sissy. I won't stay long. But Molly just told me—"

"Too many damn people tell too many things around here!"

Ellen smiled. "True. Also true of every other place on Earth. Caro, just listen to me for five minutes."

Caro nodded, because what else could she do? Lyle Luskin declared himself astonished at the speed of Ellen's further recovery since she began "visiting" Angelica. To Caro, however, Ellen still looked fragile. Or—she heard this in Molly's voice inside her head—did Caro just need her to be fragile?

Damn your interference, Molly.

Ellen said, "I realize how much I owe you, and I hope you know that I realize it. Without your financial help, I couldn't have cared for Angelica at home as long as I did. You arranged for that wonderful hospital on Grand Cayman, and you took care of Kayla while I was there. I know Julian paid for things, but I'm guessing that's because you made me a condition of you doing surgery here. And most of all, I owe you for giving me back Angelica. I know she's not really dead, just living and healthy and happy elsewhere, because death doesn't really exist. How could there be any greater gift than that? I owe you everything, Caro."

Caro's throat thickened. She couldn't find any answer.

Ellen said, "But that's exactly why I want to stay here, even after you get a real job back home someplace. I want to stay partly to go on seeing Angelica whenever I can, but also because I love it here and so does Kayla. Tomorrow I'm flying back to Fairleigh to get Kayla's school records and deal with that storage locker Julian rented for my furniture and stuff. There's a lot of things to wrap up. Lorrie will help me, and Jasmine will stay with Kayla. I need to ... Don't be angry, Caro, *please*. I need to do this on my own. To show myself that I can."

"You won't be alone. You'll be with Lorraine." Immediately Caro wanted to cut out her own tongue. Petty, spiteful, selfish ...

But Ellen only smiled. "Lorraine can never replace you, Caro. No one ever can. But she's at loose ends herself, and we can help each other."

"Doesn't she teach somewhere? Some college in the States?"

"She resigned. That isn't where her spirit is anymore."

"And so you'll support her?"

"Lorraine and Julian have family money. I'm sure you already know that. She can pay her share. But not mine. She won't be taking care of me the way you did. If anything, she's the one who needs me while she figures out what to do with the rest of her life."

"Which you already figured out for your life."

"I'm trying. You *are* upset. Please don't be. I love you so much." Ellen put her arms around her sister and hugged her tight.

When Caro could trust her voice, she said, "I'm glad we talked like this."

"No, you're not," Ellen said, sounding exactly like the old Ellen, Caro's Ellen. "But maybe you will be glad later. And everything will be all right."

≡

When Trevor returned from Boston, he knew instantly that she was troubled. Caro told him about Ellen's decision, about her own confusion. "I keep thinking I should stay here indefinitely, with you and Ellen."

"No," Trevor said. "That's not you, Caro. You're not implanted, you don't want to be implanted, and you want to do more ambitious surgery. Your skill—and gods know you struggled hard enough to acquire that skill—needs a more varied arena. You won't lose me, or Ellen. Not ever."

His understanding, his emotional generosity, overwhelmed her. "I don't think Ellen needs me anymore."

"Maybe not," he said, "but I do."

42.

Every technology is used before it is completely understood. There is always a lag between an innovation and the apprehension of its consequences.

The quote from George's book popped into Caro's mind as Trevor was being wheeled into the OR. Who had said it? Leon Somebody, Whistler or Wenter or Weister, something like that. She had no idea why she recalled it now, but it had something to do with Trevor looking small and helpless under a heated white blanket. He wore a hospital gown, a catheter, and a smile for her that could have ignited a supernova. Caro's heart tore down its seam.

"Hi, Doc," he said.

"Ready?"

"Yes. Cut away."

As Molly put Trevor under and Ralph Egan stood by as backup, Trevor kept his gaze locked on Caro until the last possible moment. When he was out, Caro's mind clicked into professional mode and he wasn't Trevor any longer, he was a skull and a brain—mostly, anyway.

The implant went flawlessly. She left Ralph to close, went into the scrub room, leaned on both hands against the sink, and closed her eyes for a long moment. Then she stripped off her gloves and gown and shoved them into the biowaste bin. Trevor could now enter into a world of his own making, or imagining, or something. And Caro could not.

Always a lag between an innovation and the apprehension of its consequences.

Leon, baby, you had no idea.

≡

The day after Trevor's surgery was publication date for George's book, *The Primacy of the Observer*. Caro organized a small celebration at dinner in the refectory. George smiled when toasts were made. He handled the one copy he had of his book with pleasure. More copies were delayed somewhere in transit. He made a short speech of thanks to everyone involved in the project, despite getting some of the young techs' names wrong. George seemed happier than at any time since the FBI agents had shown the Alternate Mayhem video, and Caro was glad for him.

Trevor recovered well from surgery. Five days afterward, he had his first session in Wing Three. Uncharacteristically, his expression gave nothing away. However, because Caro knew him so well, she sensed his suppressed excitement, his intense concentration, his determination to assess the experience as objectively as he could.

He lay on the cot and Aiden hooked him to the machinery. Caro's stomach clenched. What if—a fear that she finally admitted to herself—Trevor's session changed him, as Lorraine had been changed? Trevor, with his irreverent wit and sharp mind, but also his youthful desire for monkhood ... Was there a possibility he could become as smoothed out, as otherworldly, as Lorraine? Caro loved Trevor as he was. She did not want to find herself dating the Great Cosmic Everything.

Then the moment she always disliked, but never more than with Trevor: his mind departed. His face emptied of everything that made him Trevor.

The screen brightened.

The image of Trevor rose from the bed, but, unlike every other implantee, he did not go toward the door. He walked to one of the chairs against the wall, carried it to the center of the room, and stood behind it with one hand resting on its back. He turned toward the door, looking expectant.

What was he doing?

The door opened and Julian walked in. Caro felt the jerk of surprise from the Julian in the room with her—the "real Julian" in her mind—and then his displeasure. So he hadn't known that Trevor was going to put him into this alternate universe. The on-screen Julian crossed the room and shook hands with Trevor, leaning awkwardly over the chair between them. Then Julian left the room.

George entered—another start of surprise beside Caro—shook hands, left. Aiden, then Barbara ... What was Trevor doing? And was she next?

She was not. James was next, then Molly. After Molly left, Trevor walked around the chair and stared at it for long, silent minutes.

What the hell ...

It was a completely unremarkable chair, of the kind found throughout the compound: steel supports and arms, fake leather seat and backrest, both dull black. More just like it stood against the far wall. Caro had sat in at least one of them before, maybe this one.

The session abruptly ended.

Julian said, "What the fuck was *that*?"

"An experiment," Trevor said from the cot. His voice sounded thick.

"An experiment? How? You never left the room! And the test-subject agreement you signed forbid any creation of anyone in the compound that—"

"I know," Trevor said, "but I didn't do anything with any of you except shake hands. You weren't the focus of the experiment."

"We weren't the—"

"No. The chair was."

Trevor sat up, and Caro got a better look at his face. She'd seen faces like that before, but not for a long time. Ellen, decades ago, on Christmas morning. Ethan, Kayla, maybe even Caro herself. A child gazing at wondrous, miraculous gifts heaped under a tree ablaze with lights.

"It's real," Trevor said. "It *is* real. I created that chair in the branch universe. There were only four in this room and in my branch there were five."

Caro tried to remember how many chairs had appeared on the screen. She hadn't noticed.

"Six people entered that room and saw that chair. They had to, where I positioned it. After each of them left, I tried to change the chair any way I could, to imagine that it was green, or wicker, or Louis Quatorze. I'm an adept at lucid dreaming, studied it for years. If this had been a dream or a hallucination, I would have been able to alter the chair at will. I've done it nightly in dreams ever since I read George's book. But I *could not alter the chair*, because six other observers had contributed to its decoherence, and it existed as reality, not as hallucination or dream or drastically heightened imagination. As real as anything in this room, right now. If the chair is real, then so is the rest of that branch universe. George's theory is right. It's *right*, Julian."

"I never doubted it," Julian said tartly, but she sensed the complex emotion under the tartness, including chagrin that he hadn't thought of this experiment himself. He said, "Barbara?"

"Caro and I need more time with the mapping data, of course, but at first glance it resembles everybody else's session except for increased activity in that part of the frontal lobe that handles judgment and reasoning."

Caro felt cold. This was … What *was* this? Trevor's gaze was on her. She smiled at him, but her first coherent thought was: *Jesus Carrots, wasn't this universe hard enough to live in without adding any other universes?*

Jesus Carrots. Her father's favorite exclamation. She hadn't thought of it in years and years. It had always sent her, Ethan, and even toddler Ellen into gales of laughter.

Ivan rushed into the room and handed Julian a piece of paper. He read it, and his eyes darkened from turquoise to navy.

George said, "Julian? What is it? What's happened?"

"Meeting. Now, with all of you. Aiden, unhook Trevor. Ivan, you too."

They followed him to the big conference table, and Julian read the paper aloud.

It was a printout of an article in the *Florida Town Crier*. The headline screamed in thick black letters: NOBEL LAUREATE'S SECRET MIND-CONTROL EXPERIMENTS PROVE LIFE AFTER DEATH! FBI INVOLVED! The brief article, equally sensationalized, made the compound sound like a cross between a Satanic cult and *The Manchurian Candidate*.

Barbara said, "Nobody trusts the *Crier*. It's a yellow-journalism rag just one step above a supermarket tabloid. Maybe not even one step."

Julian said tightly, "Better journalists will investigate. Because of Sam's name."

Ivan said, "If they find the Dark Web stuff ..."

"They might, even though the FBI keeps taking down the website. Then the bastards put it up again under a different name."

George, bewildered, said, "But they don't need to 'investigate' anything. It's all there in my book already! We *want* the public to know about my theory!"

"Not like this," Julian said. "Also, the article has details about the project that only someone in the compound would know. Did any of you talk to the reporter? Or anyone else?"

Indignant denials. Julian said, "I didn't think so, but we need to talk to everyone who's ever set foot in Wing Three. I'm afraid a shitstorm is about to break over the entire project."

43.

Julian was right. Three days later, Susan Crittendon, Pulitzer-winning journalist at the *New York Times*, called Julian. "Someone contacted her directly," he said, "a source she won't name, but she says it's someone intimately familiar with the compound. She profiled Watkins once, two decades ago. Now she's reading George's book and she wants to talk to us—me, George, and the 'hospital surgeons.' Her source told her that we're doing scientific research into death."

George said, "But that isn't—"

"Not our main focus, no," Julian said. "But 'universes created by the primacy of the observer' is too intellectual. Death is visceral. Greater public appeal."

Caro said, "I won't talk to her."

"Fucking right you won't. Nobody will, except me. All information goes through me. And I'm going to find out who inside the compound is Susan Crittenden's source." His handsome face looked as contorted as it had after Ben Clarby's disappearance and subsequent murder.

Trevor said slowly, "If she finds out about the Dark Web site ... She's an experienced and respected journalist. She may very well have sources in the FBI."

"Yes," Julian said. "I wanted to release our story in ways we can control, when we were ready. *Not* like this."

The *Times* article appeared a week later. Julian and Bill Haggerty had warned off Susan Crittendon, saying that writing anything about Alternate Mayhem would interfere with an on-going FBI investigation. The journalist apparently got around that by first leaking to a TV station, which let the *Times* jump in with her much fuller print version because the story was already public.

"SCIENTIFIC" FACILITY IN CAYMANS IMPLANTS COMPUTER CHIPS IN HUMAN BRAINS

Deceased Nobel Laureate Funded Bizarre Experiment

by Susan Crittenden

On the tropical island of Cayman Brac, a popular tourist destination in the Caribbean, stands a facility founded by late Nobel laureate Samuel Louis Watkins and staffed by an eclectic collection of software experts, doctors, and physicists. The facility serves people willing to have their skulls cut open and their brains implanted with pre-programmed, permanent computer chips. Wires lead from the chips to a connector terminal on the top of each subject's head. When not in use, the terminal is covered by a tiny titanium box. When in use, the wires directly connect the subject's brain to a bank of computers.

Why would anyone create this experiment in sci-fi cyborgs? And why would anyone agree to become an experimental subject?

The answer begins not with Watkins, the famed creator of the molecules that led to the development of Achino, the most popular anti-viral drug in the world. Before Watkins, there was his close friend from their university days at Oxford. George J. Weigert, 76, a distinguished physicist who has published many studies in peer-reviewed journals, created a theory called The Primacy of the Observer, which is also the title of his recent book from a prestigious academic press. The book has raised many eyebrows throughout the scientific community. The heart of Weigert's biocentric theory is that instead of matter and evolution giving rise to consciousness, the truth is the other way around. Consciousness gave rise to both matter and time. Nothing—not the Earth, the galaxy, your kitchen, or even your brain—existed before human consciousness created it. Weigert's book, well written and full of references to accepted science, explains this in great, if esoteric, detail.

The story does not stop there. Eventually Watkins and Weigert joined forces with Julian Dey, 38, once a rising star in the tech world of Silicon Valley. The three built a secret compound on Cayman Brac and launched their project. According to a person who has been implanted with one of their chips, they succeeded in creating software that lets an implantee be connected to programming that activates "alternate universe algorithms" in the brain. The subject then can visit—not just visualize, but actually visit—alternate universes in which things have turned out differently than in the universe the rest of us inhabit. "There, you can be well again if you're sick here," the implantee said. "You can meet people who have died here. You can visit a world that looks like this one, but is kinder or more beautiful. And it is real."

There is no doubt that the speaker believes all this. So, presumably, do the roughly two dozen other people thus far implanted with computer chips. Very advanced image-reconstruction software even records what is going on in the brain while the subject is "away" from this world. "You can revisit not only the other universe," the implantee said, "but can view your recording again and again."

The brain chips are allegedly implanted by licensed surgeons; so far the Times has not learned their names. None of the experimental subjects have, according to this reporter's source, paid any fee for the surgery, computer chip, or digital-equipment use. All necessary permits for a scientific research facility are on file with the Cayman Brac government, and the facility pays the necessary taxes. The Cayman Islands, long known as a haven of very loose regulations on finance, medical research, and visa requirements for those with enough money to buy their way in, has raised no objection to, or perhaps has no knowledge of, the activities inside the walled compound. But others clearly do.

Blood And Murder In An Alternate Universe

Currently the FBI is conducting an investigation into a Dark Web site that also promises trips into alternate universes. The site has gone by various names and is not easy to find unless you already have access code words. The Times was able to learn only that it offers to implant subjects, for a hefty fee, with computer chips similar, or possibly identical, to those used on Cayman Brac. Speculation is that software was stolen from the original facility by someone familiar with it.

The Dark Web site lets its implantees, armed with weapons created by their consciousness, to "enter" another universe and kill, maim, or torture without consequence to the implantee after he "returns" here. Conduct a school shooting, run a concentration camp, torture an enemy. If the Cayman Brac facility says it is expanding the world through hallucinations cherished by the hopeful, the Dark Web site is exploiting those whose hopes represent the worst that humanity is capable of.

But is any of it "real"? Or does it all, knowingly or not, traffic in high-tech snake oil? Reactions to Weigert's book have varied widely. Eminent Yale professor Thomas Donovan, himself a Nobel laureate for his work on gravity waves, said this yesterday to the Times ...

Reporters and TV crews began to arrive at the compound. Julian said, "Nobody talks to any media. In fact, nobody leaves the compound or talks to anyone at all. Camilla, instruct your nurses and orderlies. James, send home everyone that doesn't live in Wing One, and everyone who does live here but won't or can't stay inside for a few days. Tell them they aren't to talk to anyone about anything they've seen or heard here. Not *any-one*, even family members. Threaten them if you have to."

Caro said, "Julian, you can't threaten people. You'll only make the situation worse."

He glared at her. "Worse? And just how would that look, Caro? We're doing something good here, something revolutionary and ground-breaking that can bring hope and insight to the entire fucking world. And now the story is going to be some sensationalized woo-woo spiritual out-of-body astral projection, combined with gore and blood. Our work was supposed to be established first with the scientific community and then, as they were won over by sheer irrefutable logic, they would help bring it to the popular press in a respectful and prestigious way. *That* was Sam's vision. Not this."

Trevor said quietly, "We can weather this."

Could they? Caro wondered. And what would happen if they couldn't?

Trevor added, "Julian, you need another lawyer besides Bill Haggerty, one that specializes in defamation. And you need to hire a PR firm."

"I already have," Julian said. "One with experience in cleaning up corporate messes on all platforms, including on- and offline. Their people will be in and out of the compound, but I don't want anyone but me talking to them, either."

Caro was fine with that. She wondered, however, how different her life would now be if she'd had the money to hire an online PR person to fight the social media attacks against her after she'd filed her sexual harassment charge against Paul Becker.

Another branch of a different universe.

≡

Caro said to Trevor, her naked leg flung over his on her bed, "Why do you think the project can weather all this negative publicity?"

"Because truth will out. Eventually."

She raised herself on one elbow to see his face. "Do you really believe that?"

"Yes. But only if people fight for it. I don't think there's any chance that Julian won't fight. And he has the resources—money, connections, solid research, and sheer animal cunning—to fight like hell."

That she didn't doubt. She said instead, "Trev, who do you think leaked the story to those two reporters?"

"I don't know. But I know who's the most upset about it, and it isn't even Julian. It's George."

"I talked to him today, for a long time," Caro said. "He's heartbroken."

≣

Weigert did not understand.

This was not what he had envisioned. His theory, his precious discovery and Julian's application of it, was a force for *good*. It described the world as it actually was, of course, but it also had the power to remake the world. It restored humanity to the center of reality, because it was life—us—that created reality. It removed barriers between a human being and nature. Surely that must lead to care of the environment, because the environment was *you*. One doesn't war on oneself.

He'd imagined a world where, as people began to see the truth of a consciousness-centered universe, they would come to understand that other people, too, were intimately connected to them. They would then become kinder to each other. All men would truly become brothers because they were all sharers in the consciousness that shaped the world.

And death! Death, too, would no longer trouble the human mind, wrapping it in a shroud of fear. Weigert had talked to Rose. Ellen Kemp had held her dead baby. Consciousness, not being material, could not die. It was even possible that Sam, if his body died during a session (Julian still denied this), had found himself in a state that was the superposition of all possible worlds, all possible experiences. And that his consciousness had collapsed into the single determined experience of his session. There was no way to be sure, of course, since there was no way to have communication between branches. But ... it was possible!

And then this journalist, this Susan Crittendon—she had read his book, she said so in her *Times* article—willfully misrepresented it all. Why couldn't she see all the good that a consciousness-centered explanation of the world could bring? He did not understand how an obviously intelligent woman could be so blind. Could write ... *this*.

Rose, what should I do?

Nothing, my darling. Just wait and see what happens.

Not enough, this Rose in his mind. He wanted to talk to the real Rose, hold her in his arms, smell her vanilla-and-roses hair. Weigert wasn't scheduled for a session, but he would get a tech to hook him up and supervise. He would *bully* a young tech into doing it, if necessary. After all, he was the author of *The Primacy of Consciousness*. His book was remaking the framework of contemporary physics, and he wanted to see his wife.

44.

Internet sales of George's book skyrocketed, until it temporarily reached number four on the non-fiction bestseller list,
behind two racy Hollywood memoirs and a diet book.

Online reactions to the *Times* article were ubiquitous,
heated, and often vicious. Mind control! Human lab rats!
Death cult! Caro realized that the battle for the project's public
reputation was going to be fought not in the scientific journals
but where all battles were fought now, in the media.

She stood in the security office and surveyed the scene
outside the compound gate as captured on external cameras.
Reporters had accumulated like beach flotsam after a storm
at sea. Vans and cars parked willy-nilly with a big tarp strung
between two vans to create shade, lawn chairs crowding
underneath. A woman sunbathed in a tiny bikini on a huge
beach towel. Reporters talked into booms suspended over
their heads by sound crews. An enterprising Island truck
sold coffee and sandwiches from its open side. Styrofoam
cups littered the ground. A Honey Bucket shed stood under
a tree.

Through the chaos, Ellen threaded her way toward the
gate, immediately set upon by people shouting questions.

Julian said to Caro, "And she didn't tell you why she's coming?"

"No. You said that cell conversations might be picked up
with the right equipment. She just told me that's it's urgent but
isn't about Kayla or Lorraine."

The mob tried to follow her inside but were pushed back and the gate closed. Ellen, swollen-eyed and pale as beach sand, looked even worse than Julian. She was trembling. "Sissy?" Caro said, and moved toward her. But Ellen looked straight at Julian, who seemed to have turned to stone, and her voice held steady.

"It was me, Julian. I leaked about the project to a *Florida Town Crier* reporter that I happened to sit next to on the plane to the States. And when that article was so awful, I called the *New York Times* to get a better reporter. It was me.

"I didn't know all this would happen, or anything about the horrible Dark Web stuff. I just wanted people to know that their dead loved ones aren't really dead. I just wanted to share this incredible miracle you all created because it seemed so wrong to keep it to ourselves. I just wanted to help with other people's terrible grief, like you helped with mine.

"I just wanted to help."

Caro couldn't find words. She stared at her sister, who stared back for a long moment and then began to sob. "I'm sorry! I'm sorry! I didn't realize!"

Familiarity rushed over Caro like a spring breeze. This she understood. Ellen was in trouble, and Caro again had words, actions, attitudes.

"Don't," she said to Julian, who'd opened his mouth to speak. "She only meant to help." Caro put her arms around Ellen, and Ellen, taller by six inches, bent to bury her head in Caro's neck and hang on.

George—and where had he come from?—said quietly, "Take her to your room, Caroline, and stay under the walkways. There are drones with cameras flying around out there."

By the time they'd reached the safety of Caro's room— that's how she thought of it now: "safety"—Ellen had stopped sobbing. She sank into Caro's desk chair. Caro took the bed.

Ellen said, "I didn't think it would go like this."

"I know you didn't. I know that."

"What do you want me to do?"

Caro tried to think. "Where's Kayla?"

"At the airport. She and Lorraine are going to board a plane in less than an hour."

"A plane?"

"Yes. I don't want all those reporters with their TV and online shows bothering Kayla. They would, wouldn't they? I'm sending her and Lorraine back home. Mrs. Foster said she'd put them both up until we can make other arrangements. I called her."

It took Caro a moment to remember who Mrs. Foster was. The leader of the church ladies, Ellen's former neighbors who'd organized Angelica's funeral. Napoleon with a stew ladle.

"Where did you get the—"

"Lorraine paid for the airline tickets. Caro, I'll do whatever you and Julian want me to."

"I don't know what that could be. But Ellen—"

Caro couldn't say it, not any of it. This was Ellen, who always acted from the heart, and that heart a generous one filled with concern and kindness for other people. For her father, bullied and belittled by his wife. For Angelica, a child so disabled that most mothers would have institutionalized her. For all those people out there who grieved for their dead. There wasn't enough kindness, enough genuinely sweet natures, in the world. Caro knew that she herself did not possess one.

Nor did Julian. He would throw Ellen to the journalistic lions if it would help the project: *Not a reliable source, recent mental patient, misunderstood the work here ...*

"You're going to need to leave Cayman Brac as soon as possible," Caro said.

"But you said Julian would have to decide what—"

"*I'm* deciding. I don't think the two reporters you talked to will reveal their sources, but you just walked into the compound ten minutes ago, so eventually the others in that mob out there will identify you as my sister."

"How?"

"I don't know how they do those things—facial recognition software, maybe? But they do it. We have to get you out of here." She thought quickly. "I'm going to talk to James."

Ellen left the compound in a grocery delivery truck, dressed in work clothes supplied by James, with a plane ticket to follow Lorraine and Kayla off-island.

Julian, to Caro's surprise, did not berate her for this: "As long as you're sure she won't do any further blabbing!"

It was a measure of his agitation that he used an un-Julian word like "blabbing."

"She won't," Caro said.

The PR firm crafted an alternate view to the *Times* article, designed to accomplish three things: put the project's work in positive terms, sound scientific "rather than woo-woo New Age," and offer the public something they might want. PR did a credible job, although Caro and Trevor were surprised to discover that the project now had a catchy name.

"RealityCheck?" Caro said. "Wasn't that a rock band in the 1990s?"

"I don't know, and how do you know? You were in grade school!"

Ethan, six years older, had liked Reality Check.

Trevor said, "The PR people are creating an interactive public website for us—which, incidentally, is putting Julian's techies in a snit since they're all convinced they could do it better. The PR cyberpeople are also manipulating what comes up on Google and other search engines. I don't know how they do that, but apparently only 47% of Google users go beyond the first two search results, and 89% don't look past the first page, so they want to control what is seen first. At the meeting you skipped— No, it's all right, Caro. There's no reason for you to go. I'll be your conduit for information."

YouTube videos were made. Statistically valid samples of posts on Facebook, Instagram, Twitter, and selected other social media were analyzed. The dominant reaction was skepticism, which at least was better than vicious contempt, although there was enough of that to sicken Caro.

Trevor said, "Schopenhauer: 'All truth passes through three stages. First, it is ridiculed. Second, it's violently opposed. Third, it is accepted as being self-evident.'"

"I don't think," Caro said, "that these trolls have read Schopenhauer."

"No. But Julian's PR people are going to launch phase two: mounting a serious campaign in serious popular venues. That's what Julian told me he'd really wanted to do in the first place. And, of course, he was right."

"What serious venues?"

"If they can get it, *60 Minutes*. With, depending on the content, as many as ten to fifteen million viewers."

Caro blinked. "Really? Is this PR firm that good? Can they really get *60 Minutes*?"

"No," Trevor said, "I don't think so. Not for this, not unless reporters tie Ben Clarby's murder to Alternate Mayhem, which so far they haven't done. And let's hope they don't. That kind of publicity we absolutely don't need."

45.

The story about RealityCheck stayed hot, until it didn't. The mob of reporters thinned, then vanished. The PR firm's tallies of stories in print and on the air—neatly divided into "favorable," "unfavorable," and "mixed content"— lessened in number. Camera drones, which had zoomed overhead, dwindled but did not disappear completely; those remaining were mostly from curiosity seekers, not press. The PR people called only rarely, and then the calls came from assistants-to-assistants.

But online the compound was not only debated and reviled, but also threatened.

Julian called together senior medical and software staff. Standing in front of an oversize computer screen in Wing Three, he said, "The FBI called this morning. Agent Kaplow sent me posts the Bureau is monitoring across various platforms. I want you all to see a sampling. You have the right to know this." The screen brightened.

- @realitycheckmustdie You don't have much time now, suckers
- @realitycheckmustdie Soon
- @realitycheckmustdie And the infidels will die in blood and fire! Believe it!
- @realitycheckmustdie Those two so-call doctors who put chips in head—it's mind control
- @realitycheckmustdie Fuck all of them
- @realitycheckmustdie Soon now, real soon

- @realitycheckmustdie That so-called physicist is the Antichrist!

Molly blurted, "Those fuckers!"

Barbara, visibly shaken, said, "What is the FBI doing about these?"

Julian said, "All Agent Kaplow would tell me is that 'they're working on it.'"

Caro said, "As most of you know, I've been through online threats before, at Fairleigh Memorial. But nobody ever physically attacked me, or anything close to it. It was awful, but nothing ever went beyond talk."

"That's what everyone hopes. If I hear more from the FBI, I'll let you know. Meanwhile, I want everyone to stay under the walkway eaves when you move around inside the compound. Do not leave the compound without first discussing it with me. Caro, inform the rest of the medical staff of that. Aiden, do the same with the software techs. I'll talk to James. But first, you need to see one more thing, a video. This was taken by the upward-facing security camera on the north wall just after dawn."

Empty blue sky. Then a drone traversed the screen and exited at the left.

Julian said, "The FBI enlarged the image to examine the drone. It wasn't launched by some curious amateur. It's an older model of military-grade surveillance drone, which can be purchased on the black market."

No one spoke until Caro said, "If you didn't expect this, then why is there a surveillance camera pointing upward at the sky?"

Julian gazed at her. Finally he said, "Because what you don't expect is often what gets you."

≡-

Then, all at once, the reporters were back, along with phone calls and press drones overhead and camera crews stalking around the building shooting what had to be dull footage of windowless walls. Especially aggressive news people pounded on the front gate. They interviewed bewildered delivery truck drivers unloading supplies on the loading dock.

Caro and Trevor cornered a frayed-looking Julian, shouting into a phone in the security office. "You said the investigation was undercover!" He listened, looking angrier every moment.

Ivan and Sophy sat monitoring screens. Trevor said to Sophy, "What happened? Why are those reporters back?"

"The *New York Times* printed an article about the FBI investigation of Alternate Mayhem. Somehow the paper found out that the FBI tied Alternate Mayhem to Ben Clarby. And to his murder. And so to us."

Julian shouted into his phone, "And if the Bureau security is so bad, why would we trust you with ours? That leak came from you. We *don't* want more publicity; you goddamn know that!"

Trevor said, "That other phone is ringing."

Ivan picked up, just as tech reinforcements arrived noisily in the crowded office, and slid out of his seat. He wedged himself into a corner of the room, uncharacteristically silent as he strained to hear. "Yeah ... yeah ... okay ... I'll get him! Julian, you gotta take this."

Julian punched viciously at his own phone, ending the FBI call. "Not now!"

"No, you really gotta," Ivan said. "It's the PR woman."

"I said *not now.*"

Nothing daunted Ivan, immune to social cues even when they tried to punch him in the solar plexus. "No, now. She says your best chance is a high-profile attack and she thinks she can get you *60 Minutes* after all if you—"

Julian grabbed Ivan's phone. Instantly his voice was controlled, polished, even silky. "Deanna, this is Julian. I'm glad to hear from you."

Caro's eyes widened. How did he transform himself so completely, so fast?

Trevor said quietly to Ivan, "If what?"

Ivan looked confused.

Trevor said patiently, "You told Julian that Deanna said she can get us *60 Minutes* to explain this mess 'if.' If what?"

"Oh," Ivan said, as if it were trivial, "if we can implant a really important person whose not connected with the project in any way and who everybody has already heard of and will be impressed by. I don't know who she meant. The president, maybe?"

Aiden had arrived. "Ivan," he said, "there's a code glitch you need to help Coe with. He's waiting in Wing Three. Go. I'll see that your shift is covered here."

Ivan's eyes lit up. "A code glitch?' He raced off.

Julian finished on the phone. His third expression, following utter fury and genial business mode, reminded Caro of a wolf focused on prey. "We need a high-profile, trusted, impressive volunteer to be implanted, undergo a filmed session, and go on *60 Minutes* to give a totally objective report on what we're doing here. And it needs to happen in the next week. That's the only way *60 Minutes* will give us an interview and so the chance to clear the project's name on national TV. I don't know anybody to ask. Caro, I know you don't, and Trevor, you've spent the last years in jungles. That leaves George. I don't think another physicist will do, but if George has British or American political connections from his Oxford days who are curious enough about his theory ... Although they'd have to be really aged, so maybe—"

Trevor said, "I might know someone."

≡

The woman who arrived by helicopter—helicopter!—at the compound was not what Weigert expected.

She was not a young journalist. Weigert had vaguely visualized someone like Woodward or Bernstein breaking the Watergate scandal, a feat of reporting that had greatly impressed George as a young man. After Trevor Abruzzo said that Stephanie Kathleen O'Malley would let herself be implanted, and *60 Minutes* had agreed to do the show if it included Ms. O'Malley's reporting, Weigert read her Associated Press series about Médecins Sans Frontières doctors in the Congo. The series had not only surprised but also shocked him. She'd written about the doctors as if they were *criminals*. Well, no, not that. She described the wonderful medical work they did, the lives they saved, the risks they took for their patients. But she also reported bribery of government officials, pilfering of supplies, heavy drinking, drug use, wild sex. Weigert had had no idea. It was not Florence Nightingale.

Had Trevor Abruzzo … Weigert didn't want to know. He liked Trevor.

Weigert joined Julian, Caroline, and Trevor to meet the journalist at the front gate. Ms. O'Malley looked what Rose would have called "a hard fifty," with sun-damaged skin, muscled arms, and short reddish hair that blew wildly in the wind from the helicopter blades. She wore a tee shirt and shorts with a dozen pockets. Her eyes in a snub-nosed, sharp-chinned face were a startling blue, as vivid as Julian's and, to Weigert, just as theatrical. He'd gotten used to Julian's flashy looks, but he didn't think he'd ever get used to this woman. Everything about her seemed alien to him: her aggressive stance, her twangy voice, the battered canvas duffle bag that was her only luggage. And why was there a small scorched hole in it? Also, her history. She'd written about murderers, heroin dealers, the IRA, dictators, sometimes risking her life to live with them for a while. She made Weigert feel provincial.

"Hey, mate," she said, hugging Trevor.

Mate? But she wasn't Australian, was she? Weigert was sure she wasn't.

Trevor laughed and hugged her back. So it was some sort of joke between them. When it was Weigert's turn to be introduced, he said, "Welcome, Ms. O'Malley. I'll—"

"Call me Step."

"Yes. Well." Step? He was not going to do that. "I'll be orienting you to the science behind the project and how we've applied it to—"

"I read your book. I don't need orienting and I'm on board with the surgery. Hey, the worst it can do is kill me, right?"

Trevor grinned. Another old joke? Evidently. Caroline said, a little stiffly, "I'll try to avoid that."

Ms. O'Malley said, "I have complete confidence in you, Caro. When do I go under your knife? Trev, you'll be there, right?"

"I'll be assisting."

"Just like old times. You assisting that old drunk, Johann Lundberg."

Weigert frowned. Why was an "old drunk" performing surgery? And Trevor would be assisting *Caroline*, who was hardly an old drunk. Had Julian made a mistake, trusting the reputation of their project to the reactions of this strange, intelligent, combative woman? Even though her work seemed to be acclaimed and noticed everywhere?

How could one even tell anymore?

≡—

Stephanie O'Malley had a surprisingly strong grasp of Weigert's theory and the science that supported it. A layperson's grasp, of course, but accurate as far as it went. Her curiosity seemed genuine and her questions shrewd. If she hadn't smoked throughout the entire hour-long interview, which Weigert insisted be outside at a picnic bench in the Wing One courtyard, he might have even enjoyed talking to her. He tried to sit upwind of her smoke, but there was no wind.

She noticed his discomfort; she seemed to notice every-thing. "Bad habit, I know. But in Africa and Afghanistan ev-erybody smokes. Helps with the tension."

"Doctors, too? Medical doctors were smoking?"

She grinned at him, and Weigert was sharply reminded of the indulgent smile that Rose sometimes gave him. Not that this woman was anything like his wife. She was, in fact, Rose's complete opposite.

She said, "You should at least give me credit for reining in my profanity. Another tension reliever in the middle of war."

He said primly, "Trevor was there and he doesn't use pro-fanity."

That smile again. She ground out her cigarette in the sau-cer of her coffee cup. "Not here, anyway."

Weigert was glad that Ms. O'Malley seemed like a fair and intelligent journalist, and even gladder that the interview was over.

46.

Step O'Malley's pre-surgery workup was the fastest Caro had ever done. Imagery and bloodwork looked fine. Worried by Step's constant smoking, Caro did a lung X-ray and EKG; lungs and heart were healthy. Some bodies could, unfairly, get away with anything. Julian worked with Step far into the night to train the DIR on her thought patterns. As Caro walked into the scrub room before Step's surgery the next morning, Ivan bounded up to her. "Hey, Caro, Julian says to find him as soon as you're out of the OR."

"Is anything wrong?"

"Nah. He just needs to tell you something."

Well, obviously. But she had no time now to question Ivan. Step was prepped and Trevor was already scrubbing. "Thanks."

"Oh, and YN!" Ivan said. And then, after a quick glance at her face, he added kindly, "It means 'Fingers crossed.' You probably didn't know that."

"No," Caro said. "I didn't."

"That's okay. You can't help being so old."

≡

Step's surgery presented no complications at all, and she was out of Recovery in minimal time. Caro—herself with a sturdy constitution and accustomed to being surrounded by other sturdy bodies since no one made it through med school, internship, and residence without the stamina of a draft horse—

was nonetheless surprised by Step's resilience. Med students had nothing over war correspondents.

She left Step with Trevor and found Julian in the security office, standing behind two monitoring techs who, eyes assiduously on their screens, had the air of being very careful not to attract their boss's attention. The skin around Julian's eyes was stretched taut. He said, "Step is okay?"

"The nurses are trying to keep her in bed, and she's firing off enough emails on her phone to start a conflagration."

"Good." He didn't smile, making no attempt at his usual charm. Caro discovered she liked him better this way.

"Ivan said you want to see me."

"Yes. I need to show you two things. Coe, bring up the FBI communication and the news reports. Hannah Kaplow sent all these this morning. The online attackers are getting worse. And now various newspapers and TV anchors are running with the story, or what they're making into the story: 'RealityCheck creates murderers in both virtual and real worlds!' Read the screen, Caro."

She did, and her stomach went sour. The leak about Ben Clarby's murder being linked to his data theft, which Agent Kaplow had said was "under investigation" by the FBI, had given rise to both legitimate and illegitimate speculations about the entire project. The FBI sent Julian a sampling, with hit numbers. As always, the illegitimate ones, vilely sensationalized, were winning.

"You can watch the TV cable stuff at your leisure," Julian added. "I forwarded links to you and Trevor and George. There's also this. Coe, the FBI email. It came in this morning, sent to the FBI but addressed to me by name. Hannah says she can have at least this link traced."

Mr. Julian Dey—I see your name online you are boss of RealityCheck to go in different universes and see dead. My boyfriend do this and kill people there. Now he talk

about killing you. I am scared. Please please please tell
police!! I write this at library computer.

Julian said, "Hannah is sending agents here to investigate
whether the leak about Ben came from inside the project. I told
her she fucking well better also investigate whether it came
from inside the FBI. I want you to re-emphasize to the medical
staff that nobody leaves the compound, that they walk under
the walkway overhang instead of crossing the open courtyard,
and that everybody be careful."

"I will."

Julian pulled at the skin on his face, a new gesture. "I need
to warn George. Hannah said he might be a particular target
of these fuckers. So much depends on Step O'Malley. If in her
session she finds us credible, we can get *60 Minutes*. That's our
best chance to reframe our story, vouched for by someone the
public can trust, and to get a big outside audience to hear it."

"There's George's book," Caro said, wanting to offer him
something in case Step decided her session was an illusion.

Julian turned to look at her. "George's *book*? Caro, most
Americans don't read anything but fiction—certainly not
weighty scientific tomes. We need *60 Minutes*, which means
we need Step O'Malley to undergo a life-changing experience."

≡

In the session room barely thirty-six hours later, Stephanie
O'Malley didn't look to Caro like someone about to undergo a life-changing experience. She perched on the edge of the
cot while Rosita checked her vital signs. Her arm rose once
toward a pocket in her safari shirt and Trevor said, "Forget it,
Step. The cigarettes still aren't there. Go cold turkey."

"Forget it yourself, you SOB. There speaks someone with
no addictions except being right. The second I'm outside
again, I'm smoking."

"You're wasting a golden opportunity to quit."

"Not in this life. Or any other you try to pitch me into."

Trevor laughed and shook his head. Rosita said to Step, "Hold *still.*"

"Alien to me."

"Do it anyway," Trevor said. "This isn't a foreign war you're darting around to cover."

"Could be that it will be," Step said. This time nobody laughed.

Finally Step lay back on the cot. The room prickled with tension. Julian and Barbara stood by their screens. No one else sat down either: George, Caro, Trevor, Rosita all standing and leaning slightly forward as if at a racetrack, urging on Step to the conclusion they were betting on.

Step's face went blank, and the screen brightened.

Her image rose from the cot, glanced around, and went out the door. The courtyard of Wing Three was unchanged except for a woman sitting on a stone bench by the flower bed. The woman rose, and Caro heard Trevor suck in a quick breath.

Step and the woman stared at each other for a heartbeat, two, five. She was taller than Step, younger, with green eyes, dark skin, and shoulder-length hair of a startling rich mahogany. Blood stained the front of her white tunic.

Step burst into tears. Then they were in each other's arms, holding on as if they might never let go, rocking back and forth. Step's head came only to the woman's shoulder. She had to stand on tiptoe for the woman's passionate kiss.

Julian did something and the figures, although still present on the screen, blurred. As they sank onto the grass, he said, "Maybe some privacy ..."

Ten blurry minutes later, the screen went dark and Step's eyes opened. She lay so immobile that Camilla and Caro both moved toward the cot. Trevor was faster, reaching Step just as the journalist sat up and covered her face with her hands.

"Step?" Trevor said.

"Not now," she said, the words muffled by her fingers. "I need ... I need to think about it. She was ... It was real, wasn't it? Trevor? It was *real.*"

"Yes," Trevor said.

Caro knew what she was seeing. For Stephanie Kathleen O'Malley—war-experienced, jaded, hard-smoking Step—reality had just turned inside out, like a sock.

George said simply, echoing Trevor but meaning so much more, "Yes. It was real. Now, Ms. O'Malley, what will you say about us?"

≡-

Julian raced off to call the PR firm about *60 Minutes*. Trevor sat with Step, holding her hand. They talked softly. Caro, feeling like an intruder, went to her room and searched on her laptop for images related to "Stephanie O'Malley." Far down the scroll, she found a single image of the dark-skinned, mahogany-haired woman with green eyes. Jamila Abrika, an Amazigh, formerly called "Berber." She'd been killed in the Tunisian riots three years ago.

The links to Step's works included her piece about the riots, "Chaos in Carthage." Precisely detailed, clearly written, wide in scope, the article packed an emotional punch. It included many names, but not Jamila's. Step had kept that relationship private, even after Jamila was dead.

Did that make Step, despite her avowals, more disposed to accept a hallucination as real? Or, given the journalistic skepticism displayed in the article about pretty much anything told her by any official, *less* disposed to accept delusions?

Caro, despite Step's and Trevor's and Julian's and everybody else's certainty about their sessions, still could not decide what she believed. She just could not decide.

47.

The next few days confused Weigert. The *60 Minutes* film crew would arrive on Friday. Julian said they wanted to run the RealityCheck story on Sunday: "Strike while the iron is hot." George assumed that he and Julian and Caro would just sit somewhere with an interviewer and talk, but it was not like that at all.

People from the show arrived immediately "to take establishing shots and create graphics." Julian rehearsed Weigert in how much to say and how to say it, both of which Weigert resented. He knew his own theory, and the theory could stand on its own without the polished gestures and dramatic pauses that Julian wanted. Then Julian got busy with "refining the format," and Weigert blew out a long breath of relief, until he discovered that Julian had imported a drama coach to take his place.

Stephanie O'Malley seemed to be everywhere, and, in Weigert's opinion, she did not act like someone who had just received the greatest gift of science. She made bawdy jokes while smoking cigarettes and drinking an astonishing amount of Scotch. "She's probably different when she's alone," Caroline told him. "To her, what she experienced in session is an intensely private revelation."

"Which she's going to talk about in public to millions of people."

Caroline laughed and punched him playfully on the shoulder. Weigert was, confusingly, all at once reminded of Sam.

He sought refuge in a session with Rose. The moment he saw her standing in their living room, Weigert felt calmer. Behind her on the mantelpiece stood her mother's collection of Victorian bric-a-brac. Drawn up to the fire was his deep leather club chair, and beside it the little carved table his uncle had brought from India a hundred years ago. Peonies from the garden scented the air. Rose, in his favorite blue dress, smiled and said, "You look troubled, my darling. What's wrong?"

He told her, at length. She listened with the patience she'd always shown him, and the pragmatic shrewdness that never turned vituperative.

"George, the telly show will be fine. And your book is the true rebuttal to all this sensationalizing. Wait and see."

"How long?"

She threw up her pretty hands in mock exasperation. "Do I look like the oracle at Delphi?"

She looked like Rose. He put his arms around her, smelled her hair, and was comforted amid the chaos.

≋

"George," Julian said, closing the door to the security office, "I have Hannah Kaplow on video. She has both good and bad news and wants us to hear it together."

Agent Kaplow's image on the screen said, "Hello, Dr. Weigert. The good news is that we arrested a suspect in Benjamin Clarby's murder. That email sent by his girlfriend cracked the case for us. The suspect was charged and has confessed as part of a plea bargain."

"Wonderful!" Weigert said.

"The bad news is that he's just a lower-level freelancer. A mercenary, basically. All arrangements were made anonymously. The freelancer can't lead us to whoever hired him because he doesn't know. But that he was hired establishes that this is a criminal enterprise. I have a task force on this, and eventually we'll trace the ringleaders and arrest them all under the Rico Statutes. It might or might not be Alternate Mayhem, of course."

Julian said, "But you're betting that it is."

"Yes, I am. And before you ask, no, we haven't succeeded yet in taking down their websites. They move too fast, and the source seems to be out of the country. As to who else it might it be ... We have some candidates in mind but no definitive answers. I'll tell you when we do."

Julian said, "Thanks, Hannah."

Her expression changed. "I understand, Dr. Weigert, that your book is selling extremely well. You must be pleased."

"Yes," Weigert said carefully, trying not to show his resentment that sales were due to murder rather than to science. "It is."

The Friday taping of *60 Minutes* took place in the session room, which had been transformed with huge pieces of camera and sound equipment, dozens of strangers intently focused on tasks baffling to Weigert, and a huge screen to show graphics. Comfortable chairs, which Weigert had never seen before, stood on a hastily constructed stage. Telly people told him where to look when, the drama coach sitting anxiously to one side. All was bustle and rushing and shouted orders until, suddenly, there descended a consensual silence profound as a cathedral, and the taping began.

Weigert thought the taping went well, although he recognized that he had nothing with which to compare it. Afterward, the entire TV crew and all their equipment vanished as rapidly as they'd appeared. "Going to be a tight post-production for them to air it on Sunday," Ms. O'Malley said as she, too, left the compound. "I'm off to Venezuela. Another revolution brewing. Not that you won't have one here, too. Bye, kids!"

It was like a whirlwind leaving town.

Caroline took Weigert aside. "George, don't be too upset if they edit out some of the science. The—"

"Edit it out!"

"Maybe they won't. I just want to warn you. *60 Minutes* does much better with complex subjects than nearly any other show on TV, but it *is* TV for a mass audience. We'll have to wait and see."

Something else to worry about.

≡

When Weigert was small, his father had been assigned to temporary duty with the British embassy in Washington, and the family had moved to a house in suburban Virginia. The house had a backyard deck. Five-year-old Georgie had been fascinated by the sliding glass door, so different from the small, heat-saving windows in their century-old English house. The wide expanse of glass miraculously brought the outside inside. But he cried whenever a bird flew straight into the window and knocked itself out, its compact little body inert and glassy-eyed on the wooden deck.

On Sunday night, waiting for *60 Minutes* to start, Weigert felt like that bird. Soaring on the success of his book and a cautious but definite interest from scientists he respected, he'd smashed directly into all this sensationalistic hoopla. Also into an avalanche of email with stupid questions from believers in materialism, that doctrine—taken on just as much faith as any religion!—that nothing existed except tangible matter and its interactions.

No, not stupid questions. That wasn't fair. Rose had said as much during his last session with her. She'd pointed out that he hadn't objected to the same questions when Caroline had asked them, so many months ago. In fact, he'd welcomed them. "So, my darling, what's different now?"

Everything. Including the fact that Weigert knew, although they'd never discussed it, that he hadn't succeeded in completely convincing Caroline either.

An hour before *60 Minutes* aired, people began gathering in the refectory, where Julian had set up a huge rented screen. James's staff brought extra chairs from conference rooms, bedrooms, the hospital. Everyone crowded in except the two techs unhappily monitoring the security office.

The all-important show began.

48.

60 Minutes started with the interviewer recapping what Weigert considered the least important aspects of anything: Ben Clarby's theft of "proprietary corporate data," his murder currently "under investigation by the FBI," and a mercifully brief mention of "misuse of that data, also under investigation." If the FBI had insisted on the brevity, Weigert was grateful to them. The recitation was accompanied by shots of Cayman Brac and the exterior of the compound.

The interviewer, Richard Diaz, introduced Julian as a former Silicon Valley boy genius, Weigert as an eminent physicist, and an on-screen photo of "the late Nobel laureate Samuel Louis Watkins" as the inventor of Achino. Diaz then turned to Julian. "Tell us why your scientific research compound has attracted so much attention. What's going on here?"

"What's going on, Richard, is the most exciting medical research on the planet, rigorously developed over fifteen years. What we have discovered here is nothing less than a complete up-ending of everything you think you know about reality. *Everything*, including what you think you know about death."

"That's a lot to accept. Let's back up a bit. You, Dr. Weigert, and Dr. Watkins founded RealityCheck fifteen years ago. How did that come about?"

"As a direct result of George Weigert's theory of the primacy of the observer." Julian talked briefly about building and equipping the compound, accompanied by photos. He finished with, "You don't need a medical facility and a hospital to develop physics theories. You do need those to take theory a step further and alter how human consciousness works. But RealityCheck began with George's revolution. Every now and then, a simple idea shakes the foundations of knowledge. The discovery that the earth was not flat challenged the way people perceived themselves and their relationship with the world. Einstein's relativity theories upended classical physics, and then quantum mechanics did it again. Likewise, the primacy of the observer upends conventional science."

Diaz turned to Weigert. "And how does it do that?"

This was, for Weigert, the heart of the interview, and he'd been endlessly rehearsed in how to reply. He leaned forward slightly, paused, and said, "With the seemingly absurd idea that the universe springs from life, not the other way around."

Another pause before he continued. The next speech had been written by Julian "to be accessible to the layman." Weigert had argued for more fundamentals of science, but he'd had to give in. After all, the speech was accurate, even if it did present mostly conclusions and not the necessary scientific steps to reach them.

"Switching our perspective on the universe from physics to biology shatters everything we have ever known about reality. We think life is just an accident of physics, but a long list of experiments suggests the opposite. Amazingly, if you add life and consciousness to the equation, you can explain some of the biggest puzzles of science. For instance, it becomes clear why space and time—and even the properties of matter itself—depend on the observer. It also becomes clear why the laws of the universe are fine-tuned for the existence of life. Until we recognize the universe in our head, attempts to understand the world will remain a road to nowhere.

"We are taught since childhood that the universe is divided into two entities—ourselves, and that which is outside of us. This seems logical. 'Self' is commonly defined by what we can control. I can wiggle my fingers, but I cannot wiggle your toes. The dichotomy is based largely on manipulation, even if basic biology tells us we have no more control over the trillions of cells in our body than over a rock or a tree.

"Consider everything you see around you right now—your chair, the TV cameras, your own hands. Language and custom say it all lies outside us in the external world. However, everything you see and experience is a whirl of information occurring in your mind. You *are* this process. Your eyes are not just a portal to the world. You cannot see anything through the bone surrounding your brain. No, what you are seeing is a construction inside your head.

"One simple example: the sky. You see it as blue, but the cells in your brain could be changed so the sky looks green—or even red. In fact, with a little genetic engineering I could probably make everything that is red vibrate, or make a noise, or trigger a desire in you to have sex, as color does with some birds. Your brain circuits could be changed so that on a sunny day, it looks dark out. This logic applies to virtually everything. Bottom line: what you see could not be present without your consciousness."

Diaz said, "I never thought of it that way."

"No, most people don't. Julian already mentioned how shocked the scientific world was at the experimental findings of quantum physics. That was because in the early twentieth century, science was still operating with an outdated paradigm. Now, we still believe there is an external world that exists independent of the perceiving subject. But philosophers and physicists from Plato to Hawking have debated this idea. Niels Bohr, the great Nobel-prize-winning physicist, disagreed."

Flash on the TV of a picture of Bohr, looking avuncular, with his words underneath. George gave them in voice-over: "'When we measure something, we are forcing an undetermined, undefined world to assume an experimental value. We are not 'measuring' the world; we are creating it.' At their legendary debates, Einstein—"

Another photo, with the iconic wild hair.

"—presented ingenious ideas supporting the idea of a 'real world out there,' but Bohr shot them all down and gradually won over the physics community. Wigner, winner of the 1963 Nobel Prize, insisted that the very study of the external world leads to the conclusion that 'the content of consciousness is an ultimate reality.'

"However, today most people still believe there is a real world out there—despite the scientific evidence. We look at the world like—for example—a squirrel. The squirrel opens its eyes and sees an acorn just miraculously sitting there. The squirrel grabs it and scurries up the tree without further thought. But experiment after experiment shows that the acorn is made of particles, and not a single particle exists with real properties if no one is observing."

Diaz looked genuinely interested. Was he pretending? Weigert couldn't tell, although of course these media people were all actors. Diaz said, "Tell us about the scientific evidence." He smiled reassuringly at the camera. "Briefly, anyway."

As Weigert spoke, spectacular graphics appeared on the screen, illustrating his points for an untrained audience. The drama coach had rehearsed Weigert to allow enough time to let each animated graphic complete its motions.

"Consider the famous two-slit experiment, which has been performed a number of times in various ways. When scientists watch a particle pass through two slits in a barrier, the particle behaves like a bullet and goes through one hole or the other. However, if you do not watch, it acts like a wave and can go through both holes at the same time. But how can a particle 'out there' change its behavior depending on whether you watch it or not? The answer is simple—reality is a process that involves our consciousness."

He leaned forward slightly in his chair, as he'd been coached to do.

"Consider Heisenberg's famous uncertainty principle. If there really were a world out there with particles just bouncing around, then we should be able to measure all their properties. But you cannot. For instance, a particle's exact location and momentum cannot be known at the same time. But why should it matter to a particle what you decide to measure? Again, the answer is simple—the particles are not just 'out there.'

"So it really does not take a quantum physicist to realize that reality is a process that involves our consciousness, which is why we need to replace the old physics with a new biology."

"All right," Diaz said, "you've just annihilated matter. But how about space and time? Surely they are 'real' in the sense that ordinary people mean."

'No," Weigert said. "Space and time are not hard, cold objects like the shells you pick up along the beach. Starting in the 1920s, experiments have shown just the opposite. The observer critically influences the outcome. Space and time are simply the mind's tools for putting everything together.

"Consider the electron, which has turned out to be both a particle and a wave. But how—and more importantly—*where* such a particle will be located is dependent upon the very act of observation. These and similar experiments, including Einsteinian relativity, point toward an inescapable conclusion: the observer is what determines space.

"We've come to regard space as a sort of vast container that has no walls. However, multiple illusions and processes are what give us that false view of space. For example, distances between objects can and do mutate, depending on a multitude of conditions such as gravity and speed, with the result that no 'bedrock' distance exists anywhere, between anything and anything else. In fact, quantum theory casts serious doubt on whether individual items are truly separated at all. We 'see' separations between objects only because we have been conditioned by language and convention to draw boundaries.

"The same is true of time. Quantum theory increasingly casts doubts about the existence of time as we know it. When people speak of time, they are usually referring to change. But change is *not* the same thing as time. To measure anything's position precisely, at any given instant, is to 'lock-in' on one static frame of its motion, as in a film. Conversely, as soon as you observe movement or momentum, you cannot iso-late a frame—because momentum is the summation of many frames. Sharpness in one parameter induces blurriness in the other. Time is simply the way we animate events—the still frames—of the spatial world. It, too, is a tool of our mind."

Diaz shifted on his chair. Weigert held his breath. Caro had warned him that parts of the science might be edited out, but surely not this next critical aspect of his theory!

It wasn't gone.

The on-screen Weigert continued, backed by graphics even more colorful and frenetic. "Consider an experiment published in the prestigious scientific journal *Science*. Scientists in France shot photons into an apparatus and showed that what they did could retroactively change something that had already happened in the past. You heard that right! As the photons passed a fork in the apparatus, they had to decide whether to behave like particles or waves when they hit a beam splitter. Later on—well *after* the photons passed the fork—the experimenter could randomly switch a second beam splitter on and off. It turns out that what the observer decided at that point determined what the particle actually did at the fork *in the past*. At that moment, the experimenter chose his past."

Another pause, this time by the interviewer, who finally said, as if he had just thought of it, "But all this takes place in the microscopic world. Isn't it true that our macroscopic world, the world we experience every day, behaves different-ly?"

"That's what was believed for a long time. But the idea that there exists one set of laws for small objects and another for the rest of the universe, including us, has no basis in reason and is being challenged in laboratories around the world. Quantum entanglement, in which two objects are 'entangled' and what you do to one affects the other no matter how far apart they are—"

More graphics, these definitely too gaudy, but Weigert had lost that particular argument.

"—is another refutation of the idea of space. Scientists have succeeded in entangling three-millimeter-wide diamonds, entangling huge molecules called 'buckyballs', entangling even crystals with entanglement ridges a half-inch high. What is done to one item in the entangled pair *instantly* affected the other item, even at a distance. Both the microscopic and macroscopic world are generated by consciousness."

Diaz nodded. "Which brings us to what I found to be the most startling image in your book: the disappearing kitchen. Tell us about that."

Now a very detailed graphic appeared, a cartoon kitchen with stove, sink, refrigerator, dishes on shelves and cookbooks on a counter. A tea kettle the color of a fire engine, an overhead light big as a wagon wheel, and a cartoon avatar. The onscreen Weigert began his voice-over speech in the slightly too dramatic way that the drama coach had insisted on.

"Take the seemingly undeniable logic that your kitchen is always present. You think its contents assume all their familiar shapes and colors whether or not you are in it. But consider: the shapes, colors, and forms known as your kitchen are seen because particles of light from the overhead bulb bounce off the various objects and then interact with your brain through a complex set of retinal and neural intermediaries. But on its own, light doesn't *have* any color, or any brightness, or any visual characteristics at all. It is merely an electromagnetic phenomenon. So you might think that the kitchen was 'there' in your absence, but the unquestionable reality is this: nothing remotely resembling what you can imagine could be present when a consciousness isn't interacting.

"Quantum physics agrees with that startling statement. At night, as you click off the lights and leave for the bedroom, you expect that the kitchen remains there, unseen, all through the night."

The cartoon avatar sashayed out of the kitchen, hitting the light switch. Weigert winced.

"But, in fact," said his voice-over, "the refrigerator, stove and everything else are composed of a shimmering swarm of matter/energy."

The kitchen dissolved into a silver-gray blur.

"Proven physics tells us that not a single one of the subatomic particles that make up your kitchen actually occupies a definite place. Rather, they exist as a range of possibilities— as *waves of probability*—as Max Born demonstrated a hundred years ago. The particles are statistical predictions—nothing but a *likely outcome*. In fact, outside of that idea, nothing is there! If they are not being observed, the particles cannot be thought of as having any real existence—either duration or a position in space. It is only in the presence of an observer— that is, when you go back in to get a drink of water—"

Cartoon figure returned, flicked the light switch, and the kitchen reappeared.

"—that the mind sets the scaffolding of these particles in place. Until it actually lays down the threads—somewhere in the haze of probabilities that represent the object's range of possible values—they cannot be thought of as being either here or there, or having an actual position, a physical reality.

"Of course, once the wave function of the kitchen has collapsed, a record of it remains in our memory, and when we return to the kitchen our memories agree with it. In scientific terms, the 'kitchen' degrees of freedom recorded in our memory collapse the first time we observed the kitchen.

"Another way to think about this is to think about watching a DVD. When the player is off, there is no movie. But when you return to the room and turn the player on, it leaps back into view. No matter how many times you turn the player on or off, the movie does not change—Emerald City is always at the end of the yellow brick road."

Another dramatic pause.

"The conscious observer is primary. It creates everything else."

Diaz looked directly into the camera. "Ordinarily our time for this segment of *60 Minutes* would be over, but we haven't even reached the most important aspect of this, so stay with us for more."

Cut to a commercial. A babel of voices around Weigert, which he ignored. As far as he was concerned, they'd already covered "the most important aspects," however hastily.

Caroline leaned over his shoulder and said, "George?"

"It was acceptable," he said, and he could hear the smile in her voice when she said, "Good."

After the commercial, Julian gave a polished, comprehensible explanation of the computer chips he'd developed to alter the way the brain processed information received from the senses. There was a clip of Caro and Trevor, masked and gowned in the OR, leaning over a table that Weigert knew had been filmed with no one on it. Back to Julian, who finished with, "—insert the programmed chips into the brain. It's an operation that is no more dangerous or difficult than routine insertion of Direct Brain Stimulation to control the tremors of Parkinson's disease. The result is a direct lead from the brain to an unobtrusive control box outside the skull. See, here is mine."

Julian leaned forward and parted his hair with his hands. The camera zoomed in. "With this implant and the extensive and proprietary programming on our computers, my consciousness can—and has—created another branch of the universe and temporarily inhabited it."

Diaz said with great animation, "Let's talk about those other branches of the universe. People who have undergone implant surgery claim that when their brain chips are activated, they can enter 'branch universes' where they see and talk with their beloved dead. Not a hallucination, not a dream about people who have passed, but actual versions of those people, solid and alive in another universe. RealityCheck also claims that these people *stay* alive in their universes after the implantee leaves. Julian, what can you tell us about how your implanted chips make that possible?"

The photo of Einstein reappeared, with a different quotation. Julian's voice-over said, "After the death of an old friend, Albert Einstein wrote, 'Now Besso has departed from this strange world a little ahead of me. That means nothing. People like us ... know that the distinction between past, present and future is only a stubbornly persistent illusion.' All the evidence Dr. Weigert just explained tells us that Einstein was right—death *is* an illusion.

"Our classical way of thinking is based on the belief that the world has an objective observer-independent existence, and so we think life is just the activity of carbon and an admixture of molecules—we live a while and then rot into the ground. We believe in death because we associate ourselves with our body and we know bodies die. End of story.

"Only the story is *false*, and primacy of the observer tells us death may not be the terminal event we think.

"Scientists have puzzled for a long time over why the laws, forces, and constants of the universe appear to be exquisitely fine-tuned for the existence of life. This could be just an astounding coincidence. But science doesn't like astounding coincidences. The simplest explanation is that the laws and conditions of the universe allow for the observer *because* the observer generates them. Like space and time, they are simply tools our minds use to create reality. Death doesn't exist in a timeless, spaceless world. Immortality doesn't mean a perpetual existence in time—it resides outside of time altogether.

"We generally reject the multiple universes of science fiction, but it turns out there is scientific support for this popular genre. As Dr. Weigert just explained, one well-known aspect of quantum physics is that observations can't be predicted absolutely. Instead, there is a *range* of possible observations, each with a different probability. One mainstream explanation, the 'many-worlds' interpretation, states that each of these possible observations corresponds to a different universe—the 'multiverse.' There are an infinite number of universes, and everything that could possibly happen occurs in some universe.

Death does not exist in any real sense in these scenarios. All possible universes exist simultaneously, regardless of what happens in any of them.

"When we die, we do so not in a random-billiard-ball universe but in an inescapable-life universe. Life has a non-linear dimensionality—it's like a perennial flower that returns to bloom in the multiverse. Although individual bodies are destined to self-destruct, the alive feeling—the 'Who am I?'—is just a twenty-watt fountain of energy operating in the brain. But this energy doesn't go away at death. One of the surest axioms of science is that energy never dies; it can neither be created nor destroyed.

"Time and space are simply the way our mind puts quantum information together, organizing it into the reality we see and experience. Our individual separateness—whether in this universe or between multiverses—is an illusion. The consciousness that was behind the youth you once were, is *also* behind who you are now, and who you will be anywhere in space and time. Ultimately, they are all melted together, parts of a single entity that transcends space and time. And if space and time aren't real things, in what sense can you consider yourself separate from 'another you' that exists in space and time?

"The same is true of the people you love who have died. Their bodies have died but their consciousness continues to exist in other universes. And using this new chip technology, which changes the algorithms by which your brain processes information, you *can* see them again."

A long moment of silence, before the interviewer said, "With us tonight are three people who claim to have had that experience."

The scene widened to show one of Julian's techs, Christopher Agarwal, along with Nurse Ortega and Ms. O'Malley, all seated on the stage.

"Let's start with Stephanie O'Malley, Pulitzer-prize-winning journalist and, as I can tell you from personal experience, not an easy person to delude. Step, tell us why you went to RealityCheck and what happened to you there."

The TV people had wanted to play recordings of the actual sessions, but Julian had adamantly refused. Those were private. But Ms. O'Malley's recounting of her meeting with her dead lover was vivid and gripping. Of course, she was a journalist; vividness was what she was trained to offer. Still—

The other two related their sessions. Neither had Ms. O'Malley's articulate fervor, but somehow that reinforced what the youngsters said. Their fumbling to explain what they'd experienced, their obvious awe, seemed to Weigert very moving.

Then it was his turn. As the screen zoomed in for a close-up of his face, the watching Weigert stiffened in his chair. How might they edit this?

His image said, "I saw—still see, each time I activate my chip—my wife Rose. She died of cancer sixteen years ago."

"I'm so sorry," the interviewer said, and Weigert brushed past this like the platitude it was. "As Julian explained, death is an illusion. My wife exists in another universe, and with the help of Julian's software and my implanted chip, I can again stand beside her. And I do."

The interviewer paused before saying, "So the dead are not really dead. But without RealityCheck's technology, neither we nor they can see each other."

"No," Weigert said. "But they are there. Consciousness cannot experience 'nothing' because consciousness is *defined* as being aware of something."

The cover of *The Primacy of the Observer* filled the TV screen. The interviewer said, "The full explanation of Dr. Weigert's theory is here, in his new book. I'm sure that all our viewers feel that our guests tonight have given us a lot to think about."

A commercial for toothpaste, and someone turned off the TV.

Julian turned to his techs, all bent over laptops. "Ivan?"

"Slam dunk! Huge number of online responses! Not necessarily in terms of favorability, but in ... Everybody wants to know more about the death thing. *Everybody*! Dr. Weigert, you're going to be rich!"

"Irrelevant," Weigert said, and didn't understand why everybody laughed.

Still, it had gone better than he'd expected. The interviewer had treated his theory with respect. Not enough hard science, but he'd known that would happen. The important thing was that more people would hear about, and might come to understand, what reality actually was.

That was worth having endured the drama coach.

He turned in his chair to face Julian. "Maybe we should celebrate?"

"Oh, George," Julian said. "Look around you. We *are*."

A party had erupted in the refectory. Champagne corks popped. Aiden seemed to be mixing some lethal concoction in a big metal tub. Then music, and people started to dance.

Caroline held out her hand to Weigert, and he surprised himself by taking it and swinging her into the jitterbug he remembered from his youth. Muscle memory. People laughed and cheered.

He kept it up for three minutes before, winded, he left for the session room and Rose.

49.

The next morning Caro, only slightly hung over, left Trevor asleep and went to Wing Two for coffee. She was startled to see a huge commotion spilling out from the security office, which was jammed with bodies jostling for space. Cell phones rang madly in a cacophony of different ringtones: carillons, bagpipes, car horns, rock tunes, *O Susanna*! People pointed at screens, yelling to be heard over each other. Caro, bewildered, edged into the office until she could see the computer screens surveilling the outside of the compound.

A dense mob of people, with more arriving. Cars pulled up. A helicopter without a news logo hovered low before landing somewhere off camera. Some of the crowd shouted at the compound walls, individual messages lost in the blur of sound. Others held up small signs, some hastily scrawled on cardboard:

MY FATHER DIED. HELP ME SEE HIM AGAIN!

PLEASE HELP ME ENTER ALTERNATE UNIVERSE. I CAN PAY!

MY DEPRESSED WIFE NEEDS TO SEE HER MOTHER!

PLEASE PLEASE PLEASE HELP!!!!

Ivan, feet planted firmly in front of a screen to defend his turf, craned his neck to look up at Caro from his chair. "Every single last one of them wants us to implant them! Every last fucking one!"

Someone seized her hand: Julian. He dragged her into the conference room and ejected everyone else. Last night's party must have spilled into here; the table was a battlefield of fallen plastic glasses, sticky swizzle sticks, crumpled napkins, and a vintage Brooklyn Dodgers baseball cap far older than anyone who could have plausibly been wearing it. Julian poured Caro a cup of coffee and she took it gratefully.

He said, "Where's Trevor?"

"Still asleep. What is it, Julian?"

"A question."

She guessed what was coming. "Shoot."

"I need to know long you're staying with the project. Trevor said he told you that he's committed for at least another year. He also said that you haven't made your decision yet, and that he isn't going to speak for you or pressure you. All for fairness, our Trev."

She caught the sour note in his voice. "Julian—"

"Forget it, Caro. I'm not fair and I know it. But I'm asking you professionally: Will you commit to at least another year with the project? Ellen is fine on her own now. You're a superb surgeon, and you're already familiar with everything here. Soon I hope to start taking the project commercial, offering implants to the public."

"For a hefty price."

"Of course. I have a big investment in this place, including practically every penny I ever earned. Sam's trust fund is nearly depleted. George didn't have all that much money to begin with, at least not comparatively. We have to go commercial."

"I need to talk it over with Trevor."

"Am I to believe you two haven't already discussed this? Never mind. I see you've talked; you just haven't reached a decision. Will you let me know soon?"

"Yes," Caro said, "I will."

As she sat in the refectory with her coffee and a Danish, two emails popped into her phone. Ellen praised the *60 Minutes* segment: "It was wonderful! So clear! Lorraine and I loved it! Call me!"

DeVonne also sent her an email:

Caro—

What a furor! Your unconventional compound is all over the news, all over everybody's conversation, even though of course I'd told nobody where you went after you left Fairleigh. Debate rages daily about things nobody here ever argued about before: physics, reality, meaning and existence. It's like living in a perpetual philosophy class. I bought Weigert's book, along with half the country. But I'm writing you because I have news.

We are short a surgeon. Two, actually. Paul Becker did it again, this time offering his unwanted sexual attentions to a meek little nurse who turned out to be not so meek after all. She was talked out of public sexual-harassment charges, but the Board held a hearing. You don't fire someone of Becker's stature; you promote him. So after it was suggested that he might be happier elsewhere, he moved to Mass General. Nice work if you can get it. And then, two weeks later, your old treacherous pal Vera Borella also packed up and took a job at a hospital in Boston. Who knew?

I don't know what your plans are, since you and I haven't communicated lately. Perhaps you've decided to stay with RealityCheck. But if not, I think you'd have a strong chance here. Your mapping article with Dr. Mumaw—congratulations, BTW—received a lot of respectful attention. You've obviously gained useful surgical experience. And if you happen to have in your resume a good recommendation from the late Dr. Watkins, Nobel winner ...

Also, Helen and I would love to have you back. She sends
her love.

DeVonne

"Caro?" Trevor said. She hadn't even noticed him enter the
refectory. Wordlessly she handed him her phone, still open to
DeVonne's email.

He read it. When he looked at her again, his brown eyes
were as warm, as loving as always. He said, "I've got your back,
Caro. I'll support anything you decide."

≋

She couldn't find any solitude. Leaving the compound was
out of the question. She would be mobbed; and anyway Julian's warning of potential danger filled her mind. People kept
knocking on the door of her bedroom. Aiden said that Julian
might call a meeting for this afternoon. Caro didn't want another meeting. She wanted to be uninterrupted so she could
think.

Finally, she slipped into the hospital, empty at present of
patients and so of staff, and went into a patient room. She
closed the door and sat on the edge of the unmade bed.

The visitor's chair, found in every room of every hospital
she'd ever seen, seemed to her to jump into preternaturally
sharp focus: orange, ugly, and useful. Four feet tall. Sides of
gray, epoxy-coated steel, obliquely reflecting light from the
overhead fluorescents. Footrest, seat, arms, back, movable
headrest all densely padded for patient comfort. A tiny tear on
the far left side of the faux-leather footrest. Short metal bars
at the front of each arm to attach a tray. Four lockable wheels
on swivel castors, the back two larger than the front two. A
lever on the right side so the patient, or a nurse, could adjust
the chair to sitting, half-reclining, reclining. And that hideous
color, like a diseased carrot.

Caro's consciousness had created all of that?

Along with, according to George, all the rest of the room, as familiar to her as her own body. Over-bed table holding the nurse call-button, TV control, clear plastic water pitcher, plastic-wrapped stack of disposable cups. The equipment at the head of the bed: monitor to track heart rate, blood pressure, intercranial pressure, oxygen saturation, IV pole.

This was her world. This, the OR, the scrub room, the supply closet, the ICU, the procedures of surgery. She *had* created this world, although not in the way George meant; she'd created it by choosing med school, residency, neurosurgical fellowship. She could have chosen differently, become a medical researcher, a biology professor, lawyer, or criminal. *Butcher baker candlestick maker, tinker tailor soldier spy.*

Everybody created the world they lived in.

And people could change their reality. Ellen had, moving away from her life-long dependence on Caro. Lorraine, going from desperately flamboyant to confident and serene. Even Caro, letting Trevor into her heart, had profoundly altered her personal reality. And social media changed reality every day. It had changed hers after her sexual-assault hearing at Fairleigh Memorial; it was changing the compound's reality since the *60 Minutes* episode.

But none of that erased the fact that what she'd learned of George's theory had upended her world. The ugly orange chair, and all it represented, had suddenly become a treacherous abyss. Jump that abyss and stay on Cayman Brac, with the project and with Trevor, doing easy surgery for a cause she wasn't sure she believed? Or apply for the conventional path of an appointment at Fairleigh Memorial, juggling demanding surgery and a long-distance relationship?

Trevor wouldn't abandon her; she knew that now. But wouldn't she be abandoning him?

And, even more profoundly, could Caro go on performing implants without completely believing that implants did what Julian and Trevor and George said they did? Or—and this was the most frightening thought of all—had she slowly come to believe in the primacy of the observer, but fought the belief because it meant she had to view all of reality differently?

She sat on the hospital bed, staring at the ugly orange chair for a long time. When she left the room, she still had no answer.

50.

Weigert sat at his desk, working on an answer to a physicist at Harvard who had sent him some astute questions about his book and so deserved a thoughtful answer. Most of the questions Weigert received were not astute; the majority were inane. Even accredited scientists got their knickers in a twist over the most obvious points. Weigert ignored these.

He also tried to ignore the last week's furor in and around the compound. People outside clamored to be implanted; people inside excitedly made all sorts of plans, even as others decided to leave entirely because "it was becoming too dangerous here." James was constantly interviewing and hiring new staff, and Julian's techs were busy running background checks on them. Julian was negotiating with both more media outlets and more medical personnel. Three lawyers plus Bill Haggerty were staying in Wing One, and the compound was running out of rooms. In the refectory there seemed to be a drinks party every night.

And the meetings! Julian and he, as partners in Reality-Check, called meetings every day with lawyers and Island officials and financial people and the FBI, until Weigert firmly told Julian to just arrange things without him and inform him when it was time to sign papers.

Someone knocked on his door. James, delivering another letter. "From overseas, Doctor, by *international courier*. Oh, and Julian wants you right away in the security office."

Weigert opened the letter, which was handwritten, and in French. Weigert's French was rusty but once he had been fluent, and he had no trouble translating as he read.

Dear Doctor Weigert,

I write to give to you both praise and a warning. I have read your book, which now causes such disturbance around the worlds scientific and ordinary. It is an extraordinary, if partial, job. You are to be commended. However, I hold strong reservations about places where much more experimental work must be done. I detail those reservations below.

The warning is this: You will receive great scorn for this work in some scientific quarters. Weaknesses will become exaggerated, reasoning will be found faulty, counterexamples will be given more weight than they often deserve. This will happen from those of inferior ability who will resent your achievement, from friends with sincere and genuine doubts, and—most of all—from the physics establishment, who will feel it must defend its entrenched beliefs. Already Dieter Fischer of the Planck Institute prepares a rebuttal that reads (I have seen a draft) like an attack.

You will not be able to ignore these attacks. But I urge you to try, and to continue with the refinement of your theory, in alliance with experimental physicists who can confirm or modify its major tenets. Your work is too important to stop.

We have never met. I travel very little now for reasons of health, but if you come any moment soon to Paris, I hope to make your acquaintance.

*Now, for those assertions with which I disagree.
On page 35, you write ....*

There was more, much more, pages more that Weigert would read carefully, many times. Now he just stared at the spidery signature: Jean-Luc Fournier. One of the world's most eminent physicists, the winner two years ago of the Nobel Prize for his astonishing work on anti-matter asymmetry.

Jean-Luc Fournier. Writing with praise for Weigert's theory.

Rose, it's happening.

It was bound to happen, my darling.

Weigert sat down to compose an answer to Fournier. He had just begun when James knocked again. "Doctor? The meeting in the security office?"

Weigert grimaced and laid the precious letter on his desk.

Trevor, Caroline, and Aiden stood with Julian, all of them facing a screen with Agent Kaplow's hyper-enlarged face.

"George," Julian said, "Hannah has something she wants us all to know about."

"Yes," Agent Kaplow said. "Dr. Weigert, do you recognize this man?" A photo brightened another screen.

'No," Weigert said. The man was young, in his twenties or early thirties, seated in a lawn chair among a sea of them outside the main gate. He held a video camera on his lap. "Is he a reporter?"

"He's posing as a reporter. We've identified him from the compound's security recording. He's a member of a vicious hate group."

Weigert said, "Whom do they hate?"

Julian answered before Agent Kaplow could. "Pretty much everybody. But, right now, us."

"But ... why?"

Julian said irritably, "Haven't you been following the many controversies about RealityCheck online and in the mainstream news?"

"No."

"George, you can't just ignore the outer world! Public reaction impacts what we're doing here!"

"Of course it does," Weigert said, in the tone he could muster when necessary but seldom used with Julian. Rose had always called it his please-don't-tell-me-what's-already-obvious tone. Julian flushed slightly.

Agent Kaplow stepped in. "We think this man was gathering information about the compound for a possible attack. We've picked up chatter, and we have informants. In addition, there's a stylometric match of the worst online threats you've been receiving and the group's other communications."

"Stylometric match?" Caro asked.

Aiden said, "Statistical analysis of both the words of a message and the underlying computer code."

Agent Kaplow said, "The group that your fake reporter belongs to call themselves Prophets for the End Times. They're a domestic terrorist organization that's a sort of amalgamation of white supremacists and nut-job religious fundamentalists. They hate anything they've decided contradicts their interpretations of the Biblical 'Book of Revelation.' Mainstream Christian denominations have completely repudiated them. The group posts through encrypted sites overseas, and until now we haven't identified any of the members except for an associated person in Mozambique, which doesn't honor extradition with the US.

"We think this group may be responsible for two other drone-bomb attacks, in Missouri on a psychiatrist's office, and in California on a Buddhist monastery."

Weigert was bewildered. "A psychiatrist's office?"

"Psychiatric therapy attributes evil to something other than demon possession."

Aiden said, "But what about Alternate Mayhem?"

"We're very close to making more arrests and to taking down the websites for good. But with regard to Prophets for the End Times, I wanted both to update you and to warn you to maintain vigilance. Dr. Weigert, yesterday you took a cup of coffee into the residential courtyard and sat at a picnic bench out in the open. Since you are a particular target, that was unwise."

Weigert said, astonished, "You know what we do every moment?"

"If you do it out in the open," she said. "So don't."

Weigert thought, but did not say aloud, *It was tea, not coffee.* The FBI didn't know everything.

Agent Kaplow continued, "This hate group is only a few years old but already international and well-funded. We know that in Mozambique at least they have pretty sophisticated tech, bought on the military black market."

Caroline said, "But even so, how could they ... Julian, wouldn't that new surveillance system you put in detect any camera drones? You told me it gives a twenty-second warning before a drone is over the compound."

Agent Kaplow didn't answer, but Trevor did, his gaze sharp on the screen. "They might not need a camera drone, if they're sophisticated enough to be piggy-backing on military surveillance in orbit. That happened once when I was in Africa. Agent Kaplow?"

"That's all I can tell you now." The screen went dark.

"My God," Caroline said. "If they have military surveillance, then they might have black-market military weapons, too."

"Just be careful," Julian said, and Weigert thought he had never heard his long-time partner sound so ineffectual.

After the meeting, Weigert followed Caroline and Trevor from the security office. He had to tell someone about the letter from Jean-Luc Fournier. "May I show you both something in my room?"

Caroline said warmly, "Of course. What is it George?"

"Something *wonderful*," he said. "Come with me!"

51.

Weigert was tired. He'd spent a week composing replies to physicists who deserved them, and had wasted almost as much energy fulminating about those who did not. He'd expected opposition, of course, but not this ... this irrational hatred. Not from laymen who'd never considered physics in their ignorant lives and completely misunderstood it now. Not from sociopathic groups like Prophets For The End Times (ironic name, considering that time was only an artifact of consciousness!) And certainly not from *physicists*.

He wanted to see Rose.

In the Wing Three conference room, Julian, Aiden, and Caroline studied brain mapping imagery on the efMRI screen. Caroline was saying, "Barbara and I need you to enhance the color on this cross-section here so we can— Hello, George!"

"Hello, my dear. Julian, I'd like a session with Rose, please. If you or Aiden could just—" he never finished his sentence.

A sound tore through the room, loud and insistent, beginning at the same moment that cell phones blatted. Caroline looked bewildered, so the phones must belong to Julian and Aiden ... but neither reached for their cells. Both men leapt up, Aiden so fast that he knocked his chair backwards, and raced to the session computer. A screen had sprung to life although no one had turned it on.

Caroline shouted over the din, "Is the compound being attacked?"

"I don't know," Weigert shouted back. He'd never heard that sound before, nor anything even close. Discordant, deafening ... but neither Julian nor Aiden were acting like men under attack. They stood before the bright session screen, Aiden's hand twitching toward the massive machine as if he could force it to do ... what?

Weigert and Caroline exchanged baffled glances. They went to stand behind Julian and Aiden, staring at the blank screen. The alarms— They must be alarms, but why? Warning of what?

Abruptly, the noise stopped. On screen, dots began to form. Nothing but that—five black dots against a white background:

●● ●●●

Julian folded up onto the edge of the session cot, bent nearly double, his head in his hands. His shoulders shook. He—Julian!—was crying.

Aiden's eyes had gone so wide that there was more white than iris, and the corners of his mouth kept twitching up and down, up and down.

Aiden put out a hand toward Julian's shoulder, then, from youthful embarrassment or youthful deference, pulled it back. Neither Caroline nor Weigert were afflicted with embarrassment or deference. Caroline knelt beside Julian and put her hand on his arm. Weigert marched over and pulled Julian to his feet. "*What is it? What just happened?*"

Julian regained himself, a process like assembling a jigsaw puzzle, until all the pieces of his expression were in the right positions. But it was Aiden who answered.

"Dr. Weigert ... look." He waved toward the screen.

"What is that?"

Julian said, "Sam."

"*What?*"

And then it all came out in a rush, Julian looking and sounding more like himself with every word.

"We didn't tell you because Sam didn't think you'd approve of adding yet another element to the experiment. Of bringing in another theory. And of ... more. Only Aiden and I knew, and if nothing ever happened, the experiment would stop with us. But Sam and I—"

"What experiment? Tell me!"

"I am telling you! Sam and I put extra code onto his chip. During his session, he created a universe in which there already existed tech more advanced than ours. Not the details, of course; he couldn't create what he didn't know. Just the broad outlines. The rest had to wait until he got there permanently."

Permanently.

Julian continued, "After Sam died, if his consciousness was able to create a new universe, he was going to work on the physics to manipulate particles in the cloud of superimposed possibilities. After all, his consciousness would have created both universes. He wanted to see if it was possible to manipulate pixels from the superimposed possibilities from there to here and—"

"Stop," Weigert said, more harshly than he intended. "There is no 'here' or 'there.'"

"I know that," Julian said. "I'm using shorthand to tell you what he did. He *succeeded*. I don't know how, the physics is beyond me of course, but this is the signal we agreed he'd send if he could. It's Morse code, George. Two dots and then three. 'I space S'—'I Sam.' He's alive there."

Caroline made a strangled, complicated sound.

Weigert stared at the five dots, while the room spun, righted itself, wobbled again. Could this be true? Suddenly he remembered the times he'd found Julian and Aiden conferring at the computer, discussing something they'd abruptly dropped when Weigert entered the room. The times that Weigert had felt there was more going on with the cyberteam than he'd been told.

Sam had been so brilliant ... but he was not a physicist. There would need to have been someone in that branch universe who worked with him to create this message, someone capable of what Weigert himself had not believed possible. Some young physicist, not yet tied to establishment thinking ...

A message sent between universes ...

Weigert knew, then, the thought as clear and fragile as fine crystal, that he would spend what was left of his life trying to fit what Sam had done into what he himself had achieved. But not yet. First there was something else.

After Sam died and if his consciousness was able to create a new universe, Julian had said. *The details had to wait until he got there permanently,* Julian had said. But doing that would have required Sam to die *during* his last session, while his chip with its "extra code" was still activated.

But Julian had sworn to Weigert that Sam had died *after* his session had finished.

"Julian," Weigert said, his voice gone to iron, "did you give Sam some toxin that would kill him while he was in session?"

"No," Julian said. And then, as if the words were being sucked out of him by leeches, "He injected himself."

"But you got him the toxin. You helped him."

Caroline breathed out, a heavy whoosh of air. Julian said nothing: careful to not incriminate himself, to not go on record. But his eyes told Weigert the truth.

Aiden blurted, "It was Dr. Watkins's idea."

"Yes," Weigert said, marveling at his own calm. "I believe that of Sam."

Aiden added, "He knew he was going to die anyway and he wanted to—"

"Stop," Julian said, firmly grasping the younger man's arm. "Stop talking, Aiden."

"It's all right, Julian," Weigert said. "I do believe it was Sam's doing, and I will never say otherwise to anyone. Sam wouldn't have wanted me to." *And if I spoke up, you could be charged with assisting suicide, a criminal offense.*

Julian studied Weigert closely, then nodded. "We underestimated you."

Weigert was not interested in Julian's estimates. He turned to look again at the five dots.

Julian said, "Caro?"

"You know I can't prove anything about a lethal injection."

"Do you want to?"

They stared at each other like duelists. Caroline said slowly, "No. I don't. What good would it do? My great-uncle is dead. I do believe now that he made his choice. He wouldn't be the first experimenter to risk his own life in the service of a scientific discovery. And God knows that the last thing this project needs is another murder charge."

Julian said, "You didn't feel that way before."

"No. Viewpoints can change, Julian. I would think you'd have learned that by now."

Weigert only half-listened to them. His mind raced. If he could prove this inter-universal communication true, it would change the world. *If.* Anecdotes were not evidence. To prove it—scientifically, mathematically—would take, in addition to Weigert himself, an army of young physicists with fresh ideas, a battalion of software engineers.

And yet Weigert already knew, deep in his old bones, that this bizarre, unthinkable thing was true. It had happened. Samuel Louis Watkins, who had gotten drunk with him at Oxford, who had been best man at his wedding to Rose, had succeeded at what he had planned from the beginning. Sam Watkins had not only cheated death, he'd found a way to prove it.

"Say that again," Julian said, with such intensity that Weigert was jolted out of his thoughts. He turned from the screen. Julian's laser-blue gaze bored into Caroline. Why? What was she supposed to say again?

"I said that I've made up my mind. If that's really my great-uncle, I have to *know*, really know, about ... all this. I can't leave the project until I know more about ... about what just happened. I'm staying, Julian. I'll commit to another year."

She turned to gaze at the five dots with the power to change the world. On her face, Weigert saw hope and fear and awe and skepticism and need, and knew that his own face must be a mirror of hers.

Samuel Louis Watkins had done what so many mortals had attempted and failed: to experience bodily death and then send a message back to comfort those left behind.

52.

The only other person told about the five dots was Trevor, which Caro made a condition of her staying. Secrecy suited the others. George wanted time to put equations under this new, even more radical change to physics. Julian wanted nothing to complicate and possibly derail his plans for the project's next steps. Aiden wanted whatever Julian did.

Trevor, who had much more math than Caro, spent long hours with George. "I'm just a sounding board for him," Trevor told her as he stopped by her room at the end of another long day, "but George says that's what he needs right now."

"Poor Trevor," Caro had said. "I talk at you about my decision to stay here for another year, George talks at you about physics, and two days ago I overheard you patiently listening to James's latest rant about the carelessness of the techs flinging their dirty dishes into the washing bin."

"All of it important," he said. "Well, maybe not James's broken plates. But Sam's message— Okay, I won't start in again! We've talked it out."

"I don't think," she said slowly, "that we can ever talk it out. It's too big."

"But not tonight," he said, kissed her, and left

Tonight George would have to do without his sounding board. Trevor had spent the day with him, and Caro had spent it orienting the new surgeon to the surgical team, Lisa Cummings. Short, brisk, radiating confidence but not arrogance, Dr. Cummings had asked all the right questions. Caro liked her. But for tonight, Caro and Trevor had agreed on a vacation from anything to do with the compound, and since they still couldn't leave without being besieged by reporters and implorers and general nutcases outside the gate, the vacation would happen right here in Caro's room, as soon as they returned from dinner in the refectory. Tonight was going to be free of any talk that wasn't playful or sexy, even though the occasion was a celebration of her decision to stay on at the compound.

Caro could hardly believe she'd agreed to another year at the project. But even harder to believe was that she could leave without Trevor, and without deciding, once and for all, the truth about the primacy of the observer. What could be more important than learning what reality was, what she herself was, what death was? Or was not.

Her world had been shaken to its bedrock by five dots of Morse code. And somehow the shaking had left her feeling more alert, more aware of everything around her. More real. *New.*

Would anyone at Fairleigh Memorial even recognize this new Caro? Memory was unchanged—all those years of internship and residency and surgical fellowship, of Ellen and her children. But she had stepped off the path those years were supposed to lead to, the path she had laid down for herself, and onto one as unknown and mysterious and terrifying as if marked: HERE BE DRAGONS.

"You seem different," Barbara had said. "More ... I don't know ... more alive."

"I do?"

"Yes. Ain't love grand?"

It was said playfully, but the look Barbara gave her was thoughtful, as if Barbara knew that it was more than love that had changed Caro. It was hard to not tell Barbara about the five dots, but Caro kept her promise to Julian and said nothing. Yet Barbara must have had an inkling because she glanced across the refectory at Weigert, absently eating his lunch as if he had no idea that his hand was conveying food to his mouth.

"Look at him," Barbara said softly, "just sitting there, the man who's challenging the scientific world."

Caro looked instead at Barbara—practical, calm Barbara—whose tone had just revealed a flash of a quality Caro had not realized her friend possessed: a capacity for profound wonder.

Maybe Caro didn't understand anybody. Ellen, Lorraine, Julian, even Trevor—they had all revealed themselves to be more layered than she'd known.

Her phone rang. James said, "Doctor, that case of expensive wine that Dr. Abruzzo ordered just arrived, and he's not answering his phone. If he's there, will you tell him to come get it right away before those software techs"—he said the two words as if they were *demon spawn*—"go and smash that too?"

"I'll tell him. Thank you, James."

She called to Trevor, just leaving Wing One, with James's message. Trevor grinned and disappeared under the archway between the courtyards of Wings One and Two. Caro went back into her room, leaving the door open. The room felt stuffy in the late afternoon heat.

A tiny green lizard ran across her bedroom floor, but she had learned to just ignore lizards. They were ubiquitous, like social media. Caro never looked at Twitter and all the rest, but Ellen still sent her links constantly: *RealityCheck all over every site! Look at this one! Read by over a million people!*

DeVonne said he was sorry Caro wasn't applying for the open position at Fairleigh, but he understood completely. Not true—since the five dots, not even George understood anything completely.

Another lizard followed the first. Was this an invasion? No, the lizard turned and ran back out the door.

An email from Ellen, with an attached drawing from Kayla. *Hi Ant Caro! This is a pitcher of me, Fluffy, Mom, and Dan. Rite me back! Your frend, Kayla Kemp.* Kayla was much better at drawing than spelling. The picture showed a detailed and recognizable Kayla in shorts and a ruffled purple top, Fluffy holding a squeak toy in her mouth, Ellen barefoot in a sundress, and a tall blond man with a beard. Ellen and the man were holding hands.

Well.

A third lizard darted inside. Caro caught it, threw it outside, and started to shut the door. The gorgeous waning of the day lured her onto the walkway, its cement cool under her bare feet. The sky flamed with color that would be gone in a few more minutes with the swift tropical sunset. The grass must have been freshy cut; its fragrance mingled with flowers and that indefinable promise of a summer night. The walkway lights turned on and she saw a figure rushing toward her across the courtyard. George.

"Caroline! Another letter from Dr. Fournier!"

"George, stay under the walkway!"

Trevor, his arms around a large crate balanced against his chest, emerged from Wing Two.

Blatt! Blatt! Blatt!

The alarm filled the courtyard, the sky, the world, part of the new alert system Julian had installed to detect drones. George, remarkably nimble for a man his age, darted back toward the covered walkway. The alarm allowed twenty seconds after drone detection, Julian had said. Trevor, with the wine, moved back under the wooden arch over the gate.

There were not twenty seconds. There was not a drone.

The missile hit the archway and exploded. For a moment Caro, already running toward Trevor, couldn't see through smoke and flying debris, couldn't hear anything except splintering wood and shattering glass and someone screaming. A pressure wave knocked her off her feet and fragments of something slammed into her lower body. She cried out at the pain but kept going, crawling over more fragments toward Trevor. *Let it be him screaming let him still be alive—*

By the time she reached him, he was dead.

Then other people were there, other people were— Who? Doing what? It didn't matter. Trevor's mangled body lay in a pool of blood, wine, metal fragments, shards of glass. Caro crouched beside him, and she knew that the terrible sound filling the air was coming from her. Hands pulled at her, moving her away to safety. Why? There was no safety. There was only Trevor, dead under a sky rapidly turning dark, all color fading from the world. Gone.

"She was hit, too," someone said, which made no sense because of course she was hit. She was shattered, she was in pieces. Trevor was dead.

"—was a fucking *missile*—"

"Get out of the open!"

"—hit in the head—"

"—went right through the—"

Words. Just words. Then more words. Hands on her.

"Abrasions and lacerations," someone said. "Blood in her hair."

She was under a walkway. She was being half pushed, half guided away from Trevor. "Leave me alone!" She broke free and ran back to Trevor's body. Took his pulse, tried to begin CPR.

"Caroline," someone said gently, and she was being lifted by George's surprisingly strong arms. Somewhere, sirens sounded. "Come away, my dear."

"I have to help him!"

"You can't. Caroline, come with me."

She didn't move but she sobbed against George's chest, this father who had come too late. The smell of wine and smoke filled the air. George was moving her away from Trevor but this time she went. The courtyard was full of people. She was sitting somewhere, sitting on a chair— *I might like Louis Quatorze*—and then she was fighting to not lie down, so they sat her in a different chair, large and orange, and Ralph—no, not Ralph, the new surgeon, her name was gone—was examining Caro's head, parting her hair carefully with gentle fingers, and the world turned sharp and clear and terrible as razors hidden in sweet apples.

She pushed the doctor away. "I'm not hurt! Julian! Where's Julian? I want Julian now!"

"I'm here, Caro."

Suddenly he loomed over her, Julian, who had warped and saved and manipulated her life, who had brought her Trevor. You had to bargain with Julian. If she'd learned anything here in this compound she'd learned that, and only bargaining would get her back to Trevor.

She made her voice clear and cold. "I want to be implanted. Now. This minute."

No one spoke. The silence stretched on and on, stretched to the end of the time that did not exist.

"Did you hear me? I want to be implanted now. I'm not seriously hurt, and I'm in my right mind. Do it." And to the new surgeon, "Scrub. Send for Molly."

"Caro," Julian finally said. "We can discuss this a little later. Right now the entire compound is—"

"Now!" Caro said, and as soon as she stood up from the orange chair, the pain hit.

Her abdomen. Excruciating. *On a scale of one to ten with one no pain and ten* ... Twelve. Fifteen. She managed to say, "Bleeding into capsule ... around spleen ... *Implant me!*"

Then it all went dark.

⇐

She woke and someone said, "Give her more!" More what? Pain smothered her. Then a mask came down over her face, and before she went under again and through the fog of inarticulate pain two letters came to her: *OR*. She was in an operating room and—

⇐

Caro opened her eyes. White, the ceiling was white. She tried to sit up and could not. There was pain, but now it felt distant, a fourth cousin. She couldn't move her head but someone reached for her hand. Molly's face swarmed into view. "Caro?"

"Where … wha …"

"I could tell you but you wouldn't remember."

Molly was wrong. Caro remembered everything. It came in a rush, and she opened her eyes wide. "Trevor …"

"He's gone. You know he's gone, Caro. But you're here, in Recovery. Rest now."

Caro gasped, "Implant me."

⤝

The third time she woke, it was for real. Ellen sat by her bedside, looking at her phone. When Caro's eyes opened, Ellen dropped the phone and grabbed Caro's arm. "Sissy! How do you feel?"

Caro couldn't process the question. She said, "Where … Julian?"

"I'll get him."

Ellen disappeared and Camilla took her place.

Caro said, "Implant me."

Camilla looked at her, a long moment in which Caro knew herself to be examined to the bottom of her soul. Then Camilla turned her gaze to the monitors, and Caro became aware that she was in the ICU, that she had tubes and needles and electrodes on her body. And that Camilla was not Julian. Only Julian could give the order to have her implanted. Except—

Lisa Cummings appeared before Camilla had to explain to Caro what she already knew. Lisa said, "You'll want to know what I did, Caro. You—"

"I want … implant."

Dr. Cummings's eyes were compassionate. "You just had abdominal surgery. I don't think you could survive another operation in your present condition. You lost a lot of blood, bleeding from the spleen. It had accumulated in your abdominal cavity, until the spleen ruptured. When I opened you up, it was a tidal wave. We weren't sure if you would survive, and the prognosis is still uncertain. You're just barely hanging on."

"Want ... implant."

"I'm telling you the facts, Doctor, because it's right that you know how—"

"My decision!"

"It's not," another voice said, and Julian was there. "Caro, you're too weak to survive the operation. And if Trevor were here, he wouldn't want you to take the risk."

Fury washed through Caro. *Using Trevor.* Playing the angles till the end. Was Julian thinking how bad it would look if RealityCheck killed one of its surgeons? Caro said, all too aware that her thoughts flowed better than her speech, "My ... decision."

"Actually, it's not," Julian said. "You're not capable right now of making that decision. Maybe later you can be implanted, but right now, and in the absence of a signed health proxy—"

Ellen said, "I have it here in my purse."

Julian's head swiveled around so fast that it looked as if it might ricochet. Caro found, startled, that she was too weak to turn her own head. But she heard the snap as Ellen opened her purse, the rustle of a paper that Caro must have signed years ago, given to her sister, and forgotten.

"Ellen," Julian said in his most persuasive tone, "you have to realize that—"

"Implant her," Ellen said in a granite voice that Caro would not—but should have—thought her sister capable of. It was their mother's voice. "What I have here is a—" Ellen paused, resuming in the voice of someone reading aloud "—a 'durable power of attorney for health care.' Implant Caro. She wants to see Trevor again as soon as she can. She has to *know* he's there."

Julian said, "Lisa? Isn't this your call? Medical concerns can override that paper?"

Dr. Cummings said unhappily, "A durable power of attorney for health care is a pretty powerful legal instrument but, yes, a physician can refuse to comply with it if the doctor has an objection of conscience or if the treatment is medically inappropriate."

Julian said, "There, Caro, you must see that ... I'm sorry, but it's not a good idea right now for you to—"

"But," Dr. Cummings said, "I don't have an objection of conscience, and given the circumstances, the treatment is not medically inappropriate."

Julian turned on her. "Not medically inappropriate! How can you say the—"

"Julian, we discussed all this before you hired me. You explained Samuel Watkins's situation and why implanting him was his choice, despite the great risk. You hired me over the other candidates precisely *because* I agreed with the philosophy that the patient's wishes should be supreme, not those of a doctor playing God. Caro is mentally capable of making this decision. Her sister has a durable power of attorney for health care. And 'medically inappropriate' hardly applies, given that nothing we are doing in this compound is dictated by a medical need. Nothing.

"I will do the implant as soon as her condition stabilizes a bit more."

≋

She didn't know how much time had passed, or where she was—but, then, time and space didn't really exist, did they? Did she exist? Only intermittently, flickering in and out of consciousness.

They *had* existed. The OR had existed, and her ability to speak had existed. She had spoken to people. To Julian. To Ellen. To Molly, who later—how much later?—sat beside her in the OR. Those things existed, until they no longer did, and she barely did, either.

Only one thing penetrated that fog of flickering self: Trevor no longer existed.

Did he?

Someone—who?—saying to someone else—who? "She survived the implant surgery."

371

Then those words, too, slipped away and Caro went on shifting into light and dark.

Dim light, dusky dark, nothing else. Flickering back and forth.

53.

"**I** was the target?" Weigert asked yet again.

"We think so, yes," Agent Kaplow said.

She, Julian, and Weigert sat in the conference room behind the security office. Other people had been there, too, people involved in the investigation. This was only the latest of the debriefings about the missile attack.

None of it made sense to Weigert, starting with the word "missile." Every time Agent Kaplow said the word, the images that came to Weigert's mind were of nuclear warheads, of Hiroshima and the Cuban Missile Crisis and Strategic Arms Limitation Talks and other ancient history. But Agent Kaplow was talking about something else, a missile launched from a boat offshore of Cayman Brac, guided by people on the boat who had identified Weigert in the courtyard. A missile that had killed Trevor Abruzzo and injured Caroline. A missile bought on the arms black market and deployed, unbelievably, by a group that hated him, hated RealityCheck, hated reality itself enough to try to obliterate it.

He said, "Because of my theory." The words were painful. Everything was painful, and nothing made sense. "Why not destroy Wing Three instead? With our equipment and computer records?"

Agent Kaplow said, "I'm sure your records are backed up in cyberspace, and equipment can be duplicated and replaced. You can't be, and Prophets for the End Times is convinced you're the Antichrist, using your theory to violate God's plan. They're profoundly anti-science. With the missile fragments and inter-cepted chatter, we've been able to connect them to not only you, but also an attack on a genetic research agency in Maryland."

Chatter. Another word that made no sense to Weigert. Chatter was what his mother had conducted over tea when his father had been ambassador. Somewhere in his mind he knew this other meaning as well, of course he did, but his mind felt clouded, unable to focus. All he could think of was Caroline, fighting for her life in the ICU.

Steady, my darling, his image of Rose said, and Weigert steadied.

Now Agent Kaplow was talking about things she'd prob-ably said before, details he didn't care about. Isolated words pinged against him like hail.

"—newest version Javelin missile—"

"—fragmenting steel warhead case—"

"—lock-on before an offshore launch—"

"—onboard imaging infrared system—"

"George," Julian said gently, "are you listening?"

"No," Weigert said. "All I need to know is that you caught them."

Julian said, "And just like Alternate Mayhem, they'll be prosecuted as a criminal enterprise under the Rico statutes so that— George, are you all right?"

"No," George said. He rose. "I'm going to Caroline."

Julian said, "I'll go with you. Agent Kaplow, if we're fin-ished here?"

Finished here! It would never be finished. It was Weigert's fault that Trevor Abruzzo was dead and that Caroline might not survive either. Weigert had been the target. Trevor and Caroline were, in another of Agent Kaplow's terrible phrases, "collateral damage."

It was no comfort to have Julian striding beside him to-ward the hospital in Wing Three.

He said, "George, Caro got through the surgery and has a good chance of surviving. Under the surface, she's incredibly tough."

"I know," Weigert said. How foolish of Julian to think otherwise.

But outside the ICU, Caroline's sister sat in a chair beside Dr. Mumaw, while Dr. Lewis, Camilla, and Dr. Cummings all did something to Caroline. Ellen Kemp rose. Her face looked caved in.

"Sepsis," she said. "They don't know."

$$\equiv$$

More medical personnel. More procedures on Caroline. Weigert didn't know what they were and didn't ask. He knew the medical team was trying everything they could. Weigert stood just outside the ICU and would not move when told to. He had done what he could. He had talked with the necessary people, told them to be ready. Now his job was to wait.

He waited.

"Her pressure's dropping. She's coding!"

The oscilloscope on Caroline's monitor beeped, loud and raucous. The jagged line, the line that pulsed with her life, abruptly flattened.

Paddles, electrical shocks.

The line resumed its jagged journey across the screen, the oscilloscope its regular beeping. Ellen Kemp cried out, but Weigert could hear that the cry held neither joy nor hope. But it didn't hold hysteria, either.

Mrs. Kemp, so experienced with death, knew. Just as Weigert did.

He sent a quick text and waited.

After a few minutes more, the heart line flattened again. Eventually Dr. Cummings shook her head.

"She's gone. Nurse, record the time of death."

Weigert moved quickly.

"Listen to me! Brain death hasn't occurred yet. It takes six minutes after the heart stops. Move her to the session room and hook her up. Now!"

Silence. Everyone looked at him. Julian said, "George—"

Weigert said, "Do it!" at the same moment that Caroline's sister said, "Yes!"

Julian opened his mouth to say something else and all at once Weigert wanted to punch him in those perfect teeth. Astonished at himself—he had never before even thought of such an action—Weigert turned on his partner and hissed, "Sam!" And then, very quietly, "How he died."

Julian's eyes widened. He understood Weigert's threat. Was he astonished that Weigert had made the threat, or was he weighing the odds of Weigert's actually carrying it out? Weigert didn't care which. Sam had cheated death. Maybe Caroline could too.

Julian said, "Do it."

Camilla unhooked tubes and electrodes, catheter and IV, faster than Weigert would have thought possible. Julian himself lifted Caroline's limp, small body into his arms, and Mrs. Kemp ran to open doors for him. People trailed them, but Weigert saw only Julian and Caroline.

In the session room, Aiden had all the equipment ready, exactly as Weigert had told him to do. Julian gave one startled glance at Aiden, then laid Caroline's body on the bed. Almost before she was down, Aiden had the titanium cover off her new leads and was attaching wires to them. The sight of Caroline's skull pierced Weigert: raw and red, the skin puffy around the site, not yet healed from surgery.

How much time had elapsed since Caroline's heart had stopped?

Here and now, in this universe, time mattered.

The screen brightened, then returned to black.

They were too late.

Weigert covered his eyes with his hand.

All at once Ellen Kemp cried out. "Look!"

The screen had brightened again. A dim light, but within the light a figure could be seen, wavering in and out. Weigert strained his eyes to see it better. He couldn't be sure, but it seemed to be slim but with a woman's curves ... No, impossible to tell. The image flickered and the screen went dark.

Molly Lewis cried out, "Was it her? I couldn't tell!"

Caroline's sister said, "It was. I know it was." And again, "I know it."

≡

Caro woke on the bed in the session room, bewildered and afraid, as she had never been afraid before. She was dead. She'd heard through the fog in her mind the dread word *sepsis* ...

But here she was.

She sat up on the bed, then stood. Stiffly, as if she'd been ill a long time. She *had* been ill a long time. She'd been ill, without knowing it, her whole lifetime. Like all the rest of humanity, afraid of death and, often, of life as well.

Not now.

Her strides were strong as she walked to the door of the session room and opened it. The courtyard of Wing Three was there, with its one straggly flowerbed. The walls of Julian and George and Watkins's compound, their great gamble. Grass and blue sky and a tropical breeze smelling of the sea.

And Trevor.

"You're here," he said.

"Always," she said, and moved toward him.

EPILOGUE

Kayla sat on a temporary stage erected in front of the gleaming new building. A huge crowd sat or stood in the plaza below. She was the next speaker at the dedication of the new George J. Weigert Research Center. She hadn't wanted to speak at all, not in this company. "Mom, the president of the United States is going to holo in with remarks! The president!"

"Julian ... wants ... you," her mother said. Since the stroke, Ellen's speech was halting and her movements sometimes uncontrolled, but the spirit looking out from her old eyes was as serene as before her body had begun to break down.

So Kayla had agreed to speak for her mother. First had come a performance by a high school band, one of Julian's PR moves. Then President Amy Turner Hastings had holo-ed in with congratulations, looking as solid as if she were actually present. Next had come speeches by the premier of the Cayman Islands and other important people, some of them long-winded. Now Julian, still vigorous and handsome, was speaking about the changes that would come to society as more of humanity experienced the power of consciousness to create, to share, to merge. There would come a greater empathy, a stronger identification with the planet that nourished our bodies, an inner peace.

Behind Julian, his words flashed in mid-air, glowing holograms.

Just last night, Kayla had visited with Aunt Caro, happy and alive with Trevor Abruzzo. She'd described to her aunt the new, self-controlled algorithms devised by Julian's software team. "What new algorithms?" Aunt Caro had asked. "Did you get them?"

"My chip includes the Lorraine."

"The what?"

"That's what Ivan Kyven calls it. The chief software engineer. He gives all the algorithmic variations these whimsical names. 'Lorraine,' after Mom's friend who died ten years ago in that plane crash. You remember? Julian's sister."

"I remember," Aunt Caro had said, and Kayla had not been able to read her aunt's expression.

Kayla searched for a more comfortable position in her chair. Her mind wandered. A warm, salty breeze blew from the sea, ruffling her hair. Overhead, gulls wheeled and cried.

Her attention suddenly focused. A gray-and-white seagull flew low, probably because it carried in its beak a big starfish. The starfish, orange and yellow, wriggled its arms. More seagulls pursued, screaming in envy and indignation.

Kayla couldn't resist. She bent her head to hide her face before it went blank, then activated different algorithms for how her brain processed information, including the "Lorraine." The wooden stage, the stone building, Julian and his listeners—all dissolved into a quantum blur. Kayla's consciousness and the seagull's consciousness were, of course, manifestations of the same thing, of the Oneness of the universe.

Then Kayla was the gull; the gull was she; both were the starfish squirming in Kayla's beak, and the warm ocean air rushing under the beat of her wings. Below her, the world spread out in sharp, wide-angled focus, every blade of dune grass separate and distinct, every flash of fish shoals beneath the water undulating in ultraviolet. The faint lines of electromagnetism banded across her senses, pathways in the sky. She sensed minute changes in air pressure: a storm at sea was a few days out from the coast. Everything was motion, including the wriggling prey in her beak, and Kayla was predator and prey, both, the deceptive distance between their beings erased. It was glorious.

She returned, and just in time. Finally Julian was introducing her.

"... whose aunt, Dr. Caroline Soames-Watkins, the great-niece of my co-founder Samuel Watkins, was one of our first, most eminent surgeons, and my dear friend. Please join with me in welcoming Kayla Kemp."

Kayla spoke about Aunt Caro and how the new technology had put truths into the consciousness of so many people. Truth about how reality works, truth about death, truth about the oneness of the universe created by consciousness. There had been no ethics or morality associated with the old worldview. It had set up an antagonistic outlook: man against nature. She explained how this was all changing. She finished with the English translation of a Hindu poem:

> "Know in thyself and All one self-same soul;
> "Banish the dream that sunders part from whole."

A little silence followed her words. Then: applause.

Kayla inclined her head in acknowledgment. When she straightened, she raised her eyes upward, but seagull and starfish had vanished, flown off together into the warm, bright sky.

ABOUT THE AUTHORS

ROBERT LANZA, MD is the bestselling author of the Biocentrism trilogy (*Biocentrism, Beyond Biocentrism,* and *The Grand Biocentric Design*). *Time* magazine recognized him as one of the "100 Most Influential People in the World," and *Prospect* magazine named him one of the Top 50 "World Thinkers." In addition to his groundbreaking work in the field of stem cells and regenerative medicine, Dr. Lanza has worked with some of the greatest minds of our time, including Jonas Salk and Nobel laureates Gerald Edelman (known for his work on the biological basis of consciousness) and Rodney Porter. He also worked closely (and co-authored papers in *Science* on self-awareness and symbolic communication) with noted Harvard psychologist B.F. Skinner. Lanza was part of the team that cloned the world's first human embryo, the first endangered species, and published the first-ever reports of pluripotent stem cell use in humans.

NANCY KRESS is the author of thirty-five books, including twenty-seven novels, four collections of short stories, and three books on writing. Her work has won six Nebula Awards, two Hugo Awards, a Sturgeon, and the John W. Campbell Memorial Award. Her most recent works are a stand-alone novella about genetic engineering, *Sea Change* (Tachyon, 2020) and a science fiction novel of power and money, *The Eleventh Gate* (Baen, 2020). Her fiction has been translated into nearly two dozen languages including Klingon, none of which she can read. She has taught writing in Leipzig, Beijing, and throughout the U.S. Nancy lives in Seattle with her husband, writer Jack Skillingstead.

ACKNOWLEDGMENTS

A book is always the work of many hands. The authors would like to thank Michael Signorelli, our tireless agent, and Lou Aronica, our editor. Valuable suggestions from both much improved this novel, as did the editorial help of Corinna Barsan and Pate Steele. Thanks, too, to Milan Bozic for the cover design and for his patience as we modified it.